My Own Asylum

A Novel By

Jacquelyn Schaffer

PublishAmerica
Baltimore

© 2006 by Jacquelyn Schaffer.
All rights reserved. No part of this book may be reproduced, stored in a retrieval system or transmitted in any form or by any means without the prior written permission of the publishers, except by a reviewer who may quote brief passages in a review to be printed in a newspaper, magazine or journal.

First printing

At the specific preference of the author, PublishAmerica allowed this work to remain exactly as the author intended, verbatim, without editorial input.

ISBN: 1-4241-3492-7
PUBLISHED BY PUBLISHAMERICA, LLLP
www.publishamerica.com
Baltimore

Printed in the United States of America

Part One

Pink Clouds, Purple Skies

To Be Free...

wouldn't it be nice
to be a butterfly
to spread bright wings
and fly away
away from sadness
screams and tears
away
to somewhere
where pain is not so hard
and people don't just run away
don't just run away
and leave me all alone
no, no, see if I were a butterfly
I'd never be alone
nope never alone
I would just spread bright wings
and fly away
to somewhere
and be free.
so, dear butterfly, spread those bright wings
and fly away
just fly away
and be free.

Sometime in July

July 25th

They say they want me to be independent. Responsible. But they don't know what I've done. Not that it's incredibly terrible. I like drinking and ecstasy, frankly. I have to lie to do it. Lie to get them off my back. Wish I didn't have to.

Maybe I want too much from them. Or maybe they expect too much of me. I'm not sure how that works. Maybe I am, as my dad once said, "fucking my life over." But it's **my** life I'm fucking with. Not theirs. I love my life. I'm happy with who I am.

Why isn't that enough?

ONE

It never occurred to me that I didn't have to go to college. It was just the thing to do after high school. Like a rule. Rules are things I like to break.

I was one of those rebels in high school. Got home after curfew, lied to my parents about where I was, who I was with. The normal teenage thing. It's not like I enjoyed jumping whenever they told me not to. They just said no to, well, everything. I couldn't understand why my friends were wrong, why staying out past eleven was bad, nor could I see why they were always so angry with me. Everything I did pushed some sort of button, and it got to the point where I just didn't want to deal with them.

So I didn't.

Silence became my savior, my sanity, and a one-way ticket to freedom. The summer before college I resorted to the front window of our living room. It was easy to open. Pinch, pinch, pull, and the screen was out. The leap into the bushes was exhilarating. Like an escape from prison, only it was home.

"Alright, I'm out," I'd whisper to whoever was on the other end of my cell phone. They'd pull up, turn their lights out just in case, and I'd hop in. (For the record, why would *any* parent give their teenager a cell phone? Okay, so I understand the concept of getting a hold of your kid. But are they completely clueless as to the possibilities it gives us? Must be some kind of chronic parental denial syndrome. Go figure.)

Shannon and Scott had called an hour before. They told me there was fun to be had. I said hell yes. Anything was better than home.

"So where are we going?" The window creaked as I rolled it down. Sweet, summer air kissed my face. The smell of freedom.

"Kat's house. There's a phat party tonight."

"Who's over there?"

"Everybody."

I don't know what a party meant for other kids, but for us it was like coming home. We did drugs. Laughed. Danced. Freed ourselves from the pain that bound us to reality. Free to fly far, far away. Together, we created a world of pink clouds with purple skies. Pure, innocent, untouchable.

"So Lynn, when's your curfew tonight?" Scott asked. He meant how long I had before my parents woke up.

"Four-thirty, to be safe."

Shannon laughed. "I still can't believe you get away with this shit."

"You know you're gonna get caught." Scott lit a cigarette.

"Uh-uh. Even if I do, I'm leaving in, what, six weeks? What are they gonna do?"

"Ground your ass."

"They don't do that shit."

"Not yet." Scott exhaled behind him, sending smoke directly to my face.

"Hey bitch," I slapped him lightly on the shoulder. "If you're gonna blow that shit at me, you'd better give me one."

"You fucking Jew," Scott teased. (Yes, I'm Jewish.) Then he gave me one.

"Knock it off, kids, or you're walking to Kat's house." Shannon gave me a look. I laughed.

"Yes'm." I lit my cigarette, inhaling deeply, slowly. Five months later my father would tell me to quit or he'd take me out of college. I still smoke. "What are we doing tonight?"

Shannon regretfully lowered the volume. She's an 80's fiend. "What?"

"Drugs? Alcohol? Glue?"

She laughed. For some reason glue sniffing's a big joke with her. "All of the above."

"I hear Erin's got some good E," Scott said.

Shannon laughed. "Damn E-tard."

"She's coming?" I asked, surprised.

"Yeah. With Nate."

"Could get interesting."

It's funny. Senior year we called ourselves "the drama duds," yet the dramatic performances on stage were nothing compared to our reality. There was always something going on. That's how it is for most teenagers, I guess. But I wasn't prepared for any of it. For the heartbreak, the intensity such closeness throws upon our lives. It felt like an X-rated soap opera.

We pulled up to Kat's street.

"Take that one!" I screeched, pointing to a lucky spot right by the stairs. Kat lived in an apartment complex by practically everything, so it seemed everyone was there all the time. Summers proved some major parking challenges.

"Lock the door," Shannon reminded.

"Yeah, yeah, yeah."

We trudged up the stairs, through the gate and towards Kat's door. It opened. An older man in gray sweats stood in the doorway. He reeked of alcohol and body odor. Kat's much older brother. Yuck.

"Hey Doug."

"Lynn," he greeted drunkenly. "Where've you been? Missed you."

"Around."

"Going out tonight. This girl's dancing." A stripper. Supposedly, Doug was friends with all the strippers in town. Not that we believed him. He was too creepy, even for strippers.

"And?" Scott replied. "We're trying to get inside. Could you move?"

Scott was such a bitch sometimes. I loved it.

"Oh, right." Doug's glossy eyes were staring at me. He swayed. "Was leaving anyway. See ya, Lynn."

"Later."

"Fucking perve," Shannon whispered.

"No shit."

"Did you hear what he did to Orea?"

I shook my head. Shannon lit a cigarette.

"Can I bum one? I'm out."

"Yeah. Let's sit."

We wandered to a set of stairs near Kat's apartment.

"I think it happened a couple days ago."

"What happened?" It wasn't my voice. We looked up to my ex-boyfriend Rick. He was accompanied by his "boys," as they so lovingly called themselves. Rick, "Big Tall White guy," Jay, "Big Black guy," and Tony, "Little Mexican guy." Like three little Indians.

"Oh. Hey guys."

"You fuckered up yet?" Rick asked. That was the main topic whenever he and his buddies partied. How messed up they got. A stupid competition in my opinion.

"Nope," I said, trying hard not to smile. I always smiled when he was around. A stupid habit of mine. "Just got here."

"You just gonna talk all night?" Jay lit a cigarette.

"Possibly."

"There's some bomb shit tonight." Tony blew smoke out of his nose. He had a really big stupid grin on his face. It was hard not to laugh.

Rick looked at me. Smiled. Turned his head. Looked back again. "Does anyone else see purple shit when they do this?" he asked.

"Uh. No."

He turned his head again. "I am *fucked* up," Rick laughed.

"Yup."

"Fuckered up, yo!"

"Fuckered up."

Shannon and I looked at each other. She put her cigarette out on the stairs. I did the same. Don't get me wrong, we loved hanging out with the boys. But one can only take so much testosterone.

"We're going inside now," I announced. "Don't have too much fun out here."

I'm sure they had some kind of sarcastic response, but I wasn't listening. By the door stood Erin, one of my oldest friends—and the one with the supposedly awesome ecstasy. We walked towards her. She was talking to Orea.

"I can't believe her." Orea flicked her cigarette angrily. "Who the fuck does she think she is?"

"I know." Erin tried to be soothing. "It's Kat. It's how she's always been."

Suddenly Orea noticed we were there. "When'd you get here?"

"A little awhile ago," I told her. "What's up?"

"Kat's just causing drama bullshit again."

Not surprising. As much as we loved her, Kat was the kind of person who insisted on being the center of attention. When she didn't get her way, she made it known.

"What'd she do this time?"

Orea made a face. "Fucked Josh."

We couldn't believe it. "*Your* Josh?"

Orea nodded.

"They weren't together then," Erin added.

"That doesn't matter." Orea looked pissed. "She's supposed to be my friend, you know? Fuck that."

"Have you talked to Josh?" Shannon asked.

"Oh yeah. He said he feels bad about it."

"Do you believe him?"

"Yeah. What can I do? I mean, I still love the guy. Can't blame him for Kat's shit."

I didn't understand. Shannon voiced my concerns. "It takes two to tango, Orea. He stuck his cock in her, too."

"I know. He told me he wanted to make me jealous. We had a fight. He was just trying to prove shit to me. I know it's stupid, but I can't be mad at him."

"Whatever."

The Indian clan headed towards us.

"You're still out here? You're such a Jew." Jay gave me a look.

"Yo' momma," I replied.

"I don't give a shit. I hate my mom."

We went inside.

Lights flickered to the pounding rhythm. Feet glided with the beats of trance. Strung out on psychedelics, mood enhancers, uppers and downers, we laughed. An organized chaos bursting at its seams.

"Hey Lynn!" I turned to see who called my name. It was difficult to isolate a single voice with so many people. "Lynn!"

Angie. My friend for ten years and future college roommate.

"Sup girlie?"

"Got something to show you."

She led me to the only available bathroom. We shut the door. Scott grinned at me from the edge of the bath tub.

"Check it out."

On the counter rested several strips of white powder. I looked at Angie. "What is it?"

"Crank, you goober."

Crank. "What is it, though?"

Angie smiled. She adored my naivety. "Speed."

"But better." Scott stood up and handed me something. It was a dollar bill rolled tightly together, like a straw.

"Close one nostril and put the bill to the other," Angie instructed. "Like this." She demonstrated. I did the same. "Now just sniff a line really hard."

"And quick." Scott pointed to a smaller bundle. "Try that one. It's a good first line."

I eyed the powder nervously. Speed wasn't something I knew much about. I wasn't sure what to think of it. The hesitation didn't last long. Leaning forward, I sniffed as hard as I could, following the strip of powder with the dollar bill.

"That a girl."

A sudden burning shot through my nose. It felt good. Eyes watering, I did another line.

"Did it all go in?"

I sniffed. "Think so."

"Put some water up your nose. It'll help the drip."

Drip? I did as she said. Thick, sour liquid edged down my throat. God, it tasted like shit. I made a face.

"Fuckin' nasty, isn't it?" Angie laughed. Then she did some lines. So did Scott. There was one left. They looked at me.

"Want it?"

Fuck yeah. Snort. Water. Drip, drip, drip.

"Try not to swallow." Scott handed me a cigarette. It was a menthol. "Let's smoke."

I'd done my share of drugs. Ecstasy, acid, shrooms, pot. Each included some glorious moments of insight, giggles and randomness. Marijuana. Munchies. Laughing because nothing makes sense, yet somehow a light bulb ignites and all the universe could come together if only each individual could embrace peace and humanity could just appreciate the beauty of the earth. Or something like that. Mushrooms. Acid. Both psychedelics. Rainbows in the ceiling. Pink and yellow butterflies dancing in the air. Body pulsating to the beats in the room, surging energy through to the toes. Adventuring into a magnificent palace of lights (any parking lot or lit area will do) or running around in circles because it's fun. (Hey, it happens.) And then there was ecstasy. My favorite. The physical explodes into a world of soft and fuzziness. Lotion balls, Vicks vapor rub and lights. A burst of happiness and sudden love for everyone you know. (And even those you don't.) The world's your best friend for at least six hours.

Crank was different. It was the biggest rush I had ever felt. Brain cells popping, veins bursting, skin crawling. My eyes snapped open. Everything was crisp, clear, defined. Filled with new founded energy, I wanted to do everything. Fast.

"So what do you think?" Scott exhaled deeply. So did I. Smoking was heavenly. "Isn't it rad?"

"I love it," I said. "It's better than E. Everything's just so…different."

"I know."

Three figures emerged from the shadows. Orea, Erin and Shannon grinned at us, their smiles illuminated by a nightly glow. I looked closer. They looked different. What could it? Aaah. They were on something.

"What?"

I blinked.

Erin raised an eyebrow. "You're staring."

"Oh. Sorry. Brain fart." Pause. "What are you on?"

"Double stacked Mitsubishis," Erin said. Translation: hard core ecstasy. "So is Shannon. Orea's frying."

Fabulous. "Hey Orea," I called. She looked up. "Come here." Time for some fun.

"You guys on anything?" Erin asked.

Scott and Angie glanced towards me. I didn't know what to say.

"Just E," Angie lied.

At that moment it was decided that methamphetamines were different. Something to be kept hidden from anyone who didn't use it. Our little secret.

"Who'd you get it from?"

"James." James worked with Angie. I'd met him once. A decent looking guy who had a thing for Angie, which she refused to admit. I wondered if she really did get the crank from him.

I took Orea's hand. "Come on."

"Where are we going?"

"I don't know. Just come on."

I started skipping. She laughed, shaking her head at my "bubbly Jewishness." Everything had to do with that. I was the only Jew they knew.

We stopped in front of Kat's apartment. "What do you see?"

Orea looked around. "Orange x's and green o's."

"Orange x's and green o's!" I made my move. Tickled the sides of her ribs. Orea screeched and ran into the house.

"Orange x's and green o's! Orange x's and green o's!"

"Aaah! It's the Jew!"

We chased each other through the living room, laughing, tickling, pouncing.

"You enjoying yourselves?" Kat sat on the couch, arms crossed. I stopped.

"What is it, Kat?"

Tears swelled in her eyes. She was upset. Probably because Orea wasn't talking to her. Surprise, surprise.

"Ask Orea."

Orea rolled her eyes. "I don't want to talk about this now."

"Well I do."

They stared at each other hungrily. I stood there, silently watching their anger and pain fizz into the air. Let the drama begin.

"You have no right to be angry with me," Orea snapped.

"Fuck you."

"What? What the fuck did I do?"

"You're supposed to be my best friend, Kat! And you just fucked my boyfriend."

"But you weren't together then!"

"That doesn't matter."

I wanted to tell them to shut up, that he wasn't worth this. The hate. Nothing was worth that. But my mouth shook beneath the weight of my words.

Kat shook her head. Paced. "No. It does matter. I think you're jealous."

"You're such a cunt." Orea blocked Kat's path.

Kat moved closer to Orea's face. "Why? Cuz I slept with Josh after you made him feel like shit? Oh yeah, Orea, that's so fucked up."

"Bitch fight!" Rick called. I sighed at the distraction, even if it came from the boys. They loved drama. Especially when it involved tits, fights, or better yet, both. That damn testosterone going off again.

"Shut-up Rick." Kat was pissed. So was Orea. It didn't look like either was going to back down.

"Stop it." Nate, Erin's boyfriend, stepped bravely in between them. "Can't you go somewhere and talk about this like normal people?"

"Keep drama out. That's the rule." Erin took the girls gently by the hand. I watched them go to Kat's room. They closed the door.

Phew. That wouldn't have been pretty. Later congratulations were definitely in order. Tension hung thickly in the air despite the dramatic exit. God, it'd be nice to have another line. A few, even. Shit, at that moment I could snort all night.

"Lynn." Just the person I wanted to see. Scott motioned me to the bathroom.

"You read my mind," I told him as we shut the door. Angie was taking the powder out of the bag. "Who do you get this from? I want some. Is it expensive?"

"Becky's boyfriend sells it." I didn't know Becky. "So does James."

"This costs about forty bucks," Scott said, holding up the rest of the bag. Not a bad deal.

"Do you know how to do it?" Angie asked me.

I shook my head. Angie motioned me to the counter. "All you need is a dollar and a driver's license."

She used the driver's license to break the crank. I watched her crunch the small, white rocks into smooth powder. She did it over and over and over. Perfection was a necessity.

The powder was made. She divided the newly formed crank into several strips, carefully scraping the driver's license diagonally against the counter. Six thick, beautifully even lines were formed.

Scott handed me a dollar. I looked at him blankly. "To snort with. Roll it up as tight as you can."

"But not too tight," Angie said. So many complications. I did as they instructed, rolling the bill like a sleeping bag. At least, that's the image I came up with.

They seemed please. We passed the newly formed straw around.

Snort. Water. Snort. Water. Drip, drip, drip.

Ah, heaven.

We left the bathroom. Scott and Angie went to smoke. I was tired of bumming, so I set off to find a walking partner.

"Where've you been?" It was Shannon. Wanted to talk to her anyway.

"Oot and aboot." I imitated a Canadian accent. Another joke. Shannon laughed. "Come walk with me."

"Where are we going?" Shannon asked.

"I need to buy smokes."

"I'm out too."

"Alrighty then."

The Shell station was only a couple blocks down the street, right next to Denny's. Good ol' Denny's. Open 24 hours and always available to us drug fiends. The memories were endless.

"You never told me." I watched the cracks in the sidewalk brush past my feet. Even walking felt different.

"Told you what?"

"About Orea."

Shannon thought for a moment. "Oh. That. I guess she was lying on Kat's couch when Doug started whispering shit."

"What kind of shit?"

"How he loved her. Read her some wannabe love poems he supposedly wrote."

"Gross!"

"I know. She pretended to be asleep. He left after awhile. Drunk fuck."

"Poor Orea," I sighed, picturing the grossness of Doug just watching her sleep. "That's not the first time she's had to deal with him. Did you hear about him threatening Josh?"

"What?" Shannon gasped. "No."

"Orea, Josh and Kat were in Kat's room. Doug was drunk as usual and he just started throwing shit at Kat's door. Said he loved Orea and it was either him or Josh. He tried to start a fight. Orea and Josh had to sneak out Kat's window."

"Goddamn. Why does he still live there? He's what, forty?"

"Cuz he's a drunk. I don't know."

"We deal with so much crap in this group."

"I know! It's ridiculous."

"*Ricauculous*," Shannon corrected. One of her favorite words.

I laughed. "Ricauculous. Right."

We crossed the street.

"Owww!" Some guys whistled from some wannabe tight-ass car. A couple of grease balls. Eww. "You chicks going somewhere?"

"Not with you," Shannon replied. I snickered.

"Awwh, come on baby. You know you want it."

"Whatever!" I laughed. "You wish you had something to give, huh?"

"Shit, I'll whip it out right here."

"Not with her, you won't." Shannon grabbed my hand, pulling me inside the Shell station. "I'm glad I was with you this time."

"What do you mean?" I asked, taking a bottle of water. I followed her to the candy aisle.

"You know how you are." She held up a blow pop. "Want one?"

"No thanks. Are you talking about the time when I brought those guys to Kat's house?"

"Yeah. Or those guys you met on the freeway and they followed you to the gas station."

"And then ran away from the cops," I giggled, remembering. "Okay, okay, you're right. I've got issues, girlie. You know that." Boy did I ever. Not that

I didn't have good reasons to be passive with the males, but sometimes I let it get a little out of hand.

"Here." I snuck Shannon a five dollar bill. She stared at me blankly. "For the smokes." I was only seventeen.

She laughed. "You youngin'."

By the time Shannon and I had returned to Kat's, Erin and Nate had left to take Orea to Josh's. The boys were gone. Kat slept heavily on the couch. It was strangely quiet.

"There you are." Angie and Scott wandered towards us. "We waited to make sure you were okay."

"Thanks." I tried to remember how long we were gone. Apparently a lot longer than I thought. "What time is it?"

Shannon checked her watch. "Four."

Shit. Curfew. "I've gotta go."

"I'll call you tomorrow night," Angie said. "We'll hang out." I thought she meant snorting crank. I hoped she did.

"Okay dude," I replied.

Shannon laughed. "You dork. Let's go."

Before I knew it, there we were. Home sweet home. We said our goodbyes.

"Later."

"I'll call you."

My feet swept cautiously through the dampened lawn. Past the bushes at the front of the house. Up to the front window. Looked at it.

I hated this part. Coming home. Blah. I slid the glass down and climbed in. Thump!

My foot knocked against the lamp. Shit. I pulled down the shades and hid behind the couch. Were those footsteps? I held my breath. Nothing. Reached around the blinds to reattach the screen. Pull, pinch, pinch. Shades down. I silently slipped my shoes from my feet. Tip toe, tip toe. Into my room. Door shut. Pajamas on. In bed. Lights out. Safe at last.

But my eyes wouldn't close. Memories began dancing along the ceiling. Suddenly, I was lost in my head. Lost in my past. Lost.

It wasn't my idea to sneak out. For the first two years of high school I was actually willing to do what my parents told me. Until I met my theater friends, anyway. They had such independence. I wanted that. One night Rick gave me the idea of the window. We were together then.

"Come on, Lynn."
I sighed against the phone. *"But I can't. You know that."*
"Are you always going to do what your parents tell you?"
"Shut up."
"I'm coming over."
"Rick, no. Please don't."
"See you in twenty." He hung up.
Dammit.

My parents slept near the back of the house, and though they claimed to be very light sleepers they didn't seem to hear much. If they only knew.

Was that him? A car pulled over across the street. No, a truck. His truck. (For a long time he insisted on a large vehicle. Some people say men do that to compensate for lack of something. Hmmm.)

My cell phone was ringing.
"Hey," he said.
"What are you doing?"
"Coming to see you."
My fingers twirled a piece of my hair. *"I told you I can't leave. The alarm's on and my dad'll notice if I turn it off."*
"What about the window?"
I looked around. *"What window?"*
"The one in the living room, dumb ass. Take out the screen."
I went to it. Opened the window and stared at the screen. *"How?"*
"Is there anything on the side holding it on?"
"Yeah. These two black things."
"Pinch them. It'll loosen the screen."
I followed his directions and put two fingers around the black pieces at the edge of the windowpane. *"They won't move."*
"Pinch harder."
Crash. The screen fell to the floor.
"Fuck," I laughed.
"What?"
"I dropped the screen. Ssh. Hold on." I waited. Silence. *"Ok."* I placed the screen behind the bushes. *"I'm climbing out."*

I still can't believe how easy that was. As many times as I did it, they never caught me. Maybe they didn't want to. They didn't want to see their oldest daughter sneaking out in the middle of the night with her rebellious boyfriend. They didn't want to see the drugs. The anger. The pain. It was their lack of vision that hurt the most. At first I did it to get away...and then I thought I was proving something. I was leaving when I wasn't supposed to. Doing things I knew they wouldn't approve of. They had their authority and I was going against it. Going against them.

Rick was waiting for me across the street.

"Where are we going?" I asked, closing his passenger door.

He grinned mysteriously between drags of his cigarette. I didn't smoke then. "You want to go swimming? Nobody's home."

I flashed a fake smile as a rock smashed against my insides. I didn't want to go. I was afraid to be alone with him. Afraid of getting close. Afraid of sex.

"I can't. We've got to go back."

"What? Why?"

Shit. Excuse. "I just have this feeling my mom's going to wake up." I hated lying, but I couldn't bring myself to admit the truth. I'd sound like such a loser.

"Come on, Lynn." He looked disappointed.

"Please take me back. I promise we'll do this again."

His eyes changed, like he was trying to see through me. I stared back, willing my eyes to beg into his. He looked away. Turned his over-sized vehicle around and parked across the street again.

"I'm sorry," I said. At least those words were true. "I just have this feeling. I don't want to get in trouble."

"It's okay. Tomorrow night?"

"We'll see."

We kissed...and that was it. I watched through the window as he drove away. And then I felt guilty. Called him to justify the lie.

"She came into my room." I hid under the covers so my parents wouldn't hear.

"Who?"

"My mom, doofus. Not even five minutes ago. Weird, huh?"

Lying got easier the more I did it. It was my way of hiding, of running away. My shrink said it was an attempt to gain control. "Manipulating your outsides to avoid the inside." Her fancy words coated my truth. I was afraid.

Beep. Beep. Beep. Beep.
My father's alarm clock. 5:30 AM.

"The only way I'd be up at five thirty in the morning is if I haven't gone to bed yet." That was Jay's philosophy, and it generally applied to the rest of us. Usually sleep wasn't in the party life agenda.

"Amen brother," the boys toasted.

It was New Year's Eve, a count down to the new millennium. Shannon was throwing a party to celebrate. Video games, glow sticks and other accessories included. The best part? No parents. Score.

So of course they said I couldn't go.

"I don't want you going anywhere. Crazy people are out." This was my mother's philosophy. *"You could get shot in the head."*

"I'm not going to get shot in the head."

"These guys," my dad began. The over protective father to the rescue. *"How long have you known them?"*

"A year and a half."

"They're not spending the night."

"Uh...I think they are."

"Then you're not."

"Why? They're my friends, Dad. I don't think they're going to hurt me. If anything they'll protect my head from getting shot at."

"This is not funny," my mother snapped. She was not in a very good mood. *"You're under 18, Lynn. If you're raped we'll go to jail. Do you want us to go to jail?"*

Jail? How did a high school New Year's party end in gunshots and the state pen? Were my parents mental?

"Her older sister's going to be there." Lie. Shannon doesn't even have sisters. I tried to convince someone to pose as a parent over the phone, but the plan fell through. An older sibling was the next best thing. *"She's twenty three."*

"That doesn't matter. We've gone over this before."

Ain't that the truth. My parents refused to trust anyone but fellow parents. Understandable, but not exactly smart. Not every parent is fit to raise a child.

"Are you listening?"

And then it dawned on me that they were pulling these stupid excuses out of their ass to keep me home. Another aspect of chronic parental denial syndrome, I suppose.

I sighed. *"Fine. If you don't want me to go to this party, I won't. Can I just go to Dee's?"*

That seemed to relieve them. Danielle was my best friend since ninth grade and the only friend my parents seemed to trust. I felt bad for ditching her on New Year's. We would always spent these kind of nights together. But this year was different. New friends. New parties. New drugs. A grand ole way to start the new year.

"Alright Dee," I said loudly enough for my parents to hear. "I'll see you soon."

She pulled up in her brand new Daewoo. The latest present from her father. Don't get the wrong idea—this girl wasn't spoiled...just a daddy's girl. I envied her for that. What was I? The bad apple of the family, of course. Go me.

Danielle dropped me off at Shannon's apartment complex. I could taste the freedom from the sidewalk. Freedom to try a new drug: shrooms.

They didn't taste too bad. I had heard horror stories of shoving mushrooms in peanut butter sandwiches or brewing them in tea because the taste was so rancid. Or maybe I was just so eager I didn't care.

When I felt the lightness in my step, the colors in my eyes, it was like everything I knew had disappeared. Life was brighter. Safe. I could dance there. Laugh with my happiness. I had almost forgotten it existed.

"Dude!" Josh pounced behind me. Orea, Angie and I looked up. "Chad just peed in the closet!"

"What?" Orea asked.

"Chad just peed in the closet."

"We heard that part." I laughed. "Where is he?"

"In the kitchen."

Angie grabbed my arm. "Come on!"

There he was, Danielle's future husband, standing drunkenly in the kitchen. The boys were with him. This should get interesting.

"Hey Chad. You want a donut?" Tony opened the box and waved it in front of him. "Which one do you want?"

"That one," he pointed, selecting glazed. Tony held it out to him. I suppressed a giggle as the donut's glossy surface melted into swirls of pinks and yellows.

Chad must have seen something too. He was just staring at the donut. Staring like it was moving or something.

"You gonna eat it or what?" Rick asked, raising an eyebrow.

"You gotta kill it first!" Chad hid behind the counter. His eyes were bulging. "The heart. It's still beating. Can't eat it when the heart's still beating."

Everyone was laughing.

"Chad. It's a donut." We waved it in front of him. "It's already dead, see?"
"No it isn't! Kill it! Kill the heart!"
My insides felt like they were going to explode. This was too funny.
"Bang!" Jay roared, pointing his finger at the center of the innocent donut.
"Again! Again!"
"Bang bang bang!"
"I think it's dead now," Angie told him.
Chad touched it lightly with his finger. Paused. Nodded. Ate it.
"That boy's fucked up!" Orea laughed.
"I want to show you something." Josh pulled me by the hand. Lead me to the hall.
"Lie down," he told me.
I did as he said.
"No, not like that. On your stomach."
Oh.
"Now give me your hands and close your eyes." His hands held mine. I let my eyes close. Felt Josh raise my arms above my head. "I'm going to make you the floor."
"You're what?"
"Shh!" he hissed. Ever so slowly, he let my hands down through the air. The carpet should be there soon. Where was it? Everything was just air.
"Where's the floor, Lynn? Where's the floor?"
"I don't know! It's gone."
"You're the floor, Lynn."
"I'm the floor!" I screeched. "I'm the floor!"
Angie laughed. "Josh, play spit with me. I'm bored. "
"Guys, what's up?" It was Kat. I gave her a huge hug. "Haven't seen you in awhile," she said. "Wanna smoke?"
"Fuck yeah." Orea looked at me. "You coming?"
"In a minute." I wanted to check on Erin. She told me she didn't want to be there. She'd asked me to watch her, but I'd forgotten.
"Shannon, where's Erin?"
She didn't even look up. They were playing Super Mario Kart. Scott was winning.
"In Mel's room, I think."

Melanie was Shannon's roommate. She was supposedly out with her boyfriend that night, though no one had ever seen the guy. Shannon thought Melanie was really a lesbian. Another mystery in the lives of the drama duds.

I opened the door. It was dark. Erin was curled up on the floor. She was sobbing. I had never seen her cry like that before.

"Erin?"

She didn't answer. I crouched down beside her, waiting for her to say something. But she just kept crying. Why was she crying? I wanted to ask, but I didn't. I didn't think she'd want to talk about it.

"Nate's sad," she told me through her tears.

Oh. "Do you want me to get him for you?"

"I'm here." Nate was standing in the doorway.

Damn. He must have some kind of boyfriend ESP or something. Wish Rick had something like that. Guess you can't have everything.

6:15 AM. The shower was running. My mother was probably awake. One hour to go.

Erin and I did talk about that night, though it took a lot longer than I expected. It happened during a four hour phone conversation. I miss those.

"Do you remember what I told you? About Chris?"

I didn't remember.

"Chris, Lynn. The guy who made me take a shower with him. He wouldn't give me back my clothes. He—"

"Erin, it's okay." I didn't want to hear her talk about it anymore. "I remember."

"I wasn't crying about Nate that night. I was crying about that."

"Why didn't you say that then?"

"Because there's more. Chris didn't do all that shit to me." I could hear the tears in her eyes. "Rick did."

Nothing. There was nothing. I was numb.

"Lynn?" She was crying now

Rick? My Rick? That mother fucker I just broke up with?

"I didn't want to lie to you. I thought I was protecting you from him."

It was hard to breathe. Rick. I could picture him. His face. His smile. The way his lips felt. His kisses were so soft.

"*Lynn?*"
I let him touch me.
"*Can you ever trust me again?*"
Fuck me.
"*Will you say something?*"
He took my virginity.
I swallowed my pain to speak to her. "Of course I trust you. I'll always trust you."
"*I'm so sorry.*"
"What happened?" The words came out too fast. I didn't want to know. Didn't want to see it in my head. Feel him hurt her.
Erin sighed shakily. "Rick told me to come over. He said we were waiting for...someone." Sighed again. "I got drunk. He got me drunk. I didn't know it was going to happen. I didn't know what to do."
I saw her there with him. Saw the fear inside her skin. The sadness. The shame. "Oh, honey, I'm sorry." I wanted to hold her. Take her in my arms and steal her pain. "It wasn't your fault, okay? Tell me it wasn't your fault."
"I can't," she cried.
"Yes you can. Tell me it wasn't your fault."
"It," she sniffed. "It wasn't my fault."
"Remember that. I love you, okay?"
"I love you too."
We never talked about it again. Erin wanted to forget it. So did I.

7:30 AM. Two cars drove away. The garage closed. Finally, I was alone.

July 26th

Snorted crank. A few times throughout the night, actually. That shit tastes *nasty* at the back of your throat. She told me it was really addictive. I said if she becomes an addict, I'll be one too. It's weird. A part of me knows how dangerous this is. How stupid and harmful. A part of me is scared and worried. But I don't feel any of it. I don't feel anything at all.

Maybe that's the crank talking. Or maybe not. But I think I'm done writing for awhile, though I'll be awake for a long ass time!

TWO

Someone should have warned me. Coming down from crank was fucking awful. I didn't want to move. Couldn't feel anything. Didn't care. Just stared in the dark and prayed for the sleep I knew I couldn't have.

"Lynn, come on."

I forced myself to look up. Looked away again.

"You've been sleeping forever. Come watch a movie with me." Halley, my youngest sister, was standing in the doorway. No, I wasn't sleeping. But she didn't know any better. She was only eleven.

"Where's Elle?" I asked. Our other sister, age fourteen.

"On the phone."

I grinned. That girl amused me to no end. More like a teenager than I could ever imagine, Elle infatuated herself with styles, makeup and shopping. My parents used to joke that the only thing we had in common was our hair. But there was more to her than that. Much more.

"What movie are you gonna watch?"

"*Now and Then.*"

I rolled my eyes. "Halley, you've watched that movie every day for two weeks. I'm surprised you haven't memorized it by now."

She stood there, eyes defiant, her arms crossed. A stubbornness all three of us inherited. I knew she would stand there all day if she had to.

"All right," I groaned. "I'm coming."

"Yay!" She skipped out of the room. What a goober.

So I sat on the couch and watched *Now and Then*. Or tried to. It was difficult to concentrate on the girls running across the television. My thoughts kept bouncing back and forth between past and present. Present and past. I focused on the couch, the walls, but the images were still there...

"What should we do with this room?" Kat looked around, tilting her head thoughtfully.

about this." Orea began to pace. "Move this here. And this, um, ver there..." We hauled the furniture across the room, transforming my parents' house into the ultimate party setting.

"I can't wait," I grinned, looking around. The couches were moved against the wall, creating a huge space for dancing. I could picture everyone there. Could see them laughing with their drugs.

"It's perfect, Lynn." Orea skipped along the hardwood floor. "Why haven't your parents left you alone before?"

"Cuz they're her parents," Kat told her. "You know how they are."

"Yeah. They don't trust her worth shit."

"You gotta be fucking holy for that. Guess that makes us the devil."

"Probably are to her parents."

I didn't bother to correct them.

"Rick's not coming, right?" Kat asked suddenly.

"No," I said. "He's out of town."

"Good. I hate that asshole."

"Kat," Orea gave her a look. They both knew how I felt about him, despite what he had done.

"What? She should know what a piece of shit he is."

"You don't have to make her feel worse about it. She can't help how she feels."

"That's bullshit. Even if she does still love him, I think it's fucked up to even want to talk to him after what he did." She paused. "You don't think he raped Shannon, do you?"

I wanted to slide under the floor.

"This has nothing to do with that," Orea snapped.

"Oh yes it does." Kat crossed her arms. "You wouldn't be defending him if you didn't believe it."

"I'm not defending Rick, Kat. I'm just sticking up for Lynn."

"You both make me sick."

"Why?" I asked. I was tired of this.

"Because you still let that bastard control you," Kat was angry. She stopped to look at me. I could feel the fire in her eyes. "Especially you, Lynn. He's fucked you over a million times and you still think you love him."

I looked away from her.

"How can you let someone have that much power over you?"

"Do we have to talk about this now?" I asked. The pain was getting stronger.

"Yes. Answer the question."

My insides were burning. Tension hung thickly in the air. It was difficult to think straight. I went outside to smoke. They followed.

"Do you think I like this? Being attracted to a fucking rapist? I know what he did to Shannon—whether or not she said 'no' doesn't matter. He took advantage of her the same way he did Erin...and me. But I love him, okay? So just leave me the fuck alone."

Those were the thoughts that screamed in my head. The thoughts I couldn't say to her. God, I wanted to. I wanted to tell her I was ashamed. Ashamed of who I was, afraid of who I'd become. That I just wanted her to hold me. Tell me everything would be okay.

"I don't know," I said.

We sat in silence, listening to the day fall, waiting for that warm darkness to melt into the sky.

"Come on," I told them, putting my cigarette out in the grass. "It's getting late. We've got more stuff to do."

"Hey, Lynn. When'd you wake up?" Elle entered the family room, the phone still glued to her ear.

"A little while ago."

"Do you have to work today?"

I worked at a video store whose name I'd rather not mention. "No," I replied.

"Good. Would it be okay if I went to Kendall's? You'd have to be with Halley till five."

"That's fine." I didn't mind watching my youngest sister, though I thought it was a little ridiculous that my parents couldn't leave her home alone for more than ten minutes.

"Thanks."

"How long are you gonna be gone?" I asked her.

"I'm spending the night."

"You asked Mom, right?"

"Yeah."

"Just checking."

Elle laughed at my attempt at being the responsible older sister. Responsibility and I didn't exactly get a long. Just last week, Orea and I had driven her and several friends to teepee a girl's front lawn, and a week before that Elle covered for me while I was trying to sneak out of the house. We shared a bond of secrets and love, the special kind that only sisters have.

"Hey Lynn." Halley glanced at me. "You hungry? I'm hungry."

"No." It took me a moment to realize that methamphetamines completely eliminated all appetite. Score. Much more effective than diet pills. I didn't eat for the rest of the day.

"But I want a grilled cheese sandwich. Will you make me one?"

I didn't want to move. "Can't you make something yourself?"

"I haven't had your grilled cheese in forever. It's so good." She gave me her cute little pouty face. "Please?"

Grrr. "Alright." I forced myself to stand up. My body felt heavier than usual. I wondered when Angie was going to call. "You want American cheese, right?"

"Yeah."

I stepped into the kitchen. What was I doing? Oh yeah. I slowly pulled out the necessary ingredients. Cheese, bread, butter, pan. Went through the motions, not really aware of what I was doing. Too much thinking. Another memory floated into mind.

The doorbell rang, startling the few of us still in the hall. No one had bothered with the doorbell before. What if—no, we weren't that loud. Not many cops came around my neighborhood anyway. Still.

I peered through the peep hole. Sighed. It was only Ryan and his girlfriend, Lisa. I'd known both of them since the eighth grade.

"You guys scared the shit out of me," I told them, opening the door. "Thought it was the cops or something."

Ryan laughed. "That's funny."

"Shut up, bitch." I slugged him lightly in the arm.

"Come on Lynn." Shannon pulled me from behind. "It's time for the rounds."

I followed her into the kitchen where Scott was distributing little white pills. He collected crisp, twenty dollar bills in return.

I put the ecstasy in my mouth. Used sink water to wash it down. Time for the fun to begin.

"Uh, Lynn?" Ryan was tapping my shoulder. "Lisa's puking in your bathroom." How lovely. "She had ten shots of tequila in, like, two minutes, so, um, she'll be in there for awhile."

I couldn't help laughing. "Thanks for the warning, Ry. Just make sure she's okay. No deaths tonight."

Someone wrapped their arms around my neck. I turned around.

"Hey lil' sis!" It was Adam, another theater friend who happened to be dating Angie. They seemed to fit pretty well.

I gave him another hug. "Sup, Adam! Where's Angie?"

"She's talking to Erin. So," he went on, without bothering to take a breath, "your parents' house is a rad party place."

"Isn't it?"

"I love your backyard." He grinned mischievously. Uh oh. "Can I climb the deck?"

"You monkey," I laughed.

"You didn't answer the question. Can I climb onto your roof?"

"No, Adam."

"Come on, just a little? It'd be so easy to just swing onto that post and—"

"Sorry. I don't want your broken drunk ass to be on my conscience, thanks."

"Who said I was drunk?"

"You didn't have to. You're always drunk."

The phone rang.

"I'll get it, Hall. Your sandwich is ready." I picked up the phone. It was Angie. "I've been waiting for you," I told her. "What's up?"

"You wanna hang out tonight?"

"Yeah."

"Is this sneaking out or are your parents gonna let you stay the night?"

I laughed. Angie knew me too well. "I'll call you back. You'll be home, right?"

"Yup."

I braced myself and called my mother. Assured her it would be after they got home. No, I wouldn't leave Halley home by herself. And then she said yes. Sweet!

Called Angie. She said she'd pick me up at seven. It was two o'clock. Five hours and counting.

Happy hardcore flooded through my veins, tingling my body as I danced and danced and danced. Everything was perfect, pure, innocent. Energy pulsated with every word, giving my heart a reason to soar.

Angie was sitting on the couch by the corner of the room. She was sitting there alone. I stopped dancing and went up to her.

"Ang, what's wrong?"

She shook her head.
I sat beside her. "You can't be sad tonight. It's a party."
Silence.
I touched the edge of her hair. It was soft. My fingers played with the strands against her shoulder. "We're going to live together soon. And, well, maybe it'd be good to tell each other things. Just in case. Maybe I can help you."
There was a long pause. I waited.
"I did something a couple days a go." She wouldn't look at me. "Something I shouldn't have done." I stared at my feet. "I took some pills." She touched my leg. I looked at her. "A lot of pills." Her eyes were sad.
I wanted the sadness to stop, to let Angie see the light again. "Why?" I asked softly.
"I didn't want to live," she said.
How could someone want to die? To just give up the everythings in life? Too much to let go that way. "Why?" I asked again.
Angie took my fingers from her hair and held them in her hands. Looked into my eyes. She was so sad. It crept into my heart, leaking its tears inside my high. Made me fall inside myself, inside my pain. I was raw.
No. I was supposed to be happy. It was a party. My party. I couldn't do this. Not now.
Angie was still looking at me. "Living's too painful," she whispered.
I looked away.

"Lynn, I'm bored." The movie was over. Halley stared at me from the other end of the couch, waiting for some brilliant revelation as to what she should do.

I rolled my eyes. "Watch another movie. Play a game. Read a book. Go online. I don't know."

"No." She crossed her arms. "I want to go out."

"Then call a friend. It's not *that* hard. We have a phone, you know."

She stuck her tongue out at me. I grinned, and suddenly she was laughing, trying to escape the fingers tickling her sides.

"Okay, okay, I'll call!" she gasped.

Before I knew it, our black lab Casey and I were the only ones in the house. I glanced at the clock. 3:17. Three hours and forty-three minutes. God, that was a long time.

"Hey Casey!" She looked up. "Come outside with me." She wagged her tail into the backyard. I sat on the steps of the deck and lit a cigarette, watching her attempt to sniff out a squirrel. It felt good to be outside.

"Dude, Lynn, you have to come smoke with us." Orea was tugging at my arm.
"But I just went outside."
"Does it look like we care?" Kat was on the other side of me.
"Okay, okay, I'm coming."
We joined the other fucked up folk on my parents' deck.
"Hey Lynn," Erin sputtered through a mouthful of food. "Eat some of this tangerine. It'll help your trip."
"What is it?" I giggled. That word sounded so funny.
"A tangerine."
"Tangeriiiiiiiiiiiiine!!!" I squeaked, bouncing on the deck.
"You're a loony," Erin said.
"Lynn!" Shannon ran outside, a concerned look spreading on her face. She didn't wait for a reply. "You have to ask someone to leave. I mean, this is your house and he won't listen to what I say."
I looked at her, dumbfounded. "Who?"
"Jack."
"Who's that?" Erin asked.
"This guy I invited. I didn't know he was so fucking dumb."
"What'd he do?"
Shannon looked around. Nobody was listening.
"He called Scott a faggot. Said he wasn't going to be hanging out with any homos here. Told me if Scott doesn't get out he's gonna kick his ass."
"Did he say this to Scott?" Kat asked.
Shannon shook her head.
"Good," I heaved a sigh of relief. I wasn't sure what Scott would do if he heard something like that.
"Where is this guy?" Orea and Kat were angry. They were quick to defend anyone regardless of consequence.
"Dancing, I think. But shouldn't Lynn—"
"We got this. Lynn shouldn't have to deal with that shit."
I didn't mind. Shannon lead them back in the house. Erin and I watched them go.
"Where's Scott?"

"I don't know."
Erin looked at me. "I'm glad he wasn't around to hear that."
"Me too."

I put my cigarette out under the deck. My parents still haven't discovered the butts. Casey was staring at me, an inquisitive look in her eyes. A tennis ball was lying beneath her feet.

"Sorry, puppy. I'm not really in the mood to play with you today." I opened the door. The phone was ringing.

"Hello?"

No answer.

"Hello?"

"Hi," a woman's voice said quickly. "Are you interested in a new cable access?" She didn't wait for my reply. "Here at (*fill in the blank*) we'll give you all the basic channels for only thirty dollars a month for your first three months, and—"

"Excuse me, miss, um…"

"—only forty five after that. Right now, installation's free with purchase of at least two extra channels, only ten dollars each per month."

Was this woman deaf? "We're not interested, actually…"

"Or if you'd like I can interest you in our other sales options, such as digital access for your own PC. Did you know we're the first company to—"

"I'm sorry." I hung up the phone. It seemed America was overpopulating itself with telemarketers. What an annoying new trend.

The phone rang again.

"What?"

"What do you mean, what?"

My father. Oops. "Sorry, Dad. Telemarketers. They won't leave me alone."

"Oh," he replied, not sounding very amused. "Listen, Lynn, since your sisters are out for the night, Mommy and I are going out to dinner. Do you want to come?"

"No, thanks though." An excuse. Quick. "Angie just called and asked if I could come over early so we could go out for pizza or something."

"Oh, okay. That sounds good."

"See you tomorrow."

"We have Angie's number?"

"I have a cell phone, Dad, remember?"

"Oh, right. See you tomorrow."

We hung up. I checked the clock. Five fifteen. Why was time moving so slowly?

My cell phone was ringing. It had better be Angie. Fucking people calling me and shit.

I looked at the caller ID. It was her.

"Angie!" I squeaked. "I thought you weren't coming till seven."

"Change of plans. You can go out now, right?"

"Yep."

"Okay, um, I'm going to get in the shower. I'll be over in, like, half an hour."

A cigarette of celebration was definitely in order. I lit it cheerfully on the deck, my cell phone beside me in case Angie needed to call.

The phone rang, but it wasn't Angie. Rick's name flashed on the phone. I picked it up.

"What are you doing?" I asked.

"Jack shit. I need a job."

I grinned. "Yeah you do. Then you wouldn't be bugging my ass so much."

"You Jew. What are you doing?"

"Waiting for Angie."

"You hanging out tonight?"

"Yeah."

"Right on. Me and Jay were looking for something to do."

"Is that a hint?"

"You could say that."

I tried to imagine Rick and Jay in the corner of the bathroom watching me snort some white shit up my nose. They would probably kick my ass. "Sorry Rick, no boys allowed." Another lie.

"You serious?"

"Yeah. Me and Angie and the rest of the girls are having a thing."

"A thing?"

"A thing. Chick flicks and junk food and all that shit."

"That's gay."

"It's better than your fucking hangouts."

"That's what we want you to think."

I laughed. "Sure, dude."

"Well you have fun tonight at your lame ass chick festival."

"Will do." That was probably the only truthful thing I told him.

I took a shower hoping it would pass the time. But it didn't. Twenty minutes later, and she still didn't show. Dammit. Maybe I could walk there. Angie only lived a few blocks away. But that required moving. Without the crank I was a lump of lazy. So I sat on the front porch instead. Pulled out a cigarette.

Another memory.

Orea handed me her lighter. I lit my smoke. Closed my eyes as the cool breeze of 1:00 AM played with my hair. The ecstasy was still strong.

"I still can't believe I'm with Josh. I've been wanting to be with him for so long." Orea paused. "He was my first, you know."

"Serious?" I exhaled a heavenly cloud of smoke.

"Yes."

I thought of Rick. Of my first time. Shook my head. "Did you cum?"

Orea smiled. "The first time. I hear that doesn't ever happen to girls."

"It hasn't to me. He must be good."

"He is."

We smoked in silence, drinking in the fluffy thoughts of love. I couldn't believe she had orgasmed the first time she was with him. I wanted that.

"Where is he tonight?" I asked her.

"Sleeping. He's got to work at seven."

"On a Sunday?"

"It's the Fun Center." Crazy people. No one should have to work that fucking early.

"So you're happy with him?"

"Yeah. Really happy."

I paused. Felt the void inside of me. The void stained with what I thought was love. "How do you know?"

"That I'm happy?"

"That he fits."

Orea held her cigarette mid-air as she thought. "When I'm with him I just feel whole. Complete. You know?"

No, I didn't know. I'd never felt that way with Rick. The most I ever had were waves of giddiness that sparked when I looked into his eyes. Sometimes I felt happy with him. Safe. But never complete. Was that love? It didn't sound good enough. Not for a rapist. I laughed bitterly inside my head. Rapist. God, I was a moron.

"It'll be two months on Tuesday."

"Good…" My voice trailed off. A truck drove past my house. Was that Rick's truck? It looked like it. A guy was driving. It was Rick. I watched him stop a few houses away.

"Fuck."

"What?" Orea asked.

"Rick's here."

"What?" She stood up. So did I. We watched Rick strut towards my front door.

"What am I gonna do?" I whispered, glancing behind me. Kat, Shannon, and Erin were in there. In there on drugs. They would kill me if they saw him here.

"Don't worry about it," Orea insisted. "You just keep him out here for awhile." And she left.

Rick crossed my lawn. He was holding something. It was a giant pink butterfly. He put the butterfly in my arms "I won this for you."

I gazed at him. He smiled. My fingers lightly touched the glittered wings. They felt silky.

"Thank you." I paused. "I thought you weren't coming back till Monday."

He shrugged. "Family shit sucks after awhile. I got bored." I didn't believe him. He had called me almost every day when he was gone. Told me he and his brothers were having a great time. But I didn't ask.

"Can I get a kiss?" He was looking at my eyes. I didn't want him to stop. I sucked in my breath. "No."

"Why? You're having a party and you didn't invite me."

I stared at the ground. "You were out of town."

"So? Were you just gonna lie to me about it?"

"Rick."

"I just think I deserve a kiss."

Fear pricked the sides of my skin. He was doing it again. "We're not together anymore. I can't kiss you."

"You're not kissing me. I'm kissing you." His fingers twirled a piece of my hair. "Just a small peck on the cheek?"

I hated when he played these games. I just wanted him to stop. "Fine."

He leaned towards the side of my face. Turned his head. Pushed his lips against mine. My insides jumped. His lips were so soft. Gentle. God, I missed him.

No. Stop! I shoved him away from me. His taste lingered in my mouth. "You suck."

Rick grinned. "I know. Let's see the fucked up peeps."
He started to move past me. I stood in front of the door.
"Don't," I said as firmly as I could.
"Don't what?"
I crossed my arms. "You know what I'm talking about. Don't go in my house."
"What, are you too good for me now? Come on, Lynn."
He started to open the door. I closed it.
"What the fuck? Why can't I go in?"
"Cuz I said so."
"Who's here?"
"Nobody."
He leaned over and stared into my eyes. His breath smelled like cigarettes. I backed away. He moved closer. "Don't lie to me, Lynn. I'll leave if you tell me why the fuck I can't go in your house."
"No."
"Dammit Lynn, fucking tell me. You know I don't deserve this."
I remembered his kiss. His smell. Saw the way the pain reflected his eyes. "I'm sorry," I told him. And I was. It made me sad.
"Why?"
I sighed, trying to make the sadness go away. But it wouldn't. "I don't want to deal with the shit, okay? Kat's been saying—"
"Fuck Kat!"
I watched him pace in front of my house. He lit a cigarette. "Kat's a lying sack of shit, Lynn. They all are. And for you to turn against me like this—"
"Stop it!" I yelled. Everything felt so heavy. Cold. My eyes started to water and I couldn't stop them. "Don't do this to me, please? Not right now. I can't handle it right now."
"Why not?"
The sadness was eating me alive. "I'm on ecstasy, okay? I just...I can't do this. Please."
He just stared at me. Spoke. "You know, I come over all excited to see you and you pull this shit. I can't believe you. I shouldn't have even brought you that stupid butterfly. Fuck this. Have fun at your party." He walked away.

"I'm sorry."
But he didn't look back.

"Lynn." Angie was standing in front of me. "What are you thinking about?"

I looked at my cigarette. The ash was piled in a line. I flicked it, watching the bits of gray fall onto the concrete. "Nothing." I stood up and followed her to her car. She was talking, but I wasn't paying attention. Just wanted to fly away.

We were there in fifteen minutes. Angie practically jumped from the car, anxious to feel the energy again. I wasn't far behind her.

"Hey Becky," she said to the girl who opened the door. Becky smiled.

We followed Becky through the house and to a door near the back of the hall. She unlocked it. We stepped into a cramped yet cozy bedroom.

"This is Carlos," Becky introduced, pointing to the guy sitting in front of the television.

"Hi," Carlos mumbled. His didn't look up from his video game.

Becky unraveled a small baggie filled with that wonderful whiteness I had been craving. I didn't realize how much I missed it. How much I wanted it. I wanted it all.

Becky took out a straw that was cut a little at the end. She used the end of the straw to pull the rocks of crank out of the bag. Placed the rocks into a glass pipe. What was she doing?

"Here." Angie handed Becky a twenty. I did the same. Carlos took the pipe from Becky and held it above a purple lighter.

I couldn't wait any longer. "What's going on?"

Becky gave Angie a look of what seemed to be excitement. "She's never done this?"

"She's snorted," Angie explained. "Hasn't smoked it."

Becky grinned at me. "Just you wait."

I was tired of waiting.

Carlos handed the pipe back to Becky, who fit it on the outside of something resembling a bong. She gave me the finished product.

"Okay," Angie said. "This is kind of like smoking weed, but you've got to do it really slow. And make sure you don't hold it in too long."

"Wait for Carlos to light it," Becky added. "He'll tell you when to start."

I put my mouth around the tip of the bong. Carlos lit it, and soon smoke was slowly trickling into the air.

"Go."

I sucked gently, slowly, filling my lungs with thick, white smoke. When I could breathe in no more, I let it out. I was surprised how much smoke came out of my mouth.

"Good," Angie approved, taking the pipe for herself.

"There's no drip," I said. No nasty liquid at the back of the throat. Much better than snorting.

Go.
Inhale.
Exhale.
Pass.
My eyes popped open.
Go.
Inhale.
Exhale.
Pass.
Veins were alive.
Go.
A rhythm. Like a clock.
Inhale.
Suck. More. Don't stop don't stop suck suck suck.
Exhale.
Alive. Fast. Fingers tapped against the floor.
Pass.

Becky stopped the cycle. "Save some for later," she said, taking the meth away. But I didn't want to stop.

Took out a deck of cards. Shuffled. Dealt. Card down. Another card. Back and forth back and forth. Slap.

Faster, faster, faster.
Go.
Inhale.
Exhale.
Pass.
Go.

Inhale.

Exhale.

Pass.

And then we were out. Becky, Angie, and Carlos stood up.

"Where are we going?" My voice sounded different. Higher, like a mouse.

"To play pool. Come on."

Angie drove. Conversation bounced between us. Talked to hear our voices. Get our thoughts out of our heads. Didn't matter what we said. Talked talked talked. Talked through the lights the sounds the everything was fast and around us and we were the sole receivers and I wanted more.

Pulled into the parking lot. There were people over there. I knew them. Didn't I know them? Angie jumped out of the car.

"What are you two doing here?" Angie asked. I bounced back and forth in the parking lot. Adam and Kat were standing in front of the pool hall smoking cigarettes. I bobbled to them. Gave them hugs.

"Playing pool," Kat replied. "Duh." She looked at me. "You feeling better now?"

It was a look I wasn't sure how to read. "I guess. For now. Have you talked to Josh?"

"I don't want to talk about it."

"Fine." Fine fine fine. Whatever.

We went inside. Adam was at one table, Angie, Carlos and Becky had the other. I followed Kat to where Adam stood. He gave me a cue stick.

"We playing cut throat or nine ball?" I wondered. The lights were cool in here.

"Cut throat."

"You sure you want me to play?" I asked, rubbing my cue with chalk. "I'm not very good."

Kat laughed. "Yeah, we know. We'll just kick your ass, is all."

"Move aside, sis." Adam leaned over, preparing to break. "It's show time."

The balls flew across the table. Two of them went in. I checked to see what they were.

"A three and a seven," I told him.

"Guess I'm eleven through fifteen then." Adam went again, aiming for the nine ball that lingered near a corner pocket. He shot. Missed. Cursed. Kat asked if I wanted to go next.

I shook my head. Smiled. "Let's save the best for last."

"Riiight," Kat grinned, hitting the nine ball Adam had attempted to clear. She made it. "Who's your daddy?" she teased, claiming one through five for herself. Adam pretended he didn't notice.

That left me with six through ten. I was already losing. Oh goody.

"Okay, Lynn. Let's see what you can do."

Ball twelve caught my eye. I thought that if I aimed my cue just right, then maybe...

"Good job, lil' sis!"

I couldn't believe it. The ball had done what I wanted it to. I looked at Kat questioningly.

"Must be beginner's luck," she said.

But it wasn't. I was playing better. It was the crank. It had to be. Score. Aim. Hit. Aim. Hit. Aim. Hit. Couldn't wait for my turn. For the ball to go in. For my turn again. I wanted more more more.

"One down, one to go." Adam grinned sheepishly, staring at ball two. Kat's last one. Two of my balls remained, and Adam had three. He paused. Shot. Missed again.

"That's right, bitch," Kat laughed, aiming for one of Adam's balls.

"Watch out, Adam. She's gaining on you," I teased, watching Kat sink two in a row. She missed the third.

My turn. Adam's last ball sat plainly in the corner. I held my breath. Aim. Hit. Sunk it.

"Oh!" Kat yelled, giving me a high five. "Adam got beat by a couple of chicks."

Kat sunk my ball moments later. Game over. Angie, Becky and Carlos were still playing, so the three of us went outside for a smoke.

"So." Adam lit his cigarette. "Have I ever told you my joke?"

Kat handed me her lighter. "What joke?"

"The one about the nuns."

Kat and I exchanged glances. "Nuns? Nope. Never heard that one."

"Okay." Uh oh. This was gonna take awhile. "An Irishman and his friend go into a church. The Irishman finds a nun and says:

'Top o' the mornin' to ya, sister. Do ya know of any nuns, *any* nuns at all that are only t'ree feet tall?' The nun says no, but to go to the main church in town. The sisters might know of one there.

So they go.

'Top o' the mornin' to ya, sister. Do ya know of any nuns, *any* nuns at all that are only t'ree feet tall?'

She doesn't know. They go to the city.

'Top o' the mornin' to ya, sister. Do ya know of any nuns, *any* nuns at all that are only t'ree feet tall?'

She doesn't know either, but tells them to go to a church a couple of miles away.

'Top o' the mornin' to ya, sister. Do ya know of any nuns, *any* nuns at all that are only t'ree feet tall?'

'No, and we know all the nuns in the city. Try the Father,' she says. 'I'll show you to him.'

So he says to the Father, 'Top o' the mornin' to ya, Father. Do ya know of any nuns, *any* nuns at all that are only t'ree feet tall?'

The Father looks at them and says, 'You know, I don't know. Ask the Pope.'

And so the Irishman and his friend find the Pope.

'Top o' the mornin' to ya, Father. Do ya know of any nuns, *any* nuns at all that are only t'ree feet tall?'

He thinks about it. Says 'No. There are no nuns that are three feet tall.'

So the Irishman's friend looks at the Irishman and says, 'See? I told ya you fucked a penguin.' "

Adam laughed at his own joke.

I shook my head. Fucking Adam.

Ten fifteen rolled around. Carlos and Becky left to find more shit. Adam challenged Angie to a round of pool. Kat went outside to smoke. I followed. We sat in silence for awhile. I didn't like it. Wanted to talk. Too much energy. I tapped my feet against the sidewalk.

"If I tell you a secret, will you promise not to tell anyone?" Kat asked.

"Yes."

She paused, then lifted her skirt. A long, dark red line stained her upper thigh. I gasped.

"I did it last night. Haven't done it in awhile, but…oh well."

"What'd you use?" I wondered.

"Glass."

"Why'd you do it?"

Kat shrugged. "Feels good."

"But it's not good."

"Don't. I know it's bad, but it's something I did and I wanted to tell you. That's all."

I took a drag. Tried to imagine the pain. The pain to make you cut yourself. "What hurts so much?"

Kat exhaled slowly. "Josh. Orea. Shannon. You. Rick. Kenny."

"Kenny?" Kenny was her ex-boyfriend. They broke up the week before. His real name was William, but everyone called him Kenny. Don't ask.

"I don't want to talk about this anymore." She sounded angry.

"I'm sorry. I didn't mean—"

"No, it's fine."

She was pushing me away. I knew what that was. Knew what it really meant. She wanted to talk but couldn't find the words. Didn't want to deal with it. Didn't want me to see what was really inside.

I wanted to tell her I knew what she meant. But I couldn't. I was too fucked up and she wouldn't hear me anyway. Maybe I could try. "I'm here," I told her, putting a hand on her leg. It shuttered. I took my hand away. "I don't know what I can do, but I'm here."

"I know."

Silence again. I wanted to talk, but I didn't know what to say. I was afraid of hurting Kat again. She broke the silence for me.

"Lynn," she began hesitantly, "you're leaving in six weeks. I just realized that. It's not very far away."

I nodded.

"I'm not sure what to do without you."

Didn't want to think about this. Talk about it. But my mouth moved without me. "I'll be around. It's not like I'm leaving the country or anything. Just a few miles."

"A hundred miles."

"I'm going to miss you."

"No you won't. You'll have a whole new group of friends there. Smart kids. You need some of them in your life."

"Shut up. You're just as smart as them. It's just another fucking school."

"You know what I mean. It'll be good for you."

I sighed. Threw my cigarette into the street. Lit another one. "But you're not going to be there, Kat. None of you will."

"What about Angie?"

"It's the group thing, though. All of us together. I mean, what if it's not the same when I come home?"

"Honey, it won't be the same. You know that."

"I don't want things to change."

"It already has. High school's over, Lynn."

"I know." Took another drag. Tried to silence the fear. "I'm just scared. Scared of losing you. Scared of being alone."

She put her arm around me, and I huddled close to her. Tried to be still. It was hard. My body wanted to move. I wanted to be held.

"You'll never lose me," she said, playing with a piece of my hair. "I'll always be here for you, okay?"

"Okay. Me too. I'll be there for you, I mean."

She pulled away from me. Used her cigarette to light another one. "At least you'll be on your own. You won't have to sneak out the fucking window anymore."

I grinned. "Seriously. No more curfews."

"Or telling you how shitty your friends are."

"Or what time to go to bed. Finally I'll be a fucking adult. Who would have thunk?" I wanted to bounce in the parking lot again.

"Don't forget about us, though."

"Fuck no." I tapped my feet on the concrete. Felt better. "I could never forget about you."

I thought I heard my cell phone ringing. It was Shannon.

"Hey you," I said.

"Hi." Her voice sounded funny. Something was wrong.

"What is it?"

"I just...I need to talk to you."

Kat looked at me questioningly, wondering who was on the other end. I told her to wait.

"Do you want me to come over?" I wondered.

"No, it's okay. Are you busy?"

"No."

"It's, um, about Rick."

Fuck.

"Last night I couldn't stand being around him, Lynn. It just brought everything back and...and I don't think I want to talk to him anymore. I can't do it. It's too hard." She was crying.

"It's okay, Shannon." I wasn't sure what to say. "I understand. You don't have to talk to him if you don't want to. You don't have to do anything you don't want to."

"I know. That's not it."

I waited.

"I don't think I can handle being around someone who still talks to him. It's just another reminder that he's in my life and I can't heal." She paused. "Do you get what I'm saying?"

"You don't want me to talk him anymore?"

"Not just you. Erin, Kat, Orea…I've talked to them about it a little. Erin doesn't really talk to him much anyway, and Kat's pretty much over it. Orea, well, she doesn't really like talking about it. I don't think she wants to get involved."

"And me?"

"I wanted to tell you last. I know you still think you love him, Lynn, and I've been waiting. But it's been almost six months and I can't do it anymore."

There must be some mistake. She couldn't be asking me this. Anything but this. "So…you're saying it's either you or him?"

"Yes."

I didn't know what to say. Just sat there, unable to move. Pain hung in the distance, but the crank pushed it aside. I was numb.

Drugs. Wanted more. More more more. I had to have them. I had to have them now.

"I've gotta go. I'll talk to you about this later."

"Lynn, don't hang up. Please."

"I'm sorry. I can't do this right now. I'll call you later, okay?"

"Okay."

Hung up the phone.

Kat put her arm around me. She knew. "It's all for the best. He's no good for you, for any of us. You know that, right?"

Drugs.

"He's an asshole, Lynn. A fucking rapist. He raped Shannon, he raped Erin, and he raped you."

Drugs. "No he didn't, Kat. He never raped me. Manipulated me, yes. But he never fucking raped me."

"Are you sure?"

Rape? This was too much. I wanted some fucking drugs. "Where's Angie?"

I didn't wait for Kat's answer.

They were at the register waiting for the total. Fifteen dollars and sixty-seven cents.

"You need any money?"

Angie shook her head.

We went outside. Kat immediately began telling them about Shannon's phone call. I stopped paying attention.

"Why won't you say yes?"

It was late. Rick and I were on the phone. He wanted to date me again.

"I told you."

"You haven't told me shit, Lynn. All you've said is 'I don't know.' That's not an answer."

"Fine. You really want to know?" *I could hear him breathing. Slow. Deep. Defiant.* *"I don't trust you, Rick. That's why."*

"What the fuck? That's the most retarded thing I've ever heard." *He paused. Waited for me to say something. I gave him silence.* *"Why don't you trust me? Is it because of Shannon? You think I raped her, don't you?"*

I sighed. "I never said that."

"I told you what happened. She wanted it just as much as I did. The bitch was moaning!"

"Don't call her a bitch."

"Whatever. She never said no. It's not like I was holding her against her will."

I didn't say anything.

"Why don't you trust me?"

Fuck. I didn't want to talk about this anymore. *"Something you did to someone else."*

"Who?"

Silence.

"Come on, Lynn, who?"

"I can't tell you."

"Why?"

"She trusts me. I can't."

"Who could this be? Is it Kat?"

Tired of his games. He always won them. Always. *"I'm not going to tell you."*

"Orea?"

"Stop it."

"It can't be Danielle."

"No, it's not. Can you stop guessing now?"

"Then who?"
More silence.
"I know. It's Erin, isn't it?"
"I told you I'm not telling."
"It's her, isn't it? Is she why you don't trust me?" Fuck. He won.
"Yes," I whispered.
"What did I do to her?"
"You don't know?"
"Remind me."
I was angry now. *"She came over to your house, Rick. Just the two of you. You...did things...things she didn't want to do."*
"Come on. She was drunk. We both were."
"You made her touch you."
"We were in the shower and she wanted to feel my dick. What was I gonna do?"
"She said no."
"Not that loud."
I wanted to rip out his throat through the phone. *"I don't give a fuck how loudly she said it, Rick. No means no."*
"Okay, okay, you're right. No means no. But she could have gotten out of the situation."
I couldn't believe him.
"Remember that night? When you and I were in the car and you didn't want to do it? You left. You got out of the car and fucking left. She could have too. Really, Lynn, I didn't do anything. I promise. You can trust me."
I don't remember the rest of the conversation, but in the end I believed him. I always believed him.

"What are you going to do, Lynn? You going to stop talking to him or what?" They were looking at me. I didn't know what to say.
A ringing broke the silence. Angie's cell phone. Thank God.
"What's up." Angie said. "You ready? Okay, we'll be there."
It was Becky. They had the shit. I wanted it all. I wanted it now.
I wanted to fall into myself and never ever come out.

July 27th

I'm just sick of all the bullshit. Every time I fucking breathe there's something else to deal with. I can't handle it. Swear to God it's making me crazy. I feel alone and bitter again. I look down and let the emptiness take over.

That's why I like drugs. I really do. And I think that should scare me. But it doesn't. I enjoy the feeling of being away from my conscious self. The feeling of happiness. Pure, innocent happiness. Maybe the only way to feel again is with drugs.

THREE

Five in the morning.

Angie, Becky and I sat in a circle, playing another game of cards. It was my turn. I put down a card. Jack of Spades.

Angie's turn. Jack of Hearts. Two in a row.

I moved to slap. Becky got it first. Dammit, that was a good one.

"So what should I do?" I wondered. Angie and I had just filled Becky in on the Shannon vs. Rick situation.

"It depends on what you want." Becky laid down a six, giving me the rights to the pile.

"But that's the point. I don't know what I want."

"Do you love him?" Angie asked.

Love. I had never loved a guy before, and I wasn't really sure how it was supposed to feel. "I think so."

"But you don't know."

"No."

"Then you should choose Shannon."

"But what if I do love him?" I lit a cigarette. Becky opened the window above her bed. "I don't want to do this. I shouldn't have to. I mean, normal people aren't forced to do shit like this."

"Who said we're normal people?" Angie said.

"Good point." Becky grinned, aiming to slap another pile. Angie got it first.

"You're not helping." I told them.

Angie turned towards me. "Listen, Lynn. The situation's shit but that's how it is. All I've got to say is don't let anyone tell you how you feel about him. If you love him, then you love him. You can't please everybody all the time."

"It's not like you have to decide now, either," Becky added. "Give it some time."

Pain was lingering beneath my skin. I could feel it there, vaguely. Knots at the pit of my stomach, an antsiness in my chest that made me want to run. But it was distant. It was always distant now.

The moment passed as the subject changed, and, with the help of more crank, I forgot about it. Hours flew by.

"Come on," Angie whispered. "It's nine o' clock. Let them do their thing."

Angie took me home. I lay in my room, alone, haunted by thoughts I found harder and harder to control.

Rick.

No, didn't want to think about him.

Shannon. Rape. No! I tried to make my head shut up.

Rick or Shannon. Shannon or Rick.

"He raped you," Kat had said. No he didn't.

Did he?

We drank together. Laughed. Flirted. Got lost in the happiness new relationships share. I loved it. Loved how he made me feel. How safe it was. Warm.

He said we should go swimming. We kissed under water. Danced in the pool. Showered. Went to his bedroom.

I was sixteen then. Young, vulnerable, and a virgin.

"I really want you." Rick's hardness bulged beneath the sheets.

"I see that," I giggled, slightly buzzed.

He began massaging my shoulders. "You sure you want to do this?"

"I already told you I do."

Without another word, he slid himself inside me.

God, it hurt.

"You okay?"

"Yes," I lied. I wanted him to stop, but I let him do it, lying there like a rag doll. I could have said no. If I had, he would have stopped. Honestly, he would have. But I didn't say anything. I thought he deserved me.

"You fucking sissy," a voice accused. The voice in my head.

I didn't know what I was doing, I told it. *I just wanted to make him happy.*

"You're an idiot, you know."

"Leave her alone," somebody else chimed in. "It's not her fault."

"Yes it is. She let him do it. She wouldn't stay away from him. She still can't stay away from him. Stupid bitch. She doesn't even hate him."

Yes I do. I tried to defend myself. *I hate his guts.*
"See? She hates his guts."
"Then stop talking to him, dumb shit."
*I can't. I—*I stopped. I was having a full blown conversation with the voices in my head. And then I realized I hadn't slept in over 48 hours. Hadn't eaten either, and now there were people inside my head talking to me.

No more. Well, at least not for a couple weeks.

I closed my eyes. Felt myself drift into a shallow sleep, barely grazing the surface of the darkness I longed for.

"Lynn." I raised my head slightly. Halley held up the phone. "It's for you." What now? "Hello?"

"Hey Lynn. It's Jasmine from work. I've got to leave early today, so I was wondering if you could come in at one instead of three. Tom said you could leave around eight if you do."

Shit. Work. I forgot.

"So, um, what do you think?"

"Sure," I cringed.

"Right on. So, I'll see you in, like, two hours?"

That soon? "Yep."

"Thanks. I owe you."

I hung up the phone. Picked it up again and dialed.

"Hello?"

"Hey Scott," I said quickly. "It's Lynn. I need some shit."

"Now? I just woke up, hon. Give me a couple hours."

"I can't. I've got to work at one and I don't think I can make it."

Silence. I could feel myself starting to panic.

"Please, Scott? I won't ask this early again. I promise."

"I'll make some calls."

"Thank you."

"How much do you want?" he asked.

"What you guys got the last time."

"Forty?"

"Yeah."

"Okay. I'll come over when I get it."

"I'll be waiting."

Waiting is a pain in the ass that comes in all shapes and sizes, but waiting for drugs was the biggest wait I'd ever had. It was horrible. Paced because I couldn't sit still. Snuck cigarettes when my sister wasn't looking. Ten minutes passed. Twenty. I was afraid to shower, afraid that I would miss him. I did it nervously, jumping at every sound. Forty-five. Still nothing. Sixty. I started to get nervous.

The doorbell rang. Finally. I gave him the money.

"Where have you been?"

"This shit takes awhile," he said, following me down the hall. "Where are we doing it?"

I opened the bathroom door. "In here, you greedy bastard."

"You don't mind, do you?"

I shook my head. "You gave me shit last time, remember?"

Scott took the baggie from his pocket. It was hard not to grab it from him.

The rounds began. I snorted more and more and more. So did Scott. We were both going to be pretty spun.

"You wanna smoke?" Scott asked.

"Yeah. Let's just make sure everything's clean first. You don't see anything on the counter, do you?"

"Lynn, we've wiped it off already. It's fine."

"You sure?"

"Yes. Here." Scott handed me the rest of the bag. There was still a lot left. "You ready?"

"For what?"

"To go to my house. There's no one home."

"Oh. Sure." I grabbed my work shirt and headed towards the front door. "Hey Hall?"

She poked her head up from the couch.

"I'm going to Scott's before work. Mom should be home in a few hours. She knows I have to work today. You gonna be okay?"

"Yeah," she mumbled, her eyes still glued to the television.

"Of course you are," I grinned. "You can just watch *Now and Then* a couple more times."

I gave her a kiss, and we were off.

Scott lived with his grandparents in an apartment complex a few blocks away. One day his grandparents asked him to house sit, and when they got back Scott just kind of stayed there.

We were greeted by an old cat's meow, followed by a light snore from the couch. Scott's grandfather was home.

"Hey Sadie" I cooed, stroking her back.

"Ssh!" Scott hissed. "Come on. Let's go out back."

Scott shut the glass door as soon as my feet hit the patio. "I thought you said no one was home," I said through attempts at lighting my cigarette.

"He wasn't supposed to be."

"Oh. Well, I'm sure it'll be fine."

"I hope so. You have to be at work soon anyway."

"Can't wait to get rid of me, huh?"

"Yep." Scott paused. Flicked his cigarette rapidly as if he was debating something. It's difficult to hold things in when you're tweaking. I waited.

"Have you talked to Erin lately?" he began.

"Kind of."

"I mean really talked to her." As in a heart to heart. About life. Personal life.

"No. Why?"

"Well..." He hesitated. "Don't tell anyone."

I gave him a look. "It's me, Scott. Besides, I probably know anyway." I knew I didn't. Erin and I hadn't had a conversation like that in a long time. I just figured saying I knew would make him feel better.

"Do you remember how Erin was senior year? Kinda depressed?"

I nodded.

"She's like that again, but worse."

"What do you mean?"

"She's..." he paused. "She's bulimic."

"She told you this?"

"Uh huh."

Shit. "I knew she was thinking about it, but she was supposed to tell me if she was gonna do it." I wondered what changed. Was it Rick? Maybe she was still remembering. It could be Nate. Were they having problems? She was so good at hiding things. I thought about calling her. Asking her what was wrong. But what if it was me?

"You knew she wanted to?"

I looked up. "What?"

"You knew she was thinking of throwing up?"

"Yeah." I sighed. The crank was starting to work. "We both want to lose weight. She was gonna puke and I was gonna starve myself. It was sort of a joke. I mean, I didn't think we were really going to do it."

"But you *are* doing it."

I looked at him like he had spoken another language.

"You're being anorexic."

"I am not."
"When was the last time you ate?"
I had to think about that one. "Tuesday."
"And what day is it?"
"Thursday."
"And you're not going to eat today, are you?"
"Probably not."
"That's anorexic, Lynn."

I should have cared, but I didn't. I liked the idea of losing weight. My entire life I had felt like a tub of lard. I remember being six years old and wanting to quit ballet because I felt too fat in a leotard. Looking at the pictures now, I was actually pretty average.

Kinda sums it up, doesn't it?

The crank made me feel empty, weightless. I suddenly felt thinner than I'd felt in a long time. It was a good feeling. "We're not talking about me," I told him. "Erin's the one who needs help."

Scott sighed. "It's not like we can do anything."

"Just be there for her if she wants to talk or anything. That's the only thing you can do, you know?"

He nodded. "It still sucks, though, knowing she's hurting herself like that."

"I know."

"Hey, what time is it?"

I looked at my phone. "12:30. Do you wanna do some more real quick and then I'll go?"

"You walking?"

"Yeah. Unless you want to drive me."

"It's right down the street."

"Exactly. You should walk with me."

"Okay."

We crept in the house, past his snoring grandfather. I closed my eyes in case he woke up. Snorted lines in the bathroom.

Set out to walk. Within five minutes we were there. I tried to remember whether it normally took that long, but my thoughts were going too fast.

"God, work is gonna suck," I moaned, taking another cigarette from my pack. There were only two left. Had I smoked that many already?

Scott glanced at his watch. "Lynn, it's 12:55. You should get going."

"What are you doing tonight?"

"I don't know."

"I'll call you."

I watched him walk away. Slipped into the store.

"Hey Lynn." Jasmine waved from behind the counter. She looked all too eager to leave. I knew exactly how she felt.

"Thanks," she said and walked out the door.

I stood behind the counter, permanent smile on my face. It was hard to keep still. My feet tapped the floor, alternating with my nails hitting the register. It was going to be a long shift.

I stared at the digits ticking in the corner of the monitor. Maybe if I stared hard enough, the digits would move faster. My eyeballs started to hurt. It wasn't working.

A customer distracted me. But only for a moment. Twenty minutes passed. Tap tap. My muscles ached from repetitive movement. Forty minutes. Seventy-five. One hour, fifty minutes. All I wanted to do was smoke. Maybe I could get away with one.

"Brett," I called, shifting my gaze to the guy stocking shelves. He looked up. "I'm gonna take a smoke break. Is that cool?"

"Yeah, sure," he said, walking towards the register. "Don't take too long. I want a ciggie too."

"A ciggie?" I grinned. "That's funny."

"You've never called them ciggies before?"

"No."

"What kind of smoker are you?"

I smiled, logged off, and left the building. God, it was good to walk again. I felt like a caged monkey or something. I put my hand in my pocket, brushing the bag of sweet, sweet whiteness. It was a comfort knowing it was there. Took out my pack of smokes. I forgot I only had two left. Dammit. I lit one and inhaled quickly. Tobacco had never tasted so good.

An older man walked past me. Stopped. Turned around.

I looked away. Waited for him to leave and turned around again.

He was still there, watching me with eyes reeking of hunger.

Panic. Why was he still staring at me? I was afraid of this man, afraid of his thoughts. I didn't want him looking at me anymore. But I couldn't leave. So I sat on the curb away from his gaze. Smoked my cigarette and pretended he didn't exist. It wasn't working very well.

"You have the most beautiful hair I have ever seen." His voice was raspy. If the guy wasn't so creepy, I would have laughed. What a cheesy pick up line!

He moved closer. Sat right beside me. I couldn't move.

"You're so pretty. So innocent. Like an angel. What's your name, angel?" His hand moved towards my cheek. I turned away and puffed anxiously on my cigarette. "Hey. I don't bite. Turn around."

I ignored him. Or tried to. It was hard to forget the panicked beats of my heart, the fear prickling my skin. I edged away from him. He followed.

"Are you afraid of me? Come on, kid. I'm not gonna hurt you. I just wanted to feel your skin. It looks so smooth, like a baby's ass." He chuckled at himself. "Sorry if I scared you. I'll make it up to you if you give me your number."

I shook my head.

"What, you don't have a telephone? Come on, cutie. You won't regret it. A nice guy like me could do a girl like you a lot of good."

I put my cigarette out and stood up. I probably could have had a couple more drags, but I didn't care. Half ran inside.

He followed.

"Oh, you're working. Well, if you won't give me your number," he reached into the breast pocket of his work shirt, "here's my card. Call me sometime. Or email me. It's all on there." He started to walk away. Came back again. "You will call, right?"

I nodded, my eyes firmly glued to an ink stain on the counter. I should clean that.

"My name's Kevin. Kevin Baron. And you are?"

"Lynn." My voice was shaky. Quiet.

"Lynn," he repeated, rolling my name on his tongue. "I like that."

Then he was gone.

Drugs. The desire to drift away flew strongly towards me, and I let it in without hesitation. The employee bathrooms were the kinds without stalls. It was one room with a lock and a counter. Small. Private. Perfect.

"That guy was creepy," Brett announced to the silence.

Thank you Mr. Obvious. "I've gotta go to the bathroom." I walked past him towards the back of the store.

"Hey Lynn, what about my cig?" he called. I didn't answer.

I couldn't get the baggie out of my pocket fast enough. My body ached for the whiteness my shaky hands attempted to smooth out. I realized I didn't have a dollar. It almost made me panic when I noticed a crumpled piece of paper halfway buried in the trash. It was a receipt. I didn't think twice about it. Used it as my straw. Put it to my nose when I remembered I didn't clean the counter. Fuck it. Whatever's there couldn't be half as bad as what I was doing. Would probably add to the high.

Was that someone outside?

I stopped, straining my ears through the silence. Someone might be listening. Maybe Brett was standing at the door, ready to knock me over for a cigarette break. Or worse, Kevin could try getting my number again. I shuddered at the thought. Someone could definitely be there.

But probably not. Just in case, my foot caused the toilet's flush the minute I began snorting. I was able to finish off all three lines before the water's rushing ceased. Beautiful. I grinned at my own small light of genius. Sniffed the water up my nose, washed my hands, and went back to work.

Time went by quickly for awhile. Apparently everyone wanted to rent movies after 3:00. I didn't mind. 4:16. 4:59. My last cigarette came and went. 5:07. 5:30. Brett and Rachel smoked pot in the back. A crowd gathered, and I ran around to accommodate them. Register, membership, question, register, register, question, register, membership—

"I had to see you again."

It was him. I looked at the clock. 6:00 PM. Not even four hours and he was back. I tried to work, to look away, to think…but I just stood there. Trapped.

"I have to work." That voice didn't sound like mine.

"No you don't," he said. "There's no one here. Take a break."

I looked. He was right. The store was empty. Fuck.

"What are you doing tonight?"

I could feel his breath on me. Thick and sour. It made me nauseous.

Anything. Quick. Why was it so difficult to think? "I've gotta go home…parents…"

He nodded, smiling stupidly. He had two silver teeth, bottom row.

Neither of us spoke. I tapped my fingers in a scattered beat. Tried making patterns on the counter. Traced the word *help* over and over and over.

He just kept staring at me. My eyes. My lips. My chest. I wanted him to leave. But I couldn't say it.

"I think I have a daughter your age."

Save me.

"Lynn." Orea and Erin entered the store. I could have kissed them.

Kevin eyed them for a moment. They stared back. Erin raised an eyebrow. My nails tapped the counter. Orea looked at me. At him.

"Do you want something?" Orea demanded.

He glared at her. Orea didn't flinch.

"What are you staring at?" Erin spat.

He left without saying a word. I watched him go, wishing I had the guts to say something like that. I couldn't even look at him.

Orea spoke first. "Who was that guy?"

I shrugged.

Erin shook her head. "He was creepy." She saw the anxiety on my face. "Was he bothering you?"

Another shrug.

"He was."

"Don't worry about it," I told her. She eyed me suspiciously. I quickly changed the subject. "Orea. I never got to ask what happened with you and—"

"Hey." It was Rachel. "No guests. Tom'll be here soon. You know how he gets."

"Can I go outside then?" Anything to get away.

Rachel crossed her arms. I begged. And won.

"What was he saying to you?" Erin handed me a cigarette. I didn't even have to ask.

"It's fine. He's gone now." I held it up to my lips while Erin tried to light it. My hand was shaking.

"I don't believe you."

I didn't say anything.

"Orea, you and Josh okay?" I asked her.

She puffed silently for a moment. Spoke. "We're doing better. It's going to take a lot of time. He's gotta earn my trust back, you know?"

"Yeah." I paused. "What about Kat?" Thought about last night. About the cut on her thigh.

"Fuck her. I don't even wanna talk about that bitch."

"I think you should give her a break."

"Why?"

"She's..." I trailed off. I had promised Kat I wouldn't tell anyone.

Orea sighed. "You're such a nice person, Lynn. It doesn't surprise me you don't see it."

"See what?" I glanced at Erin. She was watching us with hard eyes. I wanted to kiss her cheek and tell her I'm here, that everything was going to be okay somehow. But I didn't. I mean, I couldn't. The thoughts rolled to Kat, to Shannon, to Orea and all the pain flowing through our veins.

I wanted it all to stop.

"Kat's just trying to get attention," Orea explained. "She doesn't give a shit about anyone but herself. All she wants is that fucking spotlight and she'll do anything to get it. Put other people down just to satisfy her own fucking self. She doesn't care who gets hurt."

I shook my head. "She cares about people."

"Bullshit. You wanna know how the fuck I found out about Kat and Josh?" Orea was practically shouting now. "Kenny walked in on them together. It was, what, a week after they broke up? And Kenny said it wasn't really even a break up. She just wanted her space. Yeah, some fucking space that was."

Space.

Rick had wanted space one time. I was going to an International USY convention (a Jewish youth program for all you goyim). Was going to be gone for a week. Why not grab an excuse to fuck someone else? He wasn't getting any with me. Asked us to take a "break" from our relationship.

That was when Erin happened. Some fucking break he had. This was December of last year. Shannon wasn't too far after that. February. Maybe three weeks after I broke up with him. If that. Wasn't he on a fucking roll?

Sat down to forget my thoughts. Erin sat next to me.

I looked at Erin and remembered him. Kevin. He left a foul taste in my mouth. I realized I was sitting exactly where he was. Could smell his sour stench. It made me feel sick. I stood up quickly.

My head felt hot. Dizzy. I sat down again. Held my head in my hands.

"Lynn?"

A hand was on my back, another on my leg. Orea's face poked through my fingertips.

"I'm going to get you some water, okay?" Orea smiled. "Erin's here. I'll be right back."

She left. I could feel Erin's fingernails lightly against my back.

"Just breathe," she whispered. "Take deep breaths."

I did as she said. The dizziness began to subside. She gently guided my head to her lap. Stroked my hair. I closed my eyes.

"Can I ask you something?" My head rested against his chest, my hair twirling between his fingers.

I opened my eyes. "You brought me caffeine," I grinned. "Ask away."

I had an ugly essay due. It was late. Couldn't concentrate. My eyes were drooping.

So I called Rick for reinforcement. He came back with every possible caffeinated item imaginable. Coffee, three different energy drinks, an energy bar, and green tea. I was stoked.
He put his hand on my shoulder.
"You nervous?" he whispered.
"No."
His fingers touched my chest. "Nervous?"
I moved to look at him. His hand stayed where it was. "What are you doing?"
"Playing a game. Are you nervous yet?"
I shook my head no. I didn't understand the point.
He touched my stomach. "Now?"
"No." I watched his hand creep downward.
He touched my lower abdomen.
"Nervous yet?"
"You don't have to do it this way," I told him.
He pointed down the hall. "Can we go to your room?"
"You know the answer to that."
"That's why."
He touched my lower thigh.
"How about now?"
"No." This was getting annoying. I paused. "Do you always have to test the limits?"
"Yes." His hand moved again, and my heart beat faster. I was nervous. He reached underneath the waist of my sweats.
I covered my mouth.

"Drink this." A cup of water hugged my lips. Rick. I could still feel him, his eagerness to touch me. It was suffocating. I shook my head and sat up.

Orea was crouched beside me. The cup of water was in her hands. "Drink," she said again. My mouth felt dry. I drank.

"Do you feel better?"

I nodded and set the cup beside me. None of us spoke. I wasn't sure what to say.

Erin asked the question. "What's going on?"

I didn't answer.

"Is it what I think it is?"

She didn't know, did she? Did Scott…or Angie…? I bit my lip.

"When was the last time you ate?"

I sighed. She didn't know.

"You can tell us. It's okay."

They had mistaken my sigh of relief as hesitation. Good. I went with it, then realized I was hesitant. I didn't want them to worry.

"It's been two days." There. I said it.

Erin lit another cigarette. So did Orea. I took one from the pack.

"Why?"

I didn't have time to answer. Tom was walking towards the entrance. He stopped to look at me.

"Break time?"

I nodded. His eyes lingered, then looked at his watch. He went inside.

"Maybe we should go," Orea said.

I shook my head. "It's okay." I didn't want to be alone.

"You sure?"

"I promise."

Erin asked why I wasn't eating. I took a long drag and felt my emotions erupt. Suddenly everything was screaming. I wanted to tell them. The fear of crank, not being able to stop the need...and Rick...hadn't even thought about the decision. Didn't want to. It made me hurt. All of it. Everything was so intense. A chaotic monster in my gut, clawing its way through me, trampling the insides of my throat, my head—

"Maybe I should go back." I stood up. Erin stared at me for a long time.

"I'm worried about you," she said.

Orea nodded. "We need to talk, Lynn. Whatever it is...it's hurting you."

I flicked my cigarette nervously. Took a deep breath. I was afraid that once I started to speak it would all come out. Pour from my lips like a river. A river of secrets. Of pain.

Maybe I could open just a little bit. "It's Rick," I said.

Silence.

"Do you know what I'm talking about?" I asked.

Orea said no. Erin remained quiet.

"Shannon told me last night...it was either her or him."

Erin's eyes shot daggers of pain. I looked away.

"And I can't..." This was too much. Erin's pain. My pain. "I'm sorry."

I turned around, dropped my cigarette, and went inside.

They didn't follow.

"Not wanting to work tonight?" Tom asked as I slid back behind the counter.

"No." Oops. Shit. "I mean, yes. I do." I cringed inside. What the fuck was wrong with me?

"You're lucky I already told Rachel I'm letting you go home early." He smiled.

I glanced at the window. Orea was talking to Erin. I wished I could hear her.

"Paula wanted a short shift tonight." Tom was still talking. "She'll be here in about fifteen minutes. You're free to go when she gets here. Unless you want to stay, of course."

What were they talking about? Fear was slowly dripping through me. I forced a grin. "No, I'll go. Thanks, Tom."

"No sweat."

It was 6:15. I wanted to tell them I was getting off early, that maybe we could go to coffee like we used to. I'd tell them anything they wanted to know…as long as they didn't leave me.

Looked out the window again. They were quiet now. Orea took Erin's hands in hers and brushed her lips against them. Erin's cheeks were wet with tears.

"Excuse me." A kid was at the counter. Damn customer service.

When I got back, they were gone. Fucking figured. Maybe I should choose Rick. That pain would be better than this.

A normal person wouldn't have thought twice about this shit. A normal person would have picked Shannon and Erin and Kat. I knew they would all be gone if I picked Rick. A decent friend would be kissing their hands like Orea kissed Erin's. A decent friend would curse Rick to the ends of the earth and back again. But I couldn't. It was a horrible feeling. What kind of a person would even think about choosing a womanizing rapist and molester over the best friends they'd ever had?

Me.

It was Saturday. Rick finished pouring multi-colored plastic eyes into a bowl. All the crafts were out. We were ready for them.

It was a craft fair for children with mental disabilities. Our drama teacher had asked for volunteers. Rick and I were eager to help. We even got the coolest booth around. Pet rocks.

The kids came. Our cold, hard stones grew into purple aliens, spotted cockroaches and rainbow butterflies. They loved it. And I loved watching them. Especially Rick. Everything I knew to be within him poured out to those children. He amazed me that day.

"I can't do this." A frustrated boy of about seven years old threw his half done rock to the ground. Rick picked it up and crouched at the boy's level.

"What's wrong with this one?"

The boy crossed his arms.

Rick turned the rock over in his hands. *"This is the coolest pet rock I've ever seen."*

"You're lying."

"No really. You've just gotta look at it."

The child shook his head.

Rick smiled. *"Check this out."* He picked out a blue pipe cleaner, bent it in half, and taped it to the side of the rock. *"You see it yet?"*

The boy looked curiously at the newest addition to his previously hopeless pet. *"No."* But he was interested.

Rick glued a fuzzy, orange ball to the end of the rock. *"Now?"*

Suddenly the boy's eyes lit up. *"Yeah!"* He grabbed the rock from Rick's hand and ran to the other side of the table.

Rick glowed when he smiled at me. Turned to another kid. Helped her make a yellow cat. It was at that moment I realized I loved him.

He asked me out three days later.

6:25. Five more minutes and I was home free. Paula walked into the store. I sighed. Orea and Erin should be here to celebrate. I wished I knew where they had gone, why they left without saying goodbye. Maybe Orea was now on their side. I was losing them.

We recounted the drawer, I changed my shirt, and walked out. It felt so good to be moving again. I had forgotten how antsy I felt. A cigarette would be fabulous right now. Dammit.

Wait.

Brett was at the counter.

"Mommy! You promised!" A little girl flew to the woman in front of me. She was wearing a pink dress, dark hair tied loosely behind her ears. A giant candy bar was in her hand.

"Give it to me then," her mother said, taking the candy bar from the child.

It was almost painful to see her. So much innocence. I wished I could be that way again. Untouched by the pain life brings. The pain of growing up. I wished she didn't have to see it. That she could stay that age forever.

The child turned and saw me watching her. A single strand of hair fell perfectly in front of her piercing eyes. Was I ever that beautiful?

Her eyes stared thoughtfully into mine. Maybe she saw me. Saw what was underneath the mask I wore.

I was the first to look away.

"Aleesiya!"

The girl ran to her mother. Took her hand. I searched for a memory of my own mother, hungry for the comfort Aleesiya had. But there was nothing. I was numb to my mother. Numb to myself.

Aleesiya glanced back at me as her mother pulled her out the door. She waved. I waved back.

"Didn't you just leave?" he asked.

I stared at him for a moment. Oh yeah. Cigarettes. "Can I bum a smoke for the way home?"

"Don't you have your own?"

"Can't buy them yet. I'm not eighteen."

Brett laughed. "Sucks for you."

Not cool. "Please? I'll give you money."

"I don't want your money." He gave me two.

I sighed. "Thanks dude."

"Go home."

Home. Where was that? "Bye Brett."

I started to walk. Everything seemed strangely quiet despite the chaos of a Thursday evening. Maybe it was me. Maybe I had blocked out the world. I tried to think about everything, organize my thoughts so that somehow something made sense. But there was nothing there. It's funny how when all you want is silence the thoughts don't stop, yet the desire to think leaves utter nothingness. Whatever. I started to like being numb.

The emptiness floated with me as the streets blurred together. Almost home. It felt like forever since I'd been there. Not since I…

SHIT. I was high. I was going home and I was high. Shit shit shit.

I called Angie. It rang and rang as I paced in the middle of the street. Was I acting high? I had to be. Oh, fuck what if they found out? Didn't want to think about it. The phone kept ringing. Pick up, dammit!

"Hi."

"Angie!"

But it wasn't her. It was her answering machine. I hung up and dialed again.

"Don't tell me you ran out already."

I ignored him through my panic. "Scott, I'm high."

Pause. "Okay."

"I'm going home right now."

"Okay."

I bit my lip to hold back whatever was growing inside my throat. "I can't go home high. Can you come get me?"

Another pause. "I'm kinda far away, hon."

My hands shook as I attempted to light the other cigarette Brett had given me. I flicked it over and over, trying to get the antsiness out through my hands. I couldn't stop moving. My chest felt tight, like there was something too big living there. I tried to force my panic into one word. "Please?"

"I can't right now. Did you call Angie?"

"Yes. She didn't answer."

"Just go home, Lynn. You'll be fine." Fine? Didn't he hear it? The fear?

Fine. He didn't want to help. I didn't need him. Made myself feel numb again.

"I'll talk to you later okay?" He hung up.

I sat on a curb and smoked, trying to contemplate the consequences of getting caught. Dealing with my parents, anything's possible. Rehab? Jail?

It's not like it mattered anyway. I'd be lost no matter where I went.

I threw my cigarette into the street and went inside.

"Hi." My mom was reading on the couch in the living room.

"Hi." I hurried past her. Didn't want her to smell the smoke on me.

"How was work?" she called.

"Fine," I yelled across the house. "I'm gonna take a shower." I grabbed some clean smelling clothes and shut myself in the bathroom. The sound of the shower felt loud inside my head. Like pounding fists against a cement wall. I closed my eyes and let the water drown me.

His naked body looked small and fragile, his back hunched in embarrassment against the shower wall. I gently washed his chest. His shoulders. His arms.

"You're beautiful," he whispered. I smiled. His fingers brushed the sides of my face. "I don't even want to do anything. Just look at you." His blue eyes pleaded with me, asking for love. I leaned forward and kissed him.

Suddenly I was on the floor. Dizziness fought my attempt to stand. Rick took my arm and pulled me up. His face was angry.

I wanted to leave. My hand touched the glass door. He took my hand away.

"Where are you going?"

My lips moved but nothing came out. Everything was hazy, like I was drunk or something. Did I drink? How much did I have?

He was still holding my hand. I tried to pull it away, but his grip was firm. He yanked me towards him and forced my fingers in the last place I wanted to touch.

"No." I tried to pull away again. My head was pinned against his chest as he forced me to stroke him. I closed my eyes. Didn't want to see him. Didn't want to see myself.

"Come on Erin. I know you like it."

Erin?

I was alone. The showerhead was laughing at me, spitting water in my face. I couldn't breathe. My fingers found their way to the sides of the tub as I sat down. The tile was cold but I didn't care.

Me, then her. Or was it her then me? It didn't matter. He hurt us both. I had never thought about it before. How she must have felt. How he was with her.

But he was so gentle to me. So loving. Patient. Why? Why the fuck was I so special? Why did I still have to love him?

My body shook as the tears erupted. I didn't realize I was crying until the salt invaded my tongue. I don't know how long I sat there, crying in the shower. Felt like hours and hours and hours.

In the end there was nothing left. Maybe the pieces got washed down the drain.

July 28th

I've never been so scared before. Scared that if I give him up, then all the wonderful moments we've had together will have been a lie, that my love for him is a lie...that his love for me is a lie. I'm scared that if I let him go I'll fall so hard that I'll never be able to pick myself back up again. That maybe I'll completely lose myself in drugs, that I won't care about anything or anyone. That I'll feel empty and worthless inside. I know I'm not happy and every day I put myself in more and more danger. And I want to stop that, but that road is so long and dark and scary. I just feel like I'll get lost. I'm not strong enough.

FOUR

I didn't want to wake up.

Waves of pain lapped in and out of my head. It felt like a hangover. I wish. Hadn't been drunk in forever. Gotta remember to have some old fashioned fun sometime. If I ever got out of bed. I pulled the covers over my head and stared at the darkness. Wiggled my fingers in front of my face. I could barely see them. I remember doing that as a child. Being friends with the dark made me feel better then too.

The phone was ringing. Who the fuck was calling me so damn early? It wasn't even noon. The screen flashed Kat as I threw my phone back on the floor. Let me hide.

He was laughing at me. I shook my head.

"You're drunk," he said. Drunk. Was I? Maybe. My fingers touched in front of my eyes. Rick smiled. "Yup." He took my hand. I followed.

Up the stairs. One. Two. Three. He was going so fast. By the time we reached the top it felt like everything was swaying. I closed my eyes.

"You tired?" His voice was far away.

I nodded. His fingers rubbed a strand of my hair. My eyes stared into his. And then he leaned in and kissed me. I pulled away.

"We're not supposed to do this," I said.

Rick raised an eyebrow. I attempted to stand my ground.

"We're not together. We haven't been for a long time. You know that."

"So?" he asked.

I shook my head slightly, trying to remember what I was saying. I paused. "Lynn?" His lips were pulling towards me again. I turned away suddenly. "Don't kiss me."

Rick took my hand and pulled towards the doorway. "I wasn't."

My legs were numb and full of weight. He gently pushed me on the bed. Hopped over to the other side. I watched him nestle under the covers and close his eyes. I knew he was pretending.

"You're not sleeping," I said. I could feel him grinning through his silence. He was playing a game. I didn't want to be there, was tired of his fucking games.

I knew my decision.

I wanted to call Shannon and tell her that I was sorry, that I would never give her up for anyone. Especially him. But my body was heavy, my eyes unwilling to focus on the ground beneath my feet. I couldn't remember where I put my shoes.

"Where are you going?" His head poked from beneath the blankets. I shook my head. "You should get some sleep." He put his arms around my waist and pulled me onto the bed. The ceiling was spinning. So were my thoughts. Rick turned his back to me. I lay there, my mind swirling in rippled shouts.

His fingers touched the edge of my shirt. Underneath it. His skin brushed my navel. I went rigid.

"What are you doing?" My words were blurred together. He pulled my shirt up to my chest. I touched his hands and pulled on them. "Don't."

He put his finger to my lips. I looked at him. Hard. His eyes were so blue. I tried to sit up. To get away. But I couldn't move

He leaned over, his lips again connecting with mine. I could feel his tongue leak through my teeth. I shook my head. Attempted to speak, to move. Anything. But my hands were numb against his weight. He was on top of me, covering my will.

I wanted to cry.

Fingers grew hard against my skin. He was everywhere, his lips, his body pushing and nibbling. His pants came off. My insides were screaming. I could see them splattered on the ceiling. But they were silent screams.

He took off my jeans.

The words flew into my mouth. "STOP!"

And he did, staring into me. My cheeks were wet. He kissed a tear away.

"You owe me," he whispered as his pelvis rocked again.

I woke up. Looked around my room. It *was* my room. My bed. I could still feel him there. His breath hot against my neck. That shit felt so fucking real. But it was just a dream.

Elle and Halley were on the couch watching *Golden Girls*. I flopped next to them. My stomach growled. Suddenly I was starving. I hopped to my feet.

"Are you—"

"No. I'm not making grilled cheese," I told Halley. Elle laughed.

I rummaged through the kitchen. Nothing sounded good but I wanted to eat everything at the same time. There was a box of oatmeal in the swinging door under the counter. Fabulous.

Food hadn't tasted this good in awhile. I chowed down on three packs of Quaker's apple cinnamon, laughing with my sisters at Rose's vacant expression as Blanche sauntered across the room in another outrageous outfit. It felt good to laugh. Almost safe. Reminded me of the summers that seemed so long ago, when Elle and I would play make-believe while Halley struggled to play a part. She was so young then. We all were. I sighed and wondered where my innocence had gone...if it was ever really there to begin with.

Elle grinned at me. I missed her.

"Maybe we could talk later?" I asked.

Elle shrugged. "About what?"

"Ssh!" Halley hissed. We ignored her.

"I don't know," I said. "Whatever. Life."

"Okay. Cool."

"Guys!" Halley whined.

I laughed. "Sorry oh mighty queen of television."

She threw a pillow at me.

We watched another couple hours of old TV reruns. It was kind of nice just being home. I fucked around on the internet, munched on toast with honey, wrote in my journal, took a nap and found other ways to waste time. Forgot how necessary wasting time really was. We should have it penciled in every few days. For mental purposes.

Elle beckoned me to her room. "Shut the door."

I did as she said and crossed my legs on her bed. Elle drew her knees to her chest and stared at me.

Uh. "So? How's life?"

"Okay," she said.

"Just okay?"

"Well...I kinda need to ask you something."

I waited.

She bit her lip. "Have you ever done drugs?"

Wow. Should I lie? "Why?" I asked carefully. "Have you?"

Elle shook her head. "Anna has." Her best friend. "She wants me to do it with her."

"What kinda drugs?"
"I don't know. Smoke pot?"
"That's not that bad," I told her. "You just get kinda light headed and laugh a lot."
"You've done it?"
"Yeah."
Pause. "Have you done ecstasy?"
I sighed. "Does she want you to do that too?"
"A lot of my friends do it. They say it's really fun. Anna wants me to try it with her. You know, so it can be both of our first times."
"You're in ninth grade."
"When'd you start?"
"Eleventh."
"That's not that much different."
"Two years."
"So you've done it then?"
"Yes."
"What was it like?" she wondered.
As I described it to her, I realized I didn't want my sister doing E. I didn't want her to slip. To be like me.
"Sounds cool," she said.
"It's not that cool."
"You like it."
"Yeah. You're probably gonna do it no matter what I say, so if you do…be careful."
"I know."
"No, you don't." I figured I should tell her what someone should have told me. Tell her how to keep herself safe. "Always make sure someone you trust is with you. Someone who will take care of you. Drink lots and lots of water. And get it from someone you know."
"Okay."
"And Elle? Don't try crank. Or any of that other hard shit. Stick with ecstasy or mushrooms or even acid. Or just pot. Promise me you won't do more than that."
"Why?"
"Just promise."
She shrugged. "Okay. I promise. What's so bad about them?"
"They can get you hooked."

"Have you tried it?"

The truth lingered on my lips. But I couldn't say it. I didn't want her to know who I had become. That she had a sister addicted to drugs.

"No," I lied. "But I know people who have. Just trust me."

Wait. Addicted. Was I?

"How's life with you?" Elle asked. "I mean, besides you leaving."

I didn't want to be an addict. I thought of my stash. Maybe if I got rid of it things would be okay. Maybe I'd be okay.

"It's all right," I answered, trying to make my voice sound as normal as possible. "I'm trying to hang out with my friends as much as I can. I mean, I don't know how much longer they'll be my friends." Words that burned the roof of my mouth. "It's hard."

"I couldn't imagine leaving my friends. I mean, I kinda am for high school. Not everyone's going to the same place. But I'll still be here, you know?"

"Yeah." I kept staring at the door. Felt the panic again.

"What are you thinking about?" Elle asked. Her cell phone rang. She picked it up. "It's Anna."

"Answer it."

"You sure?"

I nodded and left, closing the door behind me. Where was my shit again? I checked the pockets of the jeans I wore yesterday. The crank wasn't there. Fuck. I threw clothes behind me in a desperate search. Where the fuck was it? My parents didn't find it. I wasn't that stupid yet.

I could see the baggie underneath a sock at the other end of my closet. Grabbed it and ran to the bathroom. Locked the door.

This is it. I'm not doing it anymore.

I lifted the seat of the toilet. Held the crank up to my eyes. "Good riddance," I told it. Dropped the baggie inside.

It floated at the top.

I poked at it, trying to get it to sink to the bottom of the bowl. But it bobbled up again. I stared at the powder for awhile, remembering how it felt. The high.

Maybe I shouldn't get rid of it.

But I had to. The rush that I knew felt distant, drowned in the fear of wanting it. Needing it. I wanted control of my life again. Before I could think about it anymore, I flushed.

There was a knock at the door.

"Lynn?" It was my father's voice. "Get out here when you're done. We need to talk."

Talk. Talk about what? Shit shit shit! I was watching my sanity swirl down the toilet.

It's okay. I needed to do this. Needed to get rid of it. I was doing the right thing.

But my lungs were crying. Needles crawled under my skin. Anxiety and panic and fear screamed in my head. What was I doing?

I reached down and grabbed the baggie just in time. Luckily I had tied the shit closed. I opened the bag quickly to make sure the crank wasn't wet.

Should I do some now?

"Lynn! Your mother and I are waiting!"

Tempting, but no. After them. Give myself a reward.

I cleaned the baggie with a towel and shoved the shit in my pocket. Washed my hands. With a heavy sigh, I opened the bathroom door.

They were at the dining room table, calendar out, chatting like nothing was wrong. I poured myself a glass of lemonade and waited for them to notice me. They didn't until I started to leave.

"We're talking in our room," my father said.

Are we now?

We walked to the other end of the house. My father opened the door. He was staring at me. I slid past him. Settled in a nice corner on the floor.

"Lynn, get up off the floor." My mother crossed her arms as my father shut the door. I was stuck there behind the bars of parental steel. Do not pass go. Do not collect 200 dollars. All the food I'd chowed felt like it was creeping up my throat. I cringed and sat at the foot of the bed.

"What do you do when you go out?" my mother asked.

I swallowed. "Hang out with my friends. Nothing really." Silence on the other end. I hesitated, wondering if I kept silent if they would too. "Why?"

"We think you're going out too much," my father said.

"You're never home, Lynn." My mother's eyes looked sad. "Do you hate being at home?"

What the fuck was this? Some kind of parent intervention? Yes, I hated being at home. I couldn't breathe. "No," I lied. "I just...I'm just trying to see my friends as much as I can before I leave." Why did I have to keep saying that? It hurt.

"We're not important enough to spend time with?"

"I didn't know you wanted to." Oops. My parents' glares penetrated my brain. I reminded myself they couldn't see my thoughts.

MY OWN ASYLUM

"You're too busy hanging out with your so called friends," my father said.
So called friends? Oh hell no. I didn't answer that.
"We don't like your friends, Lynn." My mother's voice was bitter. "We think they have bad judgment. We don't trust them."
"Except Rick," my father added. "I like him. He's a good guy."
I tried hard to keep myself calm. It was a tie between laughing in my father's face or hurling my fist into it. Of all the fucking people!
"Say something," my mother begged.
I put up the biggest front I could. Stone cold. "So I have bad judgment. You don't trust me."
My mother sighed. "We never said that."
"Yes, you did. If my friends have bad judgment, then so do I. I pick my friends, don't I?"
"That's not what we meant. It's just—"
"It's just nothing."
"Hey! Let your mother finish. And watch your tone." My father was getting angry. His whole body leans forward and his eyes bulge when I push his buttons. It's pretty interesting, actually. Something the *Discovery Channel* might like to study.
"It's not that we don't trust you. It's that we don't trust everyone else."
Same lame excuse as New Year's Eve.
"Do you understand?"
Not really. "You don't want me hanging out with my friends anymore?" I asked.
"No, Lynn. We wouldn't do that."
Lucky for you, cuz I wouldn't listen. My friends are my life.
"We just want you home more."
"I'm home a lot," I protested. Like an eternity.
"This isn't funny."
"That wasn't a joke."
"Hey!" My father was angry now. He was completely hunched forward, and I swear the veins in his neck were starting to show. "I'm tired of your bullshit, Lynn. This isn't a goddam joke. You're leaving for college in six weeks and you need to start acting like a fucking adult."
I hated when he cussed at me. He only did it when he was really angry. Like that made it okay. No matter how angry I got, I never cussed at my parents. Ever. But I guess that didn't matter.

I sighed. "I'm trying to enjoy being a teenager—"

"You're fucking your life up!" he yelled. "Your friends don't care enough to see that you need to stop playing their stupid games and grow up. Just because they can't go to college doesn't mean they should stop you."

I bit my lip and tasted blood. The pain felt good.

My mother attempted to soften the blow. "Honey, we're just worried about you. We just want to make sure you're doing the right thing. Okay?"

Fuck you. I continued to stare at my knee.

"Okay?" My father's voice. His buttons were bulging.

"Okay," I whispered.

"Okay."

We sat in silence for a moment. My mother got up. "I'm going to make dinner." She left.

My father put his arm on my shoulder. "I'm sorry for yelling. I just want what's best for you." He paused. "Are you mad?"

Duh. I was fucking pissed. But I knew if I told him that he'd just yell again. So I lied. "It's okay Dad. I understand."

"Good." He gave me a hug and left the room.

I ran to my bedroom. Shut the door. God, I was so angry at them! This shit happened all the time.

Someone knocked on my bedroom door. It was Halley.

"Mom and Dad were fighting over you. They're crying now. Just thought I'd let you know."

Halley was ten at the time. Wished she didn't have to see this. I wanted to take her in my arms and shield her from them. From the fear. The pain. But it was too late. I thanked her and waited for them to come.

They did.

"We need to talk." My parents sat on my bed. I was on the floor, knees to my chest, waiting.

My dad did most of the talking. "We had an argument. Your mother doesn't want you going to your rehearsal tomorrow. She doesn't trust you'll come home."

I was sick, and sickness wasn't taken lightly in my house. Each parent had their own reason to be afraid. My grandmother died of breast cancer at thirty-six, and my grandfather passed away from heart failure when I was thirteen. My parents' anxiety shifted to their children, to me.

"I don't think you'll come home," my mother said.

"I just said that." My father gave my mother a look. She stared at the floor. "I don't think it's that big of a deal, but she obviously does. I got angry, and—" his voice was choking up— "your mother thought I was going to hit her." I stared out the window. A butterfly was outside. One of those monarchs. It was watching me. I wished it could take me away. "If you would just do what we tell you to this wouldn't have happened. If your mother was able to trust you, if you could just be a little more responsible, then your sister wouldn't have had to see me like that. I'm really trying to work on this, Lynn, but your fucking up doesn't help anything." He paused, looking towards his wife for guidance.

My mother didn't say anything.

The silence was getting to me. "So can I go to my rehearsal or not?"

"Yes."

"But you come home right after that, understand? I want you to call one of us when you get home."

"Fine." My voice was cold. I don't think they noticed. Or maybe they did. I don't know which hurts more.

My phone had four missed calls. The first was Kat from this morning. Then Rick. Then Kat again. And again. I dialed her number.

"Is Kat there? It's Lynn."

I waited.

"I need to talk to you," Kat said.

"I'm here."

"No. In person. Something happened."

I held my breath. "Are you okay?"

"No. Can you come over?"

Dammit. "My parents just yelled at me for being out all the time. I really pissed them off…there's just no way they'll let me out."

"Can you ask them?"

"You know I can't. Why can't you tell me now?"

She sighed. "I'm pregnant." I could hear her tears. "I'm getting an abortion."

I couldn't speak.

"It's a boy. I know it. His name is Asher. Asher Logan. Stupid to name him, huh?"

"No. He's your child."

Silence.

"Is it Kenny's?" I asked.

"Yeah."

Pause. "Does he know?"

"No. I don't want him to."

"I won't tell. I won't tell anyone."

"I know."

"I'll sneak out tonight if you can get me a ride."

"Sienna could drive us. She's staying with me 'till I get it." Sienna was a close friend of Kat's. We were decent friends, but I didn't really get to know her until college.

"When are you…?" I couldn't say abortion. I didn't want to remind her again.

"Monday."

I told Kat to pick me up at midnight. A car pulled up at 11:45. They were early.

It wasn't until after I got outside that I realized it wasn't Sienna. Rick was sitting in his truck, smoking a cigarette and staring at me. I didn't move.

We stood there for awhile. I pictured myself jumping back through the window. Locking him out of my house. My head. My life. But I just stood there like always.

He got out of the car, took a last drag of his cigarette, and threw it in the street. Walked towards me.

"What the fuck's going on?"

My eyes shifted to the ground. He was glaring at me. I could feel it.

"So you don't want to talk to me anymore?"

"I never said that." I could barely hear myself speak.

"You never say anything!" He was loud. I glanced nervously at the house. "When the fuck are you gonna start sticking up for yourself Lynn? Goddamn!"

I shook my head.

"This is bullshit." He crossed his arms. Grabbed a pack of cigarettes from his pocket.

"Can I have one?"

"Yeah whatever." He handed one to me.

We smoked in silence. I couldn't look at him. Couldn't see the ugliness inside his chest, the look in his eyes.

"Could you really just…stop? Pretend I don't exist anymore?" Rick's voice was quiet, like a child.

"I don't know." There were tears on my cheeks. I turned around to wipe them away.

"Are you crying?"

"No." I wiped another tear. His hand was on my shoulder.

"You're shaking." His fingers brushed against my arm, gently making patterns along my skin. I shivered despite the summer heat. He turned to face me. Was that a tear in his eye? It had to be the light.

He touched the wetness on my cheeks, a half-smile etched on his face.

"What?" I whispered.

He pulled a strand of hair out of my eyes. "What?"

"Why are you smiling?"

His breath was warm against my face. "You're beautiful, Lynn. I don't know what I'd do…" He leaned forward. His lips touched mine.

I shoved against him and he staggered backwards.

"What the fuck are you doing?" I was yelling but I didn't care. It was just like my dream.

"What am *I* doing? *You're* the one who wanted this!"

"Wanted it? I…why is this on me? I didn't do anything!" It was all coming back, like I was with him again. Suddenly I felt so small.

"You're overreacting, Lynn."

My insides were exploding. I wanted to run. Without thinking, I sprinted across the lawn.

"Where are you going?"

Away.

"Lynn!"

The air felt cool against my skin. Energy caved into the pain, and for a moment it felt like I was flying.

And then I was on the ground. Rick was breathing heavily on top of me, his arms pinning me against the sidewalk. I gasped for air and attempted to push him off of me.

"I can't breathe with you like this," I wheezed.

"You promise not to run away again?"

I nodded. The weight was lifted from my lungs. I sat up and stared coldly into his eyes.

He lit a cigarette and threw one at me. It fell in the grass.

"You want it or not?"

I grabbed the smoke and stood up, leaning as far away from him as I could while he lit it. Time to be strong. I took a deep drag.

"I can't talk to you anymore."

Rick was silent.

"Did you hear me?"

"Fuck, Lynn. Yeah I heard you."

"Don't you want to know why?"

"I already do." He was pacing in the street. I stayed on the sidewalk, watching him.

"Tell me why then."

" Cuz they told you not to."

"They? Who's they?"

"You know. Kat, Shannon, Erin…all those fucking bitches."

"Hey! Be nice."

"Why should I when they…I shouldn't even be here."

He cared about me enough to let me hurt him. He had let me in. Tears stung my eyes. "This is my decision, Rick. Okay? Mine."

"I don't believe you."

"Why not?"

"Cuz you're here, that's why! If you really didn't want to talk to me, you'd be gone by now."

My stomach churned uncomfortably. He was right. I was still here. Well fuck then. I started walking back towards my house. Kat and Sienna should be there soon anyway.

"I thought you promised not to run away."

He caught up with me, his pace equal with mine. I sped up. He followed.

"I'm not running."

"You know what I mean."

I turned to face him. "Look. I love you." His eyes squinted a little. "Oh come on, Rick. You know that. But I just can't talk to you anymore." My throat was burning. Lots of pain now. "I have to make a choice and it's not you."

"What kind of choice?"

"Never mind, okay? It's over."

"Well I want to know what the fuck I did wrong!"

I didn't have a chance to tell him. Kat and Sienna were walking towards us. They didn't look happy.

"It's the bitch squad," Rick growled.

"Shut up, Rick," Kat hissed. Her eyes were glaring at him. He glared back. I pleaded silently to Sienna. She looked at me sympathetically.

"Why are you here?" Kat demanded.
Rick crossed his arms. "I came to see Lynn."
"Well she can't see you anymore."
"Fuck you! You her lawyer now?"
"This isn't a fucking joke, you piece of shit rapist!"
Rick stepped closer to her. "So this is why she can't talk to me, huh?" His presence was towering.
"Just try and deny it."
"I didn't do it."
Kat coiled her hand into a fist. Holy shit.
"Stop this!" I forced myself in between them. "Look, I made my decision. Now leave it."
Nothing happened. I pulled Kat on the arm. "Let's go." She didn't move. Sienna tugged on her other side.
"Kat, come on."
Slowly, Kat unclenched her fist. Followed us to the car.
"This is it, Lynn!" He was shouting. "You walk away now, you're out of my life!" His voice was quivering. It sounded like he was crying.
"Don't look at him," Sienna whispered. God, but I wanted to. Numbness was spreading through my veins. I wanted to see him while I still loved him, while I still let myself feel. Before he didn't love me anymore. If he had ever loved me at all.
I'm pathetic.
He was still there when we got into the car.
"Don't drive by him." Kat's voice sounded far away. I couldn't stop looking at him through the tinted windows. Maybe if I stared hard enough he'd stay there forever.
And then it hit me. I had really said goodbye this time. Goodbye, with a capital G.
"Can you turn up the radio?" I asked them. I didn't want them to hear me cry.

August 23rd

I need some fucking drugs.

God, I want some crank right now. Crank would be nice. I'm just so antsy. I can't stop shaking or pacing or moving, my heart's going. I feel like an animal locked in a cage, just waiting for the right moment to pounce. Damn it! I need some drugs. That's all I can think about. The feelings it'll bring. The body high. God, I've gotta stop or I'll drive myself crazy.

Dude, I must be fucked up, craving drugs like this. A psycho bitch drug addict or something. Whatever. What the fuck ever. I don't give a rat's ass anymore. Damn it all...just...fuck. I need to get out. Now. Sleep Mom, sleep. Maybe I'm addicted to crank. Oh, won't that be fun. There goes my life, down my fucking nasal cavity.

Ha ha, that's funny.

FIVE

The next four weeks went by in a blur. Maybe I made it that way. Didn't want to feel whatever was inside my head. Not that it mattered. The shit just kept piling on.

Kat had her abortion the Monday after I said Goodbye to Rick. Do not turn back, do not collect two hundred anything. Well, maybe pain. It numbed me to that point where everything just kind of floated. The world could end and I'd only remember watching. No feelings here. Maybe that's why I was able to go with Kat to the abortion clinic. Held her hand while they took her baby away. There were no tears, even when Kat cried out to her dead fetus that Mommy was sorry, that she would always love him. She said she'll never feel whole again. Sienna did most of the talking after that. I counted the cracks in the linoleum floor.

Kat's life wasn't the only thing falling apart. Shannon was struggling. She called me one night to tell me she couldn't do it anymore.

"I thought of cutting myself," she said.

Why did people do that? Kat had hinted she'd done it again, maybe even more than once. I hoped Sienna knew because I didn't care enough to do anything about it. Danielle used to cut the tips of her fingers with a nail clipper during Honors English. Once a drop of blood stained her pants. She lied and said it was ketchup. I was the only one who knew the truth. But that was a long time ago, when she told me things. Apparently, she broke up with her boyfriend. I had heard about it from Ryan two weeks after it happened. Heard it. This was her first real relationship and I didn't even know it had ended. Whatever. Guess I pushed away first. Maybe I wasn't her best friend anymore. I didn't even know if she was mine.

"I don't know what to do, Lynn," Shannon was saying. "I see him everywhere, even in my dreams. There's this part of me that's screaming and I don't know how to make it stop."

"What if you cry?" I asked her.

"I can't. Maybe all the tears are gone."

Silence. I wasn't sure what to say to her, mainly because I was feeling the same way. We were both falling yet didn't have the strength to hold onto each other before we hit the ground. I guess I was too tired to reach out. Or maybe the bitterness had already melted through my skin.

"I can't do this," she sighed.

I hesitated as the worst swam through my head. "Do what?"

"Be here. Just knowing he could see me driving down the street makes me nauseous."

Or something like that. But I didn't want to talk about Rick, let alone help someone else deal with him. It was hard enough in my own head. "Where do you wanna go?"

"Jacksonville," she answered. "That's where I'm from anyway."

"Where's that?"

"Illinois."

This was unexpected. "I didn't know that."

"Yeah you did. I've told you before. It's where my mom was from."

Shannon's mom had died a couple years ago in a car accident. The road was slick and a big rig was going too fast. She died in the operating room right before Shannon could get there. It happened the week before finals during her freshman year of college. She couldn't go back there again.

"I remember," I told her.

"I bought a plane ticket."

Holy shit. She was really doing this. "When would you leave?"

"Maybe two days before you. I want to get there before school starts."

"School?"

"Yeah. They're letting me enroll again."

"That's good." I wanted to be happy for her. Or sad she was leaving. Would be nice to feel something.

"We should have a going away party."

I think I felt myself smile. "Sure. That'd be cool."

"So when's this party?" Orea coated her toe with another layer of light purple polish. A trail of purple ran down her skin. She wiped it away, taking a drag of her cigarette as she held it between her teeth. I tried to keep mine in my mouth like that, but the smoke kept getting in my eyes. I ended up putting it on the sidewalk, catching it several times before it rolled into the street.

"She didn't say," I told her. "Soon, though."

"Well you're leaving soon."

I didn't say anything, pretending to concentrate on keeping the polish on my toenails. Actually, it wasn't too difficult to pretend. I've never been very good at polishing nails. It gets everywhere regardless of how careful I am. Sounds like a lot of other things.

"I saw Jay yesterday. He told me something about Rick." She paused and looked at me. I wiped some extra polish around my little toe. "You wanna know?"

Crap. My foot knocked black polish all over the concrete. I rescued about half the bottle. We moved to another part of the sidewalk, toes spread out like chicken feet.

"Tell me."

"He's seeing someone."

I stopped.

"Her name is Chastity."

"That was fast." I held my breath. Something had gurgled in my gut. It bubbled and rose until I was laughing. Really laughing, the kind where your breath has to be sucked in increments as your body shakes. God, was I going crazy?

Orea smiled. "That's better."

I followed her into her house. She took a soda from the fridge and looked at me questioningly.

"Grab me a root beer."

I made my way to the bathroom and locked the door. The baggie came out before my stomach could fall into the sink. Everything I had been suppressing over the last few weeks came back with that stupid laugh. Fuck happiness. It only coats the truth.

I turned on the water and made my lines.

"Lynn." A voice was right behind me. I turned around, but there was no one there. Strange.

"Dammit!" I covered my mouth to stifle the rest. My arm had brushed against a line, splattering powder all over the carpet. I reshaped what was left of it and snorted. Then another line, and another. I picked up whatever pieces I could from the carpet and shoved them in the bag. There was a towel on the floor. I wet it and rubbed it around. Washed the towel and hung it up to dry.

I put some water up my nose, flushed the toilet, and half bumped into Orea's mom.

"Sorry," I mumbled, doing my best to avoid her eyes. It felt like she could see through me.

"Be careful."

I didn't stop to figure out what she meant. Orea was in her room.

"Can we smoke again?" I asked quickly, the crank already coating my throat. She raised an eyebrow. "Suddenly Rick's not so funny anymore."

The words had more truth than I realized. It hurt that he was with someone else even though I knew he had every right to be. I couldn't stop him from being with anyone anyway. Shit, I didn't even do that when we were together.

The first time he cheated on me he told me he had kissed this girl. Her name was Pamela. I still hate that name.

Rick was drunk. It was just one time and he didn't mean to do more than kiss. He cried when he told me about it. Said he was sorry. I forgave him, of course, and unknowingly gave him permission to fuck other women. Once Rick had the nerve to ask if we could have an open relationship, meaning he could get what he wanted and still be with me. Erin was furious when I told her. She asked if I said yes. And I had, mainly because I figured if he was with other girls, then maybe he wouldn't pressure me so much. Maybe it could just be us without sex reigning over our heads.

I regretted it the next day. Every girl I saw him with, I wondered if he had touched her. If he liked her skin more than mine. Wondered if he'd leave me. I told Erin how I felt. She told Rick to knock it the fuck off, and I thought the problem was solved. Little did I know, he solved it by fucking girls behind my back. That's why we broke up, or rather, why I broke up with him.

Jay called to tell me something was up—that he had caught Rick fucking some other girl. I made up some excuse to my parents and headed over there.

It was difficult to look him in the eyes.

"I want to break up," I managed to say.

"Why?"

I thought of Jay, of him walking in on them having sex. Whoever she was. I wondered if Rick liked her more.

"You cheated on me," I said.

He stepped back. "Who told you that?"

I didn't want to tell him. Jay was one of his best friends. He had betrayed Rick to help me. "Don't start that," I said. "I know you did it."

"Whoever it is fucking lied. I've never cheated on you. I never could."

I wanted to believe him. Broke up with him anyway. It was a good thing, too. I found out later he had cheated on me two other times that week alone—

all with different girls. Talk about a great boost of confidence. I did a lot more drugs after that.

"You're thinking about him." Orea was sprawled on the lawn. She handed me her lighter. "It's been over a month. You did the right thing."

"I know. But it's still hard. You think about Josh, don't you?"

"All the time. He's stopped talking to me."

"At all?"

"Yeah. One day after we fuck he just decides he doesn't want me in his life anymore." She took a furious drag of her cigarette and sat up, her knees against her chest. "I think he likes someone else. Or maybe he's afraid of loving me. I don't even know anymore. He's a fucking moron and I hate that I still love him."

"Oh, honey." I leaned against her. Wondered if she felt the same way I did.

"I think I'm gonna take a nap," she said. I nodded. My way of saying I understood. She wanted to escape. I gave her a hug and called my mother for a ride.

I wanted to believe I was over Rick, that I hated him for what he did. But I knew I wasn't. I wanted to see him again. Call him or something. Maybe I could get Angie to drive me past his house. Maybe he'd be there.

But then what? Never mind, I didn't want to say goodbye to you? I don't hate you for raping my friends? Can we get back together so you can fuck my life up again?

Stupid. All stupid. I needed to focus on something else. I searched my cell phone. Angie? No, she was hanging out with her parents today. Sucked. My shit was almost gone. Could call Becky and get more. But I had no way of getting there.

I kept going down my phone list. Stopped at Danielle's name. I missed her. Pushed the call button and waited. Got her answering machine. Might as well leave a message.

"Dee? Hey it's Lynn. I was just calling to see what you were doing. It's, um, been awhile. Give me a call." I paused. "I'm having a going away party. It's this Saturday at Shannon's house. She's leaving town too. Call if you need directions, I mean, if you want to go." Another pause. "I'd like it if you came. Love you. Bye."

Stuck at home again. God, I wanted a fucking car. But I wanted a lot of things.

So I sat in my room and stared at the wall. The pink butterfly he had brought me was hanging on the knob of my closet. Its glossy eyes stared at me. They looked like his eyes. I turned the butterfly against the closet and left my room.

I decided to do more lines out of boredom, hoping it would pick me up from whatever hole I had fallen into. I closed the bathroom door and set up my shit the usual way. Stared at it, holding the dollar bill in my hand. For a second I wondered why I was going to snort. I almost didn't want to. Imagined the burning, the taste in my throat, the antsiness...I shook my head, leaned over, and let it all in.

The door opened.

I looked up, the dollar bill half hanging from my nose. Elle was standing there, her petrified expression shouting at me from the doorway.

Holy fuck. My sister was watching me use.

"What are you doing?" I yelled. "Get out!" I slammed the door in her face and leaned against the counter. My hands were clammy. So was my forehead. I wiped the moisture above my eyes and caught a glimpse of myself in the mirror.

Was that really me?

Frizzy, tattered hair outlined a pasty, hollowed face. Dark circles were etched beneath my eyes. I ran a finger through my hair, and a small clump of it came out with my fingers. Probably cuz I hadn't brushed it in a while. I licked my lips and gave myself a serious look. I looked dark. Mysterious. My face looked thinner. Was I?

The scale was hidden in the cabinet beneath the sink. Elle had put it there last year because she was afraid of getting obsessed with it. I already was.

My heart pounded as I stepped onto that cold surface. The arrow swung past the usual lines. Stopped at 130. Or was that 129? Impossible. Could I really be 129 pounds? I hadn't weighed that little since...I couldn't even remember. Middle school?

So it was working. I was finally going to see what it was like to feel thin, to look in the mirror and not see my layers of fat. A rush of confidence seized me. It felt good to have something to smile about.

I quickly snorted the rest of the line.

Elle was pretty easily convinced that what had happened in the bathroom was no big deal. I told her I had only done it once before.

"But why did you have to do it here?"

"I don't know," I replied. "Cuz I'm stupid." At least that part was true.

She hugged her arms tighter around her pillow. "I thought you said you've never done crank."

I stared at the carpet. "I lied."

"Why?"

"Cuz I didn't want you to look down on me."

"I won't if you tell me the truth." She paused. "How can I trust you if you lie to me?"

I shrugged. "I guess you can't. I mean, it's not like I care if you know. It's just that I don't want you to think that I'm addicted."

"Well you've only done it twice, right?"

I swallowed and nodded in agreement. "It's not even that great."

"Do you promise not to do it again? Cuz I won't tell if you don't do it anymore."

"I won't if you won't try it."

Elle made a face. "No way. I'm not that dumb." She looked at me. "Sorry."

I laughed. "Don't be. You're right. I am pretty fucking dumb."

"No you're not, Lynn. You're just…special."

"Thanks babe." My voice was pure sarcasm, but there was more relief to that sarcasm than I would have liked to admit. I could have gotten fucked over that day. Why didn't I lock the door? Or maybe I should just do it in my bedroom. Away from my sister. Away from the world.

I was running out of time. The closer I was to leaving for school, the further I wanted to be from feeling. So I used as much as possible.

But that wasn't good enough. My friends were drifting into their own lives and I was left alone. I only had ten days left. You'd think they'd be trying to spend every possible moment with me. But as they say, life is full of disappointment.

Kat was busy pursuing a guy named Trevor and some other dude whose name I can't remember. Sienna said being with other guys was Kat's way of dealing with the abortion. I think Kat was trying to forget it.

Orea told me Josh had suddenly started talking to her again. I guess that meant it was okay for her to ditch me in order to soak in every possible moment with him. I tried to understand and give her the space I thought she needed. I even made the effort to hang out with both of them. We ended up watching a movie on Josh's bed. They kept giving each other those annoying puppy dog eyes. Barf. By the time it was over, the sexual tension was so thick it I could almost touch it. So I left. The whole situation made me angry.

Maybe I was being selfish, but Josh wasn't going anywhere. Even if he was, he didn't deserve to be around her. I would never hurt her like he did. But I guess that doesn't matter when it's a guy.

The list went on. Erin and Nate had sunk into drunken isolation and it felt like I couldn't get through. I called her to see if she wanted to go to the park or something, but she said she needed to save money on gas. Oh, and she and Nate were drinking later and needed money for that too. But I would understand, right?

Shannon was consumed by packing and spending time with old friends, but mostly she wanted to get used to being away from everyone. Isolation helped her ignore the pain of leaving.

Maybe I should just get used to being alone.

But what if I didn't want to be alone anymore? I hated being stuck at home with nothing to do but stare at the memories crawling on my carpet. Packing the past was more painful than facing the future. I didn't want to choose what to take with me and what to leave behind. Everything held some kind of meaning, an emotion that tugged at the core of who I was.

Maybe this was a chance to free myself. I could throw away everything Rick chained me to, toss the pain of leaving my friends and family behind...but then what would be left of me? I felt raw without everything coating my walls. It was this fresh, gray mass that had been shriveled and torn into something I couldn't even recognize. I needed something to run to, and everything my fingers grasped was slipping away.

So I put on a half used smile, spent time with my family, and got high with Scott and Angie. It felt good to feed my veins the adrenaline I couldn't manage on my own.

"Are you scared of leaving?" I asked Angie as she, Scott and I smoked on Scott's patio.

Angie took a thoughtful drag of her cigarette. "I would be lying if I said no."

"Everyone's scared of change," Scott said.

I nodded, but it wasn't exactly change I was so afraid of. It was leaving. Leaving meant losing everything. It was getting lost in the nothing inside of me.

"But what if it doesn't work?" I asked them. "What if I hate it?"

"You won't." Angie patted my leg. "I'll be there. And if it sucks, well, we'll make it fun."

But what if all I wanted to do was run away?

"Your phone's ringing." Scott dug my phone from my purse and handed it to me. It was Danielle.

I lit another cigarette and wandered out of ear shot. "Hi."

"Hi."

"I'm glad you called. I've missed you."

"I miss you too," she said.

Pause. "How are you?"

"Good."

"That's good."

Another pause. I bit my lip.

"Actually, I'm not good. I'm crappy. I saw Eric again." Her ex-boyfriend. "I know he saw me too, but he pretended he didn't."

I took a drag of my cigarette. "What a dickwad. I'm sorry, honey."

"Why did my first boyfriend have to be so stupid? Or maybe I'm stupid."

Exhaled. "You're not stupid."

"If only I could've found someone who actually wanted a relationship, who didn't dump me cuz he wanted to look good for his friends."

"I thought you broke up with him," I interrupted.

"Who told you that?"

"Ryan."

"Oh." She sighed. "That's not how it was supposed to happen."

I knew what she meant. "It's okay," I told her. "We've been drifting. You don't have to tell me everything."

"But that *is* everything. I mean, getting dumped by my first boyfriend is huge. Normally, you'd be the first one to know." She sighed again. "I guess I've been mad at you."

"Why?" I knew why, but I wanted her to say it.

"You're not around anymore. You don't have to hang out with me 24-7 or anything, but it'd be nice once in awhile." Was she crying? "It's not the same as it used to be. You've changed."

That scared me. Had I really changed that much? "Not as much as you think. I just hang out with weird people and do drugs all the time."

"And I don't."

"You're not missing much. Shit's been really bad lately."

I told her about Rick. It was weird telling it to someone from the beginning, someone who hadn't been there to see it. It felt like I was talking about someone else. A very fucked up someone.

"And that was the last time you talked to him?" she asked.

"Yeah."

"Wow."

There was silence for a moment, and I thought I felt her hostility melt through the phone. I hesitated. "Does this mean you're coming?"

"Yes."

I smiled. Hadn't lost her yet. A sigh rippled through me. Friends are so easy to lose. I remembered Danielle in the peak of our friendship, how much she was willing to help me. When my father made me so angry that I couldn't cry, she brought me to her mother's van and sat with me while I told her what he had done. We drank apple juice and nibbled oatmeal cookies. But she was the one who ended up in tears. We laughed how she had cried instead of me, and then she hugged me. It was the kind of hug that wraps the love around. And I felt something lift. Something small inside my gut. A part of the pain. And I knew I felt better because of her.

I hung up the phone and wandered back to Scott and Angie.

"Danielle's coming," I told them, taking a cigarette from the pack on the table.

"Good." Angie stood up. "You wanna do another round?"

"But I just started smoking."

"Come back to it." Scott gave me the ashtray and I put my cigarette out. "I wanna get high."

It was Friday afternoon. Two days after talking to Danielle and my first sober day in two weeks. I thought I should rest up before Saturday night. Didn't want to hinder my options of fucked-up-ness, although looking back I was so fucked up one day wouldn't have made much difference. But I wanted to feel like I had control.

I had made sure to tell my parents well in advance about this party so they couldn't give me an excuse not to go. Their condition: I had to pack. So I locked myself in my room, blasted my angry and depressing music, and started the process of re-organizing my life.

I noticed the concept of packing is a lot simpler than its reality. The idea is to take a bunch of shit and cram it into a suitcase to the point where you have to sit on it to make it close. The reality is the shit never ends up in the suitcase because you end up finding things you had forgotten about all over the room. The memories found hidden in the nightstand or the shelf of junk inside the closet suddenly consumes whatever thoughts you previously had. A quick jog down memory lane inserts the tears in your eyes and you put it in the I'll-deal-with-you-later pile. And the more you sort through, you realize the pile of the past has set up camp on over half your floor.

Momentary determination takes hold of the garbage bag and things get tossed. But then the letter an ex-boyfriend wrote trying to get you back slaps you in the face. Or, in this case, the poems Rick had given me two weeks after I broke up with him. I read them over and over, the tears running words together into single, blue blobs. The numbness inside my gut growled and broke into a hard pain I could no longer avoid. Anger seized me, sending my fingers ripping through his heartfelt words. Or whatever they were. I shred his poems until there was nothing left. Threw his pink butterfly across the room. It slammed into the wall. I chucked it in the garbage bag.

I wiped my eyes and stared at the bag, then dug the butterfly out again. Put it in the I'll-deal-with-you-later pile.

"Lynn?" There was a knock on my door.

"Yeah?" I turned my music down as my mother stuck her head through the crack of the door.

"You have a visitor."

It was Erin. I smiled. "Thanks Mom." She closed the door behind her. Erin was looking at all the shit I had piled on the floor.

"Looks like my room."

We sat on the bed. Erin picked at the dirt beneath her nails. "I've been avoiding you."

I waited for her to continue, but nothing came out. "Why?" I asked.

"Because you're leaving. Because it hurts. Because I don't want you to go." She wiped a tear from her eyes. "Also cuz I know you're starving yourself and I can't do anything to stop it."

I put my knees up to my chest.

"I know how you feel, Lynn. About being thin. I know what it's like to look in the mirror and hate what you see." She looked at me. Her eyes were sad. "I'm bulimic."

I chewed on my lip, wanting a cigarette but knowing I wouldn't be allowed to leave the house. Maybe I could get my mother to change her mind.

"I've been wanting to tell you for awhile, but I've been scared."

"Scared?" I asked. "Why?"

Erin looked away. "No one likes admitting their faults. It's a weakness."

"But you don't have to be strong with me."

"Yes I do. Someone's gotta keep you from falling apart."

Too late.

I asked her if she wanted a cigarette. She nodded. My mother said yes to a walk around the block, and soon the nicotine was hugging my lungs. It felt good to breathe again.

"How long have you been throwing up?" I wondered.

"Awhile. Senior year mostly."

"Why did you start?"

"A hangover, actually. I was drinking vodka third period to try and get rid of it, but it just made it worse. So I puked in the bathroom. You remember how I put vodka in those water bottles?"

I nodded. "I had my first vodka experience that way. Remember? Right before math with Mr. Grant?"

Erin laughed. "Yeah. I don't think I was sober at all senior year." She paused. "It hurt too much being sober."

"It still does."

She took my hand and squeezed it. "After I puked that first time, I realized how easy it was. That's why I only ate burritos and milk chocolate. It was better coming back up."

Eew. "So you still do it?"

"Sometimes. It's nice to feel empty, you know?"

"Yeah."

"What do you use? To starve yourself, I mean. Do you use anything?"

"Diet pills." I couldn't bring myself to tell her the truth. It made me feel guilty. Erin had just revealed one of her deepest secrets and I didn't have the guts to tell her mine.

"They're working. You're skinny now."

No one had ever called me that before. Skinny. I felt a smile creep up on my face. "You're not too shabby yourself." I told her. She hugged her waist and smiled.

It was comforting to know someone else had fallen into the jaws of weight obsession. Erin and I had thrown our self-worth into the hands of our mirrors. It's amazing how much power a mirror can have. How thin I felt changed how much I ate, if anything at all. What Erin saw determined if she threw up once, twice or five times that day.

Looking in the mirror after a long day of starvation somewhat appeased the hole inside. Or maybe it fed it. I suppose every adolescent goes through a variation of this at some point. The satisfaction one minute and disgust the next. We all have expectations of ourselves that aren't met, whether it be physical or otherwise. I guess it's just up to the teenager how the void within is dealt with. Some push harder in school, others lose themselves in sports or that computer club everyone thinks is lame, and there are ones like me who drown themselves in anything that hurts. For some it eventually goes away, and others just pretend it isn't there. I still feel disgusted looking at myself sometimes. Maybe it's a curse of the human race. Looking okay on the outside is what makes us feel human on the inside.

"I have something for you." Erin stopped on the front lawn and dug something out of her purse. "It's something that'll help you when you feel alone."

She handed me a CD.

"These are all of our songs," she told me, putting a strand of hair behind my ears. "I have a copy too. That way we can listen to it together even when you're not around."

Something hit me. Hard. I could feel the water splash my cheeks. Erin was crying too. It made me realize that maybe I wasn't alone after all. At least, not as much as I thought. The ice inside me cracked enough to let her sunlight in.

"I thought you didn't care," I sputtered through the salt in my mouth.

She hugged me. "Silly rabbit. Don't you know me by now?"

I watched her drive away. Re-entered my room of cobwebbed memories. My steps were a little lighter. I put Erin's CD in my player and blasted her love. Threw that stupid butterfly into the garbage bag. And this time I didn't take it out again.

I sorted and packed and sorted again until Saturday evening. The party was at Shannon's apartment. She had called to see if I could help her set up. I told her I'd be there around 6:30. It was 6:00. I was finishing my make-up when my mom came into my room.

"Dinner's ready."

I started applying black eye liner on my left eye. "I'm not eating here."

"Where are you going?"

"Shannon's. I told you about this, like, three days ago."

"And I said you could go if you're packed."

I turned to look at her. "I am."

She came into my room. My to-be-sorted-later pile was replaced by a to-be-packed pile. The garbage bag was gone. Things were already half-folded in suitcases or shoved into duffel bags. It seemed like enough payment to exit the house.

My mother didn't seem to see it that way. "This isn't packed, Lynn. There's stuff everywhere."

"No there isn't. It's all organized. Look." I pointed at my half stuffed suitcases. "I'm almost done."

"Almost isn't good enough. You're not leaving until you're finished."

You've gotta be kidding. "Mom, it's Saturday. I'm not leaving until Thursday, right? That's five days away. Why can't I go to my own going away party with my friends, who I won't be seeing for I don't even know how long?" I swallowed thickly, trying not to think about the meaning of my words.

"And what about your family?" my mother snapped. "When are you going to spend time with us?"

"I've been home for the past two days!" I protested. "What do you want?"

My mother crossed her arms. Uncrossed them. "I want you to like being home. I want you to love this family like you love your friends. I want you to be the daughter I know for five minutes before you disappear again."

"I'm not leaving yet, Mom."

"You left a long time ago."

How could I argue with the truth? "And this is my fault, right? I wanted to leave."

She winced. "What did we do to make you feel this way?"

My father entered the room. "What is all this shouting?" He looked at me. "You're not going anywhere tonight."

I looked away. "Yes, I am."

"No, you're not."

This was not happening. "Dad, we had a deal. You and Mom told me if I was packed, then I could go. Well, I'm almost packed and I still have five days to finish. My going away party is tonight and I have to be there."

"When will you finish?"

"I don't know. Tomorrow. Just let me do this."

"When are you going to spend time with this family?" my mother asked. She was crying. Shit.

"Why is your mother crying?" my father yelled.

"She thinks I love my friends more than her."

My mother sniffed. "No. I'm crying because you're leaving in a week and you don't care."

Bubbles of anger swallowed my tears. I couldn't speak.

"That's not true. Lynn cares. And she's going to prove it by staying home tonight." My father's eyes bore into mine. "Right Lynn?"

I shook my head. My father's veins began popping from his neck.

"Yes, you are."

My mother put a hand on his shoulder. "Hold on, honey. Lynn and I were talking about why she feels like she can't be home. I want to know her answer."

My parents stared at me. I struggled to find my voice. "I want to be home."

"That's bullshit," my dad countered. "You hate it here."

You make me. "I don't hate it. I just like being with my friends, and I guess it seems like I'm with them more than I'm here."

"You *are* with them more then you are here."

Yeah, so what? What the fuck did they want me to say? "I'm seventeen!" I said. "Isn't this what's supposed to happen?"

"Being a teenager doesn't give you the right to be a bitch, Lynn." That was my father. This was pushing his buttons.

I didn't care anymore. "Why, cuz I don't do everything you say?" I glanced at my mother. "You moved out when you were my age."

Her tears started again. Fuckin' A.

"I hated my mother at your age," she whispered.

I wanted to roll my eyes. "I don't hate you."

"You don't like me either."

"Just because I'm never home doesn't mean I don't like you. I just feel like I can't breathe when I'm here, okay?"

"You'll just have to suffocate then because you're not leaving!" My father's yelling echoed through my head. I fought furiously to hold back my tears.

"Don't you care if I'm unhappy?" I asked him.

"No. I'd rather you be home."

Ouch.

My mother shook her head. "Let her go out tonight." We both stared open-mouthed. "If this is what she wants, then fine. It'll be her fault if she's not ready by Thursday."

Was this real?

"Fine." My father followed her out the door. Neither of them looked back.

I pushed in front of them and put my arms around my mother. Her body stiffened.

"Thank you," I whispered. Tightened my grip. But she didn't hug back. I let go.

"I love you." I told her.

"Thank you." She closed the door.

Thank you? What the fuck? She didn't say "I love you too." It all ripped holes inside my skin. Fuck them both.

I called Shannon and told her I was on my way. And did she have any cigarettes I could buy from her? She said she needed cigarettes anyway and to give her money later. The thought of doing more crank fluttered in and out of my head. I had enough for a few more lines, and I was going to see Angie tonight anyways. She could get me more shit.

No, no, no. I fought against the urge to run. I needed to hurt this time. It actually felt good to be in pain. I bathed in it as my mother drove me to Shannon's apartment complex. Neither of us said anything. Neither of us could find the words.

"Bye," I said, shutting the car door lightly behind me. I felt my mother watching me. I turned around. Her hands gripped the wheel, her head hovered in sobs.

"I'm sorry," I whispered even though she couldn't hear it. I hated seeing her that way. Knowing I had caused it.

Fuck it. I opened the gate and ran.

Shannon was smoking on her porch when I got there. She was crying.

"What's wrong?" I grabbed a cigarette from her pack.

"It just sunk in that I'm leaving. It's no big deal." She wiped her eyes. "You understand."

"Yeah."

"It just feels like no one cares."

"I know. It's like they know we're leaving but they just do whatever anyways."

"Yup."

"I wonder who will show up tonight," I said.

Shannon shrugged. "Whatever."

It didn't take long to set up the apartment. We moved the couches together to make more space in the living room and set all the alcohol on the table by the kitchen. Everything was clean by 8:00. Blasted 80's music to try and get us in a better mood. It wasn't working.

"When are people showing up?" I asked her.

"Nine."

Shannon curled up on the couch. I wandered to the newly formed bar. "You want a drink?"

"Yeah. Rum and coke." I made her one. Gave myself the same. Put them on the coffee table in front of Shannon. She hugged a pillow.

"Will you play with my hair?"

I smiled slightly and snuggled beside her. Let my fingers run through the red in her hair.

We sat in silence, each absorbed in our depression. Waited longingly for someone to come. Someone to chase the rawness of reality somewhere beyond the moment. Waited to fly away into the smiles of the past.

But the past and all its comfort had already disappeared.

September 7th

I am so dependent on my friends, it's disgusting. I depend on their love, their energy, their support and understanding...depend on them to make me who I am. I've thrown so much of myself into them I've forgotten about me. I just wish I knew who that was.

But I leave in a week. Less than a week. Weird. Kind of glad. Maybe it'll give me a chance to find myself again. I'm so lost. I've just been floating around for so long. Wandering. Searching for me, I guess. What else would I be looking for?

SIX

It was better than Shannon or I could have ever anticipated. All the right people showed up. They were even having a good time. We drank, got stoned, dropped acid, choked down mushrooms…I personally went for pot and alcohol, two things I had been neglecting for what seemed like forever. Fun things. It was the last party. I had to make it count.

I was pouring my third glass of rum and coke when I noticed Danielle and Chad standing by the door.

"Dee?" They looked at me. Danielle had never said hi. "How long have you been here?"

"Maybe half an hour," she said. "I've been talking to Chad."

"Oh." Pause. "That's good." I wondered if she could hear my disappointment. "You having fun?"

Danielle smiled. "Lynn." I could barely hear her. "I'm on ecstasy."

I looked at Chad. He shrugged.

"I wanted to see why you love it so much." She kissed me lightly on the cheek. "And now I know."

"It's fun, isn't it?" I squeaked. Danielle on ecstasy excited me. We could play. Do lotion balls and lights and all those fun things. I could show her where I'd been. Who I had become.

I smiled and took her hands. Squeezed. And then I noticed something.

"Is that what I think it is?" I asked her.

"What?" Danielle followed my gaze to the tiny red marks along her fingertips.

"You've been doing it again," I said.

She yanked her hands from mine. "I don't know what you mean."

"Cutting yourself with those stupid nail clippers."

She glanced at Chad. He was staring at her hands. She put them in her pockets. "Leave me alone."

"No."

"Why not?"

"Because that's not what friends do, Dee. You would do the same for me."

She turned sharply towards me, tears stinging her eyes. "Yeah, I would. Isn't that the problem?"

She was angry. I stepped back. "I don't understand."

"I wait for you to call or talk to me or just be a fucking friend, but you're never there."

"I told you I was sorry. You know what's been going on with me. I still love you—"

"Fuck off!" she spat. "You don't give a shit about me."

"Danielle!" I felt my eyes watering. "You're high—"

"Now you know how it fucking feels." She left. Chad wouldn't look at me as he tailed after her. They disappeared down the hall.

"Whatcha drinking?" asked Jay.

I didn't respond.

He took the drink from my hand and sipped it. "This shit is weak."

I downed the drink in several gulps and gave the cup back to him. "Make me something stronger."

He looked at me questiongly. "You okay, Jew girl?"

I nodded. "Just wanna get fuckered up, right?"

Jay grinned and poured me what he called his specialty. I didn't give a fuck what it was. Just wanted to get drunk. He opened the front door.

"Why aren't we going out back?" I asked, trying not to make a face as I sipped his death punch.

"Too crowded."

I pulled out a cigarette and lit it, letting the silence cool my skin. Tried to keep Danielle out of my head.

"Rick's dating some chick," Jay said.

I didn't look at him. "I know. Chastity."

"No, he dumped her. Now he's with some other bitch named Taffy or something."

Taffy? "Is she a stripper?" I asked.

Jay laughed. "She's hot enough."

I took a hasty drag of my cigarette.

Jay grew quiet, realizing the weight of his words. "He's just trying to deal with losing you," he said.

"Whatever." I didn't want to talk about Rick.

"Did you see Danielle?"

What was this guy trying to do to me? "Yeah."

"She looks really good." I inhaled too quickly and doubled over into a fit of coughs. Jay slapped me on the back.

"Thanks," I wheezed. "You like her?"

Jay nodded. "I've had a crush on her for a long time. She already told me she didn't wanna go out, but I still like her."

She what? More shit I didn't know. Behind the shades of alcohol I could feel the hurt edging itself closer into me. Fuck her. "You know, she's with Chad now," I said.

"That asshole?" Jay threw his cigarette on the ground.

"We can take him," I decided. "Rip off his nuts or something." I attempted to chuck my cigarette over the stairs. It landed by Jay's foot. Oops.

"You're drunk," Jay laughed.

"No I'm not." My eyes softened at the look on Jay's face. He really did like her. "Look Jay. She needs to figure this shit out on her own."

And I needed another drink. Or maybe two.

Kenny greeted us at the door, his pupils dilated with multiple drugs. I was surprised to see him here. Kat and Josh were both around somewhere.

"Kenny!" I squeaked

"Lynn!" He imitated my girlish squeal. Gave me a hug.

"I'm glad you're here," I told him. My way of telling him I was glad he existed. Just in case he needed to know.

"Hoobajah!" he yelled. He held his glass up.

"Hoobajah!" we cheered, hoisting our glasses into the air. That was a toast to, um, something. I finished my drink and put it on the table. Jay picked up the empty cup.

He opened the vodka and filled my cup almost to the top. Added a dash of fruit punch for color.

"That's a lot of shit, Jay. I've already had three, wait, five? I don't remember how many." I could feel my body swaying against the table. Jay handed me my cup.

"Chug it."

I drank it quickly, trying not to gag as the vodka crashed into my throat. I still hate vodka.

"Here." I handed the cup to Jay. "No more," I said thickly.

Jay laughed. "Check this out." He handed me a green and purple swirled pipe.

"It's pretty," I said.

He handed me a lighter. I took it. Wait. We were still inside. "Here?" I asked.

Jay nodded. "Shannon said she didn't give a shit. Just don't get any ash on the ground."

Cool.

"I'm taller than Jesus!" Tony was standing on the counter, his head crouched so he wouldn't hit the ceiling. I laughed. Took a couple hits. The weed was delicious.

"You fucking Mexican." Jay threw an empty pack of cigarettes at Tony. He jumped off the counter. Something fell in the kitchen.

"Shit!" Tony cursed. "What was that?"

"Just a cup." Angie picked it up from the floor.

"Angie!" I squealed.

She grinned as I stumbled towards her. "You're fucked up."

"Am I?" Maybe. The ground felt funnier than I remembered. "You're here," I slurred, extending my arms out so she could give me a hug. "Who have you been hanging out with?"

"People." Angie told me. Helpful. "Scott's here. So are Ryan and Lisa." Her eyes grew a darker shade of mysterious. "They're gonna do coke if you wanna."

"Coke? Why not meth?"

"Ssh!" Angie warned, making sure no one had heard us. "Cuz that's what Ryan and Lisa want. They're gonna treat, so whatever."

But don't you want it to...to...want what to? My thoughts weren't working properly. "I was gonna say something. What were we talking about again?"

Angie laughed and took my hand.

Ryan, Lisa and Scott were already in the bathroom. Angie locked the door as Ryan separated the lines.

"Those are thick," I said, leaning against the wall. Twice the size of normal lines.

"Coke's different," Ryan explained. "It's more intense. Doesn't last as long, so you can do more."

Oh.

"You wanna do the first line?" he asked.

"Sure." I steadied myself and took the straw from Scott, managing to get the whole line in one try. "It's smoother."

"Yeah," Scott said. "The drip's not as bad either."

Ryan had enough for two lines each. We thanked him and opened the bathroom door for smokes.

Sienna was in the doorway. "Oh. I didn't know all you guys were in there." She was staring at me. I concentrated on the wall behind her, although it was difficult to focus on one space. Everything was kind of shifting.

"Yeah. PC," Scott murmured. Private Conversation. I started to follow them.

"Lynn," Sienna said. I stopped, avoiding her gaze. Did she know? "You have something on your face."

Shit. "Where?"

She touched right under the side of her nose. I felt something grainy on my face. It was white.

"Did I get it?" I asked, trying to make it seem like no big deal.

"Yeah." She was giving me the strangest look. I had to get out of there.

"I'm gonna go smoke."

"Lynn?"

I forced myself to look at her.

"I, um, just wanted you to know that I'm here for you if you need anything."

My hands felt clammy.

"If you wanted to talk about...something."

Was it hot in here? I wiped my forehead with the back of my hand. It felt damp. "Thanks, but I'm okay."

"At school too. If you need me, I mean."

"Okay." I practically ran outside.

It seemed like half the party was on the porch. The lights blurred between seas of voices, playing with the steadiness of the floor. I leaned against the wall to steady the ground and lit a cigarette.

"It's Jack-o-Lynn!" Josh rounded in front of me. I gave him a funny look. "Jack-o-Lynn?"

"Jack-o-Lantern...Lynn...you know?"

I shook my head. Josh shrugged. I wondered if he had seen Kat yet. She probably wasn't too happy about Josh and Orea. If she knew. Where was Orea?

"Are you hiding?" I asked him. He smiled.

"Yeah. Are you?"

I glanced around, feeling the swarms of people wash over me. It made me feel nauseous. Maybe the coke was starting to set in. "I guess."

"Are you hiding from me?" Erin gently poked me in the ribs.

"Never," I smiled, trying to ignore the heat in my head. Something was wrong. I flicked my cigarette.

"Why don't you just stay the fuck out of my way?"

Erin and I turned to see what was going on. It was Kat and Orea. They faced one another, their bodies curved and waiting.

"I had him first," Kat hissed.

Orea looked like she was about to cry. "He *was* my first."

I glanced behind me, but Josh had disappeared.

Kat. "You liked him cuz I did. He didn't want to be with you, and I was there for him. We need each other."

Orea. "You need someone to fuck."

Kat. "And you had to beat me in something. Why are you always competing?"

Orea. "Why can't you be a real friend?"

Back and forth, back and forth. Like a tennis ball. No one cared to stop the screaming match as their voices escalated past the stars. Seemed like no one even noticed. Just like no one noticed how I reached to grab the railing in order to keep myself from falling. I felt so dizzy, and my intestines were ready to run a marathon.

The sliding door didn't want to open. Angie did it from the other side. She was smiling.

"It's not bad, huh?"

I shook my head and shifted past her. "Where are you going?"

"Bathroom," I called. Turned the doorknob quickly.

Danielle and Chad were wrapped together on the bathroom floor. Each missed some article of clothing, their tongues shoved down throats and other body parts. My stomach lurched and I closed the door.

"Who's in there?" It was Shannon. Here eyes were puffy. "You look funny. Are you okay?"

I swallowed. "Kat and Orea are fighting on the porch. Danielle and Chad are making out in the bathroom."

"Doesn't surprise me. Nothing fucking surprises me anymore."

I knew she meant something more, and whatever it was had made her cry. I was supposed to ask what she meant, but I couldn't. I didn't have the energy to hear the answer. "Is your other bathroom empty?"

She bit her lip and shrugged, hurrying to another part of the room. I would apologize later. Ask her what had made her cry. It would be stupid to neglect her over this. Getting too fucked up. Using coke and drinking and smoking weed.

Stupid.

I locked the door and allowed myself to collapse against the toilet. My forehead felt cool against my arms as I stared at the sloshing toilet water. Please, just let me puke. I wanted it out. All of it.

Nothing happened.

I thought of Erin. How she felt in the bathroom, head hung over the toilet. How much she wanted it out. Was I like her now? I shoved my finger down my throat and prayed to throw up.

And throw up I did. It came in streams, splattering against the sides of the toilet bowl. The drinks and the coke and the pot and the pasta Shannon and I scarfed before the party. The pain and the anger and the lonely parts that refused to admit they were drowning, the fear of losing everything and drifting into a nothingness too dark to see. Attempting to find the light that wasn't there. Wanting to float away through whatever it was that made me fly. Locking myself in some darkened cell so the hurt couldn't find me. So I could hide.

Because I deserved to feel alone.

Hadn't this party turned to shit? The group was gone. Numbness bled inside my heart at the thought, but I knew it was true. The family I had thrown myself inside of was dissolving into teenagers who were drifting apart. And I knew it was natural and normal and healthy, but it was killing me. There was this space inside. I could feel it swallowing me whole.

The vomit stopped after awhile. I stood up. Standing didn't feel as bad as it did before. Washed my hands. My face. Tried to get it all to fall down the drain. Some of the pieces stuck to the sink.

I opened the door. Ryan was standing in the hall. I grabbed his arm. "Do you have any more coke?"

He laughed and pushed me in the bathroom.

Time to fly away again.

Part Two

Drowning in Cake

She Dissolves

Dried rose petals
Once soft, fragrant
Sleep in the shadows
Of a blackened sky,

Burnt by rage and lies
That pound the ashy ground,
Spraying bitterness upon the sand.

Alone, she sits in murky tears,
Fingers brushing light pink petals
That melt into the earth—

And wonders if she too
Could disappear.

Early September

September 13th

Well, I'm here, lying in my college dorm room. And I love it. The people, the environment...everyone's so friendly and willing to open up. And my roommates are all really nice. And the best part is that my parents can't do a damn thing about anything I do!

Right now I'm, so happy, so much at peace. I'm not sure how long it will last, but I'm willing to work for it. I want to feel my worth again. I want to love myself again. I don't know. Maybe I do have the strength to walk the path of healing. I'm not sure what to do or how to do it, but I want to. And that just makes my heart sing.

SEVEN

So I was here. College. A four year university in the mountains with forest and ocean and deer and hippies and all the other things that weren't home. I still can't believe I made it. College is like this holy shrine that everyone talks about. Parents and teachers and people you don't even know ask you what college you're going to and what you want to major in and how your grades are and if you've taken the SAT's or the ACT's or CAT's and you just want to hold your head and scream.

And that was just the outside folk. Then there was high school. High school was *hard*. I ran around with my head cut off. Took all the honors classes, the AP classes, the extra curricular activities and all the other shit that supposedly set me apart from the rest of the brilliant students trying to get in. I found myself constantly praying to the academic gods. Asked them to get me through it. Get me to college and out of Hell.

And after hiking through Hell's fire and brimstone and those scary demons that'll turn you to ashes if you look at them funny, I had reached the light. And about damn time! I was doing a happy dance. Literally.

"You want me to play some music for ya?" Angie grinned, resting her head against Adam's chest.

"She's got the music in her head." Adam gave Angie a light kiss on the forehead.

"Dancing with no music! La la la la la!" I sang and bounced towards them, poking my head above the top bunk. "Wanna know why?"

Angie's eyes stared into mine. "Why?"

"Cuz I can!" I couldn't get over it. No more sneaking out, no more nagging, no more lying. I could be myself now. Whoever that was. Whoever I wanted it to be. "Let's do something crazy."

"Like what?" Angie asked.

Adam groaned. "I'm comfortable."

"Come on." I pulled heavily on their blankets. A pillow fell on the floor. They didn't move. "Fine. I'll go myself."

"Hey little sis." Adam held out his arms.
"What?"
"I'm leaving in, like, twenty minutes."
I gave him a hug. "When will you be back?"
"A couple weeks. Gotta fix up my baby a little bit." His VW. He was always talking about "fixing" his car. I remember him saying he wanted to put a spout of beer in there somehow. I don't think he ever did.

"Don't forget the house meeting tonight." Angie's voice had more than a hint of sarcasm.

"Sounds like fun," I told her in the same tone. Rolled my eyes and shut the door behind me.

The living room was pretty cluttered with things people hadn't quite put away, but I was still impressed at the cleanliness of our on-campus apartment. Seven girls. Five bedrooms. One bathroom. Didn't really want to think about the whole seven girls and one bathroom situation. But we had three stalls and a two headed shower, so that made it, um, better. I honestly think our entire complex was made in the hippie age, and most of the students were still living in it. They were already in the courtyard playing hackie sack, blasting Bob Marley and smoking rolled cigarettes. And I wanted to join them.

I made my way outside, smiling shyly at one of my new housemates. She was sitting on the bench that ran through our side of the complex. Her legs dangled over the side. I tried to remember her name.

"Hey Lynn," she said, not taking her eyes from the dancing beatniks across the way.

"Hi." Shit. Was it Cammy? Tammy? Something like that. I took out a cigarette and offered her one.

"Thanks," she said. I gave her my lighter. "I don't really smoke much."

"Don't start. It's hard to quit."

She smiled and took a slow drag, coughing slightly. "I don't think I want to be here."

I tried to read her expression, but her face was blank. "Wrong school?"

"Wrong life." She looked at me. "Do you ever wonder what things would be like if you hadn't done something? Or if you had said yes instead of no?"

I nodded.

"And then you hate yourself for it."

I stared at my cigarette, wondering what she'd done. Or hadn't done. I knew how she felt. How silence feels. That shallow chest pain when you can't fall asleep, so you replay the scenario over and over in your head. Fast forward the good, rewind the bad. Not that it made a difference. Life still happened.

"Life's shit and then you die." She said it like it was a known fact. "My shit stinks."

"Good outlook on life," I smirked. She laughed at me. "My shit doesn't smell too great either."

"Can't be that bad," she said, putting her cigarette out on the bench. It wasn't even half gone. Oh well. She hopped towards the sliding glass door. "You look so innocent."

Was that supposed to be a compliment? What's-her-name didn't know shit about me. Oh yeah, her name.

"I feel like an asshole," I began, catching her before she shut the door, "but I don't remember your name."

"Rhiannon." She went inside.

How'd I get Tammy?

The hippies were still playing hackie sack across the way. Their long skirts over frayed jeans, lack of shoes and mousy dreads screamed rebellion in the most relaxed way I'd ever seen. They just didn't give a fuck, and they were so happy about it. It drew me towards them, and I found myself standing stupidly by their circle.

I met a few of my friends this way. Well, my old friends. They were standing in the same circle, kicking a hackie sack back and forth while sneaking drags of their cigarettes behind a bush. They looked how I wanted to feel. Happy. Even then I could sense that bond, the tie of the group that I desperately wanted to be a part of. I needed them.

"Lynn, right?" Orea asked. *I nodded. Orea and I had gone to the same after school program in elementary school. I didn't know she still remembered me.* "You wanna play?"

"I'm Kat," Kat told me, wedging the hackie sack in between her feet. She half jumped, and the hackie sack flew towards me. *"Here."*

It landed on the concrete.

"Kick it back," said a guy with shoulder length blonde hair. And I remembered where I was. New people. A new life. It could happen again if I let it. I could start fresh this time.

I picked up the hackie sack, dropped it on the side of my foot, and kicked. A girl caught it, passed it along. I walked away.

I strolled along a path that weaved itself in and out of different apartment buildings. Trees quivered in the evening light, dancing with the fingers of the sun. I inhaled the sweet scent of redwoods and dirt and pot and tears sprang in my eyes. This was a place that allowed me to go wherever I wanted, even if it was just a walk down a hill. It was my hill now. My chance. My life.

"Is your name Lynn?"

It was a girl who said it, but I didn't see her.

"Up here."

I looked. She was leaning on the wall of the second floor in front of apartment 415. I shielded the sun from my eyes to see her better. It wasn't working. I had no idea who she was.

"Yeah, it's Lynn." I told her.

"Come up here."

I trudged up the stairs and took a good look at her face. Nope. Still no idea.

"Do you know Scott James?"

Scott. I nodded.

"He told me about you. Said you're really nice."

"Uh, thanks." I paused awkwardly. Shuffled my feet on the concrete. "How do you know him?"

"Friends of friends, I guess."

"Oh."

She looked around. It reminded me of Scott. The way he checked to make sure we were alone. I smiled.

"You smoke?" she whispered.

"Smoke what?" I whispered back.

"Well, pot. My roommate's got some."

"Well, yeah."

I followed her down the hall to 413. She opened the door without knocking. The living room looked the same as ours. Just cleaner. A few guys half waved from the couch. One of them had a shaved head and a wannabe goatee. He smiled more than the rest. His front tooth was chipped. I sped up.

She led me into a room with purple lights and psychedelic pictures. Trance echoed against the walls and through the students that sat in a circle on the floor. There was a hookah in the middle of them. Reminded me of *Alice In Wonderland*.

"Can she join us?" the girl asked.

"What's her name?"

"Lynn."

We passed the rest of the introductions in a well familiarized, first year oriented process. Like a survey. My answers were always the same:
Name: Lynn
Age: 17
Affiliated city and/or state: Somewhere in Hell.
Major: ???
Classes enrolled: Introductory Shakespeare, Psychology and Religion, Freshman Core
School of choice? Didn't think about it.
Apartment/living area: Up the hill.
The girl who was supposedly friends with Scott was named Jolan. Her name was of Armenian origin and yes, she was born in the United States. Other names consisted of Fern, Skip and Linda. Fern had taken residence in a tree somewhere on campus, but the others lived in the apartments here. How convenient.

"I don't even wanna go to college," Skip said, blowing smoke out of his nose. "But you have to if you wanna make money. And I'm gonna make money."

"Fuck that." Linda took the hose from Skip. Inhaled. "I want money, but this is supposed to be an experience, you know?" Linda was sitting next to me, her pink frilly sleeves grazing the rip in my jeans. She seemed kind of preppy. Girly. Something like that. "Just enjoy it, man. That's what my shrink says."

Right.

"I like it," Jolan grinned. "I mean, we've only been here one day, but this is what we've been waiting for. What high school was for."

"Exactly. I mean, it doesn't feel like I had a choice if I went to college or not. Not that I didn't want to come here or anything. It's all just unreal." That was me talking. I found myself absorbed in a conversation with people I had just met. And I was smiling.

"It's the greatest opportunity we'll ever have," Fern said. "Think of the things we can do for society, you know?"

"This is coming from someone who lives in a tree," Skip mumbled.

Jolan and I laughed. Fern ignored the comment. "I want to make a difference in this fucked up world," she said.

"Can anyone blow smoke rings?" asked Jolan. She puckered her lips like a fish, but the smoke still came in streams.

I laughed at the sudden twist in conversation. Now this was college.

"I've always wanted to." Linda blew her cheeks up like a balloon.

"I think you've gotta roll your tongue like a taco and move your face around." That was Fern, whose smoke came out in little puffs. I laughed. Move your face around? Kind of like one of those jigsaw puzzles where all the pieces fit in weird ways. I liked that.

I was stoned.

Somewhere down the line, maybe two bowls and a six pack of cola later, I decided that these people weren't so bad. Maybe we could be friends. Not good friends or anything, but it'd be nice to have others to talk to sometimes. It'd be nice to not be completely alone.

"Lynn?" Jolan's voice poked through my head. I looked around. Everyone else had left. Must have spaced out. I tried to stand up. Fell down. My body felt a lot heavier than I remembered. Hmm. I got on my hands and knees, and gradually pulled myself along the wall. Guess I had smoked a little too much.

"Hey Lynn." Jolan pulled on my shirt. "You should come back sometime."

"Okay," I answered thickly, my eyes droopy in the purple light. Jolan toppled onto her bed and closed her eyes. That looked nice.

My fingers guided the rest of me towards the door. Then there was a crash, and I was face down on the carpet. The trash can was on its side. Oops. I laughed and attempted to pull myself from the floor, but it was so warm and soft. I closed my eyes…

Kat and Orea were on the stairs. They were talking about….something. I couldn't understand them. Their voices fed angrily off one another, blurring into a shouting match as if they were fighting under water.

"What's going on?" I asked. Or tried to. My voice was gone. Could they see me?

Orea threw her cigarette and ran into the apartment. Kat watched her, tears flooding her cheeks. I reached out to comfort her, but she ran away from me.

I climbed the stairs and opened the door to a red room. Voices thundered off the walls, echoing in circles around my head. Orea and Josh were having sex on the floor. Angie, Danielle, and Sienna snorted lines on the coffee table. Shannon sat on the couch smoking a cigarette, her eyes glaring at a figure across the room. It was Rick. He was sobbing against the wall.

I sat next to him. His body shook against his cries. My fingers stretched to calm his tears.

"It's too late now." Erin was crouched beside him, her eyes saddened. *"He's already crazy."*

I awoke to an empty room. It was so quiet. Where did he go? It took me a minute to realize it was just a dream. I got off the floor quickly and left the apartment.

"You sleep good?"

I jumped, half tripping against that guy with the peach fuzz and wannabe goatee. The one who had smiled more than the rest. He was standing by the door.

"Sorry," I mumbled, pulling a cigarette out of my pack. He took out a lighter and waited for me to lean into the flame. "Thanks," I told him.

The smoke was harsh against my dry mouth, but inhaling felt really good. I licked my lips. He smiled.

"What's your name sleeping beauty?"

Oh God. "Lynn."

"I'm Diesel." He held out his hand.

I shook it. "Hi."

Pause. Something about this was really funny. Was I still stoned?

"You do drugs?" he asked.

Interesting way to begin a conversation. "Yeah. Why?"

"My dad sends me shit, cuz he gets all his for free." He inhaled deeply.

I lingered on that word. Free. "Like what?"

"Shrooms. Pot. Crank."

My heart jumped into my mouth. "You have any?"

"Yeah." He smiled. The back of his hand brushed lightly against my own. His fingers traced my knuckles. I stared at his hand and started to pull away. "You want some?" He tightened his grip. I let him.

"Can my roommate do some with us?" I asked as sweetly as I could, pulling a strand of hair out of my eyes.

Diesel put the hair back in front of my face. "Maybe. Are you worth it?"

So this was his game. I could play. "You'll just have to wait," I told him. And with that I turned around, hoping he'd take the hint and let go of my hand. He did.

I ran back down the stairs, up the hill, through our apartment and opened the door to our room. "Angie," I half-shouted, totally out of breath. Angie was on her computer. "You want some free shit?"

We met Diesel right where I left him.

He led us down the stairs, around the 300's building and up a path to 111. Easy room to remember. Diesel opened the door to his housemates smoking weed out of the biggest bong I had ever seen. It was clear, green, and as tall as a small child.

"You wanna rip?" one of the guys asked.

Tempting. "Maybe later," I said.

We went into Diesel's room and locked the door. Angie and I stood around while he fumbled under his bed. There was a picture above him. It looked like a family photo.

"When was that picture taken?" Angie asked.

"Four years ago," Diesel answered without looking up.

"That your sister?"

"Yeah." He set a small mirror, razor blade, and dollar bill on his bed. This guy was hardcore.

"She's pretty."

"She's in jail."

Angie didn't say anything else. We watched Diesel set up to snort.

"So your dad just sends you this shit?" I asked, staring wide eyed at the thick lines on the mirror.

He held out the straw. "When he has it. You wanna go first?"

I snorted the shit slowly, letting the burning coat my nose. God, I loved it.

Diesel took the straw from my hand. "That was sexy."

What, shoving a dollar bill up my nose? Oh yeah, baby. Angie made a face that said *you've gotta be kidding*. I smiled.

"This shit's really good," Angie said. She wiped her nose, sniffing hard. "It's clean."

"Thanks for sharing your shit," I added, anxious for another go. "You don't mind, right?"

Diesel smiled at me. "You'll make it worth my time."

I could see Angie's eyes widen beside me and pretended that I didn't. She handed me the straw.

"I don't trust him," she told me as we walked back towards our apartment. I lit a cigarette and gave it to her.

"Yeah, I know. He's a weasel." I paused. "Will you go there again with me?"

Angie stopped and looked at me. I lit a cigarette for myself. Took a drag. "He has free shit, Ang. I can't say no to that. Can you?"

She paused. "No." Paused again. "But I have shit too. We don't have to go back right away."

I shrugged. "Okay."

We walked in silence the rest of the way, waiting for the drip to pass and the high to set in.

"I think I'm over Adam," Angie told me in between cigarette drags. We were sitting in the same place that I had met Rhiannon. I flicked my lighter on and off against the bench, letting the sweet scent of burning wood fill my nose. "You're gonna light the bench on fire," she said.

"I like the smell." I put the lighter by my foot. "You've been with Adam awhile now."

Angie nodded. "Three and a half months. But it feels longer."

"Is it the long distance thing that makes you over him?" I asked.

"Maybe." Pause. "Last night, when he held me, I didn't feel anything. I used to, you know, feel something."

"Then you should break up with him."

She took a drag. Exhaled. "I think I'm gonna."

And thus it was so. Angie was a very practical person when it came to emotions. There was love or there wasn't. No in between. I'm still not sure if that's an easier way to feel.

Angie put her cigarette out on the bench. "Pyro," I said, scraping my own cigarette against the wood. "What time is it?" I asked her.

She grinned. "8:00. You ready for some fun?"

Oh yeah.

We then entered the domain of the House Meeting.

Four girls sat in various places, each looking their own version of nervous. Angie sat on the floor against the sliding glass door. I did the same.

"Hi," Angie said.

My teeth had suddenly glued themselves together.

"Hi," they smiled back, some of them more than others. I wondered if I remembered their names. Gertrude sat by the dining room table. She was the snotty one. The blondes, Bonnie and Karen, had claimed the couch. Sheena sat on the floor by the kitchen. I hoped that was right.

I tapped my fingers against the carpet. It was way too quiet.

"We're missing someone," Angie said in attempts to break the silence.

"Yeah, we know." Spoken by Miss High and Mighty Gertrude. Barf.

"There she is," half-whispered Sheena, hiding behind her mass of curly hair.

A knock rippled the glass behind us. We moved over so Rhiannon could open the sliding door. She sat on the floor next to Angie.

Gertrude sighed dramatically, "I have somewhere to go tonight."

"I think we all have plans, Gertrude," Karen said as if speaking to a small child. Bonnie put her hand over her mouth, stifling a giggle.

"Meeting to order!" bellowed Rhiannon, imitating an extremely drunk judge. Sheena laughed.

I wanted another smoke. "What first?" I asked, hoping they'd take the hint and move the meeting along.

"How about food?" began Bonnie. "Should we have some kind of communal stash, like milk and butter?"

"I'm vegan." Sheena twirled her curls around her mouth as she spoke. "I drink soy."

"So no to that one." That was Gertrude. We tried to ignore the holier-than-thou-ness in her voice. "We'll just have our own shelves like everyone else."

"Should we have a job chart?" asked Karen. "My sister had one and it worked."

"Those are dumb." Gertrude again. Karen's face fell slightly. "If we just keep our shit clean, it won't matter."

I didn't want Karen to feel like a retard. "But what about communal things, like vacuuming the living room? No one's gonna do that." Not that I really wanted a job chart. The idea made me cringe.

"Let's try it without one first and see how dirty it gets," Rhiannon suggested.

That seemed to calm all parties concerned. Angie glanced at me with eyes that begged leaving. I looked at the bench behind us. She nodded.

It was strange. Angie and I were residents of the apartment, yet we didn't really care much about what went on. It was like staring at a bunch of fish outside their tank. We just kind of watched them swim around and make funny faces at each other.

"What about toilet paper? Do we all buy our own rolls?"

"That's retarded. Well wait. Sheena, toilet paper's vegan, right?"

"Yes, Gertrude."

"Didn't want to offend your hippiness."

"Gertrude, don't be mean."

"It's fine."

"We could have a coffee can. Put the money for toilet paper in there."

"No. Whoever buys it, we should just give money to."

"That could get messy."

"So could the coffee can. How much do we put in?"

"However much it costs."

"As long as we all pay the same amount, it shouldn't matter how we do it."

"But it does. I don't want to be the one buying toilet paper all the time."

This was fucking ridiculous. I didn't want to be here. Would rather go back to Diesel. Back to more crank. I sniffed and wiped my nose.

"Your hand," Angie whispered.

There was blood on it. I touched the bottom of my nose. It was bleeding.

"I'll be right back," I murmured, shoving my hand over my nose. No one seemed to notice. I grabbed some toilet paper and pinched my nose, holding my head as far back as it would go. The blood dripped down my throat. Eew.

It was the first nose bleed I'd ever had. Probably the crank eating away at my nasal cavity, or whatever the technical name for it was. Fabulous. I edged towards the doorway and peaked into the living room.

"Okay, so we'll trade off buying. That's fair, right?"

A collection of head bobs and mhmm's.

"We should do that with paper towels too."

"And cleaning supplies."

"No, we get those from campus."

"Should we have some kind of official list?"

"For toilet paper and paper towels?"

"There has to be more than that."

I tiptoed through our room and out the back door. Whoever designed this place knew its residents would eventually need their own escape route. Each bedroom had a door to the outside world. I snuck out of ours and sat beneath the overhang that connected us to the next apartment. With toilet paper still shoved up my nose and my head back against the wall, I put a cigarette in my mouth and tried to avoid setting the toilet paper on fire.

Is this what my life was going to be like now? Me hiding in the corner, avoiding the petty bickering of new housemates as my insides slowly trickle down my face? I touched the toilet paper around my nose and felt for any signs of dampness. It was dry. I took the toilet paper out of my nose and stared at the darkened blood. My blood. A sign of life. Breath. Some kind of desire to survive.

Why could I only think about getting high?

The door opened behind me. It was Angie.

"There you are, sneaky." She took a cigarette from my pack and sat on the other side of the hall.

"Are they still talking about toilet paper?"
"No. They moved on to dishes."
"Maybe we should buy paper ones."
"Or just eat on paper towels."
"Would they charge us extra for that?"
"Probably."
Angie smiled at me. I was glad she was here.
"Do you think they're done yet?" I asked, putting my cigarette out on the concrete.
"No."
I reached for my pack. There was only one left. "We need more smokes."
"I'm almost out too," Angie said, "Wanna go downtown tonight?"
"Yeah." I paused. "Let's go now. You think they'd notice?"
Angie shook her head. "We should go back in there."
I rolled my eyes. "It's not going to matter. I don't care anyways."
"But we'll need that later, Lynn. A say in things. We'll need this to back us up."
"Why are you so fucking logical?"
Angie grinned. "You know you love it." She dropped her cigarette and opened the door. I waited.
"You go first," she said, holding the door for me. "No running away."
"Can I hide?" I asked as she closed the door behind us.
"Only if I know where you are."
I threw my bloody tissue into my trash can and reluctantly followed my roommate into the rest of the house. Gertrude, Sheena, Bonnie, Karen and Rhiannon debated our future sanity while Angie and I sat on the sidelines. We waited for the final score.
Several penalty shots and a few bruised egos later, we decided on lists, coffee cans and communal dishes. I wondered how long it would take before all of it would fall apart and Angie and I would be wiping exploding heads from the sliding glass door.

Ninety-seven minutes later. Rhiannon, Sheena, Bonnie, Karen, Angie and I were on our way downtown. We had invited Queen Gertrude, but apparently she had better things to do. So the rest of us piled awkwardly into the back of bus 1L, weighing our presence against the smell of excitement and BO. I stared at the blur of colored lights that flew along the window.

It didn't take us long to get downtown.

I wasn't sure what to expect as I stepped off the bus at the metro station. I just wanted to move. Diesel's shit was really good. I was definitely high. I pulled the last cigarette out of my pack and lit it quickly, letting the smoke calm my lungs. Angie wasn't far behind me.

"Hey." A man in a collared gray shirt walked towards us. "No smoking here. Go to the end of the street."

"Sorry," we told him, walking quickly to the outskirts of the metro station. The rest of the girls followed.

We found ourselves in the middle of a long street. Shops were everywhere, littered by wandering groups of all different kinds of people. There were bums, skaters, hippies, stoners, tourists, locals, gang bangers, college kids, and other random types. All were consumed by the energy that danced in the air. It made me feel alive.

"I wanna buy more smokes," I told Angie. She nodded. We looked at the rest of the group. "Does anyone care if we stop at the liquor store?"

The girls shrugged. "Where's the liquor store?" Karen asked.

"I dunno."

"Where's a liquor store?" Rhiannon asked the first group of people she saw. I couldn't decide whether they were skaters or stoners, but one of them was really cute. He smiled at me.

"At that light down there, across from Taco Bell."

"Thanks."

I half wanted to ask them to come. Okay, two-thirds. But I held myself back with a drag and followed the rest of the group. Karen and Bonnie snuck a few looks behind them, too.

The cute eye candy slammed into ugly old man as we passed two wrinkled hippies smoking out of organic tobacco pipes. Long gray hair draped over worn, cow-skinned jackets and dangling necklaces, accompanied by two guitars and a bad version of The Who. Their eyes were closed as they sang on the ground in front of their opened guitar case. I wondered how many years they had been sitting there. Sheena gave them a dollar.

The light was red. We waited, watching some skaters do tricks on the stairs of Taco Bell. One of them spun around, jumped, and fell on the sidewalk. The others laughed at him. So did I.

"You're mean," Angie told me as I gave her a five dollar bill.

"That was funny," I protested, shoving one of my fingernails in my mouth.

We crammed into a small liquor store, our eyes drinking the beers and other alcoholic accessories we weren't allowed to buy. Oh, to be twenty-one. Shit, eighteen would be nice.

"These places just make me wanna get stoned," Rhiannon half whispered from across the candy aisle. I giggled. Rhiannon grinned and grabbed a package of sour gummy straws. Mmmm. Definite stoner food. If only I was hungry.

"I fucking live by these," Rhiannon told me. She put the candy back on the shelf. No, wait. She didn't. She put it in her purse. I know because after she did it she wouldn't look at me.

I wondered what else she wouldn't look at me for.

I bought some strawberry flavored bubble gum and bright green mints, anticipating the moment my lungs would be full of sweet nicotine. Followed Sheena outside the store. The skaters were still doing tricks across the street. I wanted them to teach me how.

Karen and Bonnie were watching them too. Their eyes looked hungry. I laughed.

"What?" Sheena asked, pink sugar hugging the edge of her lips.

"I think Karen and Bonnie wanna go across the street," I explained

"Damn trampbeezies," Rhiannon laughed. "That's what we should call them. Trampbeezies." A sour straw was in her mouth.

"Here." Angie set a pack of cigarettes in my hand. Woohoo! I packed them quickly against my palm. Opened the pack. Lit one.

"You smoke a lot," Sheena said.

"I do a lot of things," I told her.

The trampbeezies made their way across the street.

"Should we follow them?" Sheena asked, throwing her candy wrapper in the ashtray by the door.

"Eh," we shrugged.

Eventually Karen and Bonnie decided the skaters weren't all that interesting, so we walked along the strip, oohing and aahing over silver jewelry, vintage clothing, glass blown pipes and hookahs, second hand CD's, and many other glamorous hippie accessories. My favorite was the giant, two storied used bookstore. I bought a copy of *Alice in Wonderland*. Kinda wished there were rabbit holes downtown.

We stopped to eat at the Taqueria. Well, to watch everyone eat. Angie and I just sipped horchata, bouncing our knees against the bottom of the table.

"Aren't you hungry?" Karen wondered, taking a huge bite of one of the biggest burritos I had ever seen. Angie shook her head.

"Too much popcorn before we left."

It could have been true. Angie loved popcorn. She'd eat it for meals all the time. That and frozen peas. I kept giving her funny looks until she made me try some. They're actually not that bad.

"Lynn!" I turned around. Jolan and Linda balanced plates of food behind me.

"Hey, what's up?" I moved over so they could sit with us. Angie gave me a look. "Oh, this is Angie," I told them.

"Hi."

"Hi. I'm Jolan, this is Linda."

"Hi."

"Hi."

"Jolan knows Scott," I told Angie.

"How do you know him?"

"We met at a rave."

Raves. Those parties where everyone gathers in blacklight and brightly beaded bracelets, shoving pacifiers in their mouths when the ecstasy kicks in. I hadn't been to one of those in a long time. It had been, what, two months? I had told my parents I was spending the night at Kat's, which was true if you count us getting to her house at five in the morning. God, that night was fun.

A pang thumped hard in my chest. I was already missing them.

"There's a party down here somewhere," Linda said through smacks of her enchilada. "You guys should come."

"Killer." Karen language for yes. Bonnie bounced her head in agreement. I looked at Angie. She shrugged.

"Okay," I told them. I wanted to go. Anything to move.

"A real college party?" Sheena stared at her nachos thoughtfully. "I always wondered what those are like."

Jolan, Linda, Karen, Bonnie and I had to bite our lips to keep our laughter down.

Angie just smiled. "You'll find out, won't ya?"

"I don't think I'm gonna go." Rhiannon crumpled her napkin and threw it at the trash. She missed.

"Why not?" I asked her.

"Not in the mood."

"But you have to go." Sheena looked at her with huge, pleading eyes. "It'll be fun. Please?" Damn, Sheena had that down to an art. I should be taking notes.

"It's not like there's anything else to do." That was Bonnie. She had a point.

Neither worked. Rhiannon refused our begging and hastily grabbed her purse, throwing her taco wrapper into the trash. She made it this time, but she was gone before I had a chance to tell her I noticed.

"What's up with her?"

"Who knows."

"Did we say something wrong?"

"I don't think it was anything we said."

"She must be too cool for us."

"Whatever."

I didn't say anything. In my opinion, it didn't matter why she left. It's that she did it. I wished I had the guts to just get up and walk away.

"Cigarette hour," I announced, carefully pulling my legs from the table so I wouldn't hit Linda.

"It's always cigarette hour," said Sheena.

"Damn straight."

Jolan and Linda said the party was down some side street not too far from here. We set out on the first of many adventures in locating the party of the night. I had to keep myself from walking too quickly. Diesel's shit was still going strong.

We walked for about ten minutes when our party guides decided that they were lost.

"I thought it was down this street somewhere," Jolan insisted.

"Are you sure this is the right one?" Bonnie asked.

"No."

"Seriously?"

"It's not like we've been here that long," Linda snapped.

"Nobody has." Karen said. "We thought you knew."

Oh goody. A bunch of sober, irritated girls. Fun. I was about to ask if there was anyone we could call for help or alcohol when a faint residue of voices perked my ears.

"Do you guys hear that?" I asked, hoping my brain hadn't completely eaten itself away. I was high, but not that high.

The girls stopped to listen.

"It's coming from over there." Sheena pointed behind the houses we were facing.

We followed the noise down the street and behind a house to some kind of garage. I didn't know how any of us could have possibly missed this party. People were everywhere, not to mention the music that pounded outside of the walls. I felt right at home.

Jolan lead us through the crowd out front and opened the door. There were twice as many people inside.

Sheena gave me a huge smile. "Now this is college."

It's amazing how generous people are with alcohol at these oh so fabulous events. Beer in the fridge? Take some. Or have a shot or two or ten. Mix and match and have some fun with everyone. And that we did. I was actually eager to drink, which surprised me after my going away party. But I was tired of being so wired.

"We should find a bottle opener," I told Angie when she handed me a bottle of beer.

"Give it to me."

We turned around, and I found myself staring at that boy who had smiled at me downtown. He was cuter up close. I gave him my beer. He held the top to his mouth and shoved the bottle cap between his teeth. The beer was opened.

"Aaaah," I winced, watching him bite open Angie's beer. "That's gotta hurt."

Cute Boy shrugged. "They're just teeth."

I grinned. He was funny. "I'm Lynn," I said, surprising myself at my own assertiveness. Did I really just say that?

"Ned," he half nodded. He had green eyes. "Nice to know your name."

My mouth was too dry to speak. I willed my eyes to pour my heart onto his chest, even if there was just a little bit left to spill. But he didn't have time to notice my efforts. Someone called his name and he was gone.

"You're gonna kiss him," Angie laughed, setting her empty beer bottle on the counter.

"You're done already?" Notice how I steered away from the conversation.

"Yeah." Angie shrugged and poured herself a shot of rum. "Catch up so you can drink this with me." She found another shot glass and poured the rum.

I attempted to drink as fast as I could, but anyone who has ever chugged beer knows how impossible it is. The bubbles get everywhere. As soon as I finished, Angie handed me the rum.

"Cheers."

I threw the shot to the back of my throat. Or tried to. I'm about as good at taking shots as I am at chugging beer. I have actually never managed to get it down in one gulp, so it didn't surprise me when half the rum ended up on the front of my shirt. Angie, laughing, left to find a paper towel.

"You spilled." Of course Ned had to walk up just at that moment. Why wouldn't he?

"I'm not that good at taking shots," I confessed.

"You should try again." Ned was smiling. He had really white teeth. "What do you want?"

To kiss you. "What?"

"For your shot."

"Um. Rum again, I guess." He filled two shot glasses and gave one to me. "Try not to spill this time."

Sure bud. I shut my eyes and took my swigs, managing to keep it all in my mouth.

"Nice job." He paused. "You like to dance?"

I swallowed hard. "Sure." He took my hand.

The music pumped its venom around the walls, cramming screams and stomping beats inside our heads. We moved jaggedly, brushing up against one another as the music roared. Ned was very good at sticking his knees against the back of my legs. Then it was his pelvis grinding against me. His cheeks were soft on the back of my neck. My head tilted toward him.

We kissed.

It was horrible, like some oversized tomato doing jumping jacks against my teeth. I pulled away.

"I've got to find Angie," I murmured, leaving before he had a chance to hear me laugh.

I grabbed Angie's arm and led her somewhere far away from Ned. "It was the worst kiss I ever had," I told her. "And that says a lot." We ended up smoking near the back gate where it was a little easier to hear.

"Well, now ya know."

"Apparently."

Sheena was swaying heavily towards us. She stumbled into Angie's arm. "Sorry," she slurred. "Can I have a cigarette?"

I raised my eyebrow. "You don't smoke."

"But…it looks…good…" She leaned on Angie's shoulder. If Angie moved, she'd definitely fall over.

"If you want." I handed one to her. She put it in her mouth and attempted to hold it there, but the cigarette dropped to the ground.

"I'll—" Sheena didn't have time to finish. As soon as she bent over, the girl's puke went everywhere. I had to step back to avoid being splattered.

"I think it's about that time," Angie said. I went to find the trampbeezies.

"Lynn." It was Diesel.

"Hi," I said quickly, shifting my eyes around him. "You heard about this too, huh?"

"It's the only thing going on tonight." He paused. I didn't bother to fill in the conversation. "You still high?"

"Sorta. I'm looking for people."

"I'm a people."

Karen and Bonnie were in the corner of the kitchen, their faces puckered like they had just eaten a rotten lemon. A guy was walking away from them. It was Ned. I laughed.

"I found them. See ya later." I moved past him. He gripped my shoulder.

"I'll come find you tomorrow, okay?" His fingers dug into my skin. I just wanted him to let go.

"Okay."

He released me.

I found the girls, forgetting to tell them about my Ned experience. It felt like Diesel was still touching me.

"Sheena's puking outside," I told them. "Angie's with her. I thought we should probably go. The bus should be going back to campus soon anyways."

They didn't argue. Jolan and Linda ran into us shortly afterwards, and the seven of us weaved our way between backstreets to the nearest bus stop. Angie stayed with Sheena so she wouldn't fall. I'm glad she was there. I didn't want anyone leaning on me.

Back in bus 1L. We rested comfortably against our thoughts, absorbing a truth that was slowly sinking in. We were really here.

"Let's sing something." Linda was squished against the window with her eyes half closed. None of us said anything. Linda paused. Sighed.

"*There are places I'll remember...*" She was singing.

All my life, though some have changed.
Some forever not for better.
Some have gone and some remain.

Angie and Karen joined in.

All these places have their moments,
With lovers and friends I still can recall

In came Bonnie and Jolan.

Some are dead and some are living,
In my life I've loved them all.
Do do do do do do...

I watched them sing the words of the Beatles, their heads low and soft against the glow of 12 AM. Their melodic voices wrapped my jitters in a milky thread of calm, and I could feel a layer of cold melt away. My lips started to move.

Though I know I'll never lose affection
For people and things that went before

I was singing.

I know I'll often stop and think about them
In my life I love you more...

Maybe I could let them in. Let life in. Maybe I could feel warm again.

In my life I love you more.

October 25th

Awake on crank. I'm sitting outside, smoking a cigarette alone. I have such mixed feelings about being here. I love it, but at the same time I still feel so fucking lost. More than ever, really. It's kind of sad. There's so much shit I put myself through. I'm ready to embrace the emptiness again. Why? I don't understand why it's so difficult to care about me.

Well, maybe I do. Every day seems like a battle...a battle against myself. I hate myself for loving him still, after everything. Hate myself for not being strong enough to let go, to protect myself at all. It's gotten to the point where I don't want to deal with anything. I've been thrown into a cold, dark place...alone and afraid. But I don't know what to do about it, if there's anything at all. You'd think I'd be over it by now.

EIGHT

College life was definitely everything it was cracked up to be. Freedom, parties, crazy roommates. Hard classes, papers, tests. More parties, arguments, people eating your food. Missed classes, crying outbreaks, more papers, more missed classes, more parties, more freedom…

At first it felt like summer camp and I wondered when I was going back home. But after six weeks I realized I wasn't. This was my life now. And I was living it my way.

"I hope we can carry everything," I told Angie as the toilet paper, paper towels, garbage bags, dish soap, sponges, milk, macaroni and cheese, ramen, popcorn, canned fruit, bread, marshmallow cereal, hot chocolate, toothpaste, face wash, conditioner, dryer sheets, and other assortments made their way down the checking aisle. We were used to carrying food and other personal things, but having to add a huge package of toilet paper along with the paper towels and other household goodies was not something we were experienced with.

Since the aluminum can episode (which did not work), Gertrude found herself a boyfriend with a Costco card and a truck. The two of them were the designated house shoppers with Gertrude keen on saving *every* possible receipt. It was annoying to have someone breathing down your neck for money every couple weeks, but at least the toilet paper got delivered.

And then there was last week. Gertrude decided her boyfriend was too much of a stoner and broke it off. (Jolan and I cheered him up with a round or five of greenage on our own, which Gertrude is still unaware of.) So when the time came to get more household supplies, Angie and I were left to fend for the clan. Not that we minded, except the walk from the bus stop to the grocery store was not exactly short. I wasn't looking forward to it.

"We've got our backpacks." Angie said. Yeah, but what about the toilet paper?

"Can you give us paper too?" I asked the checker, who rolled her eyes and put the rest of our goods in plastic. She handed me a few brown bags. Bitch. I contemplated asking for help out to our non-existent car.

We took the bags outside and began the ritual of re-arranging. I put as many things in a plastic bag as I could. Shoved them in my backpack. I could usually fit two or three bags of shit depending on how much I purchased. Maybe I should have held off on the milk. It went bad before I finished it anyway.

"You fit all you could?" Angie asked. I nodded. We stared at the leftovers. There were a lot. We put everything else in the paper bags. I took the toilet paper under one arm and a heavy paper bag in the other. Angie took the rest. I took a cigarette out of my pocket and lit it, the weight of one bag swinging around one arm and the unevenness of the toilet paper bouncing under the other. We must've looked ridiculous.

"I talked to Erin last night." Angie tried to light a cigarette with two bags leaning against her chest, the other barely hanging from her arm. It looked like it was going to fall. I held the lighter for her. "She said she talked to Kat and they both want to visit."

"You think they'll come?" I wondered.

"Maybe."

"They're not gonna come." I sighed at the image of seeing them again. "It's a nice thought, though."

"It's been a long time. Kinda weird."

"I know."

I hadn't been home since we left. My parents had asked me to visit awhile ago, and random friends were wondering when I was going to pop up. It was nice that they wanted me there, but I was afraid to go home. Afraid that I'd lose whatever ground my feet had fought to stand on. This was a new life. The quick sand had hardened into solid rock, and I didn't want to sink again.

Angie went back a few weeks ago to see her parents and get more shit, but that was it. I wondered if she had a similar fear. We didn't talk about home much. All she told me was she was able to replenish our stash. We were almost out again. Diesel would help with that if I asked him. I hated seeing him, but he was so willing to get us high. Especially me. Sometimes he'd find me when Angie was at class. We'd get high, then he'd kiss me for awhile. I didn't like it, but I figured if I led him on, he'd keep giving me my free fix. Kind of made me feel like some kind of drug whore. Angie didn't know. I liked it that way. It was nice to have something of my own.

We slowly trudged the blocks and blocks back to our beloved form of transportation. The bus. Waiting for the bus was something I despised getting used to. No matter what time I got there, the bus never came when I needed it. I was too early or, which happened much more often, too late. Running after the bus was an exhausting task that usually ended in failure. Sure, I'd make it once or twice if the bus driver had a triple espresso and a handful of anti-depressants. But most of the time their lives were unfulfilled and thus I must be punished for my existence. So they drove away without me, regardless of how close I was to those stupid glass doors. It seemed to match the rest of my life.

"I think I'm gonna buy a truck." Angie lit another cigarette and sat heavily on the concrete. The bags thumped loudly. "I'm tired of this fucking shit."

I eagerly followed suit, collapsing ass first on the sidewalk. The toilet paper half bounced over the curb. Angie picked it up and sat on it.

"I hate toilet paper," I announced.

"Do ya now?" she grinned. "Bet you'll change your mind the next time you take a shit."

"No, I'll make Gertrude wipe my ass."

Angie shook her head. Paused. "She made Rhiannon cry."

"Why? What'd she say?"

"I don't know. She just said it was cuz Rhiannon's a retard. I told her to shut the fuck up and went to find Rhiannon."

"Was she okay?"

"I never found her."

The bus was coming. Angie and I slowly gathered our bulks.

"You have your ID?" Angie asked me.

"Shit!"

Our school ID was a free pass to whatever bus we wanted. Mine was conveniently stashed in a pocket inside my backpack. I dropped the toilet paper and paper bag of shit on the sidewalk and pried open my overly stuffed backpack. Groceries attacked as I gallantly unzipped the pocket and retrieved my ID.

"It's here." Angie said.

I held the ID in between my teeth and attempted to shut my backpack. The zipper was stuck on a plastic bag.

"Come on, Lynn!"

I looked up. Angie was standing at the open doors. The driver, an extremely irritated looking woman, stared at me.

I yanked the zipper but it wouldn't close. I gave Angie a "help me" look.

"Are you coming or not?" That was the bus driver.

"Yeah," I told her, praying the groceries would stay in their bags as I swung the open backpack over my shoulder. I grabbed the toilet paper and paper bag and hastily climbed on to the bus.

"ID."

I tilted my head so the ID picture was facing her.

"Can you take it out of your mouth, please?"

Fucking shit woman. I tossed the groceries on the closest seat and showed her my ID. She grunted and closed the doors.

The trip back to campus was forty minutes. So that made one hour twenty minutes travel time, not to mention the hour it took to figure out what we wanted when we got there. Plus the forty or so minutes of walking there and back. Total time lost by grocery shopping? Three hours and twenty minutes. No wonder we never had any food.

Grouchy bus lady dropped us off at our designated stop, and we slowly began the journey back to the apartment. I cursed the campus that wasn't flat, the uneven wooden bridge that went over a bunch of fucking dirt, and the goddam stairs that seemed to grow ten times longer than the last time I climbed them. Apparently everything gets magnified when you've got a giant pack of fucking toilet paper in your arms. Check that off on life's list of things to know.

As we got closer to our lovely abode, it became apparent that there was a screaming match inside our living room. Goody.

"Our housemates are morons," Angie said.

I nodded in agreement, but Angie was ahead of me. I was glad she was going in first. The sliding glass door was opened and waiting. I could hear them even before my foot stepped into the house.

"This is fucking disgusting."

"Maybe you should clean up after yourself then."

"Maybe you should take that stick out of your ass and eat it."

"What the fuck does that mean?"

"It means I'm tired of you in my face."

Here we go again. I peered into our apartment and saw Sheena and Gertrude growling at one another in the kitchen. Yes, Sheena, the same curly haired mouse at the house meeting who threw up at her first college party. She had apparently disguised herself in the beginning and was really some kind of rat ninja, ready to fight the evil villain named Gertrude. It's amazing what six weeks can do to a person. I longed for her determination. Her fire. Mine was lost somewhere between here and home.

"You ready?" Angie whispered.

"No."

"Tough."

Angie plunged into the room with me close at her heels. Maybe if I hid behind Angie they wouldn't notice me. She's tall.

"Angie. Lynn. You think Sheena's a femme-nazi, right?" Gertrude asked. Shit. She saw me. The toilet paper must have given me away.

"Not really," Angie answered coldly. I didn't respond. Maybe Queen Bitch would forget I was there.

We shoved aside the half eaten pasta dishes and cups that hadn't been washed in maybe a week or two and whatever else had attached itself to our dining room table. Let the groceries loose. I watched a bag get attacked by a moldy cup.

"They can't even put the fucking groceries down," Sheena said.

Gertrude shrugged. "That's not my problem. Those aren't my dishes."

"No, they're mine. And they've got shit growing in them cuz people don't know how to use a fucking sponge." I glanced at the grayish green fuzz half hanging from the cup on the table. I felt bad for Sheena's dishes. "If we had a job chart, this wouldn't be a problem." That again. Sheena and Karen were still harping about having some kind of chore wheel. I actually thought it could work, but I never voiced my opinion.

Angie handed me the milk. I put it in the fridge and joined her in sorting through our groceries.

"We're not having a fucking job chart!" Gertrude was practically screaming. I wished we had bought a muzzle.

"Who died and made you God?" Sheena crossed her arms.

Gertrude rolled her eyes. "Nobody wants to do it."

"I think it's a good idea," Angie said.

Gertrude stood there for a minute. Sheena smiled.

"Fuck off," Gertrude pouted. She left the room

"No!" Sheena yelled after her. "I'm gonna make a chart, and we're *all* gonna do it!" Gertrude's door slammed.

I laughed. "Can we have a cigarette?"

By the time Angie and I had finished smoking and put away the rest of our groceries, Sheena had returned with a color coded chore card and slapped it on the wall.

"Now what, bitch?!" Sheena said to no one and left. Um, you go girl. Angie and I went to see what the damage was. According to the chart, the two of us had kitchen duty. I looked at the dried food and moldy dishes that cluttered the counter. Hmmm. We'll take care of that later, like sometime after we graduate.

I glanced at the clock. Shit, it was almost seven. I had a five page paper due at ten in the morning and I hadn't started any of it. It was for a class called Introductory Shakespeare. We were studying *Hamlet,* I think. I didn't really go to that class much. It was too fucking early. My TA told me I couldn't miss anymore or I'd lose half of a letter grade. That was last week. There were only three weeks left in the quarter. I could do it. Maybe.

Time to focus.

My nails tapped against the keyboard that faced an extremely blank computer screen. My mind wasn't functioning properly. There were no thoughts, no signs of motivation…nothing. I just wanted to smoke. I glanced on the floor for my pack. Fuck, maybe I'll just fail the damn class. It wouldn't make a difference. Not in the long run.

An instant message was blinking at me. It was from Heartz4No1. I laughed and leaned sideways so Angie could see me. She grinned and went back to her computer. Heartz4No1 was Angie's screen name. She was messaging me from across the room. I loved it.

Heartz4No1: whatcha doin?
Me: Not doing my paper. U?
Heartz4No1: talking to clyde.

Clyde was her latest obsession. She'd known him since freshman year of high school, but lately her knowing his existence had turned into pure infatuation. I think it had something to do with Adam…or lack of him.

Heartz4No1: he's gonna visit soon. dammit that means i've gotta diet.
Me: All you eat is frozen peas and popcorn. That's a diet.
Heartz4No1: u know how i am. gonna get some diet pills.

Have I mentioned obsessed? When she wanted something, she really went for it. At least it showed some kind of motivation, I guess. More than what I had. Well, except for losing weight and getting high. Great drives to have in life.

Me: Cool. U should share or buy me some and I'll pay u back. I wanna be skinny too.
Heartz4No1: ok. think i'm gonna smoke. wanna come?

My computer flashed again. It was from someone I didn't know. "Hold on," I said out loud.

Heartz4No1: k

The name was LordOfKaos. I clicked on it.

LordOfKaos: Hey. I know you.
Me: Um. Hi. Who are u?
LordOfKaos: A friend. You're Lynn.
Me: Maybe.
LordOfKaos: You are. I kissed you.
Me: Oh! Are you…shit…that guy I kissed at that party downtown? Sorry, I don't remember your name.
LordOfKaos: You kissed a random guy? You're gross.
Me: It wasn't you?
LordOfKaos: Hell no.

Okay, so it wasn't that guy. I didn't remember kissing anyone else. At least not since…Oh my God.

LordOfKaos: And we've done more than kissed.

I was having trouble breathing. My head felt like it was spinning inside the bottle of alcohol I wanted to drink.

LordOfKaos: Do you know me yet?

Deep breaths, Lynn. My fingers shook against the keyboard. I told myself to shut down the computer or throw it out the window or log off or do something to run away. But I was frozen there.

LordOfKaos: I'll give you a hint.

Tears dwelled at the back of my eyes. I could feel them dancing with the pain that slowly hovered inside my heart. I hated him. Feared him. Loved him. Why did he have to find me?

LordOfKaos: The last time you saw me you told me to get the fuck out of your life.

And he should have stayed the fuck out. I shouldn't be doing this. I couldn't. But I wanted to. This was a chance to talk to him again. To know him without the pressures of the past. We were in different cities now. Angie wouldn't care, and no one else would know about it.

Me: I didn't say it like that.
LordOfKaos: So you know me now.
Me: What are you doing?
LordOfKaos: Saying hi. I can't talk to you?
No, I wanted to type. Fuck no. But nothing came out. I was stuck.

"Can we smoke now?" Angie's voice made me jump. I had forgotten she was there.
"Yes," I whispered. Anything to run to.

Me: I've gotta go.

I logged out, grabbed my cigarettes, and willed myself numb. Rick wasn't going to break me.
"You wanna get spun?" I asked Angie as we moved to our usual smoking spot.
Angie raised her eyebrow at me. "I thought you had a paper due tomorrow."
"I do."
Angie grinned. "You're not gonna do it."
I shrugged. Maybe this was more important now.

I didn't go to sleep that night. Didn't write much of a paper, either. Rick kept popping into my head. I stared at the instant message program. Logged on. Logged off. On. Off. Wrote somewhere in between.

Somehow I made it. Five pages exactly, although I doubt it made much sense. Not that much can make sense at 9:30 in the morning after an all nighter. Especially an all nighter on crank. All I could think about was how I was coming down, that I just wanted a little more to pick me up again. Angie was out of her stash, and I didn't have any money to get my own. Even if I did, I didn't know anyone who sold. So I shoved my lame ass five page paper into my backpack and started the walk to class.

Okay. So maybe I had a little problem with crank. Maybe I was needing it more than wanting it. But I had known this for awhile. Called myself an addict all the time. Made jokes about it. Or maybe that was the crank, or the pain, or whatever it was that was eating me alive. I didn't know what was real anymore.

I got to class early. There was a small pond in the courtyard by our classroom. It had Koi fish and a mermaid who spouted water through her mouth. I set my backpack down and lit a cigarette, watching the large fish waddle beneath the water. It'd be nice to be a fish and swim the day away. I heard they didn't even have a nervous system. I wanted to live pain-free, too.

Ten minutes passed. It was 9:55. Time to learn.

This class was pretty small compared to my Psychology and Religion class, which had about 500 students. There I could miss class and no one would know the difference. The teacher didn't even know I existed. Yet my logic was oh so fabulous and I never missed that class, while Introductory Shakespeare was filled with a mere 60 students and they took attendance. But did I go? No.

I sat in the back row and waited for Professor Keys to whisk us away into an hour of Shakespearean fun.

"Good morning everyone. I bet you all had a refreshing sleep last night." Expected murmurs of laughter. Professor Keys grinned. "I trust you have your papers ready. I'll collect them now. Pass them to the end of your row and the TA's will take them."

I gave my half ass paper to the guy next to me and glanced at the clock. It was 9:58. Glad I wasn't late this time. One point for studiousness.

"Last class we finished tackling *Twelfth Night*, then began the discussion of Hamlet's internal struggle within Act One. You should be finished with most of *Hamlet* now."

I hadn't read any of them. Well, not since *Measure for Measure*. But that was the first play we read. I was a better student then.

"I'd like to conquer more of Hamlet's turmoil in a soliloquy I find fantastic. It happens to be in the first act, so feel lucky if you haven't finished the play." If I cared, I would have laughed. "Any volunteers to read Act One, Scene Two?"

A red headed girl raised her hand. I leaned my head back against the chair and folded my book against my knee.

"What's your name?"

"Molly." Her voice was low and sing-songy.

"Molly, please read until I tell you otherwise."

My eyes felt heavy.

"O, that this too too solid flesh would melt
Thaw and resolve itself into a dew!
Or that the Everlasting had not fix'd
His canon 'gainst self-slaughter! O God! God!
How weary, stale, flat and unprofitable,
Seem to me all the uses of this world!"

It was dark. I was running. And I was afraid.

"Don't stop." Shannon stood in front of me. She was crying. "He'll get you. He'll get you."

"Where do I go?" But she was gone.

There was a flower. A pink one with withered leaves. It was so beautiful. I reached to touch it, and the petals dissolved into cockroaches. One crawled on my hand. I ran.

Rick was standing at the edge of a cliff. His back was to me.

I walked up to him.

"Hi," I said. He didn't say anything. I sat on the edge of the cliff with my legs dangling over the side.

"Do you want to die?" His voice was soft.

I looked at the nothingness below me. "Will you push me?"

I opened my eyes. The students around me were shoving things into their book bags.

"Please be finished with *Hamlet* and at least halfway through *A Midsummer Night's Dream* by Wednesday. I want you to be caught up for the quiz Friday."

Quiz Friday? I rubbed my eyes. Must have fallen asleep again. Fuck. I did that in practically every lecture, which didn't help the effort it took to get myself to class. What was the point if I was going to fall asleep anyway? It all pissed me off.

The apartment was quiet as I opened the sliding glass doors. It was a strange silence for 11:30 in the morning on a Monday. Apparently everyone had something better to do. I dropped my backpack in my bedroom and grabbed a box of macaroni and cheese. My stomach wasn't exactly growling, but I figured I should eat something. It had been two days since I had put food in my stomach, minus the Cheetos I had snagged from Jolan when we were stoned yesterday.

I opened the cabinet below the stove. It was empty. Great. I had been hoping I could get away with not doing any dishes before using them. Wasn't my luck fabulous? I carefully searched the sink that swam with filth and mold for a decent sized pot. There was a perfect one beneath a crusted plate and a bowl that had something green, pink, and fuzzy in it. I held my hand over my mouth so I wouldn't gag. The pot was actually better than I expected. There was mere food instead of mold clinging to the bottom. I tried to find a spot big enough to wash the pot in. Had to use the bathroom sink instead. I dried the pot with the lovely paper towels Angie and I had just purchased, and filled it with water for boiling.

I thought of Rick again. Maybe he was online. I sat at my computer and stared at it, wondering what would happen if I talked to him. What he would say. I remembered his face. His lips. His laugh. God, to be there one more time.

I double clicked on the icon at the bottom of my monitor. *LordOfKaos* was online. I highlighted his name and pushed enter. The message screen popped up. What should I say? I wanted to pretend like everything was normal, like nothing horrible had happen. Even though it had.

Me: I had a dream about you. I asked you to push me off a cliff.

Shit, maybe I shouldn't be doing this.

LordOfKaos: Did I?

Too late now.

Me: No. I woke up.
LordOfKaos: Sucks. Falling in dreams is cool.

Me: I've never had one. **Aren't** they supposed to mean something?
LordOfKaos: Yeah. So why **are** you talking to me now?
Me: I don't know.

My answer for everything. There was a pause. Maybe it was a sign for me to go. But I couldn't stop.

LordOfKaos: How's school?
Me: It's okay. I like the freedom.
LordOfKaos: You don't have a window there?
Me: No I do. But I use the doors.
LordOfKaos: That's what you say.

I giggled and covered my mouth. He had made me laugh.

Me: Why did you find me?
LordOfKaos: You found me.
Me: No, the first time.

Another pause. I was afraid of his answer. The water sounded like it was boiling. I left the computer and went to put the noodles in.
"Hey Lynn." Angie was home. "Do you have a cigarette? I forgot to get some yesterday."
I nodded. "They're on my desk. Grab one for me too." I poured the macaroni in the pot. One of the noodles fell under the burner. It smelled.
"Who's *LordOfKaos*?"
Fuck. I pretended like I didn't hear her.
"He says you know why." She handed me a cigarette. "Let's go out front."
I flicked my cigarette against the side of the bench. He said I knew why. Fuck that bullshit. He was playing his games again.
"If I tell you, will you promise to keep it a secret?"
"Lynn, it's me."
"I know." I took a long drag. "It's Rick. He found me online last night."
Her expression was hard to read. "What did he say?"
"Nothing really. I think he just wants the last word."
She shrugged. "Not everything is as bad as you think it is."
"But how do I know what's bad and what isn't?"
"You don't."

By the time I got back to my computer, Rick had signed off. Just as well. The food was ready, and I ate it while staring at the wall. It didn't really have much taste. Kind of gross, actually. I ate as much as I could before I started gagging. Half of it was left.

"Hey Ang."

"Huh?"

"You want any mac n'cheese?"

"No. I've got my coffee."

Oh yeah. Angie's obsessive compulsive diet.

I went in the kitchen and threw the rest of the food away. What a waste. I should have saved it. There's not enough money to waste food like that. I had maybe thirty dollars to last the rest of the month. Fucking stupid. I thought I should punish myself for being so dumb. No food for the rest of the day.

I wondered if other people punished themselves like that. Probably not. Oh, the joys of me.

That night, after rolling my eyes through the discussion session for Freshman Core, I decided it was time for a damn good high. Hell, I deserved it. It was, um, Monday. Garfield hated Mondays.

I grabbed a twenty that I shouldn't be spending and flew out the glass doors. First stop was Jolan's apartment. One of them should have something. I knocked on the door. Waited. No answer. Knocked again.

"What?" a voice shouted.

I opened the door. Jolan's housemate was lying on the couch with some guy. They looked very interrupted.

"Hi there," I said. No response. "Is Jolan here?"

"No." Her voice was irritated. I didn't care.

"How about Linda?" I asked her.

"No."

"Nina or Rachel?"

"No."

"Do you know where they are?"

"No."

"Have Fern or Skip stopped by?"

"Fuckin A' Lynn! I'm busy."

Bitch. I shut the door. That was Patti, the only one of the five girls living there who didn't smoke pot. She needed some. Patti and Gertrude were a lot alike. Maybe we could get them super stoned and drive them off a cliff.

I lit a cigarette to avoid the panic that was slowly rising through my chest. Breathe. Take a drag. Exhale. There's gotta be something around here. I walked slowly through campus despite the fear beating through me. My skin felt prickly. Jittery. I bit my lip. Where was everyone?

"You got another smoke?" A person. He had dread locks, a Bob Marley shirt, and bloodshot eyes. Not any person. A Stoner Dude.

I sighed and gave him a cigarette. "You need a light?" I wondered if I sounded too eager.

Stoner Dude shook his head and pulled a lighter from his pocket. The bottom was scarred black. Another sign. He lit the cigarette and started to walk away.

"Wait." I shifted my feet. "Do you have any idea, um, where I could get some Mary Jane?"

He puffed silently, his reddened eyes staring into my stuttering face.

"I've got twenty bucks and another pack of smokes."

Stoner Dude tilted his head slightly. "You give me a hit and another cigarette, and I'll get you some."

Thank God. I followed his slow strut, biting my tongue to avoid asking him to move his ass. But it didn't take long. Just around a couple apartments, up some stairs and...

"Here?" I asked him. He nodded as I stared blankly at the familiar setting I tried my best to avoid. Stoner Dude had taken me to Diesel's apartment. Fabulous.

"These guys always have shit." He knocked. One of Diesel's housemates answered the door. I forgot his name. Diesel lived with six other guys.

"Popeye!" they yelled when they saw him. Stoner Dude's name was Popeye? I pinched myself to make sure I was still sober.

The housemate and the spinach freak gave each other macho hugs. I wanted to ask about Olive Oyl, but I thought it might reverse my chances of getting fucked up.

"So dude, can we come in?"

I followed Popeye into the testosterone filled domain. Some of them waved at me in half-ass recognition. They sat with their various pipes and yummy smoke that I attempted to get secondhand. After a few good breaths I checked for Diesel. He wasn't home. I sighed.

The guys were already pretty fucked up, so it wasn't difficult to trade some cigs for as many hits as I could get. We passed around the pipes and watched *The Simpsons* through puffy eyes, laughing at things that probably weren't as funny as we thought they were. I was just glad to be high.

Homer: No TV and no beer make Homer something, something.

Marge: Go crazy?

Homer: Don't mind if I do! Heeooow-yayaya-ha-hoo-ha-hoo-ha-hoo-ba-du-ba-du!

Laughter.

"Dude, that's hella me when I need some shit!"

"That's cuz you're a fucking stoner."

"So are you, asshole."

"Fuck yeah."

More laughter. My body felt heavy against the couch. It was difficult to keep my head up. I kind of wanted to leave, but my legs felt like bricks. I had smoked myself numb.

"Propane!"

"What's up maestro?"

"Light my ass, fuckers." That was Diesel. He was home. Apparently, the guys thought of him as some kind of god. Now *that* was funny.

"Sup?" He grinned at his boys, stopping when his eyes fell on me. "Ya got any shit left?"

"Only for you." They handed him a pipe and some pot in a bag.

He sat next to me, his leg practically on top of mine. I watched him pack the bowl. He took a deep hit.

"You want some?" he whispered.

"I'm good," I whispered back.

He took a couple more hits. "Have some. It's good shit."

"I know. I'm so stoned I can barely move."

He blew smoke in my face. "Breathe it in."

I wanted a cigarette.

"Where are you going?" he asked as I attempted to move his leg.

"Smoke."

"Hang on." He pressed his leg against me so I couldn't move. Took a few more hits. I could feel myself starting to panic again.

"You done yet?" I asked.

He moved and reached out his hand to help me up. I tried to get up on my own, then sighed and took his hand. We went outside. I leaned against the wall. Gave up and sat on the floor.

"You're fucked up," he grinned. I replied with a cloud of cigarette smoke. His smile faded to a serious look. "You should stay here for awhile. Take a nap."

I shook my head. It felt like I was moving it in slow motion. That made me feel dizzy. I rested my head against my knee.

"See? You can't even tell me no."

I didn't say anything.

When I put my cigarette out against the concrete, he held his hand out to help me up. I didn't want to go with him. It scared me.

"I want another one," I told him in a thick voice. My throat was dry and another cigarette didn't sound appealing, but it was a good way to stall. Why was I so fucking stoned? I didn't mean to paralyze myself.

He lit one for me and smoked one himself. I took slow, deliberate drags and hoped that the nicotine would wake me up. It made me feel nauseous.

"You look pale." Diesel crouched beside me and stroked my hair. I stared at my cigarette. "Finish that shit so we can get you to bed."

We?

I finished the cigarette. Put it on the ground. Watched it roll away. Diesel took my hand and pulled me up. Held on after I was standing. I tried to pull my hand away. He wouldn't let go.

I followed him inside the apartment, past the boys who gave us stupid grins and laughs. Got to Diesel's bedroom. I practically fell onto his bed. The door shut. I closed my eyes.

The bed rustled beside me. Fingers twisted around my hair. A hand touched me lightly on the shoulder. On my arm. It moved down the side of my ribs. I shuttered.

"Diesel," I whispered.

"Ssh," he said, his hand lightly playing the inside of my hip. I wanted to scream.

It came out as a croak. I managed to roll onto my stomach. Maybe I could roll off the bed.

"Come back here." He moved me so I was on my back and climbed on top of me. I turned my head away. He turned it back and leaned so close our noses touched.

"Don't," I whispered.

He put his finger to my lips and shoved his tongue inside my mouth. His spit tasted like marijuana and warm beer. I made a face he couldn't see. A hand traced my stomach and began climbing upwards beneath my shirt. His leg rubbed against my inner thighs.

Help me.

Diesel reached for his zipper. I could feel him struggling to undo it with one hand. He stopped kissing me.

"Stop," I gasped as soon as his lips left mine. "Please?"

His eyes stared at me through the darkness. I forced myself to look at him. He needed to see me.

"I'm sorry, I just don't…" I swallowed. "Just…please…"

He stopped. Got up, turned his back to me, and went to sleep.

I don't know how long I lay there. It was long after my breath became normal, after the wetness dissolved into my cheeks. I just stared into the darkness, the thoughts exploding in my head. I was a fucking idiot. I was an addict. I was probably going to do it all again tomorrow.

And it occurred to me, lying there next to someone I feared, paralyzed by the drugs I so desperately needed, that I was truly gone.

October 27th

I don't know what I'm doing here. I don't know what I'm supposed to be doing or learning or reaching towards. I don't want to do the work, don't care about the classes. I'm tired of giving myself hope and then letting myself down again. Tired of not being able to do the simplest shit. Tired of being tired even. So instead I go off and get fucked up. Maybe it's because I can? I love my drugs, my parties, my rebellion. A fascination with the "dark side". If I had crank right now I'd do it. I want some of that shit so bad. Or get stoned or...or anything. Just to get away from myself.

What the fuck is wrong with me? God, I want some crank! I know it's not true, but it feels like it'll somehow make shit better. Give me motivation or something. It's like I've dug myself into this hole of not giving a shit about my life. Hopefully I'll realize something that'll make me want to care. I just pray I find it before I can't find my way out of my own hole.

NINE

It was dark when I woke up. Diesel's breath was slow, steady. I couldn't look at him when I left. I just wanted to sleep. I slept through my mandatory Freshman Core class, through Psychology and Religion. After awhile it wasn't even sleeping. I just lay there. Shut my eyes against the night before. It felt like I had locked myself inside a cell. There were no doors, no windows, no light. Just a pathetic version of me curled up against a corner, not caring if I ever got out at all.

I finally left my bed around four o' clock in the afternoon and sat at my computer. Ate Lucky Charms out of the box. Checked my email. I had one from my mom. She said the family wanted to visit around my 18th birthday. I deleted it without reply. My birthday wasn't for a few weeks. I didn't have to deal with it yet.

Rick was online again. It didn't take long for him to say hello.

LordOfKaos: I had a shitty ass day.
Me: That sucks.
LordOfKaos: Work can kiss my asshole.
Me: What do u do again?
LordOfKaos: Make pizza.
Me: That's a new one. When'd u start?
LordOfKaos: A month ago.

My computer was flashing at me. Shannon was online. I clicked on her name.

TheRedQueen: Hi.
Me: Hi. I miss u.
TheRedQueen: Miss you too.
Me: How are things?

TheRedQueen: Shitty.
Me: ???
TheRedQueen: Something happened today. Shit hold on.
Me: K.

Rick was talking. I wasn't paying much attention.

LordOfKaos: I think I'm going to start my own religion.
Me: Yeah?
LordOfKaos: It's called Nahgvnafuq.
Me: I don't get it.
LordOfKaos: Not giving a fuck.

Shannon came back.

The RedQueen: Sorry.
Me: It's ok.
Pause.
Me: What happened?
TheRedQueen: I cut myself.

Rick was talking to me again. I minimized his screen.

Me: Why?
TheRedQueen: I didn't do it on purpose. Not at first. I was taking a shower and cut myself with the razor.

Another pause.

TheRedQueen: But I liked the way it felt. So I did it again. I did it 4 times.

I didn't know what to say.

TheRedQueen: Not sure why I'm telling you. I haven't told anyone else.
Me: U care about yourself. That's why.
TheRedQueen: I guess.

Me: No, u do. You're still breathing, u know?
TheRedQueen: Kinda. Don't really feel anything right now.
Me: You're just numb from all the hurt.
TheRedQueen: Yeah.
Me: You'll be ok.
TheRedQueen: Maybe.

More silence. I ran my fingers through my hair. My chest felt tight. Maybe I needed a cigarette.

TheRedQueen: Hey I'm gonna go. Tired.
Me: Ok. I'm glad u told me.

No response.

Me: Will you tell me if u do it again?
TheRedQueen: Yeah. Bye.
Me: Hey! I love u.
TheRedQueen: Ditto kiddo.

And she was gone.

My air had shattered, its pieces running sharply into the sides of my head. I couldn't think straight. Maybe my brain had spilled onto the floor. Pieces of sentences ran together as I tried to comprehend what just happened. What if she had…didn't know she was…how she got…so desperate. Why didn't I know? Was it my fault? She could have slit her wrists. An image of her body in the bathtub, blood running down the sides. I shook my head. The image was still there. And here I was in my own stupid bubble, states away from her. Totally helpless. Fucking fabulous wasn't it?

Not only that. I was talking to the guy who probably made her do it in the first place. I had promised her I wouldn't. She trusted me. Trusted me enough to tell me she hurt herself. Trusted me enough to help her heal.

Fuck fuck fuck. Rick should have raped me instead. I deserved it.

The all mighty leader of Nahgvnafuq was still flashing at the bottom of my computer. I clicked on it.

LordOfKaos: Hello? Helllllooooooo????

My chest felt like it was going to explode. So did my heart. If I had one.

LordOfKaos: I know you're there.

I took a deep breath. It came out shaky. My hands were shaking too.

Me: I can't talk to u.
LordOfKaos: Fine then. Bye.
Me: No, I mean at all.
LordOfKaos: You said that already. It was that night you told me to fuck off.

Strength, Lynn, strength. Another shaky breath.

Me: Well then I'm saying it again.
LordOfKaos: I don't believe you.

Don't play his game. Just do it.

Me: Goodbye.
LordOfKaos: You're better than those whores. Those sluts who call themselves your friends. They don't give a shit about you.

I shut his window. He popped up again.

LordOfKaos: They're fucked up in the head.

Wasn't there a way to block messages?

LordOfKaos: You're like them now. A no good piece of slut.

Panic was rising. I couldn't breathe, couldn't stop squirming in my seat. I had to get out of this. Out of my skin.

LordOfKaos: FUCK YOU.

There it was. I clicked on my mouse and he was gone.

My fingers could barely grip the package of cigarettes by my feet. Why was I shaking so much? I grabbed a lighter, ready to burst inside a nicotine stick. Finally time to get away.
The door flew open.
"Fuck!" It was Angie. She was pissed. I stood up slowly. Maybe she wouldn't notice if I left. I stepped. She was still pacing by her computer. The door that led to the bathroom was free. Another step.
"Why?!" she screamed, throwing her stapler across the room. It hit the wall above my head. I froze. "I got a fucking F on my lab. I worked so goddamn hard on that shit and it didn't make a fucking difference. Motherfucker!"
I sat down again and hid my head in my hands.
"We jump through hoops for these fucking people and they don't give a shit. We get fucking degrees and throw our asses on their silver fucking platters and they just rip our fucking lives apart. What's the point? It's not like any of it matters anyway."
My nails slowly dug into my scalp. I wanted to drown.
"Maybe there's no point in me being here. What the fuck am I getting out of this shit anyway? Let's say I graduate. Go to med school or whatever the fuck I decide to do. Then what? Do what they want when they want it? It's not like I can ever really be free in this fucking nation. Fuck it. I hate this. I go to class, I do the work, and for what? Not a goddamn thing. I hate it here. Dammit, this shit fucking sucks!"
Her voice was everywhere. It wouldn't stop. None of it would stop.
"But you know what? I might as well finish. I've worked my ass off for this place. It'd be stupid to quit now. Made it this far, you know? Should just keep going even if there is no point. I need a cigarette. You want one?"
I shook my head.
"When I get back we should do crank. I need a fucking get-a-way."
She shut the door behind her.
It was all too much. Too fucking much. I was rocking in my chair, my hands wrapped around my shoulders. I wanted to cry, but nothing came out. There was nothing there. Or maybe there was too much.
On the bottom shelf of my desk lived a small box of wall tacks. I grabbed one and pinched the end of my finger to it. It felt sharp enough. Before I knew

what was I was doing, my sleeve had been pushed up on my left arm. The tack was on my wrist. I moved it slowly back and forth, craving its pain. Counted on it.

But there was nothing. I was numb.

I continued to scrape my skin away, watching the flakes collect against sharpened metal. It wasn't enough. I had to dig deeper, find a part of me that could still feel. Soon my wrist began to bleed. I barely noticed. It didn't matter. There was no pain. I was hollow.

The door opened. I dropped the tack somewhere on the carpet and pulled my sleeve over my wrist. Angie didn't notice. She was too busy digging through her dresser. I looked for the tack on the floor.

"Found it." She held up a baggie that was almost emptied of white powder.

I saw something yellow. The tack had dug its way beneath my desk. I put it back in the box.

"You want some?" Angie asked.

I nodded, my eyes still refusing to look into hers. We locked both doors and set up lines on Angie's desk. There wasn't much left.

"I'm using all your shit," I said apologetically. She shrugged. "My birthday's coming up. I get money from my grandparents. It'll be my treat then."

"Okay," she smiled, handing me the straw. Letting me go first was Angie's way of saying she was sorry. I finally looked into her eyes. She wasn't angry anymore.

"Thanks." I took the straw and snorted as quickly as I could. The burning felt good. Real.

We took turns, three lines each. Went out the side door to smoke.

"Is there a point in being here?" I asked Angie as we huddled in our corner of the hall. "I mean, what is college really for?"

"More money." She paused, picking the black threads at the end of her sweatshirt. "More experience."

"But what if you don't know what you're doing? I don't have a fucking clue. I don't even have a major."

"No one has a clue, Lynn."

"You have a major. That's some kind of direction."

"Maybe."

It was starting to rain. The drops pounded against the dirt, wondering where to fall. Not that it mattered. Wherever the rain landed, it was swallowed by the ground.

MY OWN ASYLUM

I sniffed leftover crank through my sinuses. It needed to work faster. "Why do I feel so lost?" I asked.

"Cuz you haven't found what you're looking for."

"What's that?"

Angie shrugged. "You'll know when you find it. I'm still looking too." She took another cigarette from the pack and put it in her mouth, using the old one to light it.

"Chain smoker," I teased, reaching for my own pack. The rain pounded harder. "It's really raining."

"About time."

There was something else between the drumming of water drops against the earth. Some kind of laughter. Lots of it. And cheering.

"Do you hear that?" Angie asked. I exhaled smoke through my nose.

"It's the naked run!" Sheena and Rhiannon yelled to us from the end of the hall.

"The what?" we shouted.

They had disappeared. Angie and I went to the front of our apartment.

"What are you talking about?" I asked.

Sheena smiled. "Wait."

The cheering and laughing grew louder. It sounded like a stampede of mental patients. I wondered where I could sign up. Dammit, why wasn't I tweaked out yet?

"Here they come."

The expectation of a bunch of mental patients running around campus wasn't too far off. Naked people were running through our college. They were students. Some were wearing undergarments to hide the goods, the others had everything wide open. No wonder there were so many cheers.

"What the fuck?" That was Angie.

"It's the first rain," Rhiannon explained, taking her camera out.

"You're actually going to take pictures?" Sheena laughed.

"Hell yeah," she said and clicked away. "This is some famous shit. Haven't you heard of the naked run on first rain? It happens every year."

"Fucking hippies," Angie grinned, staring a little too long at some of the guys.

My arm brushed against the bench. It hurt. I lightly touched my wrist and wondered what it looked like.

"I'm gonna do it." Sheena's sweater was on the ground. She started to unzip her pants. "You guys should come!"

I lifted up my sleeve just a little, angling it so the irritation barely showed. The blood had dried, and the cut looked very puffy.

"Don't you think that would hurt after awhile?" Rhiannon asked.

Oh shit. I pulled my sleeve down quickly, praying she hadn't seen the cut. I was lucky. She was pointing to some of the bigger-chested girls. Their boobs bounced frantically as they ran. "They're kinda lacking support."

I wasn't listening. The crank still hadn't kicked in. Maybe the shit was bunk. Or maybe I just didn't do enough. That panic I had felt yesterday was creeping up my spine.

Maybe it's a good thing. There was a voice inside my head. Not again. *You could read that Shakespeare play.*

Oh shit. Forgot about that.

Or start that essay for Psych and Religion. Or that book for Core.

Shut-up! Shit shit shit. I didn't want to think about this.

Or that article for Core, or the three for Psych and Religion that you never read, or those three other plays. That essay's due tomorrow. There's a test on Friday. A paper due next week. No, two papers. And another test the week after. Shouldn't you be studying?

It felt like I was spinning in circles. Didn't know how to stop.

You're gonna fail.

I wasn't supposed to. Wasn't I excited about college? I thought I remembered being that way.

Then you got yourself fucked up, dumb ass. Fucked up, fucked up. Remember that?

Yeah, well, that's just me. Fucked up. I like my drugs and self-mutilation, thank you very much. They're my party favors.

You're fucked up, thinking that's funny. Crazy bitch.

Lock me up with the naked people.

So then I got high. I got so high I didn't make sense. Couldn't stop rambling. Was that something moving behind the tree? Diesel said it wasn't. Oh yeah, I went to him for more. Told him I had to get so fucked up I didn't wanna remember my name. Bet he liked that one. Maybe he'd get another chance with me. I didn't give a flying fuck.

But he didn't have any crank. I was going to scream, my insides hurt so much. I bit the tip of my tongue to keep the panic away. Looked at the bracelet I was wearing. Maybe I could use that to cut myself again.

Diesel wanted to get high too. Said he knew someone who might have really good shit. Better than his. I followed him to the other end of campus, my head getting louder at every step. Those goddamn voices wouldn't leave me alone. I didn't know thoughts could make so much noise.

"This is his dorm."

"Should I wait out here?" I was smoking and didn't want to put out my cigarette.

"If you want. You have any money?"

No. But I gave him some anyway. Another twenty bucks gone. Save the rest for smokes and laundry. It's not like I needed it for food.

I lit another smoke. Students looked at me when they walked by. I wondered what they saw. Maybe I looked like an addict by now. I leaned on a tree and twirled my finger in my hair. Oh yeah, my hair. I hadn't taken a shower yet. Wasn't wearing clean clothes either. Maybe that was why.

What was taking so long? I shifted my weight, trapped inside my thoughts. My skin. My pain. How to get away? Fly. Fall. Same difference now.

I touched my wrist. Fuck it. No one cared. I sat against the wall, my knees to my chest. Took my bracelet off and let it prick my skin. I tried to scrape, but it wasn't thick enough. I needed something more.

My studs. I took off my earring and shoved the back of it into my skin. There was pain this time. I dug in slowly, making a thick red line on my arm. God that felt good. Over and over I scraped. Scraped until the pain was gone. I wanted to be numb again.

"Lynn." Diesel. He held the door open. "The man wants a cut. Come up."

I covered my wrist and followed.

"This is crystal," said The Man as we sat on the floor in the dark. "It's better than crank. Way fucking better."

Shut up and give me some.

"You've lost a lot of weight." Sienna was standing in the doorway of my bedroom. I looked up from my book. "What are you reading?"

"*Are We Reviving Ophelia?* It's for Core."

"I remember that book." She sat next to me. "It's very empowering."

"Lynn." Someone was whispering my name. I turned. There was no one there. That was happening a lot lately.

"Lynn?" That was Sienna's voice. She was staring at me. "Are you okay?"

I picked at my fingernails. They were peeling at the ends. "I'm fine."

"I say that because, well, I don't know if you are."

You don't know a lot of things.

"I think you're drowning."

Drowning. Hmm. I saw an image of a river. A deep one. And me in the middle, clawing at the surface, struggling to breathe. I liked that.

"Thanks," I said in a smirky kind of way.

She sighed. "You know, I used to do tweak. I used to do a lot of tweak. I think I was fifteen when I started. My boyfriend was a manipulative asshole. I thought doing it would make him love me. It took me a long time to quit."

Okay. So she knew. Big deal. "Why are you telling me this?" Translation: Leave me alone.

"I just thought you should know that…that someone else has gone through it."

I forced myself to laugh. "You think I'm addicted to tweak? I've never even done it." Something cracked outside the window. Was someone listening?

"Lynn…"

I hurried to the glass and opened it, sticking my head out to the trees. Maybe it was a raccoon. I waited.

"Lynn, you've lost weight, you're hearing things, you're not going to class…you've done it."

Whoever it was had gone. I looked again to make sure. Closed the window. My cigarettes were on the floor by my bed. I grabbed the pack.

"Please let me help you."

My chest was hurting again. I wanted the last of that crystal. It was hiding in an empty cigarette pack in my sock drawer. God, I could almost taste it. Sienna needed to leave.

"So you're miss perfect now?" I spewed, my mouth shooting venom as I searched for my lighter. "Miss fucking know-it-all cuz you've been through something?"

Dude, I just bought the fucking lighter. Where…? Nevermind. Found it under a pair of jeans. My room was a fucking mess. Hadn't done laundry in, shit, three weeks? My underwear was starting to smell.

"I'm sorry you're in pain."

Oh yeah. Sienna. I had forgotten she was there. I turned to look at her. Were her eyes watering? I should care about that. Should care if she was in pain, that she was trying to help me. And in the back of my fucked up brain I knew she was right. I was losing it.

No more thoughts. Time to smoke.
"I only know what I see, honey."
"Get some fucking glasses." I slammed the door behind me.

Sometimes I couldn't feel my body. The distance between me rolled in and out, like waves. Black water, cold as ice. And I was spinning in circles, fighting the current. Drowning. Why couldn't I just close my eyes and disappear? So much around me, I'd fall over. Like paper dolls. It was too much to think. Couldn't go to class. Couldn't understand it. Couldn't remember how.

My parents called. Sienna called. Kat called. Over and over and over they called. It was just the fucking telephone. I shouldn't be running. Shouldn't be running from nothing. But my feet wouldn't stop. So I ran and I ran and I ran to the white snow that wasn't cold, making angels dance inside my nose.

My birthday was in four days. November 13th. It was on a Monday. My mother thought having the family spend the weekend with me would be nice.

"We got a room at the hotel. You should stay with us. It'll be nice to have the family together."

"I can't wait." I tried to sound excited.

A family visit meant turning somewhat normal. I ate a couple meals, slept at night, did the normal people thing. Tried laying off of the tweak for awhile. Actually stopped for almost a week, but that made me crave it so badly I had to do a few lines. Gave me the energy to clean up my fucking apartment. I bribed Angie's help with some of the crystal I had recently purchased with the money my grandmother had given me. I called her to thank her for sending it so early, that the money was a big help. I told her I spent her birthday check on food and other stuff I really needed. She was glad.

We scrubbed the bathroom, did two hours worth of moldy ass dishes that the job chart had failed to prevent, vacuumed week old crumbs, cleaned our tiny ass room, and topped it off with some lemon scented air freshener. It took three days.

It was almost time for family filled funness and stupid me had forgotten to get quarters. Didn't want my parents to smell the cigarette smoke on everything I owned. Sheena lent me enough for a load. I hid the rest of the evidence in a couple pillow sacks. Maybe they wouldn't notice. I was putting the one load of clean clothes away when my little sister pounced me from behind.

"You smell good," Halley grinned, plopping down on my bed. I sighed, knowing I had smoked merely an hour before. Showers and clean clothes can work major miracles sometimes.

The rest of the clan followed suit. Elle gave me a strange look before hugging me. I pretended I didn't notice.

"Hi honey," greeted the parents. I forced a smile, wondering if they could see me.

My mother's eyebrows narrowed. "I smell cigarette smoke."

I nodded. "A lot of people smoke here."

"Do you?"

"No." My eyes stared straight into hers. I wondered if she believed me.

"What happened to your arm?"

Elle was looking at my cuts. They all were. Shit. I forgot I had rolled up my sleeves. Fucking laundry.

"I fell," I told her, shoving my sleeve over my arm.

"You should put some Neosporin on it," my father said. He stepped closer and reached for my arm. "Let me see."

"No," I half shouted, yanking my arm away. "It's fine."

Awkward pause. Shuffling of feet.

"We should go to the hotel. Check in."

"Are you packed?"

Oops. I had forgotten I'd be spending the night with them. "No."

"Are those your dirty clothes?"

Shit. I should have put the pillow cases in the closet. What the fuck was wrong with me?

"Yes," I said. My hands were getting clammy.

"We could wait here for awhile," my mother said. "Do your laundry so you have clean clothes."

God, I wanted a line. Or a cigarette. Something. "No, it's okay. I can do it later."

"No, really. I'd like to do laundry with you." My mother smiled.

Tightness in my chest. Dammit, not now. "I don't have any quarters."

My mother dug into her purse. Pulled out a roll of quarters. "I brought you some."

Trapped.

The laundry room was empty. I supposed that was a good thing. No one there to hear me scream.

My mother began to dump my clothes inside a washer. "So how do you like college? We haven't talked much since you left."

"Oh, it's fine," I mumbled, trying to hide myself behind the clothes I dumped into another washing machine. I'm just failing everything. Totally lost. The usual.

"You're having a good time?"

Using? "Sure." Fucking shit, I wanted to use. My nerves began their dance. No, more like a stampede.

"What do you like the most?"

Voices whispered behind me. I looked, even though I knew there was no one there. "Independence, I guess." My fingernails tapped the washing machine. It echoed.

"Lynn." My mom was looking at me, a dirty sweatshirt in her hand. "All your clothes smell like smoke."

The room was getting smaller. I was chained to the wall with bars on the windows. Darkness in my head. My body was screaming.

"Are you smoking?"

"You already asked me." My nail pressed hard against the inside of my thumb. Pain tingled slightly. I dug further.

"Maybe I didn't believe you," she said.

"Maybe you shouldn't." The liquid detergent sat next to my arm. I thought about drinking it. Let it take me away. I saw my body on the tile, blood leaking from my eyes.

"Will you look at me please?" Her voice was desperate.

Well, so was I. Desperate to move. To breathe. To feel.

"You want to know the truth?" I shouted. "I smoke, okay? Just fucking deal with it." I turned away from her. Ran.

She didn't follow.

I ran through the parking lot and into the next college. They wouldn't find me there.

"Hey!" I asked the first smoker I saw. She had one. And a light. I thanked her with my back turned so she wouldn't see me cry.

In my own asylum now. Looked outside between the bars. No sun today. Only dark. It doesn't matter. I hate the sun.

"Why do you smoke?" We were sitting in the hotel room. My father's veins were bulging.

"Because." I tried to make myself as small as possible. Maybe I could disappear into the floor.

"That's not an answer."

"Maybe I don't have one," I told him.

His eyes were in my face. I leaned back. "Don't give me your fucking attitude," he barked.

"Okay."

He sat down again. I hugged my space.

"Please quit," my mother begged. There were tears in her eyes. I wanted to laugh.

"I wouldn't marry your mother unless she quit smoking," my father was saying.

My mother nodded. "I quit cold turkey after ten years."

You want a trophy or something?

"So can you."

Yeah. Sure. I can grow feathers too.

"If you don't quit, you won't be in college anymore." My father's logic.

The bedspread we were sitting on was dark green with yellow and blue squares. The longer I stared, the more the squares began to shift. They turned into ovals. The colors changed too. Yellow to orange. Blue to purple. Yellow, orange, blue, purple. I traced it with my fingers.

"Hey!" My father grabbed my arm.

Drip.

Drip.

Rusty water fell from the cracks in the ceiling. It trickled into little rivers that crawled along the floor, singing pretty hymns of pain.

I touched my lips. Felt the way they curled up at the edges. I pushed the corners of my mouth downwards and attempted to frown. But the happiness was molded there. It was fake. Made me so angry I tore it off. Threw it in my little river.

Goodbye smile. Drown inside the sad, sad, water. Just like me.

"Happy birthday to you! Happy birthday to you! Happy birthday dear Lynn, happy birthday to you!"

I stared at the candle.

"Make a wish," Halley whispered.

A star outside my window.

I wanted to hold it. Rip it from the sky. Fly. But the bars were strong on my window. I had made them that way.

My fingernails were at the walls. The floors. Scraping the concrete. Scraping a way out. I scratched until my blood leaked from the tips of my fingers. Screamed and cried and rocked against the wall.

That was me. Some pathetic piece of desperation I no longer wished to see, stuck in a cell inside my head. It's a happy fucking birthday to me.

"Bye Lynn."
"Bye Lynn. Happy birthday."
"Happy birthday."
"See you soon."
"Bye," I told them, watching my sisters get in the back seat of the car. I remembered us. Remembered us together. A family. How Elle and I would force Halley to sit in the middle because she was the youngest. We would entertain ourselves with the state license plate game while our parents argued in the front seat. Once we got 34 states. That was a long trip.

"Lynn." My father pulled me aside. "You remember what we talked about? With you quitting?"

"Yes," I said.

"Good." He gave me a hug. I stiffened. "See you soon."

"Okay."

My mother squeezed my hand. "You'll be fine," she whispered. I tried to smile.

"Bye!" they waved.

"Bye."

I waited for them to disappear before I lit my cigarette.

Alone, listening to the voices bounce between the walls. Shadows crawled along the ceiling, dripping shards of darkness on my head. I picked at the dried blood on my fingers.

Monday, November 13th.

"I don't remember what it's like to be sober," I laughed. I held the crack pipe while KJ lit the bottom. Diesel had made it from an incense holder he got from the liquor store at the base of campus. Said his dad taught him how to make them on a fishing trip he took when he was thirteen. KJ loved that story.

Said it was the classic icon of the United States of America. His yellow teeth sparkled when he grinned.

We were in this motel that KJ was staying in. KJ was this guy Angie, Diesel and I had met downtown on a cigarette run maybe four hours ago. He sold crystal cheaper when you fucked him first. Diesel and I went to get cigarettes while Angie and KJ made their deal. Angie said he had the most beautiful eyes she'd ever seen. They were brown and swirly. Like shitty water.

"Hang on, let me have another hit," I said.

KJ shook his head and pulled the pipe from me.

"Come on, man. It's her fucking birthday." Diesel sucked the end of one of my fingers.

"Well hurry up and decide cuz I want a fucking hit." Angie's face twitched. She scratched one of the scabs on her arm. She was picking at her skin again.

KJ's poop eyes glared at me. "Put the pipe in your fucking mouth."

"Thank you, KJ," I grinned sweetly, giving him a kiss on the cheek.

"Just hurry up so Angie'll quit bitching."

Out of the cell now.
Spun out of my fucking mind.
Running in circles, flapping my arms. Maybe if I jump I'll fly and not fall.
Fuck it, it won't matter. I'm flying on the ground now.

"We should get you a cake."
"It was my mom's birthday yesterday. I forgot again."
"What kind of cake would you get me?"
"Fuck moms."
"I think maybe I'll go home tomorrow."
"Raspberry and chocolate."
"Don't think that place exists."
"You think they have a pool here? I wanna go swimming."
"I'm gonna fail school."
"At least you have a fucking home."
"Cuz you never go to class."
"Fuck school too."
"I live down the street under a goddam bridge."

"I haven't gone swimming in so fucking long."
"So you want me to feel sorry for you?"
"Man, fuck bridges."
"What don't you fuck?"
"Dudes."
"Shit did you hear that?"
"What?"
"What are you talking about?"
"No. I heard something too."
"You think it's the cops?"
"What's going on?"

Diesel reached to open the door. KJ jumped behind him, throwing his arm around Diesel's neck.

KJ pulled out his knife.

"What the fuck?" Diesel shouted.

I covered my mouth with my hands. "KJ what are you doing?" I squeaked.

"Making sure we don't get caught, ass bitch."

Angie didn't like him calling me names. "Fuck you, we will if you don't shut the fuck up."

"I'm not the one making all the fucking noise!"

"Sssh!" I yelled.

"Shut up!" He let Diesel go and grabbed the rest of the crystal.

Angie stood up. "Fuck you, KJ, I bought that."

"Yeah, we should do that cuz I'm getting horny." He rubbed his thigh against Angie's crotch.

She pushed him away. "You already got that. Now give me my shit cuz I need a cigarette."

"Come on, baby, don't be like that."

"I'm going outside," I said. I went to unlock the door.

Angie shook her head. "Not till he gives me my shit."

KJ looked at her. "Can I just have one more hit?"

"Fine."

We stood there as he smoked, watching the shit bubble in the brown tinted pipe. I wanted another hit too.

"Later," Angie said when my eyes pleaded for more. She took the shit KJ gave her and put it in her pants.

Finally, KJ opened the door.

Happy birthday to me. Happy birthday to me. Happy birthday happy birthday happy birthday to me.

"So have you had a good birthday?" Angie and I were smoking in our usual spot.

"So far. Yeah. It's been okay." The roommates were planning something later. Something with alcohol. I wasn't allowed to know. Didn't really care.

"You can buy cigarettes now," Angie grinned.

"Yeah," I smiled. Should do that. Maybe I'll save the pack.

Angie flicked her cigarette against the wall. "You still haven't had any cake," she said.

"That's okay," I told her, pointing to the stash she held in her hand. "That's my cake today."

December 12th

I cut myself again tonight. Another thin curve of deep red. I've been wanting to do it more and more. I've found that, at least at the moment, causing myself physical pain is the easiest way to relieve everything. And that makes it feel so good. I can't cry. Writing doesn't do much. Even drugs and alcohol don't do it anymore. There's just so much inside. It claws at me, crying to get out. But I push it away to my little corner and lock the door. Feels like some of it manages to seep out through each layer of skin I scrape away. Almost feels like I'm digging for something. Answers? Truth? Reality? Sanity? I don't know.

I guess it's more of me melting into everything. The pain, the emptiness and desire for that sense of peace just beyond my reach. I want to just let it all go. Let it slip away and pull me along...drowning in my own ocean, my darkness, my protection and security against myself.

TEN

Finals week came and went. I was spun, of course. Wasn't really sober much anymore. Didn't care if I passed either. At least I showed up for the fucking things.

"How'd finals go?" Jolan and I were smoking weed in her bedroom. It had been awhile since we'd talked. She was busy with school.

I shrugged. "Didn't really pay attention. You?"

"I hope I did okay. I mean, I studied. I fucking studied my ass off."

"I didn't." I laughed lightly, shrugging off the part of me that was screaming.

"You going to the party tonight?" Jolan asked me through a cloud of smoke. "The last one before winter break?"

Winter break. That meant going home. Not sure how I felt about that yet. "Yeah."

"Good. It'll be awesome. There's this new drug Skip told me about. It's called foxy. You heard of it?"

I shook my head and took a hit.

"Kinda like ecstasy and acid mixed together."

"Candy flipping," I said.

Jolan grinned. "There's a name for that?"

"Yeah."

"Oh. Well I was gonna try it tonight. You should do it with me."

"Maybe."

"Linda and Sheena are gonna try."

I coughed. "Sheena?"

"Yeah," Jolan laughed. "She's so different from when we first met her."

"I know," I smiled. "I think we corrupted her."

"Life corrupted her. We were just there to watch."

185

I left to do some lines in her bathroom. It was secluded with a door and stuff. Better than our stupid stalls. Sometimes I used their shower just to pretend like I was home.

Angie had already left. Her finals were over a couple days before mine. All she could talk about was going home. I was avoiding it. Told my parents I'd leave sometime tomorrow, which meant today had to last a long time.

"You sure you don't wanna do it?" Jolan asked. She had just bought three pills from what's his face. Gary, maybe. One of Diesel's roommates. I hadn't seen Diesel in awhile. Kind of made it that way.

"Yeah, I'm sure. I'm good with Jack." I waved the bottle of Jack Daniels around. Took a swig. It burned my throat. I drank some more. Got the shit two days ago playing "hey mister" at the liquor store downtown. Offered a pack of smokes to whoever would buy me booze. I hid it under my bed. That was me, the closet user. Half the bottle was already gone.

"Cheers," they said, clanging their glasses of water together. I held up Jack and watched them pop their little pink pills. My hand touched the crystal I had bought, the crystal I had been craving. This was supposed to be really good shit. Too bad Angie wasn't here.

Too bad I was.

"Lynn." Diesel. His roommates must have told him about tonight. Jolan was at their place all the time.

"Hi," I said, instantly craving the goodies in my pocket.

"You trying that new shit tonight?" he wondered.

"Foxy?" I asked, trying to ignore his hand rubbing the side of my stomach. "No."

"So you'll take care of me if something happens then?" His lips brushed against my cheek. "Like last time?"

Last time. Last time he was drunk, and I was too spun to give a shit. Last time we fucked. I remembered some of it, but not enough for it to be okay. Not enough to stop the cuts on my legs. I used a razor. It bled more.

"I don't know, Diesel," I told him. My cheekbones grazed the edge of his nose. He kissed my hand.

"I'll give you a present."

He meant crank. Probably the same lame ass shit his dad always sent him. But it was free lame ass shit. I gave him a kiss. His tongue leaked into my mouth. I was used to that. He took my hand and led me to the bathroom. Closed the door.

"Suck me off and you get as much as you want."

"Excuse me?" He did not just say what I think he did.

"Do you want it or not?"

I hesitated. This was a step further than I had wanted to take. Fucking someone cuz you're high is one thing. Sucking someone off to get shit is another. That would make me an official whore.

"Someone'll come in before I'm done," I said.

"Not if you're good." He undid his pants, put down the toilet seat, and sat.

Okay, so Diesel plopped on the toilet with his dick hanging over the side wasn't very appealing. Yet when you're overdrawn fifteen bucks and money doesn't show up for another two weeks, sucking someone off for tweak starts to sound okay. It was survival, even if it was Diesel. He made me want to gag.

And I did. But I covered it up as best I could with moans and weird sounds that gurgled in my throat. It helped him get off, though I wasn't sure how some chick sucking dick in a dirty ass bathroom was at all hot. I felt like trash.

He came in my mouth. I spit it out when he was setting up my lines. There were a lot of them, and they were thick. Fuck, they'd better be.

I did seven lines, ignoring Diesel's wandering hand against my ass. He set up lines for himself. Snorted. Opened the door. I didn't follow.

"I'll be out in a minute," I told him. He closed the door as he left.

The toothpaste was in the medicine cabinet. I used my finger and brushed, rinsed, and brushed again. But I could barely taste the mint. His smell had squirted all over me. I splashed cold water on my face.

The door flew open. It was Jolan. She shut it behind her.

"Hi," I greeted, trying to hide the shakiness in my voice.

She sat on the bathtub. I remembered the new drug and wondered if she knew I was there. Then I saw it. There was a knife in her hand.

"Jolan?"

She touched the knife to her arm. I jumped at her and attempted to take the knife away. She wouldn't let go.

"I need to hurt," she told me, her voice lower than normal. More distant.

"Why?"

She glared. "I need to hurt!"

There was a rug on the floor. I pointed to it. "Hurt that."

She followed my gaze and crouched down, slowly jabbing the knife against the carpet. It tore. For a minute, I thought it worked. But the knife was at her arm again.

"The rug," I said firmly, guiding her hand back towards the floor.

"No!" She shoved me away and jabbed the knife into her skin. There was a mark, and it was bleeding.

"Goddamit Jolan, stop it!" I was on top of her, watching the knife edge closer towards my face. "Give me the fucking knife." My foot slid under her, and she tripped, hitting her head against the bathtub. The knife came loose. I grabbed it and threw it in the toilet.

"Ow," Jolan groaned, holding the side of her head. Her arm was still bleeding, but it didn't look that bad.

"Come here." I gently pulled her from the ground. It made me dizzy. The crank must be kicking in. That was fast. The room half spun as I pushed Jolan out the door and into the living room.

"Is anyone sober?" I yelled over the music. My body was starting to twitch with energy.

"Yeah." It was Rhiannon. I thought she had gone home. "Holy shit," she swore as I showed her Jolan's arm.

"I need to hurt," Jolan said again.

"You already did," I told her.

Rhiannon examined the cut. "We should wash it."

I nodded. "Take her to the bathroom. Her knife's in the toilet. Put the seat down. She'll just find ten more in the kitchen."

Rhiannon started walking to the bathroom, her hand gripped firmly around Jolan's wrist. She stopped. "You coming?"

My heart was pounding fast. Too fast. I shook my head. "I've gotta get out of here. Call the cops if she gets too bad."

I shoved my way through the crowd and stumbled out the door.

Woke up face first beneath a redwood tree. It was dark. I didn't remember getting there. Didn't remember anything past walking out Jolan's door.

Turns out it was 21 hours later. Fuck. I dragged myself to the apartment. My cell phone was under my bed.

"Hi Mom."

"Hi honey. Where are you?"

"I haven't left yet."

"Oh."

I could feel her disappointment through the phone. "I could leave now if you want." It was 10:00 at night. I knew she wouldn't want me to drive so late. She didn't. "I'm sorry," I told her. And a part of me was.

"Me too. I want to see you."

"Yeah." I sniffed and wiped my nose with the back of my hand. There was blood. Fabulous. I shifted the phone and got a tissue from my desk.

"Do you not want to come home?"

"No, I do. I just got caught up here." Damn, there was a lot of blood. I grabbed another tissue.

"Having fun with your friends?"

"Yeah." Fucking nose. I needed to do this shit in the bathroom. "But I'm tired," I said, faking a yawn. "I'll call you when I'm leaving tomorrow, okay? I'll be home by dinner time. Promise. Will you make mac n' cheese for me?"

Her voice softened. "Sure, honey. See you tomorrow."

I felt a pang in my eyes. They watered. I missed her. "See you tomorrow." I hung up the phone, shoved paper towel pieces up my nose, and reached in my pocket.

My crystal meth was gone. "Fuck!" I yelled, grabbing a cigarette and slamming the door behind me. Must have used it all when I blacked out. I couldn't believe that shit. Made me wonder what else I had done.

No it didn't. I didn't want to know. Fucking forget it.

I flicked my cigarette under the bench, took some aspirin with Jack Daniels, and passed out on my bed.

"You just got here and now you're walking out again!" My father was screaming at me.

I didn't stop moving towards the door.

"I don't understand, Lynn. Don't you want to spend time with us?" my mother asked.

"Not right now," I sighed, reaching for the door handle.

My father put his own hand over the door. "Stay home."

"No." I pulled the door open.

My father yanked my arm. My hand was on his hand, my nails ready to dig into his skin. "Don't touch me," I snapped. He let go. "Call me if you want to know where I am."

I smiled and slammed the door.

Inhale. Exhale. Pass. Inhale. Exhale. Pass.

"How do you like school?" Becky asked me, handing me the bong. Angie lit the bottom of the pipe. I sucked slowly, heavily. Holy shit, did it feel good.

"It's all right. Better than here. Not sure what I'm doing there, you know?"

"Becky goes to school and works two jobs," Angie said, bending her head to smoke the crank. "She knows what she's doing."

"No I don't," Becky laughed.

Inhale. Exhale. Pass. Inhale. Exhale. Pass.

"Did you know you have a bald spot?" Angie grinned.

"Where?"

She touched a part of my head. I went to the bathroom. Searched through my hair section by section. Couldn't find the bald spot, but there was this spot on my face. A pimple, maybe. I squeezed it and picked at the remains with my nail. Another spot. And another. I picked and scraped until one of them bled. Washed my face. Went back to Angie to tell her there wasn't a bald spot.

"Where did you go?" they asked, handing me the bong. Round four.

"Bathroom to see the bald spot. I didn't see it."

Angie laughed. "I forgot about that."

Becky nodded to the clock. "You were gone almost forty minutes."

Inhale. Exhale. Pass.

Inhale. Exhale. Pass.

Inhale. Exhale. Pass.

Shannon called. She was in town. I meant to call her back. Didn't get around to it. Wanted to get high.

"How old were you when you first got drunk?" Elle asked me. She sat in the passenger seat, her head out the window like a dog. She loved the icy wind.

"I don't remember. Maybe fifteen." I was driving Elle and two of her friends somewhere. Some boy's house or something.

"I beat you," she grinned.

"When did you get drunk?"

"A while ago."

Hmmm.

"I was ten," Anna said from the back seat. "Puked off some whiskey I stole from my dad's liquor cabinet."

"Fucking rebel," I teased.

Someone was on the side of the road. A man. He was standing near the edge of the sidewalk. Thought he was going to walk in the street. What was he doing? I was going to hit him. I swerved.

"What the fuck?" Elle shouted.

"Sorry, I didn't want to hit him," I explained.

Elle shook her head. "What are you talking about?"

"That man back there. He was practically standing in the middle of the street."

"That was a garbage can," Kendall half whispered. The girl Elle had spent the night with however many months ago. Elle told me they were getting pretty close.

I did a double take in my rear view mirror. There was a garbage bin on the side of the street. It was right where the man was. It *was* the man.

"How can you think a garbage can's a man, Lynn?" Elle was a little angry. And scared. "Are you high?"

I didn't say anything.

"I think Mom should drive us next time."

Voices. Voices whispering words. Screaming them. Screaming words so fucking loud inside my head. Sometimes I could hear what they were saying:

"I want some drugs. I want some fucking drugs! Give me some goddam drugs. Fucking shit, I want some mother fucking drugs!"

"Crazy. You're crazy. Did you know you're crazy?"

"Can't deal with this. Can't deal. Failing. Failing everything. Fuck fuck fuck fuck fuck. Not gonna make it. Gonna fail everything."

"You're nothing. A piece of shit nothing. Can't even control the thoughts in your head."

The sea of voices washed over my ears like waves, pounding the inside of my skull. I wanted to bash my head against the wall. Anything to get away.

I snorted another line.

Kat's apartment. Somehow my addiction had leaked out. Sienna must have told them. Orea, Kat, and Erin thought they could stop it. They thought I could be saved.

"Look at me, Lynn." Orea was talking to me.

I glared.

"You have a problem."

"No I don't," I spat, shoving Orea out of my way. Grabbed my pack of smokes and ran outside. Hid beneath a set of stairs around the corner. I reached for my cigarettes. The pack was empty. "Dammit!" I yelled, throwing the empty pack against the wall.

It almost hit Erin in the head. They had found me.

Orea took a cigarette from her pack and handed it to me. She lit one herself, then passed the pack to Erin. Kat gave me a lighter. I could barely use it. My hands were shaking too badly.

"Here." Erin reached out to help me. I turned away. Flicked the lighter again. It caught and I inhaled quickly. Erin took the lighter from my hand. I couldn't look her in the eyes.

"How many times have you shoved that shit up your nose?" Kat asked angrily.

"Why does it matter?"

"Fuck you. You know why."

I flicked my cigarette so hard it went out. "Shit."

"Trade me." Erin took my cigarette. I inhaled hers. "How often do you use?" she asked.

"All the time. Every day."

"How do you feel if you don't?"

"Like shit." I shoved my index finger between my teeth. Bit it. Hard.

"Stop that!" Erin pulled my finger away from my mouth. The skin was broken in red marks. Tears fell from Erin's eyes. "Why are you doing this?"

"Why can't you leave me the fuck alone?" I dodged Erin and ran from the stairs. Kat and Orea tackled me from behind, pushing me against the wall.

"What the—"

"Shut up Lynn." Kat was fuming.

"Don't you have something else to do?" I growled.

"I think this is pretty fucking important," Orea said. "You're killing yourself, you know." I couldn't stop looking at Orea's eyes. There was so much fire there. Life. And for a moment, I felt that strength. I felt human.

And then it was gone.

"We love you, okay?" Kat was telling me. "We're just trying to help."

I tried to wiggle myself out of their grip. "Can you let go?"

"Not until you say you need help."

I turned my head away. "No."

"Fucking say it!" Kat's words were spitting in my face. I bit my lip.

"You're losing yourself, Lynn." Orea's hands shook against my arm. Or maybe I was the one shaking. I couldn't tell. "Do you want to lose us too?"

"Fine," I said fiercely. "I'm an addict. I've been doing this shit for months."

They let me go. I took another cigarette from the pack. Erin sat on the stairs, her hands covering her mouth. There were still tears on her face. Orea's eyes were watering too. She joined Erin on the stairs.

Kat put her hand on my shoulder. "I went through this too."

I shrugged away quickly. "So you know all about me now?"

"Yes," Kat said slowly.

"Fuck you." I stared straight into her eyes. She didn't say anything. "Fuck all three of you." Orea grabbed Erin's hand. I flinched inside. "You're just as fucked up as I am. Erin pukes her guts out cuz she can't deal with shit, Kat's cutting her legs with fucking glass for the same reason, and Orea's still with some guy who fucking cheated on her because she's too goddamn scared to be alone. So until you have your own shit fucking put together, leave mine the fuck alone."

I left before I could see the hurt in their eyes. Left to melt in my addiction. My enemy. My home.

My family was watching a movie when I got there. Well, my mother and sisters were. My father had gone to bed. He didn't like watching movies during the week. Stayed up too late that way. We didn't mind. Perfect time to watch the girly movies. Shit, I hadn't done that in a long time.

I quickly changed my clothes, washed my face and arms and sprayed conditioner in my hair. Curled on the couch next to my mother.

She kissed the top of my head. Her scent wafted through me, wrapping my soul in her motherhood. I edged closer, allowing myself to fold into her arms. Melt into her love. I could breathe for a little while there. Exhale. Let go of the voices, the pain, the need...let it all sleep for once.

Saw Shannon. She asked what was going on with me. She'd heard shit. I shrugged. She said I looked like I'd been using. Said she didn't want me to get too into drugs. That it scared her and everyone else. I listened. Listened but didn't hear her. Was supposed to see Angie soon. We were gonna play pool with Becky, Carlos, and Scott. After smoking at Becky's house, of course. But we didn't even say that anymore. It was already assumed.

"Lynn!"
I looked at her.
"Nevermind." She left.
I lit a cigarette and called Angie.

Inhale. Exhale. Inhale. Exhale. Pass. Inhale. Exhale. Inhale. Exhale. Pass.

Driving in the dark. Driving in the dark high. Driving in the dark high at 95 miles an hour.

Cop car behind me. Shit. The red and blue lights shouted in my ears. I slowed towards the left shoulder of the freeway.

"Pull to the right side of the freeway!" the cop bellowed. His voice was loud. Must've had a bullhorn.

I pulled over. The cop stepped out of the car. I looked at myself in the mirror. Maybe he wouldn't notice I was tweaked out of my mind.

He knocked at my window. I rolled it down.

"License and registration."

I took my license from my wallet and handed it to him. He stared at it with his overly bright flashlight. I opened my glove compartment to find the registration.

A small bag of crank was shoved in the back.

The light from the flashlight blared in my face. I looked away and hoped he hadn't noticed my eyes. The pupils are bigger on crank.

"Registration?"

I tried not to speak too quickly. "It's here somewhere," I said hoarsely. I searched through the glove box, careful not to shift the papers too much. They were keeping the crank from falling out.

"You need some light?" The cop tilted the flashlight towards the inside of the compartment. I shoved the bag of crank under a crumpled napkin. "Lots of stuff in there," he said.

"I was going to clean it," I mumbled, finally spotting the registration. It was at the opposite end of the glove box. I handed it to him and shut the glove box quickly. He went back to his car. Holy fucking shit, that was close. I lit a cigarette and waited.

It took awhile for him to come back.

"Do you know how fast you were going?" he wondered.

"95," I answered. I didn't think I was sober enough to lie. "Though I didn't notice until you were behind me."

"Glad you saw me," he said rather cynically. "95 is way too fast, young lady."

I sighed dramatically. "I know, sir. I'm really sorry about that."

"Good. I'm going to give you a ticket."

Dammit.

He wrote out some shit, had me sign it, and I was off driving 70 like a good Samaritan. The cop was ahead of me. I got off at the next exit in a town I'd only seen through signs. It looked small. One of those stops where truckers crashed or a place for people to get directions. Or somewhere safe for a girl to get high.

I drove for a little while. Pulled over on a deserted side street. It was dark enough here. I opened the glove box and took out the bag of crank.

And then I was angry. So angry I couldn't stand it. Fuck my family. Fuck my friends. Fuck the law. Fuck me. I set up the lines on the dash board and snorted until there was no more. I don't remember getting back to school.

sitting on cold earth darkness pounding every cell inside my head screeching silence solitude everywhere the light is gone black clouds hovering laughing falling over my eyes can't see won't look at the reflection in the stillness grasping the depths of my soul so alone -why? the light's gone out where's my matches too wet to light, no hope lost all lost somewhere in darkness all darkness my mind is swimming sinking drowning in solitude burning my soul with black flames crackling sizzling darkness engulfing my light my heart my everything gone, disappeared in this cage of darkness let me out! running screaming pounding my fists they bleed dark red blood trickling melting falling in empty silence lonely silence dear God let my voice break free LET ME OUT! pacing sharp claws digging frantically digging searching for light screaming spinning falling crying dying death engulfing the air losing breath grasping choking groping for something anything walls holes doors nothing my fingers touch nothing only solitude empty solitude darkness surrounding holding me tight i close my eyes and let it take me away.

Three new classes. Life in the Sea, Intro to Acting, and Narratives of a Girlhood.

The first one sounded cool. Could have been cool. I liked the ocean. Wouldn't have minded learning about all the critters in the sea. There were even tide pool field trips. But I only went the first week or so.

Thought Intro to Acting would be fun. Hadn't done that shit since high school. But the teacher sucked and it wasn't really acting. Had to pretend to butter toast with no words like some kind of mime. I'm sorry, but if you're buttering toast in a play, you have the fucking knife and bread. Shouldn't we be concentrating on, oh I don't know, emotions or something? Ridiculous. I didn't go to that one either.

I loved the third class. It was a literature class about books written through the eyes of girls. That intrigued me. I felt like I could connect somehow. I was high most of the time, but I never missed it.

We were reading *The Bluest Eye* by Toni Morrison.

"Turn to page 39, at the top." Professor Corry loved quoting the books. She didn't do much else. *"You looked at them and wondered why they were so ugly,"* she read. *"You looked closely and could not find the source. Then you realized that it came from conviction, their conviction."*

I stared at the word *ugly*. Stared at its meaning. After awhile the curves of the *u*, the dip of the *g*, the bump of the *l* and the sudden downfall in the *y* seemed wrong. Like they shouldn't be together. The word itself became ugly.

Professor Corry cleared her throat. *"Pecola and her family are cursed with an ugliness that belongs to them through their past. The ugliness continues because of their own refusal to change it."*

I drew a face in my notebook. An ugly face with three eyes and a tiny nose. One eye seemed sadder than the rest. Maybe it saw me. Saw the ugliness on my insides. I looked at the quote again. Swallowed its words.

Then you realized that it came from conviction, their conviction.

So they convicted themselves. But who would want to be locked up with their own ugliness? I touched the scars on my arms. Felt the bumps inside my skin. It was ugly now. Tainted with bumps and imperfections. I was like Pecola, scarred with an ugliness I could not escape.

Somewhere downtown. There was this guy smoking a cigarette. He looked spun.

"You tweak?" I asked.

"You a cop?"

"No."

He tilted his head. "Yeah, I tweak. Why?"

"You have some?"

"Nah, but I can get it. Will you share?"

"Yeah, whatever." I followed him to a motel a few streets away. Room 37. He knocked.

"It's Cody. I got a buyer."

It was opened by this chick with hair to her waist and really big earrings. She looked like a hippie. "She's cute," she said, following me inside.

The place reeked of body odor. I tried to breathe less. It just made me dizzy. Three people huddled on the bed. One girl, two guys. One of the guys held a piece of aluminum foil. There was a line of crank on top. The girl was leaning over it with a straw. I watched him flick a lighter under the foil. The thin whisk of smoke disappeared into the girl's straw.

The other guy was looking at me. "So you want some?"

I avoided his eyes. "Yeah."

"How much?"

"Gimme an eight ball." I handed him the money. The bag was in my hand. "Can I do some here?"

"If you give us a cut."

"Okay." I didn't care.

"You wanna smoke it?"

I nodded. It had been a couple weeks.

"Let me finish my fucking high," bitched the girl on the bed when the dealer tried to push her off.

"It's cool," I told him. "I've gotta go to the bathroom anyway." I went inside and shut the door. My body was tearing itself apart, looking for a high that wasn't there. I couldn't wait.

Lines were on the bathroom counter. It only took a few seconds to set up now. No way to tell I wasn't really going to the bathroom. I flushed the toilet and did a couple lines, then ran the water and did one more. Cleaned off the counter, put my shit away. Opened the door and came out. Bing bang bong.

They set me up on the bed. Put a thick line on the aluminum foil.

"What's your name?" the guy who wasn't the dealer asked.

"Lynn."

"I'm Pete."

I forced a smile before putting the straw in my mouth. His name could be Donald Duck for all I cared. Just light the fucking foil.

Slow inhale as I followed the light. Hold it. Hold it. Hold it! Exhale. Relief. I grinned for real this time.

It was as though some mysterious all-knowing master had given each one a cloak of ugliness to wear, and they had each accepted it without question...
She hid behind hers. Concealed, veiled, eclipsed—peeping out from behind the shroud very seldom, and then only to yearn for the return of her mask.

"What are you doing now?" Cody asked, handing me another cigarette. His trade off for the high. He lit mine and then his own.

We were standing outside the liquor store. He wanted a beer and was old enough to buy his own. I told him I didn't want anything. Didn't want to fuck with my high.

I took a drag. "Dunno. Going home I guess. Not sure what else to do right now."

"Where's home?" He flicked his cigarette and the cherry fell onto the floor. I offered him a lighter, but he was crouched on the ground. I watched him touch the end of his cigarette to the ball of fire on the concrete. Watched the cigarette come back to life. "I smoke so much I don't even pack them anymore," Cody told me, sucking the cigarette thickly to make sure it was lit. "The cherries come off all the time."

Cody's eyes were green. Dark green, like the leaves of a redwood tree. "Do you have something to do?" I asked him.

"Hang out with you."

"Everything here costs money. I live on campus. Come with me."

"Cool."

We talked past the time it took to walk to the metro station, through the bus ride that I gave him a dollar for, through the walk to my apartment. We talked and talked about absolutely nothing. It was that connection, the tweaker spark and confidence and all the shit that wasn't real. But whatever. I hadn't felt real in a long time.

"It's messy," I told him. He didn't care. Opened the beer, sat on my bed. I sat next to him, my legs bouncing against the mattress.

"Can't sit still or something?" he asked.

"No. I'm so high," I laughed, flicking my hair out of my eyes. He put his finger on my chin. There were those eyes again.

"I'm gonna kiss you."

"Okay."

He tasted like beer and nicotine and salty tweak. His kiss was rough.

I heard the cling of his belt being undone. "I didn't say I'd fuck you," I said.

"What the fuck else did you bring me here for?" His voice was angry.

"I don't know. Talk."

"I don't talk." My back was against the wall. His eyes weren't so pretty anymore.

"Maybe you should leave. I don't fuck random guys." I made my voice sound as hard as it could, trying to ignore the quiver in my gut. I pictured Angie, how she was with KJ and the other random dirtbags. And now it was me. I remembered how I felt after I fucked Diesel. How disgusting it was to give him a goddamn blow job in the bathroom.

What was happening to me? I hadn't taken a shower in three days. Hadn't eaten, hadn't brushed my teeth. I was wasting my life in this fucking shit I called crank. Wasting my education, whatever dreams I could possibly have. And now I was stuck with this guy I didn't know and he was scaring me.

"Fuck you!" he yelled, slamming his fist against the wall.

"Where did this come from?" I asked, trying to slip away from his arms. "Why are you so angry?"

"All you fucking whores do is get me all goddam hot for no fucking reason!"

"Whores? I'm no whore."

"Yeah, whatever. You found me on the street bitch. What the fuck else does that make you?"

I straightened my fear as best I could. "Get out."

He wasn't moving.

"I said get the fuck out of here!" I screamed, pushing him back. He slapped his hand across my face.

"Don't yell at me bitch." He got off the bed and took a sip of his beer. "I want that blanket," he said, pointing to the one on my bed.

"No."

"You have another one?"

I shook my head. It was a lie. There was one I had bought in Mexico when I was fifteen. It was in the closet on the top shelf. But there was no way I was giving that shit up. Not to him.

"What about food? Do you have any food?"

"Ramen." I pulled the drawer open from under my bed and gave him three packs.

"I want beef. You got any beef?"

My breath was shaking. I handed him another one. There goes a few days' supply of food.

"Can I make it here?"

Was this guy serious? I shook my head. "Take your food and leave."

"Fuck you." He opened the side door and walked out.

I stood there for a moment. Ran to lock the glass doors up front. Locked both doors to my room. Prayed my roommates would come home.

There was a knock on my door. I knew it was Cody. Another knock. And another. I hid in my bed with the covers over my head. Hid there with my eyes closed.

The knocking grew louder. Louder. He was shouting now. Couldn't hear what he was saying. I put a pillow over me.

The knocking stopped. I sighed.

Footsteps around the front. He banged on the glass doors. Maybe someone would see him. Maybe they would tell him to leave.

He went around the side again. More knocking. I chewed on the side of my thumb.

Then silence. I poked my head out. Maybe he was gone. I got up and listened at my door. Nothing. Opened the other door and peered into the living room.

There was a noise in my bedroom. A loud one. I turned around.

Cody was coming in through my window. I put my hand over my mouth to stifle a scream. He tumbled onto the floor, stood up and smiled at me. Grabbed the beer that was on my desk.

"I forgot it," he said. Turned around and jumped back through the window.

I made sure to lock it behind him.

White powder on the desk. Scrape, scrape against the wood. Chop chop chop it smooth. Scrape chop scrape. A rolled up dollar bill. Sniff the crank up through my nose.

Scrape, scrape. Chop chop chop. Sniff.

Sigh.

There were white spots on my arm. They were flat. Round. I didn't notice them before and wiped them away. But they came back again.

"I see them too." Angie stared at me, her tongue skimming the inside of her mouth. "I don't know what they're saying all the time, but I see them. Do they tell you things?" She spoke so quickly. I wondered if I had heard her right.

"What are you talking about?" I asked.

"I started seeing them last month I think, maybe a little longer but I don't remember. Right after we met KJ. I saw him yesterday, did I tell you? He looked like such shit. All scrawny and dirty. But that's what happens when you live on the street, right?"

I looked at her. Really looked. I saw the scabs that littered her face, her arms. The way her eyes had glossed over and darted back and forth over and over. She was pale. Gaunt. Her hair was oily, her clothes wrinkled from not being washed. This wasn't the Angie I had remembered. I didn't want to know her.

"Lynn are you listening? Oh, oh, are they talking to you right now? Do you see them? Mine are right here. Look." She pointed to her arm.

I didn't see anything and shook my head. "What are you talking about?" I asked again.

"The aliens."

Snort. Water. Snort. Water. Drip drip drip.

The need to explode. So much it pounded my soul, pulsating with the face of pain, lingering on the edge of insanity's breath. Couldn't take it. Suddenly they played this song that was mine and Rick's song and I couldn't do it, couldn't handle it. Wanted to bite or claw or throw something and watch it smash against the wall.

What happened? Wasn't this way earlier today. Went to class. Went sober this time. Tried to be sober. Tried to fight it. Was okay, even happy. Then I wasn't. That was when I gave up.

Fuck fuck fuck.

Sigh. The song stopped. Breathing deep breaths. Slowly. Slowly. I was okay. The screaming had stopped. Body stopped shaking. I was okay. I was okay.

Heard the voices again. Hid in the bathroom. Angie found me asleep on the floor. I was covered in pee. Guess I was too tired to wake up. Didn't even remember falling asleep.

Snort. Snort. Water. Water. Drip drip. Snort. Snort. Water. Water. Drip drip.

Walked at night. Liked to talk to the shadows. Or were they birds? Are there birds at night? Do they chirp or was that my ears talking to me? I liked the birds at sunrise better. They're friendlier then. It's not so dark, either. Not that dark is bad. It's like the darkness in my head. Softer. Been foggy in there lately. Hard to see through the bars. Hard to see anything at all.

The damage done was total. She spent her days, her tendril, sap-green days, walking up and down, up and down, her head jerking to the beat of a drummer so distant only she could hear...

April 16th

I smell. Haven't taken a shower since Saturday. Today's Thursday. That's disgusting. Didn't turn in my paper today. Didn't even fucking do it. God, I want to bang my head against the fucking wall. I just wish I could run away, far far away and never have to worry about anything ever again. So scared. And there's just so much shit. So much shit. Why can't I be strong?

I don't know...and I don't really care. Analyzing myself just makes me run around in circles. Had some crank. I'm almost out. Have enough for the rest of the night. Do that shit too much. Way too much. I don't even feel human anymore. More like this thing that needs to be fed every so often or it shrivels and dies.

ELEVEN

Snort.

Little cockroaches inside my skin. I swatted at them. Picked to make them disappear. Picked and picked and picked.

Snort.

Lift me up. Make me fly off of the ground. Numbed emotion. Swarming chaos. Nowhere to go. Escape the mind the thoughts evading. Body spinning needing spinning needing needing more.

Snort.
Snort. Water.
Snort. Water. Drip drip snort. Water.
Snort. Water. Drip drip snort water snort water drip drip
Snort water snort water dripdripsnortwatersnortwaterdrip
snortwatersnortwaterdripdripsnortwatersnortwaterdripdripdrip
snortdripdripsnortwatersnortdripsnortwaterdripdripsnort

Is it possible to be afraid when you refuse to feel?

Maybe I should end it. Put a knife to my throat. Cut myself with something more than stupid tacks and razors. Swallow pills. Overdose on the shit I shoved up my nose or in my lungs. Something to end me.
    I started to see myself dead. My body on the floor, stiff and pale from seizing. Hanging by the sinks, my head thick and swollen from the rope around my neck. In the shower, blood pouring from my veins.
    Thoughts of when to do it. How to do it. Just to do it. Fuck the living.

I spiraled down and down and down beyond the emptiness of me. Down away from life away from thought away from anything everything all lost and drowning and couldn't I just melt into the ground? It was too much. Lost beyond lost beyond lost.

And then something happened.

It was spring quarter. I was reading for Intro to Psychology, sprawled on my bed, fighting the urge to smoke another cigarette. One more page. Okay. Concentrate. The midterm's tomorrow. You can read one more fucking page.

The cigarettes were on the bed. They were calling to me. Kept reading the same sentence over and over and dammit! I grabbed the pack and started to go outside. Turned around again. I was tired of being by myself. Tired of the thoughts in my head.

Maybe Rhiannon would smoke with me. She did on random occasions.

"Rhiannon," I sang, skipping down the hall and into her room. "Whatcha doing?"

I stopped.

She was sitting on the floor, her knees tucked into her chest. Head down. Uh oh. Something was wrong.

"Rhiannon?"

No response. She was staring at something. A framed photograph. Rhiannon and some girl laughing with pierced tongues.

I crouched beside her. She didn't even see me. "Rhiannon?" I said again, touching her lightly on the shoulder.

She threw the picture against the wall. Startled the living shit out of me. The glass shattered. "Who the fuck does she think she is?" she yelled, facing me for the first time. "How could she be such a fucking moron?!"

I chose my words carefully. "Who are you talking about?"

She ran her fingers through her hair. Sighed shakily. "My sister." Pause. "My mom just told me...she killed herself."

I wish it was me.

Did I really just think that? A pleasant horror seeped into my head. The relief it must have been, to let it all wash away like that. To just close my eyes. Peace. How wonderful it would be.

And then I saw the pain in Rhiannon's eyes. The pain of losing life, its light. I should say something comforting.

In times like these, the average person doesn't know what to say. I'm sorry? That sucks? No words can take away the pain and shock of losing someone, especially when they do it to themselves. But maybe the average person could do something to help. Say words of kindness. Comfort with touch. Something. But I was the average person fucked up on tweak. Not only was I out of words, I was void of everything. No tears. Maybe a tad of sorrow masked by a jolt inside my gut, but it wasn't human enough. I knew I was too fucked up to help her. Shit, I wished it was me who had died.

But I tried. I thought about my own sisters. How I would react. What I'd do first. "I have cigarettes if you want one," I told her. "I actually came to ask if you wanted to smoke with me." Really heartfelt.

She nodded and attempted to push herself from the floor. I had to help her up.

"I just talked to her maybe two, three days ago," she said, taking a heavy drag. "She sounded fine. She was fine. What a fucking liar."

I flicked my cigarette, allowing the rhythm to consume the desire to speak. Tried to cling to any last element of control I had left. Damn tweak.

"You think she would've told me. I don't even know why she did it." She laughed bitterly. "We used to be close. Used to talk about everything. But then she found Asshole. He cheated on her and beat her up and killed her cat. I told her to break up with him, that he was psycho and she didn't need someone like that in her life. Told her our father was enough to fucking deal with." She took a drag. Exhaled. "But she didn't give a fuck what I thought. Told me I was the crazy one and to stay out of her life." Another drag. Another laugh. "And then she called me out of the fucking blue. Guess Asshole got arrested for breaking into a house. Stole a bunch of crap. Almost killed the old woman who lived there. She said it wasn't his fault. That he was fucked up on drugs."

She stopped. I didn't want her to. I needed to know the secret. How her sister got to the point of death. What gave her the guts to do it.

"Was she using too?" I asked.

"Not that I know of. But I guess I didn't really know anything, did I?"

I lit another cigarette and handed it to her.

"So she breaks up with Asshole and moves back home. Starts talking to me again. Said she was sorry, that she should have listened. She wanted to go to counseling and start things over. That was during Christmas break." Pause. "That was the last time I saw her." Tears were falling from her eyes. She didn't seem to notice. "I tried not to let her get to me. She'd do this all the time.

Say she was sorry then fuck up all over again. But this time it seemed different. Or maybe I just wanted to believe it was."

"What's her name?"

"Gwen." Rhiannon stopped, tasting reality for the first time. Her cigarette was on the floor. Fingers hugged the edge of her hair, her face contorted in agony. In the front of our apartment, body against the glass doors, she doubled over and sobbed.

And I left her there. Went inside and did the last of my lines. Grabbed my wallet, my smokes, my phone. Stepped over her head to catch the bus.

I liked the name Gwen. Liked the way it sounded, classy against my lips. I wondered how she did it. What it felt like to die. What gave her the guts.

The bus ended at the metro station downtown. I started to walk, unsure of where I was going. Didn't really matter. As long as it wasn't where I'd been.

KJ was standing on the curb. "Long time no see," he said.

"You got any shit?"

"How much you want?"

I sighed. My bank account was overdrawn again. "I don't have any money."

"I'm not gonna just give it to you."

"I know." I paused, remembering Angie and the filth I saw in her eyes. KJ was a fucking dirtbag. Literally. But what other choice did I have? I was broke. He was there. I needed my fix. I didn't give a fuck anyway. "I'll do whatever you want for a dime bag."

I didn't come home that night. Or the night after that. Spent the hours getting fucked up however I could on the streets of downtown. Still don't really remember much of it. They say we block out our most painful memories. By then I was past pain. Even numbness hurt.

Saw Sienna leaving a sushi joint with a guy. Hid behind a car. Didn't think she saw me, though I swore her eyes glanced my way. Maybe she didn't recognize me. Maybe she didn't want to know me anymore. Maybe I was already dead.

Inhale. Exhale. Inhale. Exhale. Inhale inhale exhale. Inhale exhale inhale exhale inhale inhale inhale exhale inhale inhale exhale inhale exhale inhale inhale inhale inhale inhale exhale .

Day three on the streets. Sold myself to get my fix. Get me high. Let me run. But I couldn't. Always saw that damn reflection in the mirror. Always felt the same shit inside.

I was snorting some resemblance to white powder on the back of a toilet in a public bathroom that reeked of shit beneath a parking structure, when it suddenly occurred to me that I had missed my midterms again. I started laughing. It was really true. I was a psycho bitch addicted to crank. It was fucking my life up.

Thought about KJ, how I prostituted what seemed to be the only value I had left. Thought of the streets, sharing cigarettes and flirting drugs out of homeless guys. Pictured my life there or with Gwen's boyfriend, beating up old ladies to sell their shit to get more drugs. At first the image was funny. Guys with nylon masks tweaked out of their heads, tumbling over the broken glass ninja style, jaws grinding into their bulging eyes. The old lady screaming in a pink laced nightgown running down the stairs. The blood spilling from her head as they beat her over and over with a club or a television or whatever they could get their hands on. I stopped laughing.

My hand slipped and the receipt I was using to snort my yellow tinted crank fell in the toilet. Laughed again. The highlight of my life was dropping the receipts I dug out of the trash into the toilet. I was supposed to be doing something with my life. Chasing my dreams, riding the wind or whatever that fucking saying was.

I reached into the water and took back my receipt.

And then I saw my arm. It was red and blotchy and absolutely disgusting. My clothes were dirty. I hadn't showered in God knows how long. Hadn't slept. I didn't even remember the last time I talked to my parents. My sisters.

Oh God, my sisters. I saw their faces, their eyes. I was their Gwen. Would it be Elle crying next? Telling her friends how close we used to be? How fucked up I got and didn't have the guts to tell her? She was fifteen now. Old enough to understand it. Old enough to know the truth.

And Halley. I pictured my parents attempting to explain my disappearance to a twelve year old girl. Pictured her eyes. Her innocent eyes. Saw the sadness there.

How did it get this bad? It wasn't supposed to be this way. I just wanted to feel something other than pain. Now pain was the only thing I had left. And fear. The monster in my gut flexed its claws, rising to the inside of my throat as the panic set in. The world was spinning, and there was nothing left to hold onto. I was falling, losing ground, suffocating.

I wanted to breathe again. To be something beyond a slave to a drug who didn't even know I existed. It had chained me, beaten me, and I was dying.

I grabbed my shit from the back of the toilet and opened the stall. The door hit a girl, knocking her back a few steps.

"Sorry," I murmured, trying not to stare. This girl was the dirtiest thing I'd ever seen. She wore a skimpy half torn shirt, ripped jeans and no shoes. Thin black hair hung around dark, sunken eyes. Bony arms wiped the blood dripping from her nose. A cross hung around her neck.

"You do tweak, huh?" she said, pinching her nose to make the blood stop running. Her face twitched as she stared at me, seeing and not seeing me at the same time. She made me want to puke.

"No," I lied, moving around her towards the door.

"Don't fucking lie to me bitch. I heard you in there. I got the fucking shakes, ok? Gimme a break."

I looked closer. She was shivering.

"What the fuck you looking at?" she yelled, her body moving closer to me. I backed away. She turned to the mirror. Scratched at a red mark on her face. There were tons of them everywhere. Just like my arms.

I saw my reflection in the mirror. Standing side by side, we didn't look much different. Both had the same sunken eyes, the same stringy hair, the same picked skin. Equally dirty, equally skinny, equally foul.

"You've got the shakes too?" she asked, tilting her head and raising an eyebrow. I looked at her questioningly. "Your hands."

They were shaking against the counter. Shaking from shock. Shaking shaking shaking like my mind, my hope, my life. Everything I had been running from had found me and slapped me in the face. All the pain, the sadness, the anger, the fear. It made me sick. I couldn't be there. Couldn't look at her. Couldn't face the fact that this thing was just like me.

I did NOT want my life to be this way.

I ran from the bathroom. Ran all the way to the metro. Prayed no one would see me, would know me, would ask me to get high. I didn't want to use anymore. Had to get away.

But I knew I couldn't do it on my own. I needed help, but there was no one down here who could help me. I had to get back to campus. Had to get back home.

Angie was there. "Where the fuck have you been?" she asked, her teeth grinding.

I barely looked at her. Didn't want her to see the pain in my eyes. But she probably wouldn't notice. She was high too. Maybe if I told her my truth, she would understand. Know how to help me. Something.

I opened my mouth and closed it again.

Not her. Not yet. I needed someone else. Someone outside of me.

"Nowhere," I told her. "I'm back now."

Angie waved her pack of smokes around. "You coming?"

I shook my head and sat by my computer. "I'll smoke with you in a little while. Gotta do something first."

She left.

I stared at the screen. What the fuck was I doing? Maybe I should just smoke with Angie. I turned to grab my cigarettes and noticed my Intro to Psych book on my bed. That was an option. I could tell the Professor that I missed the midterm. Tell my teaching assistant I wasn't passing the class because I was high. They were psychologists, or at least knew enough to teach it. They would know what to do.

My fingers hung above the keyboard. I typed, stopped. Erased what I wrote.

I didn't want to do this. Didn't want to stop using. Even the thought of it pierced fear into my veins. This was my secret. Telling someone would open my cage. My cell. Let the light in.

Light.

I had been hiding in the dark too long. Too much suffering and pain and I needed to end it before it ended me. I had thought about killing myself today. More than today. Wasn't that a sign? A hint that it was time to stop?

I took a deep breath. Started to type.

Hi. I missed the midterm a few days ago, and I'd like to apologize for my lack of responsibility. The midterms are an important element to the class as well as my grade. I have read your grading policy and understand I am now at a failing status, which I have accepted. I actually need your help with another matter.

Panic. What the fuck was I doing? Shouldn't be writing this. Too much fear. Wanted to run again. Smoke with Angie. Snort her shit. Snort anyone's shit. Get lost in the high I despised. Dammit, why was I so fucking scared?
I shook my head. Forced myself to keep going.

I missed the midterm because I was on drugs. I've been addicted to methamphetamines for the past ten months. I'm failing college and I'm afraid. Please help me in any way you can, or at least let me know what I can do to get myself back on track.

Thank you for taking the time to read this,

Lynn Levy

I sent it before I could change my mind.
Angie came back. Said she was gonna do lines and then maybe play pool with me if I wanted to get high cuz she hadn't seen me in so long and did I know there was a pool table in this room hidden behind the mailbox?

They wrote back the next day.
The Professor said my situation was "sad" and he'd allow a retake on the midterm. Said good luck with everything, and he'd be there if I wished to discuss any personal matters. That wasn't what I expected. I checked the other email. It was from Kathryn, the teaching assistant. Kathryn said she wanted to help me with my addiction. She had made me an appointment with the Health Center at 1:00 the following afternoon. She would be there with me before and after I talked to someone. She would make sure I got the help that I deserved.
If I hadn't been so high, I would have cried. Finally someone had heard me screaming. Someone was there outside the bars, telling me everything was going to be okay. I was going to be okay.
I grabbed a cigarette and went out front to the benches where the sun lived. I saw the flowers and the clouds and the hippies and it made me feel a little

more human. Knowing I would be pulled back from whatever darkness I had lived in etched a smile on my lips and hope in my heart.

It didn't last long.

By noon the next day I was sober and terrified. Maybe I shouldn't meet her. I could go downtown or hit up Diesel for some shit and make my insides stop their screaming. I had never felt this anxious. Couldn't stop moving. Kept a cigarette in my mouth so I wouldn't chew my tongue off.

What was going to happen to me? Would they put me away in some mental place? Kick me out of school and send me back home? Tell me I fucked up too much already, that it was impossible to save me? Maybe I didn't want to be saved. Maybe there was nothing left anyway.

Or maybe it didn't matter. Whatever happened couldn't possibly be as bad as where I'd been.

12:50 PM. I sat there on the concrete in front of the Health Center, my knees to my chest, my eyes staring at the pavement. I hated the Health Center. Being here meant something was wrong. Okay, so it could be the flu or a sprained ankle but that's not what I thought of when I saw that place. It was for those who couldn't handle shit on their own, who were afraid of falling and didn't have the means to hold on anymore. Maybe I should leave. Hop the fence and tear into the forest. Live with the fucking deer. Live something else besides this fear.

"Lynn?"

I turned around. Kathryn was walking towards me. She was smiling. "Hi."

"Hi," I said, putting my cigarette out on the pavement.

"Are you ready?"

No. But I nodded anyway. Looked back at the fence. Sighed. Not this time. I needed to face this. Needed to fix myself.

I shoved my shaking hands inside my pockets and went inside the building.

PART THREE

Shadows Dance No More

Awakening

In her eyes she swallows,
empty sorrow becoming forever
as darkness melts into the sun.

Shadowed prisms echo
in the nothingness
that calls her name.

Tears of shame.

Breaking the pain
once bleeding from life's breath,
she takes her soul into her hands
and flies away.

                                      Middle of April

April 21st

Getting help. I don't know if I really care all that much. Feel kind of numb. Maybe my whole being has realized it can stop struggling, that someone else is going to hold my head up for me. I want to laugh, cry, throw things and curl up in some dark corner for all eternity.

God, I'm scared.

TWELVE

The carpet was white. Not even off-white, just white. If I unfocused my eyes and stared at one spot, the whiteness dissolved into purple and green. It swirled together slowly, weaving through the threads as the carpet moved. I stared at it, chewing the end of my fingernails off one at a time.

"You doing okay?" Kathryn whispered, leaning forward so our heads were closer.

I shrugged.

"You're strong, you know."

Ha. "No I'm not. But thanks."

"You're welcome." She checked her watch and sighed. "They should be done any minute now."

I bit the nail of my index finger a little too close to the skin. The edges turned a dark red. I looked up and saw Kathryn watching me. Our eyes met. She didn't look away. I put my finger in my mouth.

The door to Meredith Grimm's office opened. A guy walked out, his body slouched into the floor. Hopeful.

"Hold on," Kathryn told me as I started to get up. "She has to evaluate him first." The door to the office closed. My shoulders slouched forward, drooping just like that guy. I wondered what he was here for.

There was a clock above the doorway. 1:02. I tried not to look at it. Tried not to slow down the time. I stared at my torn fingernails. Wouldn't be able to paint them for awhile. Not that I did much of that anyways. The paint peeled off too quickly. 1:04 and 58 seconds. I scratched at my long sleeves. It was a little warm to be wearing them, but I'd rather be hot than show my ugly arms. But I didn't want to think about that. 1:05 and 16 seconds. 17, 18, 19—

The door opened.

Suddenly I didn't want to be there. I pictured myself running, calling Angie or Diesel or anyone who would give me something to make this shit stop. I wanted a line or a hit or some fucking glue.

"Do you want me to go in with you?" Kathryn asked.

I shook my head and forced myself to focus. This was my life. Mine. And I didn't want to spend the rest of it getting high.

I stood up and went into the office.

Meredith Grimm didn't look at me as I walked in the door. She was an older woman. Greyish hair, wrinkled skin. But not too wrinkled. It only emphasized the hardness in her face.

"Shut the door please," she told me without looking up. I did as she said. Stood awkwardly in the middle of the room. "You can sit down."

The chair was across from her desk. I sat down. She smelled musty.

"Your name is Lynn. Is that right?" she asked.

"Yes." My voice was small.

She studied a piece of paper. I wanted to know what it said. "I see here you're having problems with school."

"Yes."

"What kind of problems?"

I paused. "Um, I'm failing."

"Why do you think that is?"

"She didn't tell you?"

"Tell me? Who was supposed to tell me?"

"My TA. That I'm—" I stopped. Took a deep breath. "That I'm addicted to drugs. I'm failing my classes because I never go because I'm always getting high." There. I said it.

Silence.

I tapped my foot against the chair. She needed to say something before I bit my nails off again. I waited. She sighed.

"I'm sorry you're going through this. I want to help you, but your problem is beyond the means of our school. I'm going to recommend you to some outpatient care."

Outpatient. Sounded like a species of crazy.

"I have some women I can recommend. I assume you'd like to speak to a woman?"

I nodded. This whole thing felt so unreal. Maybe I was dreaming. She pulled out a small, plastic box and flipped through the index cards inside.

"Esther Agnes-Robins is an excellent psycho-therapist."

Psycho? Interesting word. A few hours ago I would have loved it. But now all I wanted to do was hide.

Meredith Grimm copied the information onto a piece of paper. "Call her first." She flipped through the rest of her cards and copied a few more names. "Oh. I'd advise you to speak to your academic advisor about your failing status. I believe you've passed the deadline for withdrawal, but she could at least decrease your course load for the time being."

My head was swimming. I took the piece of paper from her and put it in my backpack.

"Thank you, Lynn. And if you need anything, you can always make an appointment."

Kathryn stood up when she saw me. "How'd it go?"
I shrugged. "I'm an outpatient now. Got some numbers to call."
"That's good." Pause. "Did she talk to you about anything else?"
"No, that was it."
"She didn't mention any programs?"
"No." I was getting annoyed with her questions. This was bad enough without some chick squeezing anxiety from my brain.
"I can't believe that. There has to be something here."

I crossed my arms and stared at the floor, thinking about the nicotine sticks in my backpack.

Kathryn sighed. "It's okay. I'll go find out. Will I see you outside?"

I nodded and opened the front door quickly. Let the cool air kiss my lungs. I hated being cooped up in there. Hated Meredith Grimm staring at me like some kind of weird species twitching in a jar.

Kathryn emerged two cigarettes later. She looked angry. "They didn't have anything. Not even a meeting pamphlet. What the fuck do they expect people to do?" She glanced at me. "Sorry."

"It's okay." Her anger was comforting.

"I want you to go to a meeting. Sorry for taking over like this, but you need the support. I'm going to find out when they are and then I'll email you."

"Will you go with me?" I couldn't believe I just asked her that. Didn't I have control over my own mouth anymore? No, I didn't want her to go. I didn't want to go at all.

"Of course," she said.

I got high that night. Figured I was going to stop soon. Might as well go all out. Angie wanted to drive back home. Buy some shit. Smoke with Becky like old times, maybe leave the next morning. She asked if I wanted to come. Hell yes.

"Hurry up," Angie told me, shoving some things in a duffle bag. "It's already seven."

"I just have to check something." I went to my inbox for the third time that day. Wasn't sure why I was so anxious. It's not like I really wanted to get clean.

Her email was there. I opened it and skimmed the meeting times. There was one every day at noon. Most days at eight. Two at ten. Three at eight in the morning. No, not those ones.

"Hey Ang?" I asked, watching her throw the duffle bag on her bed. She opened her desk drawer. Started some lines. "When do you think we'll be back tomorrow?"

"I dunno. Why?"

I stared at the email. *I'll go whenever you want,* Kathryn wrote. *You can do this.* I turned off my computer. "No reason."

"You wanna do some before we leave?"

The piece of paper Meredith Grimm had given me was sitting on my desk. I crumpled it up, threw it in the trash can. Dug it out again. Put it in my pocket.

"Sure," I said, taking the straw.

Becky's house, three hours later. Inhale exhale pass inhale exhale pass inhale exhale pass. Over and over and over we smoked until I was flying high.

"Lynn."

I turned to see who had said my name. Becky and Angie were in conversation. Carlos was playing video games.

"Lynn."

"Did someone say my name?" I asked.

"No, why? Do you think someone's here?" Angie got up to check the door. There was no one there.

"You hearing things?" Becky smiled.

"Yeah." I didn't smile back.

"Lynn."

Spots on my arm again. I wiped them away, but they came back. Spread to my jeans. I wiped the spots again. They returned. I wanted to make them stop. Maybe if I picked them out. Picked out my skin. Make it all bleed.

Wait. This wasn't real. It was the tweak. I knew that. Knew the poison had seeped into my brain, giving me illusions, making me crazy. I wanted this to stop. The fear dripped through me. My heart was beating so fast. I looked at my hands. They were shaking.

I didn't want to do this anymore.

"I'm going to the bathroom." No response. Not that they cared. They were high.

Turned on the light. Shut the door. *Deep breaths, Lynn. You're just high.*

Just? I turned on the water and splashed my face, imagined the cold liquid washing the filth away. My filth. I looked in the mirror. Saw that girl again. The dirty one with no shoes. She was laughing at me with those stupid eyes and a stupid mouth and I just wanted to—

Her face broke into pieces with the shards of mirror that fell to the floor. Felt like my sanity, like I was just coming apart.

That's when it all exploded. The fear, the anger, the pain and hopelessness. I was drowning. My tears began to fall. I slid onto the bathroom floor with the broken glass and the soap dish I had thrown. I sobbed into my knees, my solitude, my fucked up self that twitched every few seconds from the high.

No fucking hope. Maybe I should let it all wash away. Shit, there was enough glass here. It would be so easy.

I wiped my wet hands against my pants and heard something crinkle. Sounded like paper. I pulled Meredith Grimm's list of phone numbers from my pocket and sighed.

"You looking for bald spots again?" Angie asked as I opened the door.

I didn't answer. My fingers anxiously dug through the depths of my purse.

"What are you doing?"

"I need to call someone," I said, grabbing my phone.

"Hurry up, we're gonna do another soon."

"Whatever." I shut the door.

Step One: We admitted that we were powerless over our addiction, that our lives had become unmanageable.
    —From the Literature of *Narcotics Anonymous*

Anxious. The heart pounding, lip biting, eye twitching, stomach churning, can't sit still, need to scream kind of anxious. Fuck, was this what sober felt like?

I sat on the curb by the community center where the 8:00 meetings were. Tried not to look at the addicts gathering out front. Smoked my cigarettes, flicking ashes in a pile on the sidewalk. Bounced my knees. Waited for Kathryn to come. Always fucking waiting.

"Hey," she waved.

"Hi," I said, standing up.

"We've got a few minutes. Still time to get a good seat."

I didn't say anything. Felt like if I spoke my throat would collapse on the inside of my stomach. We walked in silence towards the center. I stared at my feet.

"Who's that girl?"

"She's fucked up."

I looked up. Two girls were whispering by the stairs, their cigarettes in hand. We looked the same age.

"Hi," one of them said in an overly enthusiastic kind of way.

Kathryn said hello. I moved faster up the stairs.

The room consisted of several long tables with folding chairs. There was coffee, cookies, and the most random collection of people I'd ever seen. Old, young, middle aged, dressed in a myriad of ways with even more hair styles. I wrapped my hands around my tank top, wishing I had worn a sweatshirt to cover up my arms.

"Where do you wanna sit?" Kathryn asked.

I shrugged. Kathryn walked towards the front. I didn't move. She turned around.

"The back," I said hoarsely, sitting in a chair at the furthest corner of the room. Maybe I could hide in the wall.

Those girls came inside. They sat two tables in front of us. I didn't want to look at them, but my eyes kept glancing their way. Stared at my ripped up nails when they looked back. It was my way of pretending I didn't care.

A woman with fluffy blond hair sat at the table in the front of the room. She looked at her watch. At the clock above the door. Waited. Looked again. I followed her gaze. It was exactly 8:00.

"Welcome," the blonde woman said. "Welcome. My name's Gina and I'm an addict."

"Hi Gina," the audience chanted.

"If you could please join me in the serenity prayer."

I tucked my knees closer to my chin.

"God, grant me the serenity to accept the things I cannot change, the courage to change the things I can, and the wisdom to know the difference." So many voices chanting together. Kind of like an ocean washing over me.

"Amen," Kathryn whispered. I stuck my thumbnail between my teeth.

A few minutes of reading followed. Different people explained procedures and other concepts that I didn't understand. I was too nervous to listen. Too afraid.

"It's tradition to introduce the newcomers at every meeting. We don't do this to embarrass you, but so we can help support you. Are there any newcomers here with a clean date of less than thirty days?"

The girl who had said hi to me raised her hand. "I'm Kiki. I have thirteen days today."

Applause. More people spoke. Kiki and her friend stared at me, waiting for me to say my name. I didn't raise my hand.

"Welcome everyone," Gina said, offering more applause.

This was stupid.

I grabbed my cigarettes and left.

Kathryn came out after me. I leaned against the stairwell, a lit cigarette between my fingers. My back was to her.

"Why did you leave?"

I exhaled slowly, letting my silence fill the air.

"Lynn."

More silence.

"Was it those girls? Cuz we can go to another meeting—"

"It wasn't the fucking girls." Kathryn was starting to piss me off.

"Then what was it?"

"I just didn't want to be there."

Kathryn came to face me, to stare sorrowfully into my eyes. "I know you're scared, but—"

"You know?" I edged around the deck, ready to run. "What the fuck do you know?"

"That this is some serious shit you're in. It'll kill you if you don't stop it."

I turned away. Maybe if I didn't see her she'd disappear.

"You can't hide, Lynn. It's not going to just go away. You have to face it. You have to learn how to deal with the addiction. How to live again."

"Fuck you." I started to run. Didn't want to stop. Ran despite the fact that I couldn't breathe, that my sides were killing me. Ran and ran and ran, gasping and panting like an old man. Fuck, it hurt. Smoked too damn much for this shit.

I found myself downtown. Slowed to a walk in attempts to keep my lungs from exploding. Sat on a bench and ran my fingers through my hair.

"Oh good it's you." KJ was standing over me. "Do you have any shit cuz that guy got arrested and there's no one around here anymore and I really need some shit right now you can hook me up right?" Said it all in one breath. Fucking tweaked out of his mind.

I shook my head.

"Don't pull this shit with me." His hands gripped my shoulders. "You've gotta have some you're always fucked up goddamit Lynn fucking give me some shit!"

"I'm out, KJ." His eyes were bulging. I was afraid of him. "Let go of me."

He twitched. Tightened his grip. I bit my lip to hide my fear.

"Please?"

He lifted his greasy hands. "You're a fucking whore fuck you." Walked away.

Fuck this.

But it was just enough to want it. To need it. A plan leaked into my head. Maybe I could catch KJ. Find someone to snort with. Feel that rush again.

No.

I had to get back to that meeting. Started walking. Too tired to run this time. Wasn't sure how long I'd been gone. Hopefully they were still there.

The front of the community center was deserted. Shit. No, wait. There were people inside. They were listening to someone speak.

I took a deep breath and snuck back in, doing my best to avoid the stares. The clock said 8:45.

"I'm glad you came back," Kathryn whispered.

I settled in my corner. Exhaled. Maybe I could do this recovery thing. It was better than being out there.

"I'm glad too," I said.

"I hate this!" Angie yelled as she stomped into our room. "I fucking failed another bio lab."

I was on my bed reading *Alice's Adventures In Wonderland*. Figured if I couldn't get high, I might as well talk to a grinning cat.

"I'm sorry," I mumbled, staring at the book in attempts to shut her out. I could hear her fumbling through her dresser. One guess what she was looking for. The thought sent a shiver down my spine.

'In that direction,' the cat said, waving its right paw round, *'lives a Hatter: and in* that *direction,'* waving the other paw, *'lives a March Hare. Visit either you like: they're both mad.'*

"I think I'm gonna go home. Fuck this place. I'm not ready."
I didn't say anything. Too busy listening to the unraveling of the bag. She must have emptied some onto her desk. I could smell it.

'But I don't want to go among mad people,' Alice remarked.
'Oh, you can't help that,' said the Cat: *'we're all mad here. I'm mad. You're mad.'*

Scrape scrape scrape against the desktop. "Becky says this shit's better than last time." Chopped up crank against the wood. They must be in lines now.

'How do you know I'm mad?' said Alice.

That watery, snot filled sound echoed through the room. She snorted another line. Could picture it in my head. Snort water snort water drip drip drip.

'You must be,' said the Cat, *'or you wouldn't have come here.'*

I grabbed my cigarettes and left the room.

On the bus. It wasn't moving because traffic doesn't go anywhere at 4:23 in the afternoon. The appointment was at 4:30, and of course the bus didn't come when it was supposed to. It never did, but I still had my hopes. I was on my way to see Esther Agnes-Robbins, professional psycho-therapist. And I was going to be late. Woohoo.
I arrived at her building at 4:34. Sprinted two flights of stairs and stood completely out of breath. Leaned silently against the wall
"Lynn? Are you here?"
I wanted to run back the other way. "Yeah," I said, dragging myself into her office.

She wasn't what I expected her to be. For one thing, she looked 35 instead of 70 and wore knee high boots. Her hair was dark red and she had checkered framed glasses that hugged the edge of her nose.

"Hi. Have a seat."

A brown couch lay opposite to her large swiveling chair. I sat on the edge of the cushion.

"How are you?"

"Okay," I mumbled stupidly. Suddenly my speaking capacity had ceased its existance. I had nothing to say to her.

"Are you sober?"

"Yes." I couldn't help the bitterness in my voice.

"For how long?"

"Two days."

"How does that feel?"

"Shitty."

"Is it better than being high?"

I shrugged.

Silence as she wrote something on her yellow notepad. I hated the sound of the pen scratching against the paper. Hated that she was writing about me. Judging me. Made me cringe.

"We've got a long road ahead of us," Esther said, putting her notepad aside. "It's not going to be easy, but you've gotten through a pretty tough part of it. Do you know what that is?"

I had a strong suspicion, but I shook my head. Rather her talk than me.

"You came here. You're the one who decided you need help. That takes guts. You should be proud of yourself."

Another shrug.

"So the next step is to keep you safe. Keep you sober." She leaned back against the chair again and picked up her notepad. I put my feet on the couch and hugged my knees. "Where **are** you living?"

"On campus."

"Do you live alone?"

"No." I paused, letting the weight of what I was doing slowly sink in. "I live with my friend Angie." I bit my lip, not wanting to say it. "She's an addict too. We use together."

"I take it she hasn't been sober the last two days?"

I shook my head.

Esther sighed. "You have to get out of there, Lynn. The first rule of sobriety is not associating yourself with drugs or with the people who use them. You won't stay sober with her using right in front of you."

"She used in front of me today and I didn't." I knew that was a stupid thing to say. But I had to defend Angie, defend us. I didn't want to be alone.

"Cravings are strong, Lynn. There will be a point in your recovery, and possibly the rest of your life, in which you will use if it's available. Living with Angie is detrimental."

Detrimental. Who says that shit? I hated her for her words, for her fucking notepad, her stupid sympathetic smile. Hated her for speaking the truth.

I swallowed. "So where am I supposed to go?"

"Well, you have some options. Do you have family here?"

I shook my head. "Can't go home either. I have friends who use there, too."

"That's okay. I think it'll be good for you to stay here."

"I want to finish school," I blurted out. Not that it had anything to do with the conversation. I think it was my weird way of agreeing with her.

"Good. Remember that you said that." Pause. "Have you heard of an SLE?"

I shook my head again.

"Sober Living Environment. It's a house where recovering addicts live who, with support, are able to function within society."

Umm...

"There's also rehab. I know some great programs in the area."

I pictured white walls and people dressed in gowns chanting lyrics of sobriety. Saw my face there. Made me feel nauseous. I held my head in my hands.

Esther's voice didn't help much. "This must be incredibly overwhelming for you. And I don't want to have to pressure you, but you need to make a decision soon. The faster you get away from drugs, the sooner you can begin your recovery."

I tapped my fingers against my shoes. "So what if I choose the sober house?"

She scribbled something on her notepad. "This is the address of the head programming office. They should have a list available there."

"Okay."

Esther handed me the paper. "May I ask who finances where you live now?"

Uh oh. "My parents."

Another sympathetic look. "You're going to have to tell them."

I think the sky fell on my lap.

"I don't care where the fuck you get it. Just get me high!" I yelled, shoving aside papers in attempts to find my tacks. Dammit, where did I put them?

"What the fuck is your problem?" Angie roared.

The box was hidden in a corner. I grabbed one and pushed the tip against the soft flesh of my pinky. Pain. Irritation. Blood. I let out a shaky sigh. "I'm sorry. I just really need some shit right now."

"Yeah, well, so do I." She slammed the door as she left.

Fuck. I shoved the tack into my wrist over and over, begging the pain to dissolve the wounds inside my heart. Scraped more skin away. Tried my shoulder. My thigh. Wanted to go deeper. Further. Make my insides explode.

But it didn't matter how much blood stained my skin. I could still feel the fear, the anger, the pain and hurt the drugs had left behind. Why did it hurt so fucking much?

I didn't want to face my parents. Face their shame. Face the pain they put inside my skin. I would rather hurt myself than let them hurt me again. Shit, I wondered where Diesel went. Could use his free supply of bunk shit right about now.

And then my cell phone rang. It was Kathryn. Didn't want to face her. She was just going to badger me about a fucking meeting.

I just wanted to get high.

I silenced the call. She called back. Maybe I should turn off the phone. Slip away into my own filthy skin.

I reached under my desk to grab the cigarettes I threw there maybe an hour ago. My foot hit something hard beneath my bed. It was something flat. Square. I kicked it lightly. What I saw made my throat tighten. It was a picture of my sisters when they were young. I stared at them. At their pink night gowns, the baby dolls they held to their chests. They were laughing.

I kissed the glass lightly, my tears blurring the faces of those innocent girls. God, I loved them. Loved the dimples in their cheeks, the smile in their eyes.

I had forgotten this.

"Lynn?" Kathryn's voice echoed on the phone. "I'm so glad you called back."

"I need your help."

I still don't know how I had the strength to do it.

Kathryn suggested asking my parents to come and visit. But I didn't want to do that. Didn't want them to see how bad it really was. Yet I couldn't tell them over the phone.

Then I remembered my aunt and uncle lived about 100 miles away. It was a good meeting spot, plus the idea of having someone there to mediate the conversation was a huge comfort. There was no way I could face them alone.

I paced nervously as the phone rang.

"Hello?" It was my cousin. I asked to speak to his mom. More pacing. "Hello?"

"It's Lynn," I told her. My voice was shaking. "There's...there's something I need to tell you." I paused. Sighed. "I'm, um, I'm addicted to meth."

The longer I spoke, the faster the words seemed to spill from my mouth. I told her how I tried it over the summer, how I loved the way it made me feel. How it was killing me. She cried when I mentioned the fear of addiction, that I wanted so badly to stop but I couldn't do it on my own. That I needed her to help me tell my parents. Would it be okay if they came?

"Of course Lynn," she sniffed. "You're so brave."

I shrugged and remembered she couldn't see me.

"Do you want me to ask them to come here?" she asked.

Hesitation. That would make it easier. "No," I told her. "I'll do it. I need to do this on my own."

"You're amazing."

Whatever you say.

It wouldn't be easy getting my parents to leave their home unscheduled. Everything had to be written on the calendar or, according to my mother, it didn't exist. Our own yellow pages that drove any spontaneity out the window.

I figured getting stoned would make the process easier. Numb myself in case she said no. Or maybe it was just another excuse to get fucked up.

My mother didn't understand why this couldn't be discussed over the phone.

"Because I need to tell you in person," I said.
I could hear her breathing unsteadily.
"Please?"
"We'll have to get someone to watch your sisters. I have a Girl Scout meeting I'll have to reschedule, Elle needs a ride to dance, Halley needs to go to the library for a book report, your father will have to find time to do his errands." Pause. I suppressed the desire to hang up the phone. "Fine. We'll go."
It was two days away.

Snort. Water. Snort. Water. Drip drip drip. I had to. I was going crazy.

Two days later. Two days that went by way too quickly. I hated time.
I got in my car before I had the chance to get high. Blasted music, smoked my cigarettes, sang along the open road. I turned up the songs as loud as they would go, letting the music soak my fear. Sped up to hear the wind roar. My hands tapped against the wheel. God, I was nervous.
My aunt and uncle greeted me with tight hugs. It felt good to be held like that. I had missed them more than I realized. Missed that security family brings.
"Where are my cousins?" I asked, noticing the unusual silence throughout the house.
"With friends." My aunt smiled slightly. "We thought it'd be better with just us."
"Oh. Yeah. You're probably right." For a moment I'd forgotten why I was there. For a moment it had just been me.
"Do you know what you're going to say?" my uncle asked.
"No idea."
"I was just wondering because I think that's their car. Isn't that their car?"
Holy fuck they were here.
"I can't do this." I backed away from the window, burying my face in my hands.
"Yes you can." My aunt put her arms around me. I could feel the tears behind my eyes. No, no, not now. Not now.
"They're coming."
I broke away and ran to the opposite side of the house. Sat there frozen in a crumpled ball, wishing this was just a dream. Heard their voices at the front of the house. Closed my eyes.

No. It was a nightmare.

"Hi Lynn." My mother's voice was sing-songy. She was nervous.

My parents sat in the love seat across from me. My aunt and uncle took the couch beside me. I was surrounded.

"So what's this all about?" my father asked.

Everyone stared at me. My cheeks grew hot.

"I, um," I pulled my knees closer to my chest and stared at the carpet. My aunt's nails scratched lightly against my back. I sighed. "I haven't been honest with you about things lately." Silence. Another deep breath. "I've been using drugs for about three years."

My parents found each other's hands. "What kind of drugs?"

"Pot, ecstasy, shrooms, acid. Then I tried crank ten months ago. I got addicted. It got really bad and I, um, missed a midterm in my psych class."

"Lynn!"

"I know. I went to the health center and they got me this psycho-therapist. She wants me to move into a sober living house." Pause. "And I want to. I'm tired of living the way I've been. I want to get help." There. I fucking said it.

Silence again. Fucking say something!

"That explains a lot," my mother said.

Well that's bloody fabulous.

"You know," my father began, "I had a coke problem when I was your age."

Huh?

"It was when I worked at the studio in the recording business. Everyone messed around with that kind of thing. One night I did too much. I remember my heart was beating too fast. I was afraid I was going to die." I sat open-mouthed. I had never seen this side of my father. "As I was laying there, I prayed to God and said if I lived through this, I'd never do it again. And I haven't."

"Why didn't you tell me you used?" I asked him.

"I didn't think you needed to know." His lip quivered as he spoke. Was he crying? "I'm sorry you had to feel that."

"Oh, Daddy." I reached out my arms and hugged him. His cheeks were wet against my skin.

I looked at my mother. Her eyes were also moist with sorrow. She held out her hands and cradled me against her like I was young. And I felt that comfort. Her smell, her voice, her love. It melted into me. "It's okay," she whispered. "I'm here now. Everything's going to be okay. It's going to be okay."

Those words made my tears fall.

"Good job," my aunt whispered as I returned to my spot on the couch. I nodded, too drained to speak again.

"So." My father wiped his eyes. "What are you going to do about school?"

"Have you talked to someone about taking a break? They have to have some kind of withdrawal procedure."

I shook my head. "Not yet."

"You've got to take care of that now."

"I know—"

"What's this sober house?"

"Is it more expensive than campus?"

"How long do you think you'll live there?"

Couldn't they shut up? The room was spinning. I hid my face in a pillow.

"I think all of these questions are overwhelming her," my aunt said. Her fingers rubbed the base of my neck. It helped.

"I don't care." My father sounded angry. I imagined the veins popping from his neck. "I understand she's going though shit, but she needs to pull her head out of the clouds and think about things realistically."

"She's doing the best she can," my aunt said.

"We want to help her."

"Then let me do this," I blurted, sticking my head above the comfort of the pillow. "I'm the one that got addicted."

"Lynn, it's not that easy."

"I know." They were irritating me. "But I've got to do this on my own."

"You can't do it by yourself."

"Ask her what you can do to help," my aunt suggested, doing her best to leave the cynicism from her voice. I don't think they heard it, but it was damn funny.

My parents sighed. "What can we do to help you?" they asked, the strain in their voice echoing through the living room.

I smiled internally. "Help me move into the SLE. When I find one. And don't ask if I've found it yet. I'll tell you when I'm ready." Dramatic pause. "Okay?"

"Okay." And their voices were genuine. For once, it felt like they were on my side.

April 29th

So I've realized how much control the drugs truly have over me. How much I've lost because of it. Staying clean is really the only way to preserve who I am and what I can do with my life. It's not a very comforting thought. Scary to think of never doing it again. It shouldn't scare me, but it does. But I'm glad I'm finally taking this step for myself. Not that I want to—seen so many movies about this shit.

Feels like my life's been turned inside out and shaken, and I'm holding on for dear life. I'm still feeling alone and afraid. So afraid. But I know the only way to get past it all is to stay clean. If I can. I have to. I don't want to be afraid anymore.

THIRTEEN

It took me two days to find my SLE.

We called it the Coral House, as it was on Coral Road. But it wasn't coral at all. The house was the ugliest color green I'd ever seen. Single story, rocks and weeds in the front lawn. All women, all sober, and one bathroom. But it was right next door to 7-Eleven, so that made up for most of it. Flirted with the guys there. Got a few free slurpees, lighters, gum, chocolate, and of course, the only drug we were allowed to consume besides nicotine…caffeine. To this day, I have an untreated addiction to 7-Eleven coffee.

"So what's the deal here? What's the program like?" my father asked the head of the house. It was the same lady who led the only meeting I had been to. Gina. She looked about forty and had an extremely irritated look on her face. We, meaning my parents, myself, and Gina, were sitting in a small, empty room in the ugly green house, discussing my new, official residence. I had a feeling Gina wasn't too happy about it.

I was terrified.

"We have a few rules here. Obviously, no using." She glanced at me. I looked away. "We have frequent drug tests to ensure everyone's progress, which I'm in charge of, and we go to meetings every day. Lynn must have a sponsor—"

"A sponsor?" my father repeated.

"It's part of the program. Lastly, you must be a productive member of society."

"Define productive," my mother said.

"You have to have a job."

"What about school?" asked my father.

"That counts."

"But I'm not going to be in school," I told him.

"What do you mean you're not going to be in school?"

I already said that. "I'm taking some time off, remember? To deal with this?"

"For how long?"

"I don't know, Dad. I still have to talk to the academic advisor." Gina was staring at us. I didn't want to talk about this in front of her. It was embarrassing. "I'll find a job. It's no big deal." My father looked like he was about to speak again. I pleaded with my eyes for him to please just shut up.

He did.

I looked sweetly at Gina. "So what room am I in?"

Gina led the way into the garage that had been transformed into a bedroom. It was decently sized for only two beds. Had all the qualities one would expect. Closet, dresser, even a desk and a couple of windows. I wondered who—

Holy shit. You've gotta be kidding.

"This is Lynn," Gina said to the girls whispering on the bed that obviously wasn't mine. Yeah, you can guess. The girls from the meeting. Kiki and—

"Veronica."

"We've met," Veronica said. "You in this room?"

I nodded.

"Don't touch my shit." She and Kiki laughed as they left.

"Lynn," my mother began.

"Don't say anything," I told her. "This is fine. I'll be fine. It's all going to be fine."

"I was going to ask if you wanted help bringing your things here." Was my mother serious? She looked serious.

"I, um, sure."

Angie wasn't home when my parents and I packed my few belongings in their Volvo. Clothes, my computer, the comforter and pillow that had a cigarette burn on the side. The dishes and pots were left for the seven weeks my roommates would be living there. Well, more for Angie than any of the others. They had their own shit, but Angie and I had coordinated before moving in. I was leaving her.

"Are you coming?" my mother asked, her head poking into my empty room.

"Um, do you mind if I get there later? I kind of want to be alone for awhile."

She gazed at me anxiously.

"I'll be there later. I promise. Could you drop the stuff off for me?"

"We were going to leave after this."

"That's okay. I just need some time."

She kissed me on my forehead. "I love you."

I could feel my eyes watering again. "Love you too."

My mother closed the door as she left the room.

I stood there in the silence of my now familiar past. Every part of the room had a memory. Roasting mini marshmallows with toothpicks and a lighter on my bed. Saying hello to the raccoon that lived outside our window. We called him Ralph. Hiding behind the door, trying not to laugh at the rants and raves of our crazy housemates. Dressing me in a red sheet and dancing to the song *Lady In Red*. Hugging Angie when she finally let herself cry over Adam. We had hot chocolate and popcorn that night. Watched movies that I downloaded on my computer. We used to watch them until we fell asleep. Her throwing a stapler across the room. And a lighter. Hit me with a pillow once. But I had yelled at her too. I didn't remember why. She told me it was all going to be okay. God, I wanted to believe her. Using crank on her desk. On my desk. On the bed, the floor, the window sill. Remembering when it was still fun.

And now I was moving. All because of that stupid white shit that was probably still in her desk drawer.

"Be careful," she said. Her eyes glowed in the yellow light of the bathroom. "This shit's addictive."

"If you get addicted," I told her, "then I'll get addicted too."

I laughed bitterly.

"What's so funny?" Angie asked as she tossed her backpack on the floor. She stopped, glancing around the room. "Your stuff's gone."

"Yeah," I sighed. "I'm moving."

"Back home?"

Another sigh. "No. I'm moving to a sober house."

"A what?"

I glanced at my cigarettes. At her desk. The desire to use with her tumbled into me. To feel that one last time. Better than feeling the truth. I forced the thought aside in the effort to find our friendship again. I told her how far down crank had taken me, how I was afraid I had lost control. That I was failing school and didn't want to lose whatever dreams I had left.

"Fine. Leave." She grabbed her cigarettes and opened the side door.

I found my pack and followed. "I don't want to, Ang. But I can't do this alone."

"So you're just going to fucking leave me?"

"You use."

"So do you."

"That's the problem."

"Yeah, I got that. I'm not a fucking idiot." Angie sat against the wall and lit a cigarette.

I thought about sitting beside her, but leaned against the wall. Took a drag. "This isn't easy for me—"

"Well it's not a fucking picnic for me either. You think I haven't thought about quitting?"

I shrugged.

"I'm failing too, Lynn. You know, you're not the only person in the universe." She was angry. Angry because I had made the choice to start digging my way out from the dirt, and she was still suffocating. But I was tired of being dragged down.

"Then do something about it," I half-whispered.

"Fuck you! You're pissing me off." She stood up. Turned her back to me.

"You're strong, Ang. You don't have to do it this way."

"Don't talk to me. Have fun in your fucking sober house." She walked away.

I threw my cigarette against the wall, watching the ash spray against the concrete. Fuck her. I opened the door quickly, locking it when I got inside. She kept her shit in the top drawer under her checkbook. I shifted through it, anxiously peeking over my shoulder. No crank there.

I eyed her backpack on the floor. Opened the outside zipper. Nothing. Dug through her books, her notebooks. There was a baggie tucked in a pocket of her binder. I spread the lines out on my desk and buried the empty bag in the trash.

Three thick ones stared at me. My head pounded, the screaming echoing in my skull. Shaking hands rolled the dollar bill.

Snort. Water. Snort. Water. Drip drip drip.

Take me to Hell.

After I was high and stupid, I decided that maybe being high wasn't such a good idea. I, um, officially lived at a sober house. Shit.

"Hello?" Some woman answered the phone.
"Gina?"
"No. Hang on."
I waited, my teeth gnawing steadily on my lip.
"Hello?"
"Gina, it's Lynn."
"Hi."
"Um," I sighed shakily, "something came up and I won't be able to make it until tomorrow."
"Be here by 6:30 in the evening or I'm kicking you out. And you'd better be sober by the time you get here."
How did she know I was high? "Okay," I said. But she'd already hung up the phone.

I arrived to the Coral House at 12:30 in the afternoon, more because I was bored than anything else. Wandering through the trees and streets and smelly guys asking for cigarettes can be exciting for only so long. That and the desire for another hit of anything I could get my hands on was eating me alive. I didn't want to get loaded again. That's why I needed this. I was ready, dammit.

I had to be.

I reached for the doorknob. Stopped. Tapped the pink welcome mat with the front of my shoes. Sighed. Reached again and touched the metal with the tip of a finger.

Okay, so maybe I couldn't do this. Maybe I could just leave now and come back in the middle of the night for my shit. Run away somewhere. Live like a true junkie. Never have to feel this shaky again.

I turned around and stepped off the porch.

"So you actually showed up."

My skin jumped. Veronica and Kiki had opened the door. I stared at them.

"You think she's fucked up?" Kiki asked, sitting on one of the plastic chairs. She hit the end of her unopened pack of cigarettes against her palm.

Veronica glanced at me. "I don't care. You done packing the smokes?"

"Yeah." Kiki unwrapped her cigarettes and handed one to Veronica. "You want one?"

It took me a minute to realize she was talking to me. "Oh. Sure," I said stupidly, fumbling to grab the cigarette Kiki held out. "Thanks."

"So what's your drug of choice?" Kiki asked, her high pitched voice bouncing between the smoke in the air.

"My what?"

"Why are you here?" Veronica clarified, rolling her eyes.

I pictured myself head butting her face. I was a decently fast runner. "Crank."

"Sweet!" squeaked Kiki.

"Another tweaker," Veronica groaned.

"Three to two."

"What are you talking about?" I wondered quietly, taking a long drag on my cigarette. That way if they didn't respond I could pretend they didn't hear me.

But they did. "There's six people here, including you," Kiki began. "All of us have a drug of choice. Gina and Veronica like heroine."

"Chiva," Veronica corrected.

"Whatever." Kiki barely missed a beat. "Sandy and I tweak."

"Charlotte doesn't count cuz she's an alcoholic."

"But we think she popped pills."

"No, we *know* she did. You heard what Tisha said."

"Whatever. Anyway, you break the tie of tweaks and *chiva* users." Kiki glanced at Veronica as she emphasized the word "chiva."

Fabulous. Give me the award for the biggest loser now.

"How do you like it here?" asked Kiki.

I shrugged.

Veronica spit on one of the plants by the porch. "It sucks. I fucking hate it."

"Dude, Veronica, it's not that bad."

"Dude yourself bitch."

3:30 PM.

Gina opened the front door to the three of us sprawled across the couches. We were watching some random MTV special.

"I see you've gotten yourselves acquainted," she said.

"She only says that shit to sound smart," Kiki whispered to me. I giggled.

"Lynn, can I see you in the bathroom?" Gina announced to the room, not waiting for a response before heading down the hall.

I looked at the girls who in a mere three hours had become my official translators. It amused me how much they knew, especially about the other people in the program. Veronica said I should know an addict's life story before I even meet them. That way they couldn't get to me first. I liked that.

Kiki said she just liked talking shit. I still wasn't sure how I felt about the duo, but at least they were willing to acknowledge my existence.

"Why?" I asked them.

"Pee test," they said in unison.

You've gotta be kidding.

Gina was standing by the sink with a smirk on her face. Her hands were covered with latex gloves, like some nurse about to give a shot in all the wrong places. She was holding a clear, plastic cup. I stepped into the bathroom. She handed the cup to me and shut the door.

I took it and stared at her.

"Pee in it," she said flatly.

I stood by the toilet. She hadn't moved.

"Are you gonna stand there?" I asked her, hearing a hint of attitude in my voice. Felt like those girls had already rubbed off on me.

"Yes."

This was stupid. It wouldn't come out clean anyway. I sighed and pulled my pants to my knees, holding the cup between my legs. I could feel her eyes piercing my flesh and wondered where she hid her horns.

I took the cup from beneath my urine before it overflowed, getting the liquid all over my hand. Gross. I wiped quickly and handed her the cup.

"You'll get better at it," Gina said. I tried not to show her my tears.

She stuck a thin piece of paper with a bunch of writing on it in my pee and waited. I wanted to bite my nails, but there was dried urine there and Gina was in the way of the sink. I folded my arms instead.

"You used meth yesterday," she declared, pulling the paper out. She put a lid on the cup and leaned against the sink. "I knew you came here late because you were loaded."

More tears burned behind my eyes. I couldn't look at her.

"I'm testing you every day for two weeks. You come up dirty again, you're out."

I nodded.

"I'm going to send this out, and then I'm going to go over the rules."

Finally, she was gone. I turned on the hot water quickly, ignoring the tears that fell down my cheeks.

So maybe you're not interested in hearing the fine tuning of a Sober Living Environment. Maybe you have a right not to care. I, however, was forced to endure a twenty minute lecture regardless of giving two shits or giggles, thus I have no guilt in passing it on. But I do sympathize, so here is the condensed version in a tiny list of ten:

1. No using *any* form of narcotics. If caught using inside the house or are under the influence on the property, there is an automatic exile. The End.
2. Attend a meeting every day, even if you're on the brink of death. Okay, not really, but you've got to be bleeding buckets or a really good liar to get away with it. I wasn't either of those, so I was stuck attending them daily.
3. Curfew is 10:00 PM for the first thirty days. After thirty days, it's 11:00 PM. It's amazing how much an hour can mean. Another thirty days permits an exciting one night out per week, which must be noted on the little white board displayed by the television. If you're super good, a two night out option can be discussed.
4. A sponsor is mandatory within two weeks. A job is required within three.
5. No men allowed in bedrooms. Don't want any hanky panky. No men are allowed in the house after 9:00 PM. If a man is bold enough to enter the house when permitted, one must yell "Man in the house!" to warn all other women of the testosterone.
6. You may use one-half of a shelf for food in the refrigerator and another half in any available cupboard. Not much space for a growing teen. I resorted to storing most things in this little space behind my bed, which quickly became the designated area for midnight munchies.
7. There's a job chart, and this one apparently works. Each week, a different job is assigned. It kept some form of excitement in our lives, as in "yay, I don't have to clean the toilets this week!" Bedrooms are not included in the chart and must be kept tidy daily.
8. Dishes must be done immediately after use. Extra kitchen duty will be assigned to those who forget to wash dishes regularly. I was fortunate enough to claim excess oven and tile cleaning many a time.
9. No internet allowed. No private phones in bedrooms. There is one phone in the kitchen. It does not have call waiting, so there is a thirty minute limit. (Another use of a cell phone, check!)
10. One relapse permitted. After that, you're out.

"Look who just came in the door," Kiki whispered across the table, eyeing a heavier girl with pink streaked hair.

"Fuck," Veronica spat, shaking her head. "She better not start shit."

"I know."

I shifted awkwardly in my chair, eyeing the table I sat at the last time I was here. I could see myself there, crouched in the corner, hiding clumsily behind my hair. It seemed so long ago.

"Hello everyone," said a semi-cute twenty-something guy in the front of the room. He waved his tattooed arm around in a motion of silence. "I'm Mike. Addict."

"Hi Mike."

"Join me in the serenity prayer."

"She used to live with us."

"Who?" I asked, realizing Kiki was talking to me.

"Candy." Veronica said the name with a nasty taste in her mouth.

I raised my eyebrow.

"That bitch we were talking about. The one with the stupid hair."

Candy was sitting at the opposite end of the room, giggling with other colorful haired people. She turned her head and looked straight at us, making a very mean looking face. Her friends laughed.

"What happened?" I asked, watching Candy giggle with her friends again.

"She used in the house," Kiki told me.

Veronica glanced at Candy. Looked away. "She lied to me about what happened with her and this guy I was with."

"They fucked while Veronica was still with him."

"Thank you, Kiki," Veronica said. It looked like her eyes had watered a little. Maybe it was the light. "What?" she barked, realizing I was staring. I shook my head.

"Are there any newcomers in the room?" Mike asked. "Anyone with thirty days or less?"

Kiki raised her hand. "Kiki. Addict. Nineteen days clean."

Applause. Other addicts raised their hands.

Veronica elbowed me in the ribs. "You're a newcomer. Introduce yourself."

I bit my lip. "I don't want to."

"You have to if you're going to get clean."

I sighed and waited for a silent moment. Soon it was my chance. I took a deep breath. "Lynn. Addict. I have, um, one day."

Loud applause and cheering. I hid my head in my hands.

"You only have one day?" Kiki hissed.

I didn't say anything. My cheeks were still burning.

"Anyone else?"

Silence.

"Welcome everyone." More applause. "The topic is trust," Mike announced to the room. "The steps talk about it, our shrinks talk about it, our sobriety depends on it."

"Fuck trust," whispered Veronica. "You wanna smoke?"

"Yeah."

I hated leaving in the middle of everything. It felt so rude. But I didn't want to sit there alone.

Veronica flipped Candy off as we passed her.

"Bitch," Candy whispered.

"Slut," Veronica snapped back. Kiki laughed as we stepped outside. I leaned against the wall so I could still hear the meeting.

"You have to trust that things are going to work out," an older woman said. "Trust in something greater than yourself. You can't control everything. That's why we use. To try and control the things we can't. And we all know how that turns out."

I thought of Rick, of Diesel and the other men who had turned everything upside down. Of my friends back home, how I had abandoned them…how they abandoned me. Thought of Angie and Scott and the others I'd have to rid from my life. How unfair and fucked up it felt. Remembered my parents, my sisters. How I failed them. How I failed myself. How shitty life was. How much I wanted to get it back.

I took a drag slowly in an effort to kill the hole inside my heart. It only made my lungs hurt.

"Fuck trust," I whispered.

Therapy session number two, take one.

It was one o'clock in the afternoon. I had just finished eating three whole sushi rolls purchased at the grocery store, and my steps were a little uppity compared to my usual dragging of the foot. The sun was shining, the birds were singing…

And then I got to her office. That's when reality set in, accompanied by awkward silence that I didn't care to fill.

"So how's sobriety treating you?" Esther Agnes-Robbins asked after a few minutes, her notepad resting dutifully on her knees.

My elbows leaned against my thighs. I bounced my legs, watching the hem of my torn jeans wiggle against the floor. "It's only been two days," I mumbled.

"What do you mean?"

I hated when she asked me that. "I've done this before."

She pulled her glasses to the bridge of her nose. "Have you?"

I didn't answer. She wasn't looking at me anyway.

"When you stayed clean in the past, how many days did it take for you to use again?"

"Three," I sighed, trying not to show her how nervous I was.

"So on day three, what happens? What makes you use again?"

Shouldn't she know this? I pulled my knees to my chest. "Cravings."

"What do you mean by cravings?"

"Do I have to explain everything to you?" I asked her, my voice louder than it should be. "Fuck!"

Esther sighed and pulled her glasses back up. "I can't help you if you don't tell me what's going on."

I slapped the palm of my hand dramatically against my forehead. "I try not to talk about it," I told her.

"Maybe you should."

Pause.

"Do you want to get high again?"

God, she was annoying. "No." Another pause. Fine. I opened my mouth, wondering if the truth could see beyond my tongue. "I get shaky. My head feels like it's gonna explode. Bugs crawl inside of my skin. I want to dig my eyeballs out of my skull or smash my head into the wall. That kind of thing."

"You don't feel that the first two days?"

"No, I do. It's just not as bad." Shit. The tightness in my chest was growing.

"You're strong," Esther smiled.

I laughed, trying to avoid the anxiety in my skin. It was happening again.

"So when you feel the cravings the first two days, what do you do to stop them? Besides use, of course."

"I dunno," I sighed, wrapping my arms around myself. I wanted to run. "Wait it out. Do something else."

"Exactly. You just have to find things strong enough to get you through the rest of the time."

Voices whispered in my head. So many inside my brain, I couldn't think straight. They shouted at me, telling me to use.

"Tell me something you can do that will keep you from using."

The monster's claws tore at my flesh. My insides burned. Anxiety rushed into me. God, it hurt.

"Lynn, are you okay?"

I rocked slowly back and forth, attempting to slow the shallow breaths. Make it stop. Make it all just fucking stop.

"Lynn!" Esther's voice echoed loudly in the silence of the room.

I looked at her.

"Follow my breath. You ready?"

I nodded, watching her inhale deeply. I did the same, sucking air slowly into my lungs. Let it out. Inhale. Exhale. Inhale. Exhale. I closed my eyes and continued to breathe.

It took me awhile to realize I was okay again.

"How do you feel?" Esther's voice was quiet.

"Better."

She leaned forward, setting her notebook on the floor beside her chair. "Can I ask you to promise me something?"

I shrugged.

"When you feel that way, take deep breaths like we just did. If it stops, I want you to tell someone what happened. If it doesn't stop, I want you to tell someone how you're feeling. Talk through it. No matter where you are or what you're doing, I need you to let others help you. Do you promise?"

My head slowly shook up and down. Esther nodded with me. Glanced at the purple watch around her wrist.

"We're out of time." She stood up. I followed. "I assume you've found a sober house?"

"Yes."

"Do you like it?"

"It's okay."

"I'm sorry we didn't get to talk about your new living environment. We can discuss that next time if you like. Oh, and your parents! Did you tell them?"

"Yes."

"I'm proud of you."

MY OWN ASYLUM

Silence.

"Next time. Same time next week?"

"Sure."

"I'll see you then, Lynn. Take care of yourself, okay? Eat plenty of food and get at least eight hours of sleep at night. Your body needs time to replenish itself."

A cigarette was at my lips as soon as I reached the outside world. I just wanted to go home. Home. The word tasted foreign on my tongue. Felt like I lost it a long time ago, if it was ever there at all.

Out on the sidewalk, waiting for the bus to come. Hated waiting around here. Too many drugs. Saw some thugs across the street, all decked out in skull tattoos and chains on their belt. I knew they were high. Could probably get drugs from them right now if I wanted.

Shit, why was I thinking this way? I had to stop before the cravings came back. I could feel the need there, lurking over my shoulder with blood dribbling from its chin. Beady eyes just watching. Waiting for my strength to jump. Waiting for me to die.

Distraction. Fast. I scanned the stores across the street, looking for something to take me away from myself. There was a clothing store, a bar, another clothing store, and…duh…an arcade. I wasn't exactly a video game fanatic, but there was the minor obsession with Nintendo in elementary school. If nothing else, it would keep my hands busy.

I crossed the street carefully, doing my best to avoid the fucked up thugs. Didn't want to see their eyes, see the drugs behind their masks. Big pupils: meth. Little ones: opiates. Mine: normal. Or close to it. Apparently meth doesn't leave your system for three days. Mine was almost gone.

I fell in love as soon as I opened the door. The high pitched pings and techno sounds wrapped me in chaotic song. Teens bounced without realizing it as they fought the villains on the screen. Others moved from side to side with the virtual cars they drove. My favorite was the dancing game. Arrows dodged across the screen while feet attempted to replay the movements on a map below them. It was like learning how to dance, something I could definitely find helpful.

I fumbled for some quarters when I noticed the token sign on the coin slots. There was a token machine by the door. I took out a dollar, and suddenly noticed a red sign in the window. *Help Wanted.*

No chance to think. Didn't want to lose the motivation that suddenly dropped inside my gut. I looked around quickly and found a counter near the back.

He was the same age as me, dressed in a bright orange polo shirt. Had a small, blue name tag on his chest. A rather buff chest, I might add, with strong arms and piercing dark eyes. Day-dreamy sigh. His name was Shiloh. Shiloh was hot.

"You need change?" he asked, eyeing the dollar bill in my hand.

"Oh," I fumbled, trying to remember what I was supposed to say. That same red sign hung behind his fluffy hair. It looked so soft.

Help Wanted. Right. "You're hiring, right?" I said quietly, trying not to allow the hotness in my cheeks to show.

"Yeah."

Awkward pause.

"You want an application?" he asked.

"Um, yes please." God, I was acting like a moron! I waited nervously while Shiloh disappeared behind the counter. "How long have you worked here?"

"What?" he asked, his head popping into view.

I grinned. "I'll wait till you're done."

"No, it's okay. Here." He plopped the application onto the counter. I folded it up carefully and put it in my purse. "What'd you say?"

I shook my head. "It's not important."

"Whatever." He smiled, revealing tiny dimples on each cheek.

"You have dimples."

"I, uh, yeah," he said, smiling wider as his head tilted away from my eyes.

Shit! What did I say that for? Probably embarrassed the guy to the point of no return. I played with the straps of my purse, hurriedly thinking of ways to redeem myself.

The familiar loudness of a bus engine roared across the street. Dammit. "I've gotta go," I mumbled, bolting to the door. "It was nice meeting you!"

Shiloh couldn't have understood me over the noise of the arcade, but he must've heard something he liked. I got to see those dimples again.

May 2nd

I don't know how to express the pain. These past two days have been nothing but fucking cravings. Hands shaking like a little bitch—now they're all clammy. Then there's my body wanting it...feels like it's on it, coming down, craving more. I'm sick of it. All of it. Makes me feel like I have less control over my body than I did when I was using. At least then I was the one making my body high, and when the cravings came...no. No control there either. I just feel so helpless, powerless. I'm tired of the fear, tired of the urge to crawl into a hole and wait for it to be over. Emotions I can't control, my body screaming at me to use...

And then there's my mind. You'd think a human being could be capable of controlling its own thoughts. Been getting images in my head. Snorting it, smoking up a storm, feeling the rush. God, I want some. It's like this pull from a distance, calling me in, drawing me towards it. The cravings and withdrawals are so hard to ignore. Even harder to get through. Don't know how long I can do this. It's all so fucking hard.

FOURTEEN

Voices. They're all around me in my head. They yell but I can't hear what they're saying. Too many, all the time they scream. What are they saying? So much screaming. It hurts my ears, they're so loud. So loud! I don't want to be here don't want to hear it can't I run away? I close my ears before they bleed, close them to the voices in my head. But they get louder. Louder LOuder LOUDer LOUDER! Pounding echoing beneath my skin my heart my eyes sweat tears and there's so much pain so much pain so much pain
"OOOWWWWWWWW!"
I scream louder than I've ever screamed before. I scream on my bed and through the ceiling and through the roof and into the sky. I scream and I scream and I scream.

I woke up, the screaming still ringing in my ears. Woke up with clammy palms and shaky breath. Shaky everything. Was I really awake?

The clock said 2:24AM. The middle of the night and I was wide awake. Great. I fumbled in the dark for cigarettes, shoes and a lighter. Where was my fucking lighter? Ouch. I stepped on something metal, something round…oh, there's my lighter.

I closed the door quickly, hopefully leaving Veronica in perfect sleep. Tip-toed to the front door. Outside. I breathed deeply, the night's crisp air filling my head.

"Couldn't sleep?"

I jumped.

Gina was sitting in a chair on the side of the door. I hadn't even seen her.

"No," I said quietly, putting a cigarette to my lips. She offered her lighter. I took it despite the dull pain on the bottom of my foot from when I had scrambled to find my own.

"You've got the shakes," she noticed. I handed her lighter back. "How long has it been?"

"Six days," I told her, knowing full well she knew the time herself. She watched me piss every fucking day.

"It's gonna get harder."

Thank you Dr. Bitch. I took a deep drag, trying to ease the spasms in my skin. The bouncing thoughts inside my head. Took another drag.

"I never wanted to get clean." Gina stared blankly in the distance. "Maybe that's why it never worked." She chuckled to herself.

I sat on the edge of the porch, trying to ignore my shivering. God, I wished someone would make it stop. That someone would hold me.

"I was your age the first time. Eighteen. Stupid."

Thanks. Say something helpful maybe? I flicked my cigarette in an attempt to show my annoyance. She didn't notice.

"I had run away from home again. Been on the streets for maybe a year. Year and a half. We were tweaking out, thought we were gods, of course. My friends from the street and I. There was this guy. Hottest guy I'd met in my life. Jake. He dared me to climb the edge of this bridge. Fucking high ass bridge. I was afraid of heights. So he climbed it. Wanted to show off, I guess. He got to the top and stood there a long time. He was looking at the water. Said how beautiful it was. Like me." She smiled and took a drag. "And then, he jumped."

I turned around to look at her. She returned the gaze. "He died obviously. And I turned myself into rehab. There was no way I was jumping off a fucking bridge. Not that it worked. Got loaded the day I left. But I was young. It took me four times in ten years to get it right. I have six years clean now." She thumped her fist lightly against the side of the house. "Knock on wood."

"Does it ever work the first time?" I whispered.

"I've never seen it. But that doesn't mean it can't." She stared hard at me. "You have to really want it. Worse than anything you've ever wanted in your whole life." She put her cigarette out in the giant coffee can we called an ashtray. "Cuz this will be the hardest thing you've ever done."

I swallowed, wrapping myself with shaky arms.

"Do you believe her?" Esther Agnes-Robbins asked, pushing her glasses up the brim of her nose.

"Which part?"

"That this is the hardest thing you'll ever do."

I sighed heavily and watched my fingers toy with the hole in my jeans. "It feels like it."

"Are you still shaking?"

I held out my hands. They were steadier than I thought they'd be, but there was a definite movement that shouldn't have been there. "That's the best they've been all day."

"It's just a part of healing, Lynn. It'll stop."

"What about my head?" I asked her, remembering my dream.

"That will take some time." Esther smiled slightly. "That's why we're doing what we're doing."

"And what are we doing?" I was getting frustrated with her optimism.

"You tell me."

"I don't know."

"Well, how about this. What should we be doing?"

"Talking about something that matters. Like why I use drugs."

"Used. Past tense. Why did you use, Lynn?"

"Isn't that *your* job?" I hissed. My head hurt enough without her asking me so many stupid questions.

"No." She tapped her pen against her notepad. "I'm here to make sure you're safe, that you're going in the right direction. But you need to be the one who comes up with the answers. I can't do that for you."

I rolled my eyes.

"Would you like to discuss something else?"

"No." I sighed. "We should talk about it. I just don't want to."

Silence. I hated silence. Especially here. I ripped a thread from my jeans and twisted it around my ring finger. Pulled until the top of my finger turned a shade of pink. Felt my skin tingle.

"Do you like pain?" Esther asked.

"Sometimes." The pink was turning red. I pulled harder, wondering how long it would take to turn blue.

"Take that string off of your finger, please."

I ignored her.

"Lynn, take the string off!" she almost shouted, half standing at the edge of the chair. I shoved the thread inside the couch. Esther sat down again. "Have you hurt yourself before?"

My fingers touched the tip of my wrist. I sat on my hands. "I don't want to talk about that."

"Lynn."

"I said I don't want to talk about it!"

More fucking silence. Was it an hour yet? I didn't have a watch.

"Do you want to get better?" Esther asked quietly.

"Yes."

"I think a part of you doesn't. There's a part of you that likes this darkness, the depression. It's safe for you."

I shrugged, trying not to let my insides spill into her ears.

"I think you've been living there a long time."

"That's why I got high," I blurted out. "I wanted to run away." I paused. "But then...then it followed me. No matter what I did, it was there. The drugs just numbed me for awhile. Now they don't even do that anymore."

Esther gave me a look.

"They didn't," I corrected. "I don't feel human without them. That's present on purpose. I feel like a zombie."

"What are you running from?" Esther asked.

Another pause. "I think it's been an hour now."

Have to make it stop. The pain erupts inside my gut. My head explodes behind closed eyes. Just want to fucking use. That's all. That's all. Trying to ignore it but it won't stop screaming and I just don't think I can do this anymore. Running from the snarling mass of blood and teeth and beady eyes that chase me to the edge. Wish I had my wings to fly. They've fallen way down there somewhere. Somewhere beneath the drugs and hurt and pain.

It's taking me away.

My body rocked under the covers, begging silence beneath my tears. I was shivering again. It was three in the fucking morning. Shouldn't I be sleeping like a normal person? I tried to close my eyes but everything was just too strong. I couldn't be inside myself anymore.

The box of tacks were stashed beneath my bed. Safe keeping, I guess. Had to fumble in the dark to find them. Fumble through my need. Got one in between my fingers. The tip dug quickly through soft flesh, scraping just below my belly button. I sighed in the pain.

Happy seven days clean.

8:57AM. Dressed in a bright orange shirt and blue Dockers, smoking a cigarette on the curb. I started my first shift at FrankZilla's Arcade in three minutes. Yes, FrankZilla. Hey, at least I didn't have to wear a hotdog on my head or dress up as a giant teddy bear on the side of the road. But still, I admit, it's pretty bad. Let's call it FZ's to lessen the humiliation, shall we?

This whole job concept was almost as scary as the interview. I was sweating like a pig then, all shaky and shit. I had no idea what I was doing. Mumbled a lot. But whatever, they liked me. Gave me a drug test, which I passed by a whole day, an ugly ass orange shirt, a weird looking belt, and told me to come back on Thursday. Maybe I should have told them the last job I had I was high all the time and this psycho pedophile wanted to marry me. Or that right now I was just trying to get clean and the world was spinning and I had to double check that my shirt was right side out.

I sighed and checked the time on my phone. Shit! It was 9:01. Already late and I hadn't even started the damn job. I threw my cigarette in the street and half ran to the door. Tripped on a stick or a crack or my own foot and landed face first on the concrete.

"You okay?"

I cringed at the sound of his voice. Of course I had to fall in front of him. "Fine," I said into the ground. I lifted myself up quickly, trying to avoid his eyes. But mine kept looking at him.

"Elizabeth can't get here till 10. She's the supervisor."

"What are you?"

"A lead, but it's not that much different than a regular."

"What's the difference?"

"I get to tell you what to do." His dimples glistened in the morning dew. Okay, so there was no dew, but they were damn cute. You can tell me what to do anytime, dimple boy.

Shiloh unlocked the front doors, and I followed him into a very silent arcade. Too silent. I hated silence. It was hard to believe this was the same place I had applied for last week.

"We open at 10 AM. Opening doesn't really take an hour but they schedule us that way anyway." He hurried to the back, opened the *Employee's Only* door and punched some numbers into the keypad. "You have to clock in before it reaches the seven minute mark. Otherwise it rounds up and they know you're late. I clocked you in as a newbie, but you'll get your own numbers soon."

I nodded slowly, wondering if maybe this wasn't such a good idea. It was still early enough to go back to sleep or watch *Law And Order* with the girls at home.

"Don't look so scared."

I blinked. "What?"

"You'll be fine. It's not that bad once you get the hang of things."

Within an hour, I learned that the yellow breakers are turned on in the morning, the blue breakers should only be on at dusk or if it's cloudy or for some reason one of the yellow breaker's lights are out, and the red breakers cannot, under any circumstances, be touched at all. If they are touched Jim, the arcade technician, will hunt you down and kill you. Or at least maim you for a short while.

I laughed.

"You think I'm kidding?" Shiloh giggled. His dimples were showing again. I bit my lip.

Shiloh continued his long list of rules. All games, windows, counters, and whatever else is dirty must be cleaned with the universal glass cleaner and nappers. Nappers are merely oversized napkins that cost 10 cents each so use them over if possible. Special keys open games to get the tokens or nickels or other weird objects that kids stick in there. There are no refunds on tokens. If they want change, send them to the counter in the back. Wear closed toed shoes. Report all accidents, even if it's just a paper cut. Do that with customers too. No food. Drinks can be left at the counter.

"Oh, and watch out for the locals." Shiloh fumbled with his keys.

"The who?"

"The kids who come here everyday." He paused, nodding his head to a small pack of teens that had gathered outside the door. "They like to mess with newbies."

"Don't they have school?"

He turned the key and opened the door, letting the stampede of teenagers shove me into the wall. "Spring break."

"But it's May."

"Year round school. They get three weeks off."

Of course they did. Why not on my first fucking day?

Shiloh wasn't kidding about the locals. For the first hour we were open, those damn kids bombarded me for free credits every five seconds. The game ate their tokens. The start button wouldn't move. The game froze. The fighting buttons didn't work. The wheel overturned. One kid claimed his little brother shoved his token up his nose. No kidding. I felt like a baby sitter for a large pack of monkeys. Devil monkeys.

11:30 and counting. God, it was hot. I wanted fresh air. And a cigarette. Elizabeth was at the counter talking to Shiloh. I remembered her from my interview. She had seemed pretty cool. Maybe I could steal a break.

"Would it be okay if, um, I had a cigarette?" I asked as sweetly as my sarcasm would allow.

Elizabeth cocked her head slightly. "Hi Lynn. Nice to see you again."

"Oh, sorry. Hi."

She smiled. "It's okay. I'm just messing with you."

I sat down by the curb. It was nice to be away from the noise. I could already feel my ears ringing. I lit my cigarette and rubbed the back of my calves. Standing for six hours was not going to be fun. I wondered how long it took Shiloh to get used to it. He had the counter to lean on. Elizabeth to talk to.

Wait…they weren't…were they? I tried to remember how flirtatious their body language was, but all I could see were his dimples and fluffy hair. I'd have to look into that one. If she…they…nope, didn't want to think it. He was single. He had to be.

My cigarette was out. Shit, I wondered what time it was. Maybe I could smoke one more before going back. I reached for my purse when something caught my eye.

A tall girl with black hair was walking hand in hand with a scrawny, pimpled guy. I gasped, wondering if it really was…yes, it was. Angie and KJ were on the street together. They were walking towards me. Maybe I should run, hide behind the arcade. Tell Shiloh some tweakers were outside.

But I just sat there. Waited. Angie took a cigarette from her purse. She had seen me. I wondered if KJ would notice. Probably not. I wouldn't be surprised if he had forgotten I existed. Angie could only try to pretend.

It was time for them to pass me. I braced myself, waiting for an evil look, a raised eyebrow, a hello. I kind of hoped she would say something. I wanted to tell her I like her hair black. That it brought out the blue in her eyes.

They passed me.

Nothing. No look. No acknowledgement. Both of them had stared straight ahead as if I hadn't been sitting in the middle of the sidewalk. As if I hadn't given myself to KJ for his stupid tweak or had known Angie since the sixth grade. There were tears in my eyes. No, dammit! I was supposed to be the one to say goodbye.

I grabbed another cigarette, not caring what the time was. Fuck her. I hoped she rotted in her own addiction. Choked on her own venom for making me feel this way. Guess I was some vermin that didn't fucking matter. Made me glad I was getting clean. Glad I had a reason to forget.

"Kiki, come on! We're late already." Veronica puckered her lips and dropped her lipstick in her purse. Kiki's keys were on the floor. She picked them up and threw them at Kiki, who was still doing her hair.

The car keys hit the mirror and landed on an open compact. "Ver! You got powder all over my keys!"

"Let me try again. I'll hit your face next time."

I stood in the doorway and crossed my arms. Neither of them noticed. I watched Kiki flip her layers of hair again and again, spraying hair spray everywhere. It was a consistent hiss for at least a minute.

"You gonna use the whole can?"

Kiki looked at me through the reflection of the mirror. "Shut up, Lynn. You don't have to worry about this shit. You're not getting a chip tonight."

"Like anyone gives a shit how you look," Veronica said, although all three of us knew how untrue that was. Everyone cared how you looked. If you looked good, you were clean. Clean meant healthy and living some kind of life that wasn't fucked up like the rest of us. Even I had succumbed into makeup, although I used it to make me look as dark as possible. I wore black a lot more too. And silver jewelry. Made me feel safe, protected by the anger I wore on my clothes. It felt good to rebel like that. Maybe I should dye my hair black like Angie.

A sharp pain stung my gut. I forgot. I wasn't supposed to think about her.

"Oh my god, Kik, you're driving me crazy!" Veronica walked towards me and pulled my arm back through the front of the house. "We're smoking!" she yelled.

"Whatever! I'm almost done!"

"She said that ten minutes ago."

6:07 PM. We got there as they were introducing the newcomers. Veronica, Kiki, and I snuck quietly into the first seats we could find.

"Are there any others who would like to introduce themselves?"

"Lynn. Addict," I said quickly, pretending I had been there the whole time.

"Hi Lynn," they chimed.

"You're late," whispered a voice. I turned around. Gina was sitting behind us.

I shrugged and tilted my head towards Kiki. "It takes her ten hours to do her hair." Gina laughed and told me to turn around.

"This is a chip meeting," the secretary said. She looked tired. "You get one on every significant birthday. Thirty days, sixty days, ninety days, six months, nine months, one year, two years, and so on." She gestured to a woman beside her. "Natalie's going to hand them out." Natalie smiled shyly.

"That's our sponsor," Veronica whispered. "Mine and Kiki's."

I looked at Natalie a little more. She seemed nice enough. Her face was soft. So were her eyes.

"You think she'd want to be mine?" I whispered back.

"I don't know. Ask her."

"Anyone have a birthday of thirty days?" the secretary asked. Kiki jumped up.

"I'm Kiki. I'm an addict and I have thirty days today," she chimed, waltzing to the front of the room. Everyone clapped. Natalie grinned, handing Kiki a large, white keychain. They hugged and Kiki sat back down.

"Can I see it?" I asked her. She handed it to me. It had silver writing on it that said *clean and serene for thirty days*. I turned the keychain over and over in my hands. Almost pretended it was mine. Pretended I had the guts to stay clean for thirty days. God, that was a long time. A lot longer than my stupid eleven. I sighed and returned Kiki her chip.

"Cool, huh?" she grinned.

"It's her second one," Veronica told me.

"So?" Kiki snapped. "You've tried way more than that."

"I know."

"How much time do you have?" I asked her, surprised I hadn't thought of it before.

"Forty-three days."

"Only thirteen more than me. She thinks that makes her better or something."

"Shut up Kiki."

"Ssh!" Gina hissed. Veronica rolled her eyes.

The speaker was an old man with a storyteller's voice. I don't remember his name. He talked about his past, how he started using when he was ten. Got sucked into a gang when his father died. Stabbed his first victim at twelve, killed at fifteen. Only because they shot his "brother." He escaped from the cops that time, but was forced to kill again a year later. He got caught. Was tried as an adult, got twenty years. He was high when he did it. He said that part saved his life. Didn't know what kind of sentence he would've gotten sober. Not that it made it any better. He wouldn't have killed if he hadn't been high.

"I got out seven years ago," he said. "I had twenty-two years sober April 29th." Loud applause. "And you wanna know what keeps me there? Morality. Sounds stupid, but when you're stuck in the joint for twenty years, your head starts ticking. You start thinking about why shit got fucked up and then the anger kicks. You blame everyone you've ever met. Mother, brother, friend, dealer, prostitute, whatever. Until the lightning hits and you realize that the fucker to blame is you. It was you the whole goddamn time." He paused to take a sip of water. The room was so quiet I could hear him swallow. "Now why would a thing like morality keep an asshole like me clean?" He paused for dramatic effect. I sat on the edge of my seat, fingernails in my mouth. We waited. "Cuz I've got nothing else. I'm not who I was back then. Not a punk, not a killer, not a scared little shit with nowhere else to go. I'm a man now. I take care of myself. I want to be a good person. Want people to trust me. You know, my mom gave me the keys to her place a few years back. The fact that she trusts me with all her shit like that…reminds me of who I am. Who I want to be. I'm an addict, sure, but I don't use. I don't steal. I don't kill. I got my life back and I want to live it. I'm not who I was. I never will be."

He went on to talk about the fourth step, how important it is to do moral inventory. How the steps themselves save lives so go to meetings and respect your sponsor.

But I wasn't listening. Too busy thinking about his story. How he was who he wanted to be. I wondered who I had become. It wasn't who I wanted to be. I knew that. But I wasn't sure who I wanted to be either.

The meeting was over. We went outside.

"Wow. That guy fucked me up," Kiki said with a cigarette in her mouth. She wasn't the only one. Everyone was talking about him. What he said about morality, how it kept him clean. It reminded me of Gina, of how she tried to get clean because she didn't want to jump off a bridge. She didn't want to die.

But it wasn't a good enough reason. She got high again. I wanted to know what made her stop for good, what gave her the means to have six years clean. Did every addict need a reason? What was mine? What if it wasn't good enough?

"I think he fucked up everyone," I told Kiki.

"Lynn!" Veronica was calling my name. She was with Natalie. Dammit. I didn't think I was ready for a sponsor. Too much in my head.

"Hi," I said shyly.

"Here." Veronica half-shoved Natalie at me and walked away.

Uh.

"Hi. Lynn, right?" Natalie smiled.

"Yeah."

Silence. I could feel her looking at me. I took out a cigarette. "Want one?" I asked her.

"I don't smoke."

I put the cigarette in my mouth. Lit it.

"Veronica said you want to ask me something?"

Exhaled. "Yeah." Pause. I shifted my feet. "Do you want to be my sponsor?" It came out so quickly I wondered if she understood me. She was just smiling.

"Do you have a pen?" she asked me. I shook my head no. She fumbled in her purse. Took out a pen and one of those mini notepads. She wrote something and tore the notepad. Gave me the piece of paper and the pen. "Here's my number. Call me every day. And keep that pen with you at all times."

I put the piece of paper and the pen in my pocket. The end of the pen dug into my thigh. Should have brought my purse.

Natalie left. Veronica came back over to me. "Why are you smiling?" she asked.

I shrugged. It felt good to smile. Reminded me of how I was before all this. Before I fell. I was surprised I could remember that at all.

It was happening again. The cravings. I wanted to die. Thoughts of Jake. I saw him, faceless, standing at the top of the bridge. Saw his body fall. Saw me fall. Blood in the water.

I hated this. Hated the highs and lows. Like I was on it, touching the sweet energy inside my skull, the tingling flying beneath my skin. And then it was gone, as if yanked from my insides, spilling my guts onto the floor. I was left with the empty yearning, the wretched clenching in my chest, my mouth, my eyes. I closed them, wishing it all away. Hoping that maybe it was just a dream and I could fly.

I opened my eyes. This was no dream. This was worse than using. Worse than anything I'd ever felt. My world was spiraling in pieces around me and I just wanted it to stop. Wanted it all to stop.

Fuck it. Maybe I should just get high. Give myself a reason to feel this way. A reason to stay clean.

A reason. What was my reason?

I remembered Natalie. She would know how to help me. How to make it stop. I tore my room apart, searching for that stupid piece of paper. But I couldn't find her number. Maybe I could call Esther. Maybe she would talk to me. Had an appointment with her tomorrow, but it wasn't soon enough. I needed her now.

Worked tomorrow too. Work. Could go there. Run away to dimple boy. To video games and local kids. Run away outside of me.

But work was downtown. Drugs were downtown. KJ and Angie were downtown.

Fuck it. Why not?

I grabbed my cigarettes, my wallet, my keys. Started to walk away from myself.

My phone rang.

It was my mother. I picked it up and started crying before I could even say hello.

"I'm proud of you." Esther Agnes-Robbins grinned.

"Why?" I asked, settling further into the couch. The cushions were soft against my back.

"Well, for one, you're leaning back today." She paused. I didn't say anything. "You're usually all scrunched up. Closed off." She held her arms close to her chest and hunched over to demonstrate. I noticed I had folded my own arms. I unfolded them and put them awkwardly beside me. "Your body language shows me you're opening up. That you're getting ready to heal."

I wanted to hug my knees to my chest, but I couldn't now. I was all open and shit. I kind of liked that. Liked the idea of healing. I crossed my legs instead.

Esther smiled again. "Now it's your turn."

Huh?

"Give me a reason to be proud of you."

Silence.

"There are tons of them, Lynn."

More silence.

"Do you want me to start listing them?"

"I have twelve days clean today," I said quickly.

Esther clapped. "That's great! Do you remember the first time we talked? How you didn't think you'd make it past two?"

I nodded, ignoring the heat rushing to my cheeks. I wasn't used to praise.

"That's great." Pause. "You're great."

I shoved a fingernail between my teeth.

"I'm trying to show you your accomplishments. I want you to see how far you've come."

I shook my head. "I'm still the same. I almost use every day. At least every day."

"Almost, Lynn. That's a big word there. Almost. You're thinking twice about getting high. You don't want to hurt yourself anymore."

"But I do."

Esther pushed her glasses further down her nose. "You hurt yourself?"

I nodded.

"When ?"

"Last Wednesday. The night after I saw you."

Pause. "How did you hurt yourself?"

"With a tack. I always use a tack."

"Are you in danger? Do you think you'll do it again soon?"

I shook my head.

Esther sighed. "How else have you hurt yourself? Besides cutting or drugs."

I brought my knees to my chest. I didn't care if I was closed. I needed to feel safe. "Um," I swallowed hard, trying to get past the urge to run. It just made my heart thump faster. "Sometimes I don't eat. That's one of the reasons why I like meth. Cuz I don't eat. It's hard not having that, cuz I eat more now and then I freak out."

Esther's eyes didn't change. I had waited for them to. I thought they'd show some kind of pity or disappointment. But they were still the same. Sensitive.

I took a deep breath and continued. "Smoking's another thing I probably shouldn't do. My mom cried when I told her I smoked. My dad said he'd kick me out of college. They didn't say those things when they found out I was using." Pause. "I never thought about that. Um, I have a thing with guys. I try not to think about it, about how I let them treat me. Use me. I let them make me feel like shit. Like I deserve it. Maybe I bring it on myself. Maybe I want them to use me."

I could feel myself getting smaller and smaller, as if my body were slowly caving in on itself. I wanted to disintegrate. Let my pieces blow away. "I think the biggest thing is hiding." My voice was so quiet, Esther had to lean forward to hear me. "I even have this place inside my head." I laughed bitterly, and when I sniffed I realized my face was wet. I was crying. "It's a cell, like where they'd put criminals or something. I think it started with my ex boyfriend, but I'm not sure." I sniffed. "There's nothing there but darkness. I sit in the corner of it. Sometimes I want to and sometimes because I'm chained there. But I'm there all the time, in the dark with no way out. I sit in there and I wait. I wait for something to happen but nothing ever does and it's lonely." Sniff. "But it's safe."

"Why is it safe?" Esther's voice sounded distance. I put my cheek against my knees and felt the tears soak into the fabric.

"It's safe because nothing can touch me. Nothing can hurt me."

"Lynn." Esther was crouched beside me now. Her eyelashes almost touched my cheek. I looked at her. "This is why you started using. Why you hurt yourself. Why you hide. What put you in this cell? What are you protecting yourself from?"

The tears were falling fast. I could barely see her eyes, but I could feel their eagerness to know the truth. I could feel the same look in myself.

I shook my head.

"You can't say it?" Esther asked. "Is it too horrible to speak of?"

"No," I shook, doing my best not to fall apart. "I don't know what I'm hiding from. Isn't that stupid?"

This time Esther shook her head. "That's why we're here, Lynn. That's why we're doing this. But you're going to have to open yourself to the past. You have to open yourself if you want to stop your pain. You need to let it out. Okay?"

I sniffed. Esther handed me a tissue. I blew my nose and realized she had taken a tissue for herself. I smiled.

"Okay."

My eyes were puffy from crying. Red blotches stained my cheeks. I hoped no one would notice. And then I saw my reflection in the clothing store next to FZ's Arcade. Laughed. Okay, so they'll notice. Maybe I'll tell them I kicked someone's ass on the way over here. I laughed again. Yeah right.

Ten minutes till work. I took out another cigarette. Smoked three in a row since that talk with Esther. Couldn't stop myself from smoking. Maybe smoking was my way of covering it all up. Hiding how I felt. Hiding in my cell.

I wondered how much longer I'd be living there.

Fuck. I could feel the intensity before the desire to use surged through my body. The need. I breathed deeply in attempts to push it all away. I didn't want this anymore. Didn't need it.

But it wouldn't stop. I was finally ready to look inside my fucked up self and the cravings washed over me like a storm. Fucking figured. What if I drowned this time? Drowned in the filth and white powder and shame and fear of me.

And then I saw them. Those guys, the ones I knew were fucked up. They weren't even two stores away. It'd be so easy to walk over there. Dammit, why did I have to work downtown? Maybe I didn't really want to get clean. Maybe I wasn't ready to heal. Maybe I just wanted to sit in my goddamn cell and shove shit up my nose one more fucking time.

"Are you okay?" Elizabeth asked me from the door.

I jumped, dropping my cigarette on the ground. I picked it up and looked at her. Fuck, why was she here? I just wanted to use drugs. Do something to fill the need.

"Lynn?"

I started to panic. Didn't know what to do. How to fix this. Fix the bugs inside my skin, the shakiness beneath the mask I wore. I could feel it cracking, could feel the soft layer of fear poking through my eyes. I was falling apart. I was...

Wait. It was going away. I took deep breaths, slowly, remembering what Esther and I had done ten days ago. I was letting the moment pass. Breathe in. Out. In. Out.

I sighed, tears stinging my lashes.

"Lynn, are you crying?"

I thought about lying. Could tell her I have asthma or allergies or whatever else my fucked up brain could come up with. That there was nothing wrong at all.

I could also tell her the truth.

My thoughts went back to Gina, to that old man. How they trusted themselves enough to face life, to try and understand it. Understand themselves. They didn't have to hide in a cell with no doors or windows. Most people don't. Most people have light in their lives.

I wanted some in mine.

"I, um, sort of," I stuttered, wandering to the door. I looked inside. There was no one in there. Spring break, thank everything holy, had ended. "Can I talk to you?"

Elizabeth looked behind her. Nodded. I sat on the curb and lit my cigarette. Elizabeth sat beside me. Shallow silence hovered for a minute. She coughed. I held my cigarette away from her and blew the smoke behind me.

"Don't worry about the smoke," she told me. "My boyfriend smokes." She paused. "Ex-boyfriend. I can't believe I just called him my boyfriend."

I smiled. "It happens." Pause. I flicked my cigarette and bounced my knee. Sighed. Again. Okay. I can do this. I can heal. "I probably should have told you this before you hired me, but it's only been a week so I guess you won't be losing much if you decide to let me go."

Elizabeth gave me a strange look.

"I'm a drug addict. You just saw me go through a craving." Pause. I took a drag, doing my best not to look at her. "And I think that you just stopped me from using."

"My ex-boyfriend's a drug addict."

Our eyes met. "Is that why you broke up with him?" I asked. She hesitated. Shit. "I'm sorry," I said quickly. "It's none of my business. I shouldn't have asked."

"No, it's okay. I just…it's still hard for me to talk about it. It happened a couple weeks ago, so it's still pretty fresh, you know?"

I nodded.

"He cheated on me with this girl in New York. Found out they're having a kid together."

"I'm sorry. I've been cheated on too. That shit sucks."

"Yeah. But I guess it's a good thing. He wouldn't stop shooting up."

"He did heroin?"

"Yeah." She paused. "What did you use?"

"Meth."

"Oh. I've heard that's just as bad. It's good you're doing this, Lynn. I've seen how hard it is. Patrick couldn't do it. He tried to quit so many times. I wanted to help him, but it didn't work. He would just use again. It was awful."

I didn't say anything.

"I want to be there for you."

"What do you mean?" I asked her.

"You're doing what Patrick couldn't. You're quitting. I want to help you. I want to be there. I want," she sucked in air as if holding back tears, "to see what it was like for him. To understand why he couldn't do it."

I looked at her. Studied her face. And I saw it. That pain in her eyes, the desperation on her lips. I saw the tread marks on her skin, the wear of fear. And I realized that I wasn't alone. We both wanted understanding, to feel the warmth against our skin. We both yearned for the truth.

I smiled. "Cool."

"Cool," she laughed. Looked at her watch.

"I don't want to know," I said, shoving the end of my cigarette against the gravel.

"You're not that late," she told me, opening the door. Held it for me as I walked inside.

May 13th

I know the depression's still there. Maybe that's why I don't want to deal with anything, why lying down and staring at nothing is so comforting. Or there's the void—feeling nothing, an emptiness consuming every vessel inside. Numb to myself, to the world around me. My hands are shaking again. I wish they would stop. I wish everything would stop and I could have it back the way it was, before the drugs, before depression—when I had control. I'm just so lost.

And afraid. Afraid that something will happen and I'll fall, afraid that my lack of control will take me somewhere I don't want to go, make me do something I don't want to do. I'm afraid of what's inside, why I feel so caged up, why I can't seem to let it out. I don't even know why so much is there. Maybe there's more to this than I thought. Maybe it was there before the drugs. I don't know. I wish I could cry.

FIFTEEN

I was late again. Should implant a permanent clock on my forehead. No, I'd still be late but everyone else would be on time. Go figure.

Natalie was sitting on the patio, absorbed in a mug of tea and a college textbook. College. I hadn't thought about that in forever. Even when I was there I had forgotten about it. How much I wanted to learn, to fly beyond my dreams. Well I fucked that up, didn't I?

Shit. The academic advisor. I still had to do that. Mental note to call the campus tomorrow.

"Hey Natalie," I greeted, plopping my notebook onto the table. "I'm going to get a coffee before we start, ok?"

Natalie nodded without looking up. I skipped inside and stood in line behind a girl with really cool hair. It was dark red with deep purple highlights. I'd never seen that before.

"I like your hair," I said to the back of her head. The girl turned around.

It was Rhiannon.

I tried to remember the last time I saw her. It felt so long ago. It was when…oh shit. I remembered her. Remember her hunched over, sobbing her soul into the ground. How I just stepped over her and walked away. Walked away to get my fix, my high, my death.

Death. Her sister. I cringed tightly inside.

She was staring at me. I could feel her eyes, how they burned. She was angry.

"Hi Lynn."

I forced myself to smile, to look her in the face. Her lips were pinched so tightly together they looked white.

"Hi Rhiannon." Awkward silence burned my ears. "How are you?"

"How the fuck do you think I am?"

I could feel my smile falter, but I held on.

"My sister's still dead."

I looked away. Shoved my fingernails into my palm. Wanted to disappear.

"You're a bitch."

My heart was beating fast. It was getting difficult to breathe. To think.

"You left me there. Alone. I was sobbing my fucking heart out and you just walked away. I was there for two hours. Didn't even realize it until Sheena found me. But Sheena's not a bitch like you."

I looked at her, desperation screaming in my eyes. "I'm sorry."

"Yeah, whatever."

And then it hit me. I had left her. She needed me and I just fucking left. Left her in her rawness. Left her heart to bleed. I was the only person in the world who knew her pain, and I threw it away. Threw her away.

"That wasn't me," I whispered, trying to grasp the pieces of it all.

"Bullshit it wasn't you. Everything we do is us. I should know. I'm bipolar. You think I can just get all fucked up and crazy and blame it on something else? Bullshit. I'm me all the fucking time. I have to own myself and my actions no matter what. And so do you. In fact, I think that day you showed me who you *really* were."

"Can I help you?"

He was talking to Rhiannon. I went silent, turning my back against the counter as she ordered her soy latte.

"Did you want something?" the guy asked.

Rhiannon was waiting at the other end of the counter. I ordered a non-fat mocha and stood next to her. She didn't say anything.

"I wanted to help you, Rhiannon. That day you found out about your sister was horrible for you."

She turned her head away.

"But I couldn't. I couldn't deal with what you were going through."

"So you just fucking left?"

"I didn't know what else to do."

"Soy latte?"

Rhiannon grabbed her drink, started to turn around. But I didn't want her to leave. She needed to understand why I left. That I was really a good friend…I had just gotten lost. I needed her to tell me it was okay.

I touched her arm. She pulled away.

"I'm sorry, Rhiannon. I really am. Can you at least try to forgive me?"

I thought I saw something in her eyes. It was understanding. And she saw it in mine. And then time stood still and we saw one another as we were. Naked in pain, searching to find the reason for the darkness that devoured our lives.

But it was only a moment. Her eyes clouded over in her pain again, and she was gone.

And I was left alone with mine.

"I'm sorry you had to deal with that," Natalie told me through sips of green tea. I shrugged and tapped my fingernails against my mocha. "It hurts to face the past."

"I just wish she would forgive me," I mumbled.

"You tried. All we have is that, Lynn. All we can do is try."

"Maybe."

Silence.

"Don't think about it right now," Natalie said. "Think about yourself. Think about staying clean. How much time do you have?"

"Twenty-seven days."

"See? You're almost at thirty. So many people don't make it to thirty. Forget the past for the moment. You need to think about right now."

I nodded.

"So you're almost done with Step One. Did you answer the rest of the questions in the workbook?"

I nodded again.

"Read them to me."

So I sat on the porch of a coffee shop with my sponsor, pouring my heart's most broken moments out into the sky. I talked about surrender, how it scared me more than my addiction. *I'm afraid to lose control*, I read. *I'm afraid I'll fail. I'm afraid I'm not good enough to recover.*

Not good enough. Is that why I hid? To make myself silent because I didn't deserve to be heard?

I've been using drugs to get away from myself for so long, it's difficult to cope without them. Difficult to deal with anything.

Deal with what?

Fear. Anger. Afraid of what's inside. Angry at myself for having to do this.

I hated myself for it. I wanted to know who I was beneath it all. I wanted to see myself again. I thought of Rhiannon and wondered who I had become. I knew I wouldn't have done that sober. I knew how much I tried to be a good friend. A good person.

Was I?

The thoughts of Rhiannon drifted to my sisters. I couldn't remember the last time I talked to them. Didn't know what was going on in their lives. Shit,

Elle was a freshman in high school and I had no idea if she even liked it. If she needed help with boys or friends or adjusting to the true beginning of teenagedom. So many new things in her life. I wanted to be there for her. To be the sister she deserved to have.

The session with Natalie was over. We said goodbye. I pulled out my cell phone and called home.

"Hello?" It was Halley.

I smiled. "Hi sweetie. How are you?"

"Good." It sounded like she was eating. "I'm having ice cream with Tess."

"Who's Tess? Have I met her?"

"No. She's a new friend."

I sighed. "That's good. Are you having fun?"

"Yeah. We're watching *Now and Then*."

I laughed. "You haven't changed." I could feel the tears inside my heart. Maybe I wasn't too late after all.

"Changed? I just saw you."

"Yeah," I said, wiping my eyes. "You did." Pause. "Is Elle there?"

Halley's mouth smacked against the phone. "She's in her room. Mom and Dad were yelling at her. But I think they stopped. Hang on."

I bit my lip anxiously. Wondered what it was like for Elle…if my parents were passing on their anger. Their fears. I wanted to tell her I was sorry for leaving that shit behind.

"Hi." Elle's voice sounded cold. Not surprising after a parents' session.

"Halley said Mom and Dad were yelling at you. Are you okay?"

"I'm fine."

"Why do you sound angry then?"

"I don't want to talk about it."

I sighed. "Elle, I've been there. Maybe I can help."

"It's not them Lynn." She paused. "It's you."

"What?"

"You lied to me."

I held my breath. Tried to remember what I could have said to her. What I could have done. But I couldn't think of anything. I didn't see her enough to do anything.

"Mom told me about you. About your *addiction*." She said the word like something awful was in her mouth.

I took a cigarette from my pack. "I don't understand why that would make you angry, Elle. Maybe scared, but—"

"I can't fucking believe you."

I had never heard her like this. So angry. Her hatred was pouring through the phone. I took another drag. "Tell me what you mean."

Elle was silent.

"Please?"

"That day when I saw you in the bathroom." Her voice quivered. "I saw you getting high on crank. And you said you only did it once and it was okay and you'd never do it again."

I had forgotten that.

"I knew about it and I didn't say anything because I thought you were okay." She was crying now. "And you weren't."

Tears in my eyes again. I swallowed. "I didn't want you to know. I was ashamed of myself."

"I don't fucking care! You're my sister and we're supposed to tell each other everything and I trusted you. I shouldn't have. I should have told Mom and Dad so they could have stopped you from doing it again."

"They wouldn't have stopped me, though. No one could have stopped me." I paused, realizing what she was trying to tell me. She knew about my drug use. She had seen it. And she let me use because I told her it was okay. That trust had betrayed her, and now her sister was falling. "*You* couldn't have stopped me," I told her. My voice was desperate. "It's not your fault."

"Yeah, whatever." She hung up the phone.

I put my cigarette to my lips, tasting the salt that clung to the edge of my mouth. I wiped my face. Tried to remember what Natalie had said. The past was the past. I couldn't do anything about it now. I had to focus on the present. Focus on keeping myself sober.

But what if the past was the present and everything I knew was falling apart?

Happy twenty-seven days clean.

"Oh my God, I can't believe she's wearing that," Kiki said to no one as she flipped through one of her beauty magazines.

"Oh my God!" Veronica repeated in a high pitched valley girl voice. I laughed. Kiki squinted her eyes into an evil look.

"Do you think she bites?" I whispered to Veronica. Kiki threw the magazine at my head.

"Hi girls," Gina sighed, attempting to balance several grocery bags against her knee and open the front door at the same time. I got up quickly and let her inside the house.

"Thanks Lynn," she said as she hobbled through the door.

"Take me to your leader!" Kiki squeaked, just loud enough for Veronica and me to hear. We laughed. Kiki had overheard Gina telling Sandy an embarrassing using moment. One time on a particularly strong high, Gina had the urge to talk to the aliens that lived on a busy street. She stood on her car and held up a sign that read *Take Me To Your Leader* to oncoming traffic. Gina was indeed taken, but it was by the cops in shiny handcuffs. Apparently she had been holding her sign there for almost three hours. We thought it was one of the funniest stories we'd ever heard.

And I was starting to breathe again. The pain of Elle's words, of Rhiannon's words…it clung to me, yet somehow I was able to put it aside. I knew that eventually I would have to face that part of my life. That eventually I would have to face myself. But right now there was nothing I could do. Right now I could only stay clean and help myself get better. And that helped.

I took another breath.

The sun was setting against the row of trees and houses across the street. The three of us sat there on the porch, bathed in the golden rays of life. We smoked our cigarettes and laughed at the people who walked by. Laughed at the life we lived before, at the pain that was slowly fading like the shadows that danced beneath the rising moon. We were hopeful. We were healing. And life was somehow getting better.

I rubbed my hands against my arms. My stomach. Nineteen days since I had cut myself. Twenty-seven days since drugs. Twenty-seven days since I stayed up all night or starved myself for days at a time. More than twenty-seven days since I had done sexual favors for drugs. Sold myself to the need. Twenty-seven days of being sober. Of being me.

Almost twenty-eight, which was almost thirty. I could picture myself holding that keychain in my hands, holding the silver letters that claimed the serenity I craved. It was another step to staying sober, and I couldn't wait to see the other side.

"It sounds like you're doing better," Esther Agnes-Robbins said as she jotted her psycho notes into her notebook. "Better enough to have a session with your parents."

"Huh?"

Esther laughed. "I know, I know. It's scary. But so many of the issues you're dealing with are rooted in your childhood. The sooner you confront your parents, the sooner you can heal that part of you. And I promise, once you face that, the rest will make much more sense."

I sighed. "But that means I have to talk to them."

Esther laughed again. Nodded.

"Like, really talk." I paused. "That's not gonna make me use, is it?"

"Anything can make you use Lynn. It's the choices you make that keep you sober. I think this is a good choice."

I shut my eyes. "Okay."

"Why don't you talk to them about it and see what they say? Make it, let's say, a month from now?"

A month. Thirty days. I could deal with that. I'd have almost sixty days by then. Sixty days clean.

"Um. Yeah. Okay."

"Okay."

I picked at some dirt under my fingernails. Silence filled my ears. Fuck silence. "Can we talk about something?"

"What would you like to discuss?"

I shrugged, annoyed with her question.

"Is there anything on your mind?"

My knees scrunched themselves against my chest. I buried my face in my arms.

"Lynn?"

"I'm tired of this," I mumbled.

"Tried of what?"

"Of this." I bit my fingernail. Stopped. Bit it again. "I'm spinning in circles. No matter where I go it's the same fucking thing. I don't want to talk about it anymore. I want something to happen. I want to move on with my life."

"How do you think that can happen?"

"You're the fucking therapist."
"And you're the patient. You have control, not me."
I laughed.
"Why is that funny?" Esther asked.
"You said I have control."
"That wasn't a joke."
"But it is. It's a total joke."
"Why aren't you in control?"
"Are you seriously asking me this?" She was making me angry.
Esther just looked at me.

My feet dropped to the floor. I stood up. Sat down again. "If I had control, I wouldn't be here. I wouldn't be an addict. Shit, I wouldn't have used at all. Never would've cut myself or had sex for drugs." Stomach acid was rising in my throat. I swallowed. "I wouldn't have given up my virginity to a rapist. I wouldn't have loved him. I wouldn't be afraid of men." Another swallow. "My parents would know how much they hurt me. I'd still be in school. I'd have a life. A boyfriend who respects me." My hands gripped the edge of the couch, trying to settle the chaos in my gut. "I'd respect myself. I'd be happy. Healthy. Free." I closed my eyes. Swallowed again. It wasn't working. I was going to throw up.

"Esther," I croaked before cupping my fingers over my mouth. My stomach lurched. Esther shoved a trash can in my lap.

I puked. A purging of pasts collected in brown and yellow mush. It was disgusting. I wiped my mouth.

"Is it okay to take this away?"
I nodded.
Esther took the trash from me and tied the plastic bag. I couldn't look at her.

"Do you want to postpone the remainder of this session?"
I shook my head and hugged myself again.
"Okay." She put the trash can outside the door. Sat down again. "Tell me how you feel."

I dug a piece of gum from my purse. Shoved it in my mouth. Spread the mint over my tongue. "Like a piece of shit."

Esther picked up her yellow notepad. "Why?"
"Cuz I puked in your office. Can't even control my own fucking body."

"That's not fair. You're attacking yourself with something you have no control over anyway. You didn't throw up on purpose and I'm not upset with you. There's no need for you to be upset with yourself. Okay?"

I shrugged.

"How do you think you lost control in the beginning?"

I shook my head.

"When was the last time you had control?"

"I don't know," I said, still avoiding Esther's eyes. "I don't remember much before we moved."

"Moved?"

"Yeah. My parents had this business that went bad and some guys put a pipe bomb in our window. They threatened to kill my father. So we moved."

"Wow. Okay. How old were you?"

"Seven."

"That's a pretty traumatic experience for a seven year old."

"I guess. I don't like talking about it."

"Tell me why."

"I just don't. Feels like when I do, it's like I'm blaming all the shit in my life on it. Worse things have happened to people. Shit, worse things have happened to me."

"It doesn't demean the experience. You had to deal with something extremely traumatic that probably wasn't handled correctly when it happened. What do you feel when you think of that time of your life?"

"I told you I don't remember. I don't remember anything until we left."

"What do you remember after you left?"

"Him yelling."

"Who?"

"My father."

"When he yelled at you, what would you do?"

"Stand there."

"Would you yell back?"

"No."

"Were you afraid to?"

"Sometimes. But it was more like there was no point. He wouldn't have heard me no matter what I said."

"So your voice was taken away by your father."

I nodded.

"You lost control over your right to speak as the rest of your life was falling apart. Everything you knew was being flipped around and you weren't allowed to express yourself." She stopped and tapped the end of her pen against her lip. "What would you do to repossess your control?"

I thought about it. Saw the images collect behind my eyes. "There was a cupboard where my mom kept bags of chocolate. She would only allow us a piece a week. But sometimes I would sneak in there and eat as much as I could. It was like," I gasped, rather shocked at what I was saying, "it was like I was trying to eat the pain away."

"Escaping in the forbidden," Esther said. "How old were you then?"

"Eight, I think. Eight or nine."

"What else do you remember?"

I couldn't believe I was going to tell her. But I opened my mouth. "I had voices."

Esther raised her eyebrow.

"In my head. I had voices in my head."

"What kind of voices?"

"Nice ones."

Esther chuckled.

"I even named them, though I don't remember what they were anymore. But I remember the types. There was the mother. The angel. There was a child, a rebellious girl. They would comfort me, but they also helped me make decisions. I remember," I was laughing now, "I had this classroom in my head. When I had a problem, I would ask them to vote on it. Whatever suggestion had the most votes, I'd usually do it."

"Why do you think you had this classroom or the voices?" Esther asked.

I shrugged. "To keep me company? I was sad all the time. Felt like I didn't matter. Like no one could see me." I gasped. "They had my control."

Esther nodded. "You gave control to something outside of yourself. Same with the chocolate. It was a defense mechanism."

"Did that with Rick too," I said bitterly. "And all the other fuckheads I was with. Let them have my control. I wish I knew why I did that. It's like they made me feel safe but then they didn't but I was already stuck with them and I didn't know how to let go. I didn't know how to get back that control. Do you think it's because of my father? Because he was the first one who took it away?"

"It's possible," she said. "This is good." Esther looked at her watch. "We still have time. Is it okay if we change the subject a little? I want to get to the point where you used drugs."

"Okay."

"So your life is out of control. You're grasping for something to fix you but at the same time you can't stop giving yourself away."

"So I escape in drugs." I paused. "How is that different than the chocolate?"

"You tell me."

I rolled my eyes. "I don't know. Maybe it isn't." I shook my head. "But it has to be. Chocolate doesn't make you go to a sober house."

"Why do drugs?" Esther asked.

"Because they're addictive. Because they change the way I feel."

Esther nodded. "The term is mind altering substance. Drugs create a different reality. A reality in which you feel control."

"But I wasn't in control."

"Bingo. You found that drugs were controlling you."

"So I freaked out. Right?"

"Right. You did other things to get the control back. You hurt yourself. You put yourself in compromising positions. You starved yourself. All these things are deliberate ways of punishing. Kind of like putting yourself in a corner." Esther shook her head. "Sorry, I'm kind of realizing these things as I say them. Um, your attempts to control even the smallest pieces of your life were getting lost. So you gave up. And that's why you're here."

"Because I gave up? Isn't that accepting defeat?"

"No. It's admitting you don't have control over your life. That's the first step in your program, isn't it?"

"Yes."

"So now it's time to take it back, Lynn. Take back your control."

For some reason that scared me. Being in control. "How do I do that?"

"It's all about the little things. Make small decisions every day and stick with them. Do things because you have made the choice to do it. Take the time to believe in your truths. Take control over yourself. I want you to tell me that you are in control."

"I don't know if I can."

"Lynn. Say it."

"I am in control," I squeaked.

"Say it again. Say it louder."

"I am in control."

"I want you to stand up. I want you to stand up and yell that you are in control."

And I did. I did it without a moment's thought. I stood up and I yelled.

"I AM IN CONTROL!"

And then I smiled.

"I am in control."

My feet bounced back and forth on the carpet.

"I am in control!"

I was jumping. "I am in control! I am in control!"

"Good," Esther clapped, wiping her eyes. "Good. Remember today. Remember how you feel. You can do this. Make a decision and stick with it. Be in control."

I leaned forward and wrapped my arms around Esther's back. "Thank you," I whispered. She returned the hug tightly.

"You're the one doing this," she said as we let go. "I'm just along for the ride."

"Fasten your seatbelt," I told her. "Cuz it's gonna be crazy!"

And as I skipped out of her office, my smile was brighter than it had been in years.

The arcade was busier than I expected when I went into the back to change. Felt like Halloween in the middle of May with my stupid orange shirt. A walking pumpkin. I stuck my tongue out at my reflection, but found myself smiling again. Fucking Esther. I shook my head, the grin still plastered on my face.

It almost felt like I was some kind of human.

I clocked in and opened the employee door. Shiloh was at the other end of the arcade. His back was to me. Even the back of his head was cute. I wanted to touch him. Hug him.

Why not? I laughed inside and half ran to him, throwing my arms around his chest. His fluffy hair tickled my cheek.

"What the?" he choked. He smelled like cinnamon.

Shiloh's eyes smiled when he turned around. When he saw me. I had the strongest urge to kiss him. But I didn't.

"What was that for?" he asked, rubbing the tips of his shoulders.

I shrugged.

He shook his head. "Women." Turned around and walked towards the counter. I was smiling when he turned to look at me. He was smiling too.

"Keep walking," I teased. My feet felt like they were floating.

"Sup sexy?" said a voice behind me. I turned around. It was Shorty, one of the regulars whose real name I didn't know. He was fourteen. Short. Thought he was the coolest guy. I thought he was kind of a moron, but I have to admit there was a soft spot for him. I had a soft spot for all the stupid locals. Damn kids.

"Hi Shorty."

"Hey," he said, looking around. Not that anyone could hear us. We were in an arcade. "You got a smoke?"

I gave him a look.

"Come on."

"Turn eighteen soon," I told him, holding out my pack. He took one. Started taking another. I let him.

"You're the shit."

"You're lucky I'm in a good mood."

"Yeah? You want me to make it better?" He didn't wait for my reply. "Check this out. I know this guy, right? He hooked me up with some bomb ass tweak."

"Shorty."

"It's good shit too. But maybe you smoke dope, I don't know."

"Shorty, I don't do any of that."

"But I got your back girl. Anything you want, I'll get it free."

I think the world crashed into my head.

Anything you want, I'll get it free.

I couldn't breathe.

Anything you want, I'll get it free.

I couldn't move.

Anything you want, I'll get it free.

I just wanted to get high.

"Lynn?" Shorty's voice echoed in my ears.

"I'm gonna get a break," I told him. Walked to the counter. Walked up to Shiloh.

Anything you want, I'll get it free.

"What's wrong?" His face changed when he saw me. I wondered what I looked like.

"I need a cigarette." I tapped my fingernails on the counter. "Can I have a cigarette?"

"You just got here."

"I know." I looked behind me to see if Shorty was still there. He was watching me.

"What's going on?" Shiloh asked.

I turned back towards the counter, but I couldn't meet his eyes. Didn't want to fall apart. Not yet. "Please Shiloh?" I begged. "I just, I need a break. I can't be here right now. I can't."

His eyes softened. He smiled slightly. Nodded.

I ran out the door, pulling Shorty by the arm.

"Where the fuck is it?" I asked, shoving a cigarette in my mouth.

Shorty laughed, lighting one of the smokes I had given him. He lit mine too.

Anything you want, I'll get it free.

I just wanted to get high. Get high. Get high.

Shorty shoved his hand in his pocket. Pulled out a baggie of white shit.

"Give me some." I couldn't stop looking at it. The powder. The high inside the plastic.

Wait.

He unrolled the bag.

What was I doing?

Stuck his finger in it. Rubbed it on the inside of his gums.

I didn't want this.

Held the bag out to me.

I am in control.

I stared at it.

I am in control.

Took a step back.

I am in control.

And another.

"What are you doing?"

Threw my cigarette on the ground and ran. I ran across the street. Started running home.

Stopped.

I just turned down free shit. Turned down as much free shit as I wanted. What the fuck was wrong with me? I hurried back, called Shorty's name.

But he was gone.

Panic now. It skidded through my pores. My veins. I had to have something. Something to take me away.

There was a liquor store down the street. I ran to it. Went inside. Wasn't sure what I was doing. Too young to buy alcohol. Too impatient to find someone to do it for me. Too impatient for anything. Maybe I should run back to the arcade. See if Shorty's friends know where he went. See if they had any shit. Or anyone. It didn't fucking matter anymore.

And then I saw it.

There was a box of caffeine pills hanging above the pain medication. I grabbed them without thinking. Without caring. Bought the pills and two packs of cigarettes. Swallowed with no water.

I smoked outside the store, tapping my foot against the pavement. Started to walk. Walked across the street. The next corner. Found myself in front of FrankZilla's Arcade again.

Shiloh was in there. He didn't see me. I didn't want him to see me. I didn't want anyone to see me. I flicked my cigarette, watching the ashes fall onto the sidewalk. Wondered what to do. Where to go. I had probably lost my job by now. Lost a lot of things.

"Lynn?"

Shit. Elizabeth had come up behind me. I didn't know she was working today.

"Lynn, are you okay?"

I looked at her and let her see me. Let her see my eyes. The fear.

"What happened?"

"I fucked up." I took a drag of my cigarette, letting the nicotine soak into my lungs.

"Did you get high?"

"Yeah."

Elizabeth looked behind her. "Stay here," she told me and walked into the arcade.

I could have run. Ran down the block and to the metro. Ran to see who was there and if I could get shit and get high high high.

But I didn't. I waited. Went to the door and peeked inside. Elizabeth was talking to Shiloh. Her back was to me. Shiloh glanced over her shoulder. He saw me standing there. I hid behind the wall.

"You're coming to my house," Elizabeth announced as she stepped onto the sidewalk.

"What about the arcade?"
"Andrea's coming in a couple hours. It'll be fine."
"Andrea?"
"Another employee. She's been on vacation."
I paused. "Will I get in trouble for this?"
Elizabeth shook her head. "Frank's pretty cool about these things."
"Frank like FrankZilla? He exists?"
"Yeah," Elizabeth laughed. "He's obsessed with Godzilla too."
"Go fucking figure."

Elizabeth lived in an apartment complex a few blocks away. As we walked I could feel the caffeine pill starting to work. It was different than tweak. Not as intense. But the basics were there. The energy surging, veins popping, wanting to talk to move to smoke and talk some more. But I kept my mouth shut and watched the cracks in the sidewalk fly beneath my feet.

I had a memory. Remembered the party at Kat's house and how I tried it for the first time. Remembered walking with Shannon to get smokes. I had watched the sidewalk fly then too. It was so new. So new and so wonderful. I wondered what my life would be like if I hadn't snorted that first line. Who I'd be. It all seemed so long ago. So far away. I was far away.

"I would do this when Patrick was trying to quit. Take him to my house. Give him kava kava to calm his cravings."

"Kava kava?" I was grateful for the break in thought.

"An herbal supplement. Makes you tired, calm."

"Would it work?"

"Not really. He'd always shoot up." She paused. "Or I'd do it for him. I usually did it for him."

I tried to imagine Elizabeth putting a tourniquet around a junkie's arm. Use a syringe. Watch him leave her over and over again.

"Did you ever try it?" I asked.

"Yes. A couple times. But I didn't like it much. I'm not a big fan of drugs."

"You're smart."

"Not really. I had a junkie as a boyfriend." She laughed. "Did you ever do heroine?"

I shook my head. "I like uppers. *Liked* uppers. They made me feel, well, in control." My eyes moistened in my shame. I almost had it. Almost had a grip on my past, on myself. And I lost it again. Lost it in a stupid attempt to get high. Wasn't even the real thing.

"Is that what you're on now?"

"Yeah." One stupid pill. Had to start over, erase my time.

"What'd you take?"

I flicked my cigarette into the street and shoved my hands in my pockets. "A caffeine pill."

Elizabeth stopped walking. "Lynn. That's not a drug."

"It is. It's a narcotic. When my house manager gives me a drug test it will come out positive." Maybe I should get high for real. Go all out.

"I didn't know that."

Give myself a reason to start over.

We got to the front of Elizabeth's apartment. I wasn't ready to go inside. Took out my pack and asked if I could smoke again. She didn't care. So I took out my cigarette and I lit it, trying to calm the antsiness that had pounced onto my mind. Reminded me of those voices I had when I was little. Different parts of me screaming while I attempted to hold on.

There was a part of me that wanted to run. The rebellious girl. She wore her leather jacket and knee high boots and spat and cursed and shook the bars outside her cage. Wanted to get the fuck out and would kill anyone who got in her way. There was a part that just wanted to cry. The child. All alone in the dark, sobbing out the pain, wondering why no one was there to hold her. But the loudest was the part that wanted me to use. It didn't have a face. Just this thing inside of me that clawed the soft parts of my insides, desperate to feed. It felt the rush and the pop and the dilated eyes and it wanted more.

And I was ready to feed it.

"What are you thinking about?"

"Getting high." It came out before I could stop it. I hadn't wanted to tell her.

"Why?"

"Because I already fucked up." I took a bitter drag of my cigarette and wondered why I was still sitting there. I should have found someone by now. "Might as well go out with a bang." Be tweaked out of my brain.

"What can I do to stop you?"

I shrugged.

"I don't want you to get high."

I turned to look at her. Hardened my eyes. "Why the fuck do you care?"

"I told you," she said.

"I'm not Patrick."

"No. You're not." Elizabeth crossed her arms over her chest. Her eyes looked sad. Distant. "When I first met Patrick, he didn't seem like a heroine addict. He was fit, not too skinny. He would make me dinner. Sometimes we'd go to this spot on the cliff, the one that looks over the ocean and the city. It's beautiful. There's a bench there. We'd sit on it and I'd huddle against him to hide from the cold and we'd just talk. He would kiss me on the top of my head cuz my hair was all over my face because of the wind. I thought I loved him. He said he knew I did." She sighed heavily, her memories melting into her pain. "And then he started using in front of me. He'd use in my car, in my house. And I'd clean up after him. I'd take care of him when he was sick and when he wanted to get well. I'd stand there when he'd yell or throw my dishes or pass out in the middle of my driveway. I'd lie to his mother when she asked me where he was. I told her how happy we were, how good he was to me."

"Why did you stay with him?"

Elizabeth shrugged. "I wanted to help him. I wanted to make him better."

"But you can't. He has to do that himself."

"I know that now." Bitterness reeked in her voice.

"What happened?"

"You know how I told you he left me for another girl? How he got her pregnant?"

I nodded.

"He wanted to move to New York because he thought not knowing anyone there would help him stay clean. He said he wanted to get clean so bad. He wanted to be with me. That when he was clean for awhile I could come and visit him. We could be together, like before. But, of course, it didn't work and he ended up getting high. And then he met this other girl. They'd get high together. So when I went to visit him, he told me she was a friend of his sister's. Might really be true, I don't know. I spent time with her when Patrick was working." She made her fingers like quotation marks to emphasize the lie in that last word. "*Working* as in dealing drugs. But I was stupid and didn't see it. So I went home after he picked a fight with me. Of course he had to do it right before I left. He'd always do shit like that. I don't even remember what it was about. After I got home he called me and said he was sorry and that he had something to tell me. I asked what. He said that he was cheating on me with that other girl and now she's pregnant and they're going to have a baby." She snickered lightly.

"At least he can't hurt you anymore."

"I guess." She looked at me. "If you get high, how do you know you'll stop? How do you know you won't end up like Patrick?"

I broke her gaze and lit another cigarette. "I already got high."

"Then why do it again? Why put yourself through all of that? Why hurt the people you love?"

I hadn't thought of that. Of hurting the people I love. Not really. Listening to Elizabeth's story was sad, but it didn't hit me until now.

I *was* Patrick. I burned the people I loved. Told them lies and promised change and danced right through them. I took advantage of their generosity, stole their trust. Like with Elle and Rhiannon and a bunch of other people who I didn't want to begin to think about. I was a horrible, pathetic drug addict and I had thrown my friends and family away. I had thrown them away and I didn't give a fuck. Didn't give a fuck about anything but getting high and staying high and getting high again.

But maybe I could try. Maybe I was tired of hurting the people I loved. Maybe I was tired of hurting myself. Maybe it was time to take control. Take control the real way.

"Can you do me a favor?"

"Depends."

I dug in my purse, searching for the latest means of escape. The box of caffeine pills felt good between my fingers. Comforting.

"Lynn."

"I know," I said. My hands loosened their grip on the last drug I would ever have. "Here. Take these away from me." I put the box on Elizabeth's leg. Looked away.

"I'm proud of you."

"Thanks." Panic whispered nastily in my ear. My head. I shook it, trying to get the thoughts to go away.

"Hey." Elizabeth touched my arm. "Don't think about it. It's done now."

I took a drag of my cigarette. Threw it in the street. Wished I could do that with all the things that hurt. Just throw them away and not look back. Let them be washed by the rain.

I stood up. Fuck the street. I had a home now.

It was then I knew that something inside of me had shifted. Determination to fight. To win. To live. I wanted to find the light again. I was tired of being depressed. Tired of dwelling on my pain. Tired of letting my past carry my present. I wanted to be free this time, to fly beyond those pink clouds and purple skies I knew so long ago. Surpass that innocence that dragged me inside my Hell. I wanted to grow. I wanted to change. And this time, I was going to do it sober. It was time to take control, to kill those damn shadows that danced inside my cell. I had to find my light. Find my window. I had to face myself.

The girl inside my head opened her eyes.

May 15th

Addiction. An undertow constantly hammering our souls, waiting for that one rocky moment to drag us down. It's always there. Watching...waiting...I don't know why it's there, but that addiction was inbred long before the drugs. A disease burrowed inside. I can't stop thinking about that.

For the first time I'm sad about what I've put myself through. For so long I've bottled up all this shit. So fucking long. Now I just want to curl into a ball and cry. Let it all out. My head's going off again. I'm stuck between addiction and recovery. I guess I just need to ride it out. NOT hide. Feel it. Live through it. Heal.

SIXTEEN

The problem with admitting defeat is that it requires starting over. It's admitting to myself and everyone else that yes, I fucked up. I fucked up big time. But I was back and ready to try again.

If only it was that easy.

"You're out of here if you do this again," Gina announced to me in the bathroom as she held up my urine test. It was positive, though for what I don't remember. It doesn't really matter.

"Yes it does," Kiki told me on the way to my first meeting since swallowing that pill. "You took a caffeine pill. It's not like you were smoking crack."

"It's still getting high," Veronica said.

"But it's different. Lynn only took one pill." She turned to look at me. "Do you have any idea how strong you are?"

I didn't have a chance to answer. We had entered the realm of pre-meeting gossip. Everyone mingled on the deck with cigarettes in hand, discussing who was back, who was still high, and how many meetings they were going to. It was the same people, the same conversations, the same place I went to every day…but it felt different. I was different. I wondered if people could see it.

"Lynn." It was Natalie. "I'm glad you called me. Did you get my message?"

I stared at the ground. "Yeah."

"We should meet. Can we do that? I want to talk to you about, well." Natalie looked around cautiously. Someone was always listening here. "What you called me for. I'll call you later to set up a time."

"Sure."

"Oh, and when we say the serenity prayer tonight? Think about the words. It'll help."

I wanted to disappear.

We sat at our table. I closed my ears to the giggling of Veronica and Kiki and waited for the serenity prayer. Waited to hear the calm I craved.

God,

I closed my eyes.

grant me the serenity

Serenity. Quiet. Alone. Safe.

to accept the things I cannot change,

I saw myself inside my cell. I saw the girl.

the courage to change the things I can,

She was staring at the wall. No, it was a window. There was a window inside my cell.

and the wisdom

I wanted her to stand up. To go to the window. To look at the beauty outside.

to know

But she just sat there. Just sat there staring.

the difference.

And I didn't know why. There was my past, my addiction, my pain. All these things were permanent, a part of me and my life. They created the place in my head. My own asylum. But what I did there, whether I sat in my cell or tried to get out, to move forward, to fly…that was a choice.

And I was sitting there.

Kiki tapped me on the shoulder. I looked at her. "I know this guy." She pointed to the man at the front table. The man who was supposed to tell us his story. "He was clean for, like, fifteen years. And then he went out."

After fifteen years? How is that possible? How can someone give up fifteen years of time to get high? I stared harder, searching for a truth. A reason. He was older. Maybe mid-fifties. Tall. He had such a sad look in his eyes. I wanted to hug him and run from him at the same time.

"What'd he relapse on?"

Kiki shook her head. "Dunno. But his name is Danny."

"Hi Danny," I whispered.

"Is there anyone here with less than thirty days of sobriety?" Gina asked from the front of the room. Of course it was Gina who was secretary of this meeting, and her eyes shot flaming daggers at me. I was supposed to be raising my hand.

Veronica shoved her elbow into my stomach.

"Ow!" I winced, attempting a furious glare.

"Don't give a fuck what they think," she whispered. "You can do this."

I smiled slightly. Lowered my eyes and raised my hand. "I'm Lynn. I have one day clean today."

"Welcome back," Gina grinned. She clapped her hands. Others followed. I couldn't look at anything but the cracks on the top of the table.

"I hate this," I pouted.

"That's why some don't come back," Kiki said. "Cuz they're scared to say they fucked up."

I tried to pretend I didn't care.

Danny's turn to speak. His voice was shakier than I expected. Shaky and dry. He began with the usual drama of getting into his drug of choice. (Saying specific drugs were thought to torment the addicts involved. Not many want to hear about smoking crack and shooting heroine when they're trying so hard to bleach it from their brains.) He told us how he couldn't stop, went in and out of the program. The usual. And then he got clean and stayed clean. He stayed clean for fifteen years and has a wife and two kids and all is good with the world. Woo hee hah.

"It was my wife Kristine and my anniversary. She wanted to go out to some fancy restaurant. Celebrate us. We were sitting there and the sun was setting and she looked so beautiful that when she ordered a glass of champagne I thought what the hell? Fifteen years sober, one drink ain't shit." He pinched his lips together. Sighed. "But that was all it took. Soon as the drink touched my lips, this switch went off. Drank the whole fucking bottle. Drank ten bottles. And then I was back on the streets, doing the same shit I swore I'd never do again. Off of one fucking drink with my goddam wife on our anniversary." He shook his head. Most of the addicts in the room were shaking theirs as well. All I could do was stare. "I got almost eleven months now." Applause and cheering. "But every day I think about what I lost. How good I had it. How I can never take back that time. My kids have seen me loaded. They've seen my demons now. God it makes me fucking pissed." He scrunched his fist together until the skin around his knuckles turned white. Sighed again "Go to meetings. I know people say this all the time and you get tired of hearing the same shit over and over but it's true. Follow the program. You don't wanna end up like me. Work the steps. Call your sponsor. Don't go out for one stupid ass drink."

The applause was deafening. Some people stood up. I went outside to smoke.

The meeting was over.

Kiki, Veronica and I sat on the porch of the Coral House blowing smoke bubbles into the stars. A smoke bubble is made by inhaling a cigarette and blowing the smoke into a bubble. Hence the name smoke bubbles. I loved it.

My hands touched the sticky soap as I dipped the bubble stick into the bottle. Let it drip. Took a drag of my cigarette. Held it. Put the bubble stick up to my mouth and, as slowly as I could, blew. A circle of smoky rainbows swirled playfully above my head. Another small one behind it. They danced in the wind of the night, their colors melting in and out of clouds.

And then they popped. A poof of smoke lingered beneath the mist of the bubbles, and it was gone. I wanted the color back. Dance in it. Too bad it would only last a moment.

Is that how I felt? Like a bubble that breaks so I might as well hide until I break too?

"Why are you so quiet?" Kiki asked, dissolving the thoughts inside my head.

"Watching the bubbles," I told her truthfully. She didn't believe me.

"You're thinking about Danny, huh?"

I didn't answer. Maybe she'd forget about it.

"I'd be upset if I were you. Even though you shouldn't be. You didn't wait fifteen years to fuck up."

"She got it out of the way?" Veronica laughed. "That's great, Kik."

"It's true. And now you know you can come back." Kiki smiled at me. "You can start over."

"Not that I want to." I sighed. "I guess you're right. I just hate failing."

"You didn't fail," Veronica said. "You just fucked up for a minute. It's not permanent. You can start over."

"I don't wanna fuck up again," I said through a drag of my cigarette. I blew another smoke bubble. Veronica poked it with the tip of her finger. It popped. I looked at her thoughtfully. "How have you stayed clean so long? What's your reason?"

Kiki stopped mid-drag.

Veronica's eyes hardened. "I haven't told anyone so don't say anything."

We nodded.

"I'm pregnant."

Kiki gasped. "I can't believe you didn't tell me! Why didn't you tell me?"

"I don't know if I'm going to keep it yet. But I'm not having a crack baby."

"How far along are you?" I asked.

"Almost six weeks."

"You're running out of time," Kiki told her.

"Shut up. I know."

"I'm glad you told me," I smiled.

Veronica shrugged. "Was gonna have to tell you eventually."

Silence. Awkward silence. I took a drag of my cigarette. Looked at Kiki.

"What about you, Kiki?" I asked. "What's your reason?"

She tapped her fingers against her jeans. Stared at the fence above us. We waited.

"I guess I was tired of how I used to live. I mean, I wouldn't be alive if I didn't get clean." She exhaled a shaky stream of smoke. "I'd be tweaking so long that when I passed out, I slept for days. I really mean days. I would have to pee and wouldn't wake up. Have to shit and I wouldn't wake up. My boyfriend had to clean me off, give me a bath and I was still asleep."

Memory. I was on the bathroom floor. Angie was shaking me. I looked at her. Followed her gaze. The floor around me was wet. It smelled like urine. She said I had pee'd on myself. Helped me clean it up. Set up some lines and got high again.

"One time I was so skinny and so loaded and I hadn't eaten anything in I don't even remember how long that I passed out. I woke up in the hospital with some stranger sitting next to me. Told me he found me with a bloody nose. They called my mom and she cried so bad when I told her why I was there. She took me to rehab. I left. Went back again. Left. But one day I just got sick of it all. I went to rehab myself. Changed my mind after a week and came here. It feels safer here, I think." She shrugged. "I guess I stay clean cuz that's all I have. Everything else was taken by drugs. You know?"

"Yeah, Kiki. We know."

Two days clean.

Esther Agnes-Robbins crossed her legs and bounced her foot against her calf. She was waiting for me to say something. But my throat was dry. I couldn't talk about my relapse anymore. Relapse. That word made me sick.

"What are you thinking about?" Esther asked.

I twirled a piece of hair between my fingers. "How I'm tired of talking. I want to get better before I can fuck it up again."

"You were protecting yourself, remember? We talked about this."

"Yeah, I still think it's bullshit. I could have told someone or ran home or something. Something besides taking that fucking pill."

"You could have, but you didn't. You have to accept the mistake and do something about it. That's how you get better. You talk about your mistakes. Your fears. Your shame. Let go of the negativity and trust yourself. Otherwise all the crap inside of you just sits there, and we know what happens when it sits there."

"I run," I said in a cynical sort of way. "I use and I hide and I hurt myself." I put the piece of hair in my mouth, tasting the residue of cigarette smoke and hair spray. "It's the same thing over and over. I want it to stop. I want to be in control."

"You what?"

"I *am* in control," I corrected myself. Esther nodded. "And, um, I think I should meet with my parents. Soon, like before I have thirty days. I want to fix this. I want to fix it before I can fuck up again."

"Okay."

I couldn't believe she was going along with this. This was Esther, the one who had a poster that said *step cautiously and life will follow* on her wall.

"But you have to set it up."

I laughed unevenly. "That'll be fun."

"There are other things you can do to stay clean," she said, bluntly ignoring what I had said. And then she stopped talking and waited for me to participate. But I was still thinking about my parents. My father's veins popping in his neck. The way my mother's eyes quivered before she cried.

"Focus on what your program has to offer."

How I disappointed them. Hurt them. Lashed out my pain as loud as I could.

"Use what's available to you instead of letting it fall in your lap."

How they didn't hear me. Didn't stop me from falling.

"If you use it, you're actively changing your life."

And they were going to be here, sitting across from me. I tried to picture them watching us now.

"It'll make you feel so much better."

Fuck.

"Lynn, do you hear what I'm saying?"

I nodded slowly. "I've got to focus. I can do that."

Silence. I couldn't stop thinking about my parents. How much I wanted to tell them. How much I wanted to run. I knew I had to do it. Maybe I should do it now, before I changed my mind. "Fuck it," I said and shoved my hand in my purse.

"What are you doing?" Esther asked. I didn't answer. Where was my phone? "Should I be concerned?"

"I don't know," I breathed, pulling my cell phone out of my purse. Esther sighed. I dialed my home number quickly. They weren't home. I left a message asking them to call me about a session. Maybe they could come in a few weeks. That it was important for my recovery. I told them I loved them. Hung up.

"Congratulations," Esther smiled. I smiled back. We hugged.

"This is scaring the shit out of me," I said.

"It should. If it didn't, I'd be worried."

"Oh. That's great. Thanks."

Waiting for the bus again. Stared at FZ's across the street. Maybe if I squinted I could see Shiloh in there. I wanted to see him. To feel his fluffy hair against my skin. I wanted to tell him I was sorry.

My phone rang. It was my mother. She had just gotten home. Said she'd heard the message and it would be fine. We decided a session in three weeks exactly. Three weeks exactly. The words were spinning in my head.

"This is good, Lynn," my mother was still talking. I wanted her to stop. "I'm glad you're doing this. I'm glad you called."

"Me too, Mom. I've gotta go, okay? We'll talk soon."

"Okay honey. Love you."

"Love you too."

We hung up. My hands shook a little. I breathed. Started to take out a cigarette. Stopped. And then I was walking towards the arcade. Running. If I could I would fly.

Shiloh saw me stumbling through the door. Watched as I almost fell. Caught myself on a game and propped myself up again. I looked at him. Our eyes connected, flooding my head with heat. I could feel the red against my cheeks. Shiloh's cheeks were red too.

I walked up to him, my hands shoved inside my pockets. His face looked so soft. Concerned. I wanted to cry.

"I'm sorry," I whispered, tilting my head towards the floor. His fingers cupped the edge of my chin, pulling my face gently up to his. His breath was warm.

"What happened?" he asked with a tenderness I had never heard.

It was his voice that broke me. It had a warmth that melted the fear and shame and panic in my heart and I couldn't stop the tears from falling. So desperate to be okay. He smiled through my blurred eyes and wrapped his arms around me. I buried my face in his chest and sobbed.

His lips brushed the wetness on my cheek. It was so fast I wondered if it had even happened. If he had really kissed me.

"It's okay," he whispered, hugging my body tighter into his. "It's okay."

Three days clean.

I was ready to do this. Ready to heal and move on. I took Esther Agnes-Robbin's advice and threw myself into the program. Stopped trying to do everything on my own.

Five days clean.

I had to do Step One again. Had to admit, honestly admit, that my life was unmanageable. I was told I had to let go. Believe in something greater than myself. Natalie said that the idea of spirituality was the biggest problem for most addicts. But it was also the key to success in recovery.

"But I have spirituality," I told her. "I'm Jewish. We pray and have holidays and stuff."

Natalie laughed. "Sorry," she told me. "You're funny. Listen Lynn, just because you have a religion doesn't mean you're spiritual. Spirituality means letting your life open up to something beyond you. We as addicts try to hold on to our disease because it's what we know. It's how we attempt to control our lives. But that's our problem. Control. We have to let go."

"But I was told I have control."

Natalie smiled. "You do have control. You have control over whether or not you use today. If you go to meetings. What you eat. Who you talk to. But you do not have control over your addiction, over whatever it is that makes you use. It's like there's this battle inside of you. You fight to control your using or you break and the drugs win. Surrendering to spirituality is another option. It's letting go of the past. Of the battle inside."

"That's not true. If I stop fighting, the drugs *do* win."

"No, Lynn. There doesn't have to be a battle at all. The minute you surrender, you admit you can't control using the drugs. Then you don't have to fight to stop using. You just let go and never have to use again."

I shook my head.

"Do you believe in something greater than you?"

I thought about it. Tried to remember what I believed in. But I couldn't. It was all just so dark.

"Try. Tell me some things that are bigger than you. Things you can't control."

"I don't know." Pause. "Earthquakes. The ocean. Time."

"That's a good start," Natalie said, nodding her head in approval. "Think about it. It'll come to you."

So I tried. I tried to surrender myself to the sky and the trees and the little ants next to our ashtray, but I still craved the drugs. Craved the escape more than anything in the world. I wanted to give up so badly to whatever was out there, but I didn't know how. I was too afraid.

Nine days clean.

Gina suggested I try writing. She bought me a notebook and a pen and told me to write my thoughts every day. The darker ones that clung to the parts of my mind I tried not to see. I told her I had a journal that I barely wrote in. That I hadn't really written anything in a long time. That I lost it after I started using.

"You can't lose writing. You just stopped for awhile."

"But what if I suck? What if the best of me got lost when I did?"

She shook her head and told me to just do it. Just put down words, and eventually the words would flow into emotions and thoughts and they'd be on the paper instead of in me.

Esther thought it was a brilliant idea. She told me that addiction thrived on the anger and pain and self-loathing inside of me. Addicts breathe negativity. I had to get out of mine. So I went somewhere happy-like and pretended to write. I usually ended up drawing pictures of girls with dark eyes smoking cigarettes and looking angry, but once in awhile an idea would spark. Once in awhile it felt like I was me again. It was those times I felt something. Like a piece of my cell wall chipping away.

Fourteen days clean.

Maybe I could let it all go. Maybe I could let go without falling down.

Fifteen days clean.

Maybe not.

When I told Natalie I hadn't found the powers beyond to surrender to, she said I should speak in a meeting. I laughed. She was serious. I laughed again.

The only thing I had ever said in a meeting was my name and that I was an addict with however many days clean. Obviously, that hadn't worked very well. Yet the thought of letting my darkness out into a room full of strangers was completely terrifying. I didn't want to do it.

I told Kiki and Veronica, who would probably tell me Natalie was nuts and it didn't matter. I mean, they didn't care about meetings at all.

But they agreed with Natalie.

"Why?" I asked them.

"Cuz you can't just sit there. It's doesn't work like that."

"You have to speak out."

I didn't understand. "But you guys just talk shit the whole time."

"Yeah," Veronica laughed. "But we listen when it's important. I hate meetings, but I go because it keeps me sober. And when I feel like using, I talk about it."

"The meeting tonight," Kiki gave me her squinted look, "you're talking."

I bit the tip of my thumbnail off.

Wednesday night meetings were different than others. We called them step meetings. Whoever remembered brought their blue books and green books and we sat around and discussed one of the steps or the traditions in our program.

"So what do you think the meeting's on?" I asked Veronica while we smoked out front in an attempt to delay going in.

"I don't know."

"You're talking no matter what," Kiki reminded me. I stuck my tongue out. She did the same.

"How old are you, like four?" Veronica shook her head.

Kiki and I smiled. Felt like a normal meeting for a moment. Maybe I should run away now. Veronica twisted the end of her cigarette so the cherry fell to the floor. Threw the butt over the fence.

"Let's go."

I took one last drag and followed.

This meeting was set up more like a living room than a lecture hall. There were couches and rugs and a bookshelf in the back. The couches were all taken, so the three of us settled on the floor. I scrunched my knees in as tight as they would go. Waited.

God, grant me the serenity to accept the things I cannot change, the courage to change the things I can, and the wisdom to know the difference.

"Welcome to the Wednesday step meeting," a red head told the room. "Tonight we'll be discussing Step Three." I laughed. The red-head glared.

"Sorry," I mumbled. But I couldn't help it. Out of all the steps and all the meetings, why did this one have to be about letting go?

"Are there any newcomers here before we begin?"

"Lynn, addict." I was getting tired of announcing myself that way.

"Welcome." A few others raised their hands. Applause followed. When everyone was silent, the red-head began the discussion by introducing the two books on her lap. She called them our Literature. Told us how important it is to know what the books say. How important it is to understand the program. So we went around the room and took turns reciting from the book with the green cover.

It Works: How and Why, page 26:

"The decision we make in Step Three requires that we move away from our self-will."

"Self-will is composed of such characteristics as closed-mindedness, unwillingness, self-centeredness and outright defiance. Our self-centered obsession and its accompanying insanity have made our lives unmanageable."

"Acting on our self-will has kept us trapped in a continuous cycle of fear and pain. We wore ourselves out in fruitless attempts to control everyone and everything."

"We couldn't just allow events to happen. We were always on the lookout for ways we could force things to go as we wanted."

"I think whoever wrote this knew my name," I whispered to Veronica.

"Mine too."

"Ssh!" Some old lady hushed us from the rocking chair by my foot. I had an urge to tip it over.

"In working Step Three, we begin to learn how to stop struggling."

"Turning our will and our lives over to the care of our Higher Power provides a solution to the problems created by a life based in self-will, resentment, and control."

"We can cease questioning why painful things happen and trust that walking through the difficult times in our lives can strengthen our recovery."

"Where once we focused only on not using, we now can appreciate the many things that make our lives so valuable."

"The Third Step is our commitment to our own emotional, physical, and spiritual well-being."

Hallelujah.

And so the reading went on. We talked about different ways of letting go. How easier life becomes once one begins to ask a Higher Power for guidance.

"What am I supposed to say?" I whispered. Kiki shrugged. I thought about it. Tried to remember what I believed in. If whatever it was had helped me get clean, or if that was just me. If there was a Higher Power, why would it want me to go through this anyway? I was the one who put myself through it. I was the one who used. I was the one who would pull myself out.

Or maybe I couldn't. Maybe I had to ask for help. I remembered my discussion with Esther, how I had used drugs as an attempt to fix whatever was inside. I hurt myself to fix myself. Maybe I had to use drugs and get addicted to find some way to stop the pain. Maybe this was my only way out.

Fuck it. I was tired of hurting. There was a lull in the conversation. A silence. Deep breaths.

I told them how much I had been wanting to let go lately. That the thought of just closing my eyes and having all the burdens and pain and fear disappear kept me trying.

"Maybe I want to let go so badly it keeps me from doing it." I stopped. No one spoke. "I relapsed almost three weeks ago. I relapsed on a fucking caffeine pill when I had 28 days clean. I was so close to getting that thirty day chip. It pisses me off. And I know that if I had just told someone or had gone home…if I had let someone else help me say 'no' to that stupid tweak, I wouldn't have relapsed. But I couldn't give up my control. It's this cycle. I want control so I use and then I fuck it up so I try to make it better and I know this Higher Power thing will help but I just can't do it."

"Yes you can," said the red head. "Keep working the steps. You'll do it."

Kiki and Veronica stared at me with their mouths half open. I laughed and covered my mouth before the old lady shushed me again.

"Wanna smoke?" Kiki whispered. Veronica nodded. The two of them got up. Veronica motioned me to go with them. I shook my head.

"Are you sure?" Kiki mouthed. I nodded. For once I figured I should pay attention. The two of them went outside, and I was left alone with thoughts of something beyond myself.

Twenty-one days clean.

My parents were coming. They were coming any second. I smoked, cleaned my room, smoked, ate, smoked, showered so my parents wouldn't smell the smoke, and then I waited. Remember how much waiting sucks? Waiting for parents to arrive for a therapy session is pretty close to the shittiest waiting I've ever done. I wouldn't recommend it. I attempted to watch some reality show but I couldn't pay attention because my fucking parents were having therapy with me today. Today. Therapy. With me, in the same room. I just wanted to smoke but I couldn't because then they'd smell me and couldn't they just show up already?

The doorbell rang.

I couldn't move to answer it. My brain was frozen.

"Lynn! Get the door." Veronica called from somewhere in the kitchen. "Quit stalling."

Went to the door. Fingers on the knob. Twist. Pull.

"Hi Lynn," they greeted, smiling faces and all.

"Hi."

Awkward silence.

"Can we come in?"

"Oh. Yeah." I went back inside. "Man in the house!" I yelled to whoever was home.

My father laughed.

I showed them my room, which they hadn't seen since they dropped off my shit almost two months ago. They liked it. Thought I did a good job.

"Show us the rest of the house," my mother said.

"You've seen it before."

"I know, but still. It's been a long time."

Gave them the five second grand tour. They said hi to my housemates. I wanted to leave.

"We should go," I told them after a whole ten minutes of them wandering around. There wasn't much nail for biting left. I needed to find a new nervous habit.

They drove to Esther's office. We climbed the stairs. Walked down the hallway. The door, as always, was open. I stopped.

Esther stood up. "Hi," she said softly.

My parents half pushed me into the room.

"You must be Esther Agnes-Robbins," my father said. They shook hands. So did my mother.

"Have a seat."

My parents took the couch I usually sat on. Esther pulled a chair out for me. I put it by the door. Safer there.

"It's fantastic to meet you," Esther grinned.

My hands were shaking. I was shaking. Shaking shaking shaking.

"So where should we begin?"

"I'd like to say something," my mother said. She paused, picking the dirt from her fingernails. So that's where I got that from. "I'd like to apologize to you, Lynn." I looked at her. Looked at the sadness in her eyes. The shakiness in her voice. "I should have been there when you were going through this. I'm your mother, and…" She stopped. She stopped because the shakiness had turned to tears and she couldn't speak through them. My father held her hand.

"You don't have to be sorry for anything," I told her. "I was the one who got high."

"But it shouldn't have reached that point." Her breath hiccupped. "I should have seen it. *We* should have seen it." She looked at my father. "We should have been there."

"We all should have done a lot of things," I said.

My mother didn't say anything. The tension was starting to grow. It was gnawing the air away. I pulled on a piece of my hair.

"I think the thing we need to do," Esther began in her gentle voice, "is help Lynn find some of the roots of her using. I've been telling her a lot of her issues began in her childhood. Lynn, why don't you begin by telling your parents when you first felt the need to escape."

"Okay." I was still shaking. Tried to forget they were there. This was just another session. "Um." But their presence clung to my skin. This was absolutely terrifying. "The only thing I can think of is when my dad yelled." I couldn't look at his face. I didn't want to see the hurt.

"How did his yelling make you feel?"

"Small."

"Small?" my father asked. "Why did it make you feel small?"

"Well she was small, honey," my mother said. "You were this big guy screaming at her."

"I didn't scream."

I thought my mother's eyes were going to pop out of her skull. "You didn't scream? What, were you there?"

"I yelled sometimes, maybe, but I don't think it was that bad."

I shook my head. "I can't believe you said that." My voice was cold. Numb. "You screamed at me all the time."

"But I would come in later to apologize and you said it was okay and we hugged and then we moved on."

"You moved on."

"What, you were still angry?"

"Yes."

"Then why didn't you say something?"

"Because I couldn't do anything!" I dug my nails into my thighs. He was making me angry. "I couldn't yell back. I couldn't tell you how I felt. I definitely couldn't tell you I wasn't ready for your apology."

"Why not?"

"Because you wouldn't let me. If I yelled back, you'd yell more. If I told you how I felt, you'd yell more. If I said I wasn't ready to forgive you, you'd scream at me. And then you'd come back and say you were sorry again and I was tired of it so I just told you I was sorry so you'd leave me alone."

"Maybe that's why you have such problems with dealing," my mother said. It sounded like she was trying to make a joke. Trying to make it less painful. "Because I know that's not your best quality."

I didn't think it was funny.

"Is that why you used drugs?" my mother asked. "Because you couldn't deal with things?"

"One of the reasons."

"What were some of the others?"

"Well why did *you* use drugs?" I spat.

My mother blinked. I guess she didn't expect that. "Because they felt good. Because they felt better than everything else."

"Why would I be different? I wanted to escape the shit inside."

"But why was there so much shit, Lynn? What were you escaping from?"

I laughed because I couldn't cry. "I can't believe you don't know this! You were there too. You saw it. You saw him yell and you just stood there."

"I was scared out of my mind." Tears were falling down her cheeks. "I thought about taking you girls and leaving. I thought about divorce. I didn't know what to do to protect you."

"I was *not* that bad!" my father yelled. His face was turning red.

"You were bad enough to make our daughter want to use drugs."

"Hey! This is *not* all my fault!" He slammed his fist against the couch. It made a loud thunk. "I was working twelve fucking hours a day trying to put our family back together. We lost everything, Lynn. You are not the only person in the family here, okay?" He swallowed. "I was scared too."

"I know you were," I said quietly. My father stopped screaming to look at me. "I know you did the best you could. Mom did too. But I think," I licked my lips, choosing my words carefully, "I think that everything was just so hard and stressful that you couldn't see what you were doing. You couldn't see the effect it had on me. Both of you."

They were silent. I continued.

"I don't think I was seen. I don't think I was heard. That's what I meant by small. I felt like I couldn't say anything. I couldn't defend myself. I remember one time in eighth grade when I was on the phone with Danielle. My phone curfew was 9:00. It was 8:45 and Dad was yelling at me to get off the phone. He was tired and not in the mood and he didn't care what the rule was."

"But—"

"Let her talk."

"I talked to you about it later. I said that I didn't like you changing the rules depending on how you felt. I didn't care what time I had to stop talking on the phone, I just wanted one time. I wanted consistency. You acted like you understood me. Like you heard me. But it happened again a few days later."

"Well, I'm sorry," my father blurted out. "What does this have to do with you using drugs?"

I sighed. Dammit, I wanted a cigarette. I tapped my fingers against the tips of my knees. "I couldn't be myself around you. I had to cater to what you wanted. Everything was how you felt and what you needed and whether or not you were in a good mood and if you were going to yell at me and I couldn't handle it. I had to hide myself from you." I stopped, realizing this for the first time. "I wore a mask. And the more I wore it, the more everything inside got taken away. I felt numb. I felt hurt. And I didn't know how to deal with it except hide it. So I tried other things to make the pain go away. That's why I was never home. That's why I picked the friends I did. I felt like I couldn't breathe around you. I couldn't be home because I couldn't be me. I couldn't feel. I wanted to explode. My friends made me feel better. The drugs made me feel better. I would sneak out of the house last summer—"

"You did what?" That was my father.

"—because I couldn't even stand being there when everyone was sleeping. I hated it."

"I knew that. I knew you were sneaking out," my mother half whispered.

"You did?" my father bellowed again.

"You did?" I repeated. "You knew and you didn't do anything?"

"What could I do?" my mother asked me. "What could I have said? Would anything I have done made you stop?"

"Probably not. But you could have tried!"

"What would be the point? I knew how far gone you were. I knew you didn't give a shit and that you would just do it anyway."

"Funny. That's how I felt about you."

Silence.

I looked at Esther. She was smiling at me. Her eyes were proud and all that bullshit and that was great and fine for her but I felt like screaming. "This isn't getting anywhere," I told her.

"What do you mean?"

"We're just going around in circles and placing pain on each other and that's not what I want. It's not helping."

"You don't think this is good?"

"I think it's good to realize these things but it just brings me back and I don't want to be there anymore." My eyes were watering. I wanted to run. To run and run and not look back.

"What would you like to happen?"

I forced myself to look at my parents. To see them. Their eyes were hurt too. I didn't want them to hurt anymore. I hated our pain. "I want a relationship with you. A real one. I want to hug you and feel safe and loved." Tears burned my eyes. I looked away. Wasn't ready for them to see me cry. "I want to feel wanted. I want to get excited about telling you things. I want you to understand me. I want to be around you and feel happy instead of counting down the hours when I can get away." Something touched my hand. It was my mother. Her hand was on my hand. She was squeezing it. "And this is my fault too. I mean, I've closed myself to you. I know that. I…I want you to be a part of my life again."

"Then let us honey," she sniffed, using her other hand to wipe the tears from her face. "Let us in and we'll try together."

"I don't know how."

"That's why I'm here," Esther said, blotting her own nose with a tissue. She passed the box to me. "That's what recovery is about."

"What do I do now?"

Esther took the hand that wasn't attached to my mother's. She guided me off of the chair I was in. Took me in front of my parents. Placed my free hand inside my father's. He squeezed it gently and smiled. It was real. I smiled back. Esther moved my chair. I sat down and we became a unit of three.

"You are together." Esther's voice was soft. Soft like the atmosphere in the room. The way I felt. Soft. "I want you to see yourselves now. Feel it. You can work together and heal the pain. Heal the past. Remember how willing you are. That there are wounds but they can and will go away. You can do this. I want each of you to say a goal. Something small that you'd like to happen from all of this. Lynn, you go first."

I closed my eyes. "I want to feel calm around my parents. I want to be able to breathe and enjoy spending the time we have together."

My mother spoke next. "I want to have more of a connection with my daughter. I want to know more of her life and know she is comfortable around me. I want to be more open and understanding with her and what she's going through."

It was my father's turn. I could hear him breathing. "I want us to have a better relationship. I want her to understand where I'm coming from and I'll do what I can to understand her. I want to do more things with her. Talk to her. Know what she thinks about things."

I opened my eyes. Their eyes were closed. I smiled. Seeing them there with such willingness in their hearts made me feel special. Hopeful. Normal. I wanted this to work. It was going to be hard and painful, but I wanted to get my parents back. I wanted to be their little girl again.

And as they opened their eyes, I turned around and fell into their laps. Their arms closed around me. They kissed the dried tears on my cheeks and held me close to them. I felt their love. It was real. My parents weren't perfect but they were here holding me and I was okay.

It was all going to be okay.

June 5th

Everything I did was based around drugs. That's pretty much it. I wasn't in control of what I did, where I went, who I talked to...the addiction was. It's weird. I've never fully realized that until now. I never saw how much control the drugs really had over me. To think how much control I've lost...that I never really had it to begin with. As soon as I took that first hit, all was taken away from me, and I disappeared.

I want myself back. I'm tired of being locked up. Tired of the struggle, of the pain. Tired of being immersed in darkness and enjoying it. Not wanting to feel. Running with no destination. Using everything—body, mind, soul, family, strangers...whoever, to get away. Being empty. Throwing away dreams, away life. I'm tired of being afraid, of hiding, of sitting in the dark and waiting for some knight in shining armor to take me away. It's time to pick my ass up. No more darkness; it's the end of the road. The light is there, and I want to fucking reach it. It's time...

SEVENTEEN

Twenty-two days clean.

We were standing outside of the Coral House. My mother, father, myself. All of us. Together. At the same time. I looked back at the house and wanted to go inside. Wanted to slip away for awhile. My parents had been kind enough to let me stay there last night. Not that I was allowed to stay at their hotel overnight, but they didn't even ask me to. They knew when it was time to stop pushing. It gave me a chance to smoke. Breathe. Think. Then they came back and took me out to breakfast. We didn't talk about much, but the silence was almost comforting. It was calm. Understanding. Not the overbearing tension I had grown accustomed to.

And now my parents were leaving. They hadn't planned on staying more than two days.

"I wish we could, honey." My mother smiled slightly.

"It's okay." I sighed. "I think we could all use a break. Think about things, you know?" And sleep. I was exhausted despite the three cups of coffee I had a few hours ago. All of the truth, the past, the anxiety and pain we drank yesterday was still running through me. Falling into the soft pillows on my bed sounded very nice.

"Did you ever talk to the academic advisor?" my father asked.

Shit.

"Lawrence!" my mother yelled, slapping my father lightly in the arm.

"What?"

"We're not supposed to nag her about this. We have to be there when she asks us to and that's it."

Wow. Unexpected. I touched my mother's shoulder. "It's okay. I'm, um," I stared at the ground. "I'm kind of glad you asked." I didn't say anything else.

"Well did you?" my father wondered.

"No."

"Lynn!"

"I know, I know." I forced myself to look at them. "I'm scared to." I bit my thumb nail.

"Honey." My mother's voice was soft. "You've done all this and you're afraid to talk to an academic advisor?"

I nodded.

"Why?"

"What if it's too late? What if I already failed?" The nail was jagged. A piece came off in my mouth. I put it in my pocket.

"You don't know unless you ask."

"And if you already failed, we'll deal with it. It's not the end of the world." My father's words. I could have kissed him.

"Thank you," I said.

My eyes looked into theirs. I saw the pain, the hurt, the sadness. But I also saw something new. Concern. Willingness. Patience. They wanted to help me. Genuinely help me. And I actually wanted them to. Even needed them to. I remembered that feeling before, how I had buried it under the rocks of crystal meth. Maybe this time I could let them help me. Let them in.

I crossed my arms and dug my shoes into the sidewalk. Stopped. Showed them my eyes so they could see behind my mask. "Would you come with me? To see her?"

"Now?" they asked.

"Now."

My parents looked at each other. I wondered if it was too much. They had changed their plans for me so many times already. I tried to read them but couldn't. My mother's eyes were watering again.

"Why are you crying?" I asked her.

"Oh Lynn," she sighed, throwing her arms around me. She squeezed tightly, almost too tightly. I put my arms around her and tried to feel okay. There was panic. Anxiety. The desire to forget everything and run inside the house. Run away from them.

But I held on.

My mother pulled away. "Of course we'll go. I'm just," her voice trembled, "I'm just happy you're here. That you're back."

"You know," I said, looking into her eyes. "I never really left."

She laughed at me.

I had never met the academic advisor, though I'd heard her name floating around our college a few times. Sue Benson. I didn't know if she'd be there. I hoped she would. She should be. It was a Tuesday.

Holy fuck. I gripped the edge of my seat. It was a Tuesday on campus the last week before finals and I was going there like the stupid moron I was. Dammit, why did I have to be such an idiot?

"You okay honey?" my mother asked. I could see her eyes in the rear view mirror.

"Yeah. Sure," I breathed. I was sick of this. I shouldn't be afraid to be at my own school. Shouldn't be having to talk to a stupid academic advisor. Should have gone to class and done the work and not have failed like the pathetic loser I was. God, I was so angry!

The car stopped in the parking lot closest to my college. Lovely. I stared at the trees and wondered if they could see me.

"Lynn. Come on, we're here."

I wanted a fucking cigarette.

The parking lot was a lot emptier than I expected. Maybe students figured the last week of classes didn't matter. Shit, I never went. But I never went to anything. Neither did most of the druggies I hung out with.

They wouldn't be here, would they? What if I saw someone I knew? I shook my head. Whatever. Fuck it all.

"Where are we going again?" my father asked.

"The main office," my mother told him, squeezing his hand. Barf.

"I forgot how pretty this campus is."

"Oh come on," I hissed, quickening my pace.

The main office was at the bottom of the hill, right below the apartments I had practically lived at two months ago. I tried not to look at it, to remember myself there smoking with Angie out front, summoning the strength to see Diesel again. To kiss him and get my fix. His lips were harder than Rick's were. More rough. Or maybe I had hardened myself to him. How disgusting I was, giving myself away like that. All for some stupid ass high.

We crossed the patio. I looked behind me, half expecting Diesel to be there. Half wanting him to be. But there was no one.

What a mess.

"Do you want us to go in with you?" my mother asked.

I didn't answer. Wished I could just close my eyes and let it all disappear. Quit struggling for once.

Wait.

I remembered Natalie. Remembered our session outside of the coffee house. She had told me that when I stopped fighting, I could recover. Surrendering was the only way to move on.

How? I looked behind me. My parents were holding each other. Waiting. Waiting for me to tell them what to do. Like I knew what I wanted.

Okay. Focus. I knew that whatever Sue Benson said I had no control over. If I failed I would deal with it. My parents and I would deal with it. I didn't have to do this alone. Maybe that's what the third step meant. Letting others in. Letting shit just kind of fall into place. I looked at the sky, at whoever or whatever was out there. Maybe they would help me fly. Give me the strength to let go.

"Lynn?" My mother's hand touched the back of my head.

I looked at her. Shrugged. "Do whatever you want." I just wanted it to end. Opened the door. They didn't follow. I sighed.

A woman was behind the counter. She flashed me a super smile.

"Is Sue Benson here?" I asked her.

She was chewing gum. It smacked loudly against her lips. I wanted to pull it from her teeth. "She's booked today."

Of course she was. This was stupid. Fuck surrender. I chewed off the rest of my thumbnail and started to leave.

"Do you want to talk to June?"

"June?" I asked, turning around.

"The other academic advisor. She's kind of new."

I wondered if that was to my advantage. "Um, sure." June. Seeing June in June. I chuckled at my own joke.

The lady was still smacking. "She's ready now."

"You don't have to tell her I'm coming?" But she didn't hear me. Her gum was too loud.

June's office was behind the front desk and around the corner. I went there. Slowly. Knocked on the door.

"Come in."

I opened the door. Sat down. My knees bounced against the chair.

"What can I do for you?"

The carpet was different here. Dark blue. I unfocused my eyes. Let them wander on the fabric. But it didn't move.

June was staring at me. She wore a red hat with a purple feather in it. The feather bounced when she breathed.

"Sorry," I told her, forcing myself into the moment. Not that I wanted to be there. I was so fucking tired of sitting in offices discussing some kind of option for my screwed up-ness. "I don't know how this works, but I need a break in school."

"May I ask why?"

"I'm a drug addict."

She folded her hands on her desk. Unfolded them. Folded them again. Her feather bounced. "Okay."

"I was hoping to have one class in the fall. Start slow. If I haven't already failed, I mean." I paused. Looked at the scratch marks in the desk. "Have I failed?"

"What's your name?"

"Lynn Levy."

"Lynn Levy…" Her expression changed when she saw who I was. Saw the grades I didn't have. "You're lucky."

"Why?" I asked her, doing my best to avoid her gaze. She was trying to see through me.

"If you fail one more class, you're done."

"Oh."

Pause.

"You said you would like only one class this fall?"

"Yes."

"You'd have to be a part time student in order to do that. You don't by chance have a job?"

I looked at her. "Yes."

"Do you work 25 hours a week?"

"I can."

"Good." She fumbled through her desk. I glanced around, half expecting to see some angel with a harp in the corner of the room.

June handed me some papers. "Get these signed and bring them to the registrar. Registration's already started, so get a move on with that class."

I nodded.

"That's it," she said. "You can go."

Oh. I stood up. "Um, thank you."

She smiled. "You're the one who got the chance. You do believe in second chances, right?"

I shrugged.

"You should Lynn Levy. You are one."

My parents hugged me when I told them the news.

"I knew everything would work out," my mother said.

"Lynn."

I turned around. No one was there. "We should go," I whispered.

"When will we see you again?" my father asked. We were in the car. They were taking me home.

"I don't know," I said. "Whenever you come back to visit."

"Why don't you come home for the weekend?"

"I can't."

"Why not?"

I stared at my hands. "It's where I used meth, Dad."

"You used here."

"It's different."

"Why?"

His questions were frustrating. "Because it is. I have a sober house here. Support. I'm not friends with anyone who I used with." Except Angie. I wondered if I would ever see her again. Really see her. Like we were before.

"Your friends use at home?"

"Yes."

"But what about us, Lynn?" my mother asked. "We're your family. You can't not use for one weekend to see us?"

"No."

"That's ridiculous." My father turned around. His veins were starting their dance. "I don't believe that."

"Fine. Don't believe me. But it's true. I'm an addict, remember?"

"So you can never come home again?"

I shrugged.

"You have to come home eventually."

The anxiety was crawling on my jeans. I tried to flick it away. "Can we talk about this later?"

"Fine."

Silence followed us back to the Coral House. It was the tense kind. I was used to that.

Shit. I shouldn't have snapped at them. It wasn't their fault I couldn't go home.

My mother pulled in front of the SLE. I got out of the car. So did they.

"I'm sorry," I told them. I couldn't believe I had just apologized. Made me smile. Was this what healing was?

"We know." My mother played with a piece of my hair. "It's hard for us too, Lynn. We get scared."

I hugged her. She wiped her eyes.

My father wrapped his arms around me. "Try to answer your phone, okay?"

"Bye, Dad."

They got in their car. I waved to them when they drove off. Somehow, I was smiling.

Went back inside.

"Hey Kiki!" I yelled, throwing my house keys on the couch cushion next to her. She threw them back. They landed on my foot. "Smoke with me, bitch."

Twenty-four days clean.

On the bus again. Would have to do this a lot more now. Elizabeth said twenty-five hours was definitely okay. Shit, they'd give me thirty if I lasted long enough.

"Lasted long enough?" I had asked.

"A lot of people get fired. It's easy to steal."

I pictured myself opening a video game and stealing the tokens inside. Selling them to the locals while wearing a nylon mask. Like those tweaker guys who stole from that old lady. But I would wear purple stockings.

Laughed at my head.

"You're so pretty when you do that."

My face went numb. That voice. But it couldn't be.

"Haven't seen you in awhile."

His breath was on my neck. I could feel his smell. Beer. Cigarettes. Tweak.

"Where've you been?"

Diesel.

"I've missed you."

I was frozen. Wanted to turn around and tell him to get the fuck away from me but my thoughts weren't working right.

"You just gonna sit there?"

Yes.

"Lynn."

Maybe if I closed my eyes he'd disappear. Him and the fear and the pain and the tweak and the fucking memories and why did he have to find me?

"Lynn."

"What?" I yelled. Turned to face him. God, he looked like shit. Dark circles in his face, his skin all red and blotchy. Probably from picking at himself.

"You don't have to get all bitchy on me."

I wanted to leave. Run. My stop was soon. Maybe I could wait. I could do this.

"Lynn."

"Will you quit saying my fucking name?" I spat.

"Lynn." He smiled at me. Made me want to throw up.

"What do you want?" I asked him, though I already knew. He always wanted the same thing.

Maybe I wanted to give it. The idea of using sunk into my lips. My head. The tweak. The high. Could feel it dripping in my veins. Goddamit couldn't the bus go any faster?

His fingers touched my head. Stroked it. The grime on his skin soaked into mine. I shuddered and shrugged away. Wanted to hide.

"Saw you on campus. Called your name but you didn't see me."

I saw myself inside my cell. It was *dark dark dark*.

"I followed you home."

The dark walls dripped the pain onto the floor. Pain inside my skin my heart my mind.

"And you've got a job. FrankZilla's Arcade. I like your uniform."

Too much. Can't breathe. Tired of this, tired of here.

"Still think about that night at Jolan's place. When you, you know, sucked me off."

Dug my nails into the floor the walls my eyes and the pain splashed on the ground. No no no get me out now I want out!

"I, um," Diesel lowered his voice. "I got some tweak if you wanna, you know, do that again."

Rocking screaming crying hiding wanting to run to hide but I'm stuck back there let me bleed use get high get wasted and fly.

"Why are you so quiet?"

I was sick of this. Sick of this and sick of him. I turned around. Showed him the anger in my eyes. "I don't want to talk to you."

Something was hiding in the wall.

"Why the fuck not?"

The strength behind my lips. "I quit tweak."

It was light.

"So that means you're too good for me now?"

Light inside my cell.

The fire in my heart. "Yeah, that's what it means."

I wanted more.

"That's fucked up."

"You're fucked up," I said. Looked out the window. My stop was next. Finally.

I pulled the wire above my head.

"Come on, Lynn, don't be like that."

I stood up before the bus stopped. Wandered sideways to the front. He followed.

"You can't run from me."

"Fucking watch me."

The doors opened. I jumped. Went to the edge of the curb. A car was coming. A whole line of them.

"You're not gonna make it."

I bolted across the street, ignoring the screeches and honks flying towards me. Made it to the other side without looking back.

"Lynn!"

Ran into the arcade and over Andrea. Our shoulders collided but I didn't stop. She yelled to me. I kept going. Past the counter. Through the *Employee's Only* door. Shut it behind me. Dropped to the ground.

"Lynn?"

His voice was soft against my fear. I felt his arms around me. Felt the panic melt into the floor.

"What happened?"

"Hold me, Shiloh," I whispered. "Just hold me and don't let go."

Twenty-seven days clean.

Another night at the Coral House. Kiki and I sat on the porch in our usual spot, smoking and watching the traffic crawl by. We lived on a two lane street. It was the middle of rush hour. I was glad I didn't have a car.

Kiki flicked her cigarette over the side of the fence.

"You know we have an ashtray," I told her, poking the over sized coffee can with my foot.

She lit another cigarette. "I don't want to live here anymore."

"Why?" I asked, although I knew why. Nobody wants to live in a fucking sober house.

"I'm tired of it all. Shit, how long are we going to have to do this?"

I puffed the end of my cigarette in an attempt to avoid her truth. She had asked a question I had never thought about. I guess with all the focus on staying clean just for today, there wasn't much room for anything tomorrow. But the thought burrowed itself under my fingernails. I picked at the edges.

"I don't want to go to meetings for the rest of my life."

"I don't think anyone does," I said.

"But some people don't have to. Some people can just stay clean on their own. Live normal lives like normal people and never have to go to meetings."

"And some people can't." I paused. "How do we know which ones we are?"

Kiki shrugged. "I guess there's only one way to find out."

Fabulous.

Veronica was walking towards us. I wondered where she'd been.

"Hi dude," Kiki said.

"Guess what?" Veronica grinned, squishing in between Kiki and me. "Give me a cigarette."

I handed her one.

She lit it slowly. Inhaled. Waited. Exhaled. The anticipation was making me anxious.

Kiki poked Veronica with her lighter. "What happened?"

Veronica smiled again. "Candy got high."

"Serious?" Kiki laughed. "On what?"

"What the fuck does it matter? The bitch is gone."

"How'd you find out?" I asked.

"Carson told me. That's who I was with just now. He said he saw her at the metro with some other thugs. Candy looked tore up as shit."

"Carson's the one Candy stole from Veronica hella days ago."

"Fucking Kiki! You're lucky it's just Lynn."

"Thanks," I said.

"I got that bitch back though," Veronica told me.

"What, did you put some tar in her shit?" Kiki asked. Veronica and other heroine addicts had told us stories of drug dealers putting substances in heroine that shouldn't be there. Substances like tar. It was almost always deadly. Veronica had never said it, but I suspected she had sold some pampered heroine in her drug years.

"Fuck you, no I didn't." She paused. Took a dramatic drag of her cigarette. "I'm keeping the baby. Carson's the dad."

"Holy shit Ver! You're gonna be a mom."

"Fucking crazy, huh?"

"Candy's gonna have a fit!"

My cell phone rang. It was Natalie. Strange. I was the one who was supposed to call her.

"Hello?" I said.

"Lynn?" Her voice sounded shaky. Something wasn't right.

"Who's that?" Kiki asked. I turned away from her.

"It's me."

"Lynn, I, um." It sounded like she was crying. "I relapsed last night."

Oh my God. "Are you okay? Do you need help?" I took another cigarette from my pack. What was I supposed to say? I was the one who fucked up. Not Natalie. She was supposed to tell *me* what to do.

"What's going on?" Kiki's voice pierced the inside of my ears. I hissed at her to shut up.

"Yeah, I'm okay."

"What happened?"

Natalie sighed. "My roommate got a prescription a few days ago. Vicodin. Really strong ones. She kept leaving the shit out and I told her not to cuz I used to do it all the time so she put it in our bathroom cabinet. Last night she was sleeping and I just got this thought in my head that I could take some and it wouldn't go away. I was going crazy and it wouldn't stop so I took one."

"Come on, Lynn, what the fuck is going on?"

I turned around. "It's Natalie, okay? Just hang on! Shit!"

Kiki bit her lip.

"Sorry." I flicked my cigarette against the grass. "Are you still high?"

"No." She paused. "I wanted to be. Thought of going downtown or something. Anything. Cuz I had already fucked up, right?"

"Natalie."

"Hang on, Lynn. I didn't go downtown. I didn't use again. I didn't because of you."

My shock slid onto the sidewalk.

"You took one pill and came back. Just one. And I thought that if you could do it at 18 years old then I could at least try."

"Natalie," I whispered.

"You're amazing Lynn. Don't give up. You'll get your thirty day chip. And I'll be there to watch. I'll be there with four days clean."

Tears were in my eyes. Her clean date was next month. She would have gotten a five year chip. "I'm sorry," I said.

"Don't be sorry. Shit, you probably saved my life."

"But you're the one who said no." I wanted to tell her she was wrong, that I couldn't have that much influence on anyone. "You're the one who's still here."

"Lynn! Just take the fucking compliment."

I smiled.

"Are the other girls with you?" she asked.

I handed Kiki the phone.

Twenty-nine days clean.

"How are you?" Esther Agnes-Robbins asked, balancing her notepad on her knees.

I put my thumbnail in my mouth. Took it out again. "I think I'm okay."

"You think?" she smiled.

I told her about June and surrendering to a second chance, how I had invited my parents to be a part of it and they were. Told her about Diesel and the fear and the light inside my cell when I told him to go away. How Natalie had called, how I had made a difference in someone else's life. That maybe the pieces of myself were finally coming together.

"I'm so proud of you," Esther said. "Not only because of these amazing things you're telling me, but you're recognizing the positive in them. You just complimented yourself."

I held my head in my hands to hide the red on my face.

"Look at who you're becoming, Lynn. Look at the difference between now and nine weeks ago."

I thought about it. Saw myself before. The pain. The fear. The need to hide. "But it's all still there," I said. "I'm not better. There's still so much inside."

"And you're learning how to deal with it, how to let it go. One of the curses addiction grants is self-hatred. The more you recover, the more you'll be able to appreciate yourself. You've made some progress already, Lynn. You're learning how to face things and move past them one at a time. Have you noticed?"

I shrugged. Nodded.

Silence. It tickled the inside of my nose. I sniffed and tasted the residue of crank. Made me cringe. I thought of Angie and Scott, of the three of us standing in Kat's bathroom. Saw myself fall inside the need...but I couldn't remember how it happened. One minute I was using and then I was an addict. I wanted to know why.

"How did I become an addict?" I asked.

Esther nibbled the end of her pen. "Some say there is a gene that can be more prone to addiction."

"So you're saying I was born with it?"

"Partially. But there are many factors as to why you became addicted to drugs. How do you think it happened?"

"I liked it."

"But just because you like something doesn't mean you're addicted. You experimented with drugs. Then you abused them. From there you became addicted. It's a process. Where in your using did it cross from abuse to addiction?"

I swallowed. "I think it was when I thought I needed it to be okay. When I snuck chocolate, that was abuse. When I did mushrooms at Shannon's apartment, that was abuse. I even think it was abuse when I first tried crank. But once I associated it with feeling better, that's when it became addiction." I paused in the memories that bounced inside my head. "When Shannon told me it was between her and Rick, the first thing I thought of was using crank. And I think that was when I felt the need. That was when I became addicted. I needed it to feel better." I smiled. "I let it take control. Isn't that the definition of addiction? When it controls what you do?"

"You're unbelievable."

"Why?"

"You have this self-awareness that I just can't get over. Even when you were using, you understood yourself."

I opened my mouth. Closed it again.

"I know you're going to be fine."

I thought about Kiki, about our conversation a few days ago. "Do you think I'll have to go to meetings for the rest of my life?"

Esther looked at me. Showed me the security in her eyes. "What do you think?"

"I don't know. I don't want to. It feels like a weakness. Another addiction."

"Why?"

"If I need the meetings to stay clean, it's still needing something. How is that different than needing drugs to feel okay?"

"The meetings don't kill you."

"Okay, so that's true. And meetings don't make me go crazy either."

Esther nodded.

"But I don't want to have to depend on *anything*. I'm so tired of needing something else to make me okay."

"*You* make you okay."

I saw inside my head again. The cell was there. Dark as always. The girl stood against the wall, poking her finger inside the hole of light. She took it out and watched the yellow glow against the ground. Filled it with her skin again.

"I don't feel okay," I told Esther.

"Just look at yourself. You've conquered so much on your own."

I didn't say anything.

"You realized you had a problem and admitted your addiction. You got clean. You told your parents about your addiction and moved into a sober house. You got a job. You relapsed, got clean again." Her pen rolled off the notepad. She didn't notice. "You've re-connected with your parents, you've stopped hurting yourself, you've taken Rick and drugs out of your life."

"Okay, Esther. I get it."

"You want to do so much so quickly. Remember where you were and where you are now. Remember that you're only human and it's okay if you need to spend an hour of your day in a sober meeting to keep you safe. Just try to take things one day at a time."

"I can't. I live in my head, remember? You know what it's like in there."

"You let some light in."

"Only a little and it took forever to get it there. I'm tired of living inside myself. I'm tired of being an addict."

"That you can't change. You will always be an addict."

"How do you know?" I asked.

"Do you plan on testing this?" she wondered.

I shrugged. "What if I want to drink on my 21st birthday? Have champagne at my wedding? A beer when I graduate college? I want to live a normal life!"

Esther leaned towards me. "I understand your desire to drink and honestly, it's not irrational. But you have to be careful. Drinking lowers your willpower. You're more susceptible to using and that's dangerous."

"Life is dangerous."

"You're right, and for you it's even more so. You will always have to watch out for triggers. You will always have to worry about your darkness returning. You will always have to fight, Lynn."

"I don't want to fight anymore." I bit my lip to stop my tears. It didn't work.

"I know. And it's hard. But you're strong. You're smart. You obviously care about yourself or you wouldn't be here. The disease we call addiction does not have to control you. It does not define you and will not keep you from being who you are."

"I fucking hate it."

"And you have a right to hate it. But don't let your hatred consume you, or you will go back there. Do you understand?"

I pulled my knees against my chest. "What can I do to feel okay with who I am?"

"What do you think?"

"Don't. Just help me with this one. Please?"

Esther smiled. "I think you should use it."

"The addiction?"

"Yes. It is your ally as much as your enemy. Think about it. You have gone through so much at such a young age. You've found a strength that so many don't even know they have. You can do anything now."

I sniffed. "You sound like a *Lifetime* movie."

"Hey, I'm allowed to be cheesy. It's part of my job description."

I traced the pattern of thread along my jeans. Wondered what kind of movie my life would be.

My life.

I liked that. Liked the way it sounded in my head. Strong. Like the girl who sat in it, gazing at the hole inside the wall. Her eyes were dark. Sad. I wanted to tell her that someday those walls around her will disappear. That maybe she could have a garden and dance in the sun with flowers and butterflies and all the pretty things. That life and love will be her friends. That she could take her soul into her hands and fly away.

As I sat there in the silence with Esther Agnes-Robbins, I realized that my life was indeed my own. And, for once, that was okay with me.

Addiction

If you or someone you know needs help with drug, alcohol, or other addictions, there is hope. You can get the support you need. You don't have to do this alone.

Narcotics Anonymous: (818) 773-9999
Alcoholics Anonymous: (212) 870-3400
Al-Anon & Alateen: (888) 425-2666
Drug & Alcohol Resource Center: (800) 784-6776
Suicide Prevention Hotline: (800) 273-8255

Online Help:

Narcotics Anonymous World Services: Http://www.na.org
Alcoholics Anonymous: Http://www.alcoholics-anonymous.org
Al-Anon & Alateen: Http://www.al-anon.alateen.org
Drug & Alcohol Resource Center: Http://www.addict-help.com

FROM THE AUTHOR

August 1, 2006

Lynn's story is based on my own drug addiction. I stopped using methamphetamines April 16th, 2002. It's strange that it's already been four years. It feels like another lifetime...and yet it doesn't. It doesn't feel that long ago at all. I can still remember using, the way it tastes, how fantastic my body felt. I actually had a using dream a couple weeks ago. Some guys whom I've never met were giving crank to my dog. It was the first using dream I've had in a long time. I don't miss that part of my life much. It's hard to miss watching pieces of yourself breaking on the floor.

    I don't know how I got through the process of getting clean. I don't know why I was able to do it when I've seen so many others fail. It's strange. A couple years ago I saw a young woman walk into the arcade I used to work at. She was a regular at meetings, the kind that went in and out of sobriety over and over again. Yet her attitude was always positive. She had an enthusiasm that I couldn't find in myself. It was a love for life and everything in it. I admired her for that. Admired her strength to start over. When I saw her that day, she was trying to get well from heroine. She told me a story. Said her family didn't want her around for Christmas and she got kicked out of the last motel because she was broke and couldn't I lend her some money for the bus? But I could see the truth behind her mask because I had once shared her face. She just wanted to get high. I didn't give her the money, and when she left I never saw her again.

    Maybe she couldn't find her strength. Her reason. I strongly believe that every addict needs a reason to stay clean. The problem is finding it, as the pull of addiction is the most powerful thing I've ever felt. I'm one of the lucky ones. I remember the day I got clean. I was sitting on the floor in Santa Cruz, California. I was high on whatever means of speed I could find, wasting away on the spots in the walls I knew were in my head. Somehow, through the darkness I had learned to hide in, I realized that I was losing my dreams. I wanted to change something. To speak and be heard. I wanted to make a difference in someone else's life.

Ultimately, as cheesy as this may sound, I got clean because of you. Yes, you. You, the reader, had the guts to read my story. Regardless of what you got out of it, which I hope is something somewhat warm and fuzzy, you heard me. And that is the greatest reason for sobriety that I could ever have. I wish I could thank you. Yet how does one thank someone they have never met? I've thought about it, and maybe all I can do is attempt to share the thoughts inside of me.

I've realized that life isn't easy. Shit, it's the most difficult thing we have to face. But it's our own difficult life. It's the only life we have. So why not live it? We have the strength to survive, the opportunity to learn and grow and change. We have the ability to define who we are and what we want and how much events around us define the actions we take.

Use what you have and fly.

Printed in the United States
105045LV00001B/236/A